# charlie big potatoes

**Phil Robinson** was born in Essex and
lives in London with his wife Anna Maxted
who is also a novelist.

'This rather fine novel will not just appeal to males,
for Robinson has fashioned a character who sheds a
skewed light on the odd, code-bound world of men
who really don't have a clue about women'
***Times***

'Perfect reading . . . *Charlie Big Potatoes* is chock-a-block
with dark humour to leave you chortling into your pillow
long after you've shut the book. A sort of Bridget Jones
with testicles and a wrap'
***Ice Magazine***

'This is an entertaining, bittersweet story loaded with
black humour. It will have you laughing out loud and
wincing at its pathos, while women readers will gain
something of an insight into the male psyche'
***Waterstone's Books Quarterly***

# phil robinson

## charlie big potatoes

PAN BOOKS

First published 2002 by Macmillan

This edition published 2003 by Pan Books
an imprint of Pan Macmillan Ltd
Pan Macmillan, 20 New Wharf Road, London N1 9RR
Basingstoke and Oxford
Associated companies throughout the world
www.panmacmillan.com

ISBN 0 330 49051 6

3 5 7 9 8 6 4 2

A CIP catalogue record for this book is available from
the British Library.

Typeset by Intype London Ltd
Printed and bound in Great Britain by
Mackays of Chatham plc, Chatham, Kent

for Anna

I'd like to thank
Ali Gunn, Mari Evans, Anna Maxted
and Charlie 'Tea Time' Howgego

# 1

I am meant to be working but then I get lost in the haze, the dust storm, amongst the drugged eyes and the sunburnt faces. I have a whole list of places I have to be. I have a badge around my neck that says the name of my magazine, stickers on my jeans that affiliate me to certain bands and a white vinyl wrist strap that gives me access to all areas. It is clear to everyone here that I have an important job to do. That I am *someone*. If I wanted to, I could go and stand at the back of the main stage and watch the bands play. I won't, because it's the same from the back as from the front but you have to smile an awful lot when you're standing around famous people. You also have to nod along to their music and look *really into it*. Maybe they didn't get smiled at enough when they were kids, who knows. So I interview them, grin, nod, listen, new album, blah, blah, fall asleep, wake up smiling, yeah it's brilliant, what are your influences.

I check my jeans for the itinerary that my boss Sean had typed out for me.

'Don't fuck this job up,' he said.

It tells me who I'm supposed to be interviewing and lists the phone numbers of all the record company press officers I have to speak to in case there's a problem. I can't find it. I search myself, my jean jacket, my shirt twice. All my gear,

my phone, my notepad and pens, minidisc player and micro-
phone all seem to chase each other from pocket to pocket
like mice, turning up over and over again. Not watching or
caring much I follow a large crowd downhill, my head beginning to burn in the sun.

Without that piece of paper I'm screwed. I sit down on a
spare patch of coarse dry grass and take a blot of acid, a pill
and a swig of water. I can do this job, I think. They were
right to trust me. I can handle this. I begin emptying the
contents of all my pockets on the ground in front of me. My
head aches. I find a wad of hotel letterhead, a washed-out
tourist map of Bucharest, a twenty-pound note and the small
bag of dried mushrooms that I first started nibbling on an
hour ago, which are now grit in my mouth. I take another
swig of water. Now I am going to have to think long and
hard about what I am going to do next. I've got enough
water to keep me going, I have pens and pencils and a phone
and maybe if I sit here long enough someone will come along
who knows me, and who can sort this whole mess out.
Maybe someone I am supposed to interview will even walk
past.

'Hello,' says a female voice. 'Are you all right?'

'I needed to find something. Do you mind if I sit here for
a while?'

'No,' she says. 'You can sit on the blanket if you want, I
don't mind.'

'Thanks,' I say. 'I have to work.'

I try to make the effort to look at what I have laid out
in front of me. I spy a piece of white paper folded neatly to
a small quarter. I open it up and written in bold Helvetica
is a list of bands and times.

'Here it is.'

My words echo in my ears. This echo is the result of all the drugs I've taken today.

She smiles at me and I look down, blinking twice as the schedule melts through my fingers like a sheet of pure white chocolate. I gasp and I lie back on the blanket, mind blown.

There is musical laughter, the murmur of the crowd, the beat in the distance. She appears beside me, she is beautiful, and we watch each other and the sun sets over the field and the world around us turns purple and crimson in the darkness. I hand her my bottle of water and she smiles and whispers to me asking if I want to brush her hair. I say yes and she sits between my outstretched legs, leaning her head to the side while I gather her hair together. It is straight and long and shimmers in my hands. Each single strand is a rivulet of liquid electricity that joins us. With each gentle stroke of her brush I know her more. She is Sarah, my beating heart. Sarah, my earth. Sarah, my woman.

I stop brushing her hair and we hold each other instead. Our tight grip anchoring us to this dirt, the fabric of this globe which is spinning through space at 1,000 miles per hour. We are together whether we like it or not, clinging to the earth like a motorcycle rider on the wall of death. She takes my hand and we roll back inside the tent where the darkness is filled with a multitude of colours and spirals, endless and unbroken, and the sound of her musical laughter. Our bodies contact. And my desire, my love for her dominates, reverberates around my mind like a hymn sung in a cathedral of fire.

Sarah, Sarah, Sarah so beautiful.

I want her to be here. I tell her this will be good. Tell her that I won't let any harm come to her, that she shouldn't be scared.

'Sarah?' I say in the darkness.

'Who's Sarah?' she says.

'You're not Sarah?' I say.

'No,' she says, 'I'm not Sarah.'

□

In the back of an old Ford Scorpio streaking down the motorway, Sean's name blinks on my mobile. I missed my interviews, I lost my notes, I have nothing to say to him. I divert the call to my message service.

The girl's head is resting on my lap. I cover her up with a blanket so she can sleep.

'Haven't you got to go to work?' she says, looking up at me.

'Maybe,' I say. 'I thought you were asleep.'

*Work.*

'What do you do?' she says.

'I'm a journalist,' I say, then add, 'Why don't you come out with me tonight? I'm going to a party, it's my boss's birthday. You can relax, have a laugh.' I don't know where that came from, I can't explain that, the drink maybe. But she turns to me and says, 'Yeah, OK.'

Is she being polite? I'll give her another chance, an out.

'It's just a casual thing, some drinks, some mates, it's cool.'

'No, yeah,' she says, 'it sounds good.'

'Shit,' I say, 'I forgot to ask you what your name was, I mean I don't know.'

'Kelly,' she says.

'Kelly,' I say, touching her face. 'My name is Charlie Marshall.'

Julius the driver is kind enough to stop at an offy on the

way over so we can get some refreshments for the three-hour drive into town. I knew I had the right man when I smelt the magic tree. I like getting in cabs where the driver's got a tree swinging from the rear-view mirror. It means that despite the corporate no-smoking sign stuck aggressively to the back of the passenger's headrest, you can smoke yourself sick. Two or three magic trees means he's been smoking spliffs, you can smoke spliffs and he's probably selling it too. These are the best drivers. I don't want some stuffy old bastard, hands perfectly positioned at ten to two. Safety is not a consideration. My perfect driver is a slightly reformed wide boy, usually with a couple of kids, who's learnt to appreciate the privacy and freedom that a Scorpio with blacked-out windows brings – who knows that with a spliff and a hands-free set, the party can come to the car and so what if the price of that freedom is driving around all day with the smell of vanilla syrup up your nose and getting in your clothes. I get Julius to make a stop at my mate Ray's flat. I need to borrow some cash for tonight. I coax both of them out of the car so we can break the journey with a smoke and a cup of tea.

'I was at school with Ray,' I tell them as Ray opens the front door holding a coffee cup and wearing the same kung fu dressing gown he's had since we were fifteen.

It's best not to allow Ray time to react. I establish a military-style beachhead and start rolling first Kelly then Julius through the gap.

'Ray, meet Kelly and Julius. Julius is the one who looks like a Yardie.'

'Nice flat, Raymond,' rumbles Julius, lumbering past him.

Kelly is close behind. Full of Scotch, she gives Ray a big kiss on the cheek.

'Hello, Ray, are you as lovely as Charlie?' she says.

'I'm having a bath,' says Ray.

'Smooth,' I say.

'Great,' she says, swaying drunk.

Kelly follows Julius though the narrow corridor into the lounge, which like most lounges in most ex-council flats was decorated pre-Ikea and laid with a red, brown and mustard-coloured carpet, the kind that gets cut into squares for animals in kennels.

'Refill, Ray? Tea or coffee anyone, take a seat. Ray has the full Sky service, I'll be with you in just a moment.'

Ray pulls the lounge door shut for privacy.

'Charlie, what are you doing here? I haven't seen you in a week.'

'Lend us a C-note till Thursday, go on.'

'No. What do you need it for?'

'My horse needs an operation. What do you think? New York.' I'm standing there with my hand out. 'Don't make me stand here with my hand out.'

'What the fuck are you doing with her? And who's he?'

'She's the Lord of Sussex and he's the gay one from Steps. I'm hiding them from the papers. Ray, there's nothing in it, I'm just going to a party. Sort me out.'

'Why?'

'Please.'

'I know her,' he says. 'I know her. I've seen her in a magazine. *Razzle* or something. I've, you know, her.'

'What?'

'Mmmmmm.' He crosses his eyes and sticks out his dog-like tongue.

'Mmmm what?' I say. 'She's just normal, she's not a tart or anything.'

'You aren't humph, humph, humph? You know. With her?'

'Am I fucking her?'

'Shhh!'

Did I? Have I? I don't think so. 'No way!'

'Don't even think about it, Charlie,' he says. 'Don't fuck this up. Stay here, man, sleep. Tomorrow I'll drive you to the airport myself.'

'Ray, c'mon. I've got to go to Sean's thing. I promised everyone.'

'No. No more money.'

'Give me the paper or I'll show her the sofa she's sitting on is covered in special glue!'

He thinks about that for the moment.

'Because,' I say, 'that sofa's in a horrible way. You must brush your teeth in front of the telly a lot.'

Ray is now pink.

'I'll get the tea,' he says, 'you skin up.'

He pops his head around the door of the front room.

'Tea anyone?'

Julius looks up holding a couple of Ray's CDs.

'Have you got any biscuits?' he says.

⌂

As our taxi pulls out of the estate the big-headed dogs bark, welcoming the evening, and the boys on the bikes make off to the local Kentucky with a bit of thieving in mind. The big lads hide in clouds of acrid rubber, as they doughnut family Fords in front of crowds of girls in various states of excitement and emaciation. A city in a rut.

On the kerb outside the dark little club are the same old faces. Tuesday night is the best night. Fridays are for City boys and Saturdays are for amateurs – 'We're in the big town now, Ma!' – folk who smell of hay and Kouros. Tuesday is an evening for professionals, people who know where they're headed because they've been invited, and I don't mean to some Leicester Square dry-ice, holiday-park disco with 'free VIP invites' either.

I walk round the car, pull open the passenger door and lead the girl out by the hand. Across the pavement, past the doorman, up the stairs and into the club; two Bellinis, please. The woman behind the bar is frighteningly big. Amazonian even. She tells me to fuck off. And I order two vodka tonics instead. A rude place inside me imagines sex with her would be like trying to operate one of those giant cinema organs; working yourself into a frenzy, hands and feet flying everywhere, keys, pulleys and buttons and pedals. Honk, honk, paarp. There is a thin strand of identical male and female haircuts winding from the door along the bar to the toilets and booths on the far wall. This is it. We all look the same. Honk, honk, paarp. Every generation has its Marks and Spencer, ours will be Duffer of St George. I get us through the crowd to a table where my boys are holding court. Ben, the deputy editor, Doyle, the staff writer, and Alex, the features editor. I'm not senior on the magazine, but I'm not junior either, I'm just somewhere in between. It's a solid position, kind of like a sweeper – not a sweeper in a football team, more like the bloke who walks furthest back from the dustcart.

The boys don't pride themselves on rudeness, but nor do they go as far as introducing themselves to someone new. They are a tight group and the nucleus of a larger sprawl of do-nothing intelligent degenerates. They own no titles or land, but are an aristocracy of sorts. A contrary elite before whom you still have to prove yourself. I was lucky. When I started in the business they were willing to teach me everything I needed to know. They helped me manipulate expenses, taught me what to drink and where, how to and how not to take drugs, and when to act stupid, cut corners and play hookey. Most important they taught me how not to die on the pavement like River Phoenix. I remember that lesson. I collapsed in this same club four years ago and was resuscitated by a smack head called Ben, who pulled me into the toilets, ran my wrists under the cold tap and slapped me round the face – at the same time telling me the secrets of self-medication. I've performed the same service for others since. It makes me sad when people say that my generation has learnt nothing worth passing on.

When I first started here I'd look around the pub thinking, Would I ever be friends with these people? I didn't think so at the time, but then I began to realize that there was no hard rule against me either. Male, female it doesn't matter. Educated, Oxbridge? Gratis MA and Daddy's on the board? Not relevant. You have to fit the group dynamic, you have to be humble and appreciative at least for the first year, two years; I had to be. You see, young lions take last bite at the carcass, in this group you take last bite at the punchline.

Ben leans towards my ear, staring at me through pissed, low-slung eyelids. We're going to New York tomorrow and I want to ask him if he can sort out the taxi. That way the firm will pay for it. I burn his chin with the cigarette hanging out of my mouth, which then bounces from my knee into the darkness under the table.

'Sorry Charlie boy. I think you want to go and say happy fucking birthday to Sean.'

'No I don't.'

I reach for the bottle in my pocket, grab a drained glass that's still got some ice in the bottom and pour.

'You know . . . he's been talking about you, 'bout not pulling your weight, fucking around too much. I said I'd square it but . . . well.'

It's hard to know whether he's joking or not. I know what I haven't been doing. That Sean's been waiting for a good excuse.

Doyle's chubby high-pitched laughter breaks through my thoughts.

Alex has turned up with fresh drinks and I turn round to see Doyle spreading his generous arms around the back of the booth and Kelly acting like he's the man from Del Monte and she's got the ripe pineapples.

More drinks go down. Kelly is on slammers and is giggling now and I've got that beat in my head, the indestructible beat I get when I'm drunk, sitting comfortably and the fun is about to begin. Alex takes me to the toilet and he chops out a couple of lines on the toilet seat. It looks smeared and dirty and I get worried about hepatitis. 'Fuck hepatitis,' Alex says, and I do it all the same. Back at the table Doyle has got this game where if Kelly says something he considers to be stupid he sticks a fiver down the front of her dress. I tell him she's not a tart but he doesn't listen. Then we all start doing it. Alex, who always looks as though he's on the verge of saying 'I ain't done nothin' guv'nor' actually says 'Open wide' and drops a little something wet and slippery on my tongue. I suck on it and he nods and smiles a bowl of cream that it's all right. I feel good and I want to share it with Kelly. I tell her that she's a beautiful woman, because she really is, and I love her, even if all that is just an illusion and we don't ever love anyone really because it's all in our heads, and that

I'd never let her get hurt and she knows I'm telling her the truth. She looks at me as if to say Are you serious? You're drunk but are you serious? Shall we go somewhere now? And then I don't know what to do because I've separated her from the pack and my head is crackling, my heart is beat, beat, beating and the silence is starting to crush . . . A body breaks through the crowds around the table. Sean. Slick ginger curls and sideburns of clear glass noodles.

'You going to wish me happy birthday?'

'Yeah, yeah, in a minute, Sean, mate.'

*Go away.*

'It's my fucking party, you're drinking my booze, don't you think you're being impolite?'

'I didn't know it was so important to you.'

Brandy bottle in his hand, always half empty, always the big man.

'You ungrateful little shithead.'

'Whoa,' I say. My vision pitches to the left.

'Don't ever fuck around on a job like that again. You had a load of responsibility and you fucked it up.'

*Stay back, give me some space.*

I know he's angry, that he's probably got tunnel vision with me at the end of it. I'm drunk but he's worse. He is one gram ahead of me and he feels strong. Crystal beads of sweat against his fair-freckled skin.

'Is that where you got the tart? Were you fucking her when you should have been working for me?'

It feels like everyone in the room stops and turns round to stare at Kelly, Salem-style, demanding an inquisition. She's a normal person. Not one of us. I brought her here for a laugh, not to be humiliated. Everyone is staring at me. This is wrong. We're not in the office now. Outside the office you have to treat people with respect. He should know that. If you don't have respect you have nothing. You may as well be dead.

Sean is shocked when he feels my hands grabbing his neck. I can feel the stubble on his jaw, his strength going as I squeeze his throat. This is my boss. I'm running him backwards away from the table, away from the girl, forcing him over. His back slams into the end bar. He smashes the brandy bottle and I push his head into the candelabra, there's a flash, hair on fire. Down he goes. Rolling, studded with diamonds, beating his head. Then I'm forced backwards, legs thrashing, my arms bent behind my head, FUCK OFF! and then stairs and two men in black coats staring down and a crack like celery. I can't breathe. Suffocating. My arm is wrong, it's broken. The sharp bone threatening to split the thin skin. Alex and Ben pull me out of the road. My limp arm drags across the pavement behind me.

Sarah, I forgot about Sarah, what's Sarah going to say?

'You prick,' says Ben. 'What are you supposed to do with that? You're getting married at the weekend.'

**2**

The limo creeps through the Manhattan traffic and I know that I'm already dead. Massive heart attack, haemorrhage, aneurysm. He's watching me now. We'll stop at the next set of lights and the door will swing open and Death will step into the car, insects crawling over his wrist down to the tip of one long translucent finger and he'll point at me and say, 'TIME'S UP, SUNSHINE!'

I've got a pain down my right side, and a headache. I just need some water, some pure, middle-of-a-mountain cold water with no booze in it. I can feel my heart inflating, deflating, grating against my chest, desperately pushing the thick dark lumps of my blood upwards. Pressing the mess through the thin complaining vein in the centre of my forehead. Cocaine and sleep deprivation. You can't keep your heart beating like this. Even a donkey engine that hums for twenty years, generating only a flickering uneven light, dies eventually. And your heart never rests. Never sleeps when you sleep. Carries you through repetitive nightmares, shock, grief and mixed grills and you still trust it will be beating every morning. Yet it's not made of metal, you can't oil it. You can't lift the lid on a Sunday morning, poke it with a screwdriver while swearing into a book. It spends its life in a dark wet space, minding your business, until it stops and you stop with it.

'I want to go to hospital.'

'But you just got out of hospital.'

Ben slaps my cast. I can't even remember asking for this. I didn't want my stag night here. We could have gone to Amsterdam, which would have rendered Ben, Doyle and Alex harmless, human Sticklebricks, stuck together with dope and beer. And Ray, my best man, could have come – he could afford Amsterdam. But then they wanted New York and I went along with them. Good memories they said. Amsterdam is little England, pissed-up Scouse grannies and sixth formers retching on space cakes. I can deal with that. But I let them decide for me, I always let them decide. And I remember how too much coke can make you feel, no matter what the company. Like a scared child twisting and turning away from the shadows that crawl across the bedroom ceiling.

'Where we going next?'

'Have some more charlie, Charlie.'

Ben swigs from a bottle of Wild Turkey and hands it to Doyle who is toying with an injured TV set that will not surrender.

'Where are we going, Doyle?'

'That's a secret. I'm not going to tell you 'cause you'll get scared and run away. The groom is flagging, Alex, do the honours.'

Alex pushes his card deep into the eightball and offers me a corner loaded with sparkling wet powder. I look at it and think of Paul Newman contemplating egg forty-eight in *Cool Hand Luke*. His stomach, my brain. My nose, my headstone.

'If I do all that I'll go blind, I promise. I'll be sick and bleed all over this car if I have any more.'

'Charlie boy!'

'Make it trams, two lines enough?'

'My heart is going to burst.'

Ben leans forwards handing a small baggie to Alex. 'Don't worry, sunshine, I got just the thing for that. Gimme a pen, Alex. I'm going to write on his arm while you chop 'em out. Be careful with that.'

'Don't write anything stupid.' But I haven't got the energy to protest more. If the drugs don't get me today, they will soon.

'You know Sean lost half his hair. And you gave him a big scab.'

'What?' I say.

'When I left him at the hospital a big red scab was already forming. A big brown and red scab like a fucking bogey the size of a saucer.'

Alex and Doyle wince simultaneously.

Ben is now drawing a picture of Sean with his hair on fire. He's having trouble finding space because there is already a drawing of what appears to be a squirrel with very large testicles. And the words 'YES, I AM A TWAT'.

'Alex, gimme your phone so I can call Sarah.'

'Can't. The batteries have run out.'

'I'm serious, give me the phone.'

They all laugh. Doyle is rubbing Ben's leg pretending to be gay and winking at him. They both wink at Alex who begins shouting and trying the door handles. Ben strokes his back. He once explained to me that after enough drink and drugs your sexuality becomes a grey area. Looking at him now, I'd say all bets are off.

'You're fucking joking! Driver! Driver!'

A pack of wolf cubs yelping, rolling around in the dirt, scratching and nipping each other. Alex knows it's a game but can't be sure how far they are willing to go. He squeals.

'Mr Driver man, he's touching me in the arghhh!'

The driver heels the brakes, the limo stops and Ben steps out of it, away from the trouble. He always gets himself well clear.

'Why are we stopping here?'

The driver is out of his seat and leaning in through the door.

'I throw you out. I throw you fucking out!'

'How do you know I haven't got a gun?' says Doyle.

Sarah needs to know where I am. These are the new rules that I should live by. That I will have to learn. Married people know where each other are. At all times. They call each other from work and say they'll be late. And they make plans that shouldn't be broken at any cost because the marriage comes first. I know that I should have called her from the hospital last night but it was 4, 5 a.m. Bad news can always wait till morning when fear and panic are more distant notions.

I fall out of the limo and stumble towards a payphone. Raccooning through my jeans pockets. Rooting quarters out of a jumble of fag wrappers, foil, matches and lighters, a compass, skins, lint and ten-pence pieces. What else have I got in here? Baby magpies? I touch something that feels like a beak. When I get home I'm going to get these pockets stitched up. I'm a menace. It's all out, everything I've got. Passport, a packet of latex gloves, plasters, a small bottle of iodine, a pill bottle with someone else's name on it and a dirty old brown pipe. I'm not making a phone call; I'm holding a bring and buy sale. Ben collars me, dragging me back to the car, Alex scraping my stuff off the floor. Running along behind us, dropping half of it, bent over laughing.

'Get in the car you tramp!'

'No. No, no. Let me make the call, c'mon c'mon, one call please . . .'

They're all over me, kissing me on the head.

'You hold that,' says Alex. 'I can't hold his stuff and all these little packets. That's possession with intent.'

Doyle grabs at them.

'Don't panic, Mr Mainwaring, we'll just use the one big bag and split the rest.'

'And let you hold the big bag?' says Ben.

□

When I woke up in the hospital I didn't feel like I'd slept at all. Maybe I'd just been staring at the ceiling. Alex still won't tell me what he gave me, acid or a piece of mushroom. Maybe a mouthful of GHB. Whatever, it must have been strong, because I felt nothing when I bounced down that flight of stairs and rolled right across the pavement and into the road.

I remember that there were two ambulances and four green men. A paramedic asked me if I'd been drinking before fitting me with a transparent gas and air muzzle. Hisss. I think he strapped me onto the trolley because I tried to shout at Sean, but couldn't hear myself over the high-pitched fault-testing signal that was rebounding around the inside of my cranium. Then later, in hospital, I remember being in every-one's way because they were brushing past me and knocking my arm as they walked by. There I was, drifting through the hospital on a trolley buffeted by the able but bleeding drunks

17

with nurses coming and going and when it got to hurting too much I remember asking for water and painkillers. But I didn't get any because I'd been drinking. People were screaming at one man who was turning red, turning inside out, and then a man in a white coat arrived. A surgeon not a loon doctor, who didn't seem to speak English, but touched my shoulder and I woke up somewhere else, in a bed, in the middle of a dark ward, with a cast on my arm. I only had to follow the exit signs. Already I was starting to change. I searched for painkillers, looking for medication sitting in little plastic pots. Anything I could swallow or chew or grind up later. I found myself standing at the end of a sleeping patient's bed, becoming a giant, golden griffin. I casually followed the exit signs, carrying whatever I could pick up, leaving the rest of the customers with their heads and bellies filled with dead cells and poison, their pipes gurgling effluvia. I left as casually as I could with my giant killing talons tap-tap-scraping the linoleum. A car arrived, I don't remember from where or how it got there but I asked the driver where I was, knowing Sarah wasn't far away. But she mustn't know any of this. The driver, an old colonel type in a brown country shirt and tie, opened my door. He should be more careful, I could have any kind of disease leaving a place like this. Something I never even went in with. A copy of *The Times* sat on the front seat, and underneath it the *Racing Post*. The car filled with the sweet, dead air of pipe smoke. The colonel was a quick, clever bastard who moved in fits and spurts, making me jump. Shouting 'Left turn!' and making me bang my nose on the window as I change direction, parade-ground style. He took me to Sarah's flat to pick up my bag, passport and tickets. There was a phone message dated Tuesday afternoon from Sarah. It said that she'd left for her hen night in

Brighton and that I should be careful because I always get in trouble in New York. I remember that I have a mission, and I feel golden again. North London to Heathrow. My skull beat 400 per minute on the wet glass. Oncoming traffic jumped from the grey fog threatening to decapitate me, to turn me inside out and red.

'Which terminal are you departing from, sir?'

'Which airline, sir?'

Then I'm standing at the check-in desk. 'Did you pack all your bags yourself?'

What if I'm still golden and my new face doesn't look like my old one in the passport because I've got this big sharp beak? Feathers? The answer stuck in my metal throat. If I speak I might shriek instead.

'Do you have in your luggage any electronic equipment that has recently been out of your possession or been in for repair?'

'No!' I wanted to say to her. But it came out as: 'Reeeeeeaaaaackack!' I clamp my hand over my mouth to stop it happening again.

Then after check-in Doyle found me, mouth open and shrieking by Boots the Chemist. My miniaturized transatlantic hand luggage skittered across the cold stone floor. Travel clocks and headphones became black hard-shelled insects, that darted across the marble concourse, around and under me faster and faster with each gathering sweep of my cast. 'Shut up,' he said, and led me to the bathroom where he retied the sling holding my cast. 'If anyone asks just hiccup. Say nothing and take a drink from this bottle of water. Here.'

'Reeeeeeeeeeeaaaaackack!'

He repacked my bag, pushed me through passport

control, the gate, and into economy on the way to New York. Around then I took the first of the strange pills and lost the feeling in my legs for two hours.

☐

Ben is back in the car.

'Alex, give me the phone so I can call Sarah.'

'No.'

☐

I tried to call her from the phone on the plane but she hadn't picked up. I felt a pulse of love for her that was stronger than any part of me; it killed me that I couldn't tell her right then. I remember that the first time I told her I loved her was also the first time I made her cry. I was in the bath round at her flat, having a proper cowboy-quality, soapy-water splash-splosh using her ex-boyfriend's sport active shampoo. It was a type I would never buy. The kind advertised on TV by a smiling man throwing a javelin, then holding a baby. I was wondering whether the hero-man on TV ever got confused and instead cuddled the javelin and threw the baby when I heard her whispering on the phone. I knew who it was. He had only moved out a couple of months before and I was about to use his sponge, though instinctively this is wrong on way too many levels. (Washing with another man's sponge is probably the equivalent of playful teasing, mild petting and nuzzling.)

Then I heard his name.

'Dan?' she whispered.

You see, what most people never realize is that whispers travel further at night. They come creeping along hallways, through locked doors, through the thickest walls.

*Dan.*

There I am, lying in the cold blue suds scared of perfect Dan and all the others that have been here before me. Angry, waiting. Half an hour later she was standing over me and I was shouting about betrayal. She says she'd known I'd be like this which was why she was whispering. She was telling him that he had to come and pick up his stuff. Then she cried, and I stopped accusing her long enough to listen to what she had to say. She said that today was to be the end and the beginning, that she was going to ask me to live with her and it was going to be a surprise.

In that moment, pink, wrinkled and smelling of some try-hard baby-making rock-climbing man-scent, I swore I'd do no more wrong. I also knew that I'd never start another argument until I'd got out of the bath. And towelled off. It was only two months from the day we first met and we had already decided in one way or another that we were going to be together. Needed each other for ever. I held her while she cried some more and I wanted to as well, though I didn't. Even though we made each other so angry, I wanted her and I loved her and I was sure she loved me.

☐

'Drink, drink, drink, got to play catch-up, Charlie boy.'

A bottle is pushed into my hands, now it's champagne. Alex is still playing with the TV, holding pieces of it in his hand and looking nervously at the driver.

'Someone else must have done this.'

'You punched it.'

'I want to watch *Oz*.'

Hyper conversation rattles around the steel box, I am irrelevant.

'Drink up.'

I can't even taste it, it's lukewarm.

'You don't even know what you just drank, do you?'

'What?'

Laughing again.

Ben puts something under my nose, the corner of a credit card. *Come on, let me call Sarah.*

'Don't sneeze, sunshine, this one's very precious, you'll feel much better.'

I need sleep. Haven't slept since before the festival . . . how many hours?

□

'A bottle of champagne, the Aphrodite Suite, a sheet of plastic and some tape for my man here.'

Lights, thousands of small lights and my whole body feels warm and smells of opium and jasmine. I'm in Rome. Pillars and a beautiful woman in a toga, music like a lute and a boom, boom, boom bass but faint. She pours something into the water and she leaves me alone; this is beautiful, everyone stay away. Steam, passing upwards and swirling, becomes smoke and clouds, and the ceiling is blue, becomes sky and then the sky turns into blocks and bricks and then back into sky again. Sarah is next to me and she's touching my face and she's kissing me and I tell her I love her still, that I do miss her after all. I called her and everything is fine now, then the clouds and the sky disappear and I'm slipping, it's lovely being warm when you've been so cold.

'He was under the water, Ben, he could have fucking drowned. You were supposed to be watching him.'

Naked on these hot tiles. Economy air freshener sprayed

automatically from a rusting canister to mask the malodorous yeast, sweat and foam of human scum.

'Where was I? Where the fuck do you think I was, Doyle? Where's the girl that was with him?' shouts Ben

'Who cares?' says Doyle. 'Are you going to trust a fucking hooker? He was under the water.'

I try to say something, keep my head straight, but Ben goes to slap me again. Alex takes him by the wrist.

'Stop bitching. We keep him conscious. This shit'll keep him awake till we get home, just don't let him fall asleep.'

'Ben, I'm not fucking around, don't give him any more. Drugs, anything.'

'I'll get him some water. Now take your fucking hand off me.'

'You can't give him water if he's going to hospital.'

'He's not going to hospital. It was only a bit of smack.'

'I want to call Sarah,' I say.

'Sorry, pal,' Alex pushes a towel under my head, 'can't have the groom speaking to the bride in this condition. Let's get you straight, then you can talk to her.'

*Scared.*

'I'm going to die.'

'No you're not.'

'Get him back to the hotel, get his finger down his throat, he'll be as right as rain.'

'Look at him, Ben, he's fucked.'

'Let's take him to hospital.'

The skin on my face feels like neoprene, my tongue moulded into my teeth, blood in my mouth, not good. I feel hot . . . too hot.

'Get his clothes. Alex, pay the bill and bring the car round. I'll sit with him.'

'I'm telling you, Ben, no more shit.'

'Yes, Mummy, now fuck off.'

He is close, whispering, perspiration, watery, shining skin.

'You're all right, Charlie, listen you're slowing down too fast. Take a bump of this and you'll be all right, we went a bit silly with the brown stuff. C'mon take a bump.'

Another line, wet and thick in the steam, all clogged up, stuck in my nose. Can't breathe.

*Panic.*

'Here, lean back, lean your head back, Charlie.'

Ben drops some water into my nose, rinsing it through.

'Swallow it, swallow it now.'

Coughing, can't breathe, Ben hitting my back. Whump, whump, whump. Cough, breathing again, breathing. Breathing.

Cold air. Want to sleep but I can't now. No one is talking. At the hotel, straight through reception and up to the room. They could clean this place for another twenty years and they'd never be able to remove the film of grease that covers the surfaces, that's penetrated every fibre. Doyle is sitting on the bed next to me.

I have been reassembled by butchers from a rough schematic.

'Ben goes too far sometimes,' he says. He gets up and walks to the door.

'You're all right on your own. Don't fall over in the shower or any shit like that. You've got about three hours, no porn or minibar, the charges are on my card.'

'Can I call Sarah?'

'Christ, yeah,' he says, 'whatever.'

Want to tell her how I need her and hope that she needs me. That I'm sorry for not being there the past few months, but that I'm all right and I'll help, I'll make it up, do anything she wants. She'll see. I can do the right thing. I pick up the phone and dial.

'My God, Charlie, where have you been? What happened to you? Why haven't you called me? I haven't heard anything in a week! Your mum called, she said the hospital called her and your dad said that you fell down some steps, you've broken your arm! Do you *want* to get married? Don't you want this any more? How could you? Charlie, you could have died, you could have broken your neck. What's wrong with you?'

*She doesn't know? She wants to marry me and she doesn't know what's wrong with me?*

'I can't stand it any more, don't you realize how hard this is? And you haven't done anything. Don't you understand? We were meant to do this together! You've left everything to me. You haven't helped me with anything. Do you understand? We're getting married and I feel alone, Charlie. Don't you want this? Just tell me if you don't want to marry me any more, please tell me.'

*Don't you want this any more?*

'I do want this, I love you.'

I want to tell her everything but I can't because I have no answers. That girl I met at the festival. Kelly? I don't know her, or why I took her to Sean's party or why I attacked him. If I am destroying myself I could do it cheaper and quicker maybe with a crushed-up stick of Solidox and some sugar. I could blow my head off and still make the papers for under fifteen pounds.

'God . . .'

Silence.

What do I tell her? The truth. I did nothing with that

girl. I was being stupid. Getting myself in trouble, always in trouble.

'Don't you want this any more?'

There it is again: *Don't you want this any more?*

These words are a klaxon sounding.

She is going to be my wife. She speaks about my mother and Ray the best man, and her mother making the preparations. Already she weaves around my life. She picks up the loose ends and forgotten promises that I abandon like spent books of matches.

*Don't you want this any more?*

Have I collected my suit and my shoes? And the rings and the honeymoon tickets? There are a thousand small jobs to be done and there is no time to think.

'Well, do you?'

'I do.'

I am going to be her husband, she is going to be my wife. 'What am I supposed to do?' she says. 'I'm all sympathized out, Charlie ... You sound like shit. Just come home, Charlie,' her voice softer now. 'Just come home.'

**3**

The boys doze in uncomfortable contortions, while I remain awake, gently blast-frozen by the economy-class aircon – dusty dry eyeballs and a tongue like a crusty Russian bath plug. Ben, Alex and Doyle are asleep, knocked sideways into vacant space. Temazepam, nitrazepam. Time travel will only ever be a chemical experience.

Me? I look like an antique stuffed cat that's been twenty years by a radiator in a bucket of water. The foul glamour of drink and drugs. Maybe someone should have pickled River Phoenix like this, preserving his final narcotic grimace, and done us all a favour.

I want to sleep, I need to, I really do. But the wedding invades my mind. Guilt, and anger at the idea of going home hide behind every thought, jumping out to be greeted with tired surprise, to the point where I want to reach inside my skull and rinse my brain with soap. I put on my headphones, wrap a jumper around my head and listen to the same album again and again, waiting for the point where the clinical, hypnotic repetition of 'Kelly Watch The Stars' and the gas of Valium remove the care in me, bringing nothingness. A space where my thoughts are white noise, like the cyclic mechanical hum that fills the cabin. The end point, a bargain nirvana. A state of mind where you actually stop hating the people who can't sit still, who climb over you repeatedly – for whom the flight is one long unbroken piss.

The bad dream continues until we pass through customs. In the middle of the crowd of West African minicab drivers and families with 'How Did They Do That?' kids is my best man, Ray, holding up a piece of paper with one word written on it.

TWAT

People always say that ugly folks shouldn't have children. And Ray is proof of this. Ray has always said that if he was an accurate gene splice of his parents then he could have had a long and successful life in the circus.

I could have made Alex, Doyle or Ben best man, but it wouldn't have sat right. Ray's been around as long as my fingers and toes, which we learnt to count on together. He deserves it, he's carried the responsibility, and most importantly he's the only person who actually wanted to do it.

'The groom returns. Hey, hey, Charlie boy!'

The line delivers with it an involuntary, cold shiver. I'm getting married tomorrow. Alex, Ben and Doyle turn up having stalked through customs like an aimless Baader–Meinhof cell. Seventies menopause sunglasses, Berlin smack fashion. The mobiles are already out, message services dialled. Interpol could be round the next corner.

Ray takes my trolley and starts to push it.

'Something I said?'

'No, don't worry about it, just a bad flight that's all, I just want to get home.'

I want to keep Ray separate from Alex, Ben and Doyle.

'Did you have a laugh? I like the arm.'

'Three days on and it already smells of spam jelly. Want to smell?'

'Yeah,' he says.

I flip it over and hold the browning palm section under his nose.

'Yeah, spam. This is the fucking limit of course.' He knocks the cast away with his knuckle. 'The breaking the arm before the wedding, oh yeah. They've all been going mental. Sarah's mum wanted to cancel the wedding.'

'She's tried to do that three times already. I have this feeling I'm going to walk out of the airport and get whacked. Nice touch with the "twat" card by the way. It made me laugh inside.'

'Thanks. So what did they do to you then? Anything clever.'

*Ben tried to do me over with a hot-tub speedball and champagne overdose.*

'Nothing, some drinks, bars, same old. I haven't slept.'

'Too much to think about, eh?'

'Yeah, it makes a change, right?'

Alex steps between us, curling a bony arm round my shoulder, ignoring Ray.

'Well, well, married man, can't say I'd want to be in your shoes right now, but we warned you and you didn't fucking listen.'

Ben joins him.

'So we'll see you make a tool of yourself tomorrow then. Rather you than me.'

He slaps me half playfully round the face and my heart starts to beat faster. A rush of hot air fills my lungs and throat, I feel on the verge of combustion. Nausea. This is it. I feel like I'm going to die, go to prison or both at once.

'Pay attention,' says Ben, waving his hand in the direction of my loose shape. 'This is what happens when you get nervous and marry the first woman you have sex with. The berk.'

They all walk away laughing, leaving me and Ray standing either side of my trolley like two confused bombers who've realized that their lunch box has started to tick.

'Nice mates you've got there, Charlie.'

'Yeah, I know they come across . . . a bit harsh, but once you get to know 'em.'

Ray raises the thick eyebrows that he inherited from his father, who has the same colouring as an old Alsatian.

'I'm in no hurry,' he says.

I want to ask him if he's spoken to Sarah. He would have mentioned if Sarah had heard about the girl. Instead I say, 'Her mother really wanted to cancel the wedding again?'

'Yes,' he says. 'The van's this way. She said the cast on your arm would ruin the pictures.'

We get into the van and drive off. Ray flings us sideways out of the car park. He has to hit the brakes immediately as we join the end of a traffic jam edging towards town, heeling the brakes.

I light two fags and hand one to Ray.

'Every time you hit the brakes my delicate bones fail to mesh correctly.'

'Shut up.'

'I'll need to keep the plaster on another week if you keep driving like that.' He rolls the window down and starts beating the door in time to the radio which is running adverts, all of which Ray knows off by heart.

'They really don't want you to get married do they?' he says.

'Who?' I say. 'Sarah's parents?'

'No, Alex, Ben and Doyle.'

Ray works for my old man now, which is why he has the van. Ray drives the van because he spent most of his time at school carving penises into desks and smoking. Sometimes he even smoked while carving penises. Meanwhile I worked a little harder. I'd already worked out that you had to wait till you actually had a job before you could get paid to sit around doing nothing. The school gerbils got a better education than Ray. But then Ray is happy and I'm not, and the gerbils, well, they ate each other's brains during Easter break.

On the way home he fills me in on what's happened. He's collected my suit, paying with money borrowed from my old man, Harold. June, my mother, has been at her 'wits' end', and Sarah called to ask if Ray could find out which hotel I was staying at. She told him she was beyond crying then burst into tears.

Is there anyone I haven't upset?

'How are you, Ray? Have I fucked you off as well?'

'Shit. Everyone just wants to see you back. I couldn't have made New York anyway. I had other things to do.'

'I just wanted to do something different.'

I want to tell him that he would have hated it. But he knows that he wouldn't have fitted in. That they would've ripped him to shreds. It would have been miserable.

'It was a mistake. I'll make it up to you.'

I have all these people in so many different compartments, protecting myself. Fearing they might all meet one day and share the truth about me.

'I will make it up to you.'

'No need,' he says. 'Just get home, get some food and some kip. I've got to go and tart up my speech. Add on the bit about watching three-year-old Charlie chew and swallow an old dog's egg he found in the park. How when we found

31

him he was noshing on it like a big fat chocolate bar – got to get that one in.'

Both of us laugh.

'It was in your teeth. Your mouth was all brown. I remember it on your tongue.'

I go to lick him on his arm. 'I can still taste it,' I say.

'Fuck off, shit-eater!'

It feels good, the sunlight filling the front of the van, smoking hundreds of fags, surrounded by old newspapers and crisp packets. The heat and the laughter warm my bones, and for the first time in weeks I can remember how it was I used to feel.

The road where I was born is lined with sickly looking trees. Each blackened and gnarled and set in an identical rectangle of grey earth. Paving slabs broken under the wheelie bins. Sporadic hanging baskets overflow, giving the houses a pub-like appearance. These belong to the people who make an effort. These, you suppose, are the families who stick around, getting older and fatter like the trees. Growing outwards in concentric rings, increasing in size, experience and in dirt.

The front door opens slowly at first – in the crack, one bottle-blue eyelid winking – my mum. She swings the door open, cardigan belt twisted tight into her middle, looking this way and that as if she expects a bus to tear through next door's garden. She grabs hold of my busted arm.

'Oh, look at what you've done.'

'Watch the arm, Mum. I'm not wearing this for a bet.'

My dad appears at the door while my mum continues to strangle me.

'All right, son? Let him get his breath, woman.'

She won't let go.

'I was so worried . . . you'll be the death of me.'

'Come inside the pair of you. Ray, put his bag in the spare room.'

*Spare room?*

'Yes, boss.'

'Aren't you going to say something, Harold?'

He scans the street for window-twitchers.

'We'll talk later, inside, not in the street.'

'Why can't I have my room?'

'Dennis is moving into your room,' says Mum, addressing the pot plant.

'Where's Dennis now?' I ask. Dennis, their lodger, has been with them for nine months now.

'He's out playing badminton.'

'He hasn't moved into my room, has he?'

Dad pulls a face like he's chewing on a particularly tart piece of apple.

'He'll be home for dinner. Go and give your nan a kiss; she's in the lounge watching telly.'

'Dennis can wait a day. I'll take my old quarters, thanks. And have the staff draw my bath.'

I turn around and they've all walked off.

Ray darts back down the stairs and gives me a restrained tough-man hug. No body contact. The kind you see on the news when POWs are reunited with their old captors.

'Listen, mate, I'll see you tomorrow. I've laid everything out in the spare room and written down a list of things to remember. You'll be sound.'

'Thanks, Ray. I mean it.'

We grip each other again even though I still feel like I've been accosted.

Mum appears in the kitchen doorway.

'Of course,' she says in a vicar's wife sort of voice, 'Dennis offered to let you have his new room for the night.'

'My old room?'

'Yes, but I said no. I said you wouldn't want that, and with him paying and . . .' I never paid any rent. '. . . and you not paying any rent.'

'Yes, but I was born here. Tell Dennis if he wants to sleep in my room it'll be with me and I sleep naked.'

'Beer, son?'

'That'll be lovely, Dad.'

'Go and say hello to Nan, I'll bring you one. Glass or can? French or Australian?'

'Australian. Can, please.'

The dining-room extension ate up most of the grass and a tree had been cut down to make way for a rockery. The flower beds seem to swell that little bit more each year, bleeding colour across the grass. Lush and undisturbed. In my mind's eye I can still see the place where my climbing frame stood, and me hanging off it like a little monkey. Sitting in the shadows out of the light is Nan, slumped in a chair, her knees askew – that carelessness you adopt when you're old enough or drunk enough. She is both.

'Watching the football, Nan? Spurs is it?'

'No, Leeds. Give us a kiss. Watch my drink . . . So, I hear you've been up to no good then?' She sips a ginger ale but she smells of whisky. 'Playing silly goats, I suppose. Thoughtless.'

'You know, you look more and more like Yoda every time I see you?'

'What's a Yoda? Are you being rude?'

'You're the right size, height and colour.'

'What are you saying?'

'But you've got beautiful ears. Yoda doesn't have your ears.'

'That's nice,' she says.

'Your ears are beautiful.'

'Are you ready for tomorrow?' she says.

'What? Are you going to lend me some johnnies?' I say. 'I don't need any. I've got loads. Do you want some? I've got some if you need 'em.'

'You rotten sod. At my age? Are you ready.'

'I've got my suit. A speech of sorts. Clean drawers.'

'You'll need more than that. It's a change coming into your life, Charlie, and we don't like change, no one likes change.'

Nan's soft growl is drowned out by Mum screeching from the kitchen. 'Dinner's on the table. Haaaaaaaaarold!'

A key turns in the lock. Dennis.

'Hello, June, am I late?'

'No, Dennis, you're just in time.'

*Keen little bastard.*

'Help me out of this chair,' orders Nan, gripping my good wrist, 'although with your lame arm and my legs we might not make it to the table. How did you break it? Did it hurt much? Was the doctor an Asian?'

Dennis flaps into the dining room, legs flailing awkwardly, looking like a bat on stilts. Shiny black hair and nasty two-for-the-price-of-one glasses, head spiralling out of his V-neck like a Triffid with a red-brick education.

'Roast beef is it, June? Lovely. Your roast tops my mother's, I'll tell you that for nothing.'

'Oh don't, Dennis! What if she could hear you?'

My mother blushes, and grotesquely her schoolgirl ghost

appears. I look at my father, he stares down at his plate. Back in the bosom of home.

*I have made my choice, I am going to become this. I'll have a family and I'll cook my own roast dinners, and where Nan is sitting, in so many years' time, will be my mother or father, depending on who has the Blitz spirit to outlive the other. Then Sarah and me. And then only one of us. That'll be my family, same name, same vegetables. All these people will be dead and I'll be the sole cause of the generation that follows. My children will become me, become Sarah, more children, new blood, and less of everything to go around. Breeding for breeding's sake.*

There are large veins in the carved meat on my plate, heavy and gaping. Each mouthful rejoining, repairing, twitching in my stomach. My mind is a bobsleigh accelerating. The speed is making me sick. I put a napkin over my plate.

'These are excellent potatoes, June,' says Dennis. 'Have you tried a potato, Harold?'

'I have eaten my wife's potatoes, Dennis.' Dad realizes at once that this sounds vaguely rude, and shoves a whole potato in his mouth.

*Don't talk to my dad like that.*

'Yeah, fuck off, Dennis.'

I visualize myself being sick in his lap.

'Charlie!' My mother jumps in her skin. 'Apologize right now.'

'I'm going for a walk.'

'But you haven't finished your dinner!'

'I'm sick.'

Dennis is eating his dinner, undisturbed.

Mum drops her fork and throws me an all-purpose look of guilt.

'You've been drinking, haven't you?'

'No.'

That look of hers *would* work if it didn't have to join the back of a very long queue.

'I need to get out on my own for a bit. Nan, can I have a couple of fags?'

'There's a fresh pack in me handbag.'

'Harold, say something!'

Dad turns towards me with a smile that makes me ache, just a little bit.

'Are you sure you should go out, son? You don't seem too steady.'

'I'm going.'

'Just make sure you're home in time to phone Sarah, she'll be getting an early night tonight.'

I nod, open the front door and walk out at an escaping pace. This is the last time I'll be able to do this. This is the last time these streets will be relevant; there will be new streets to mould and define me. In minutes, I reach the copse that adjoins my old secondary school, scramble up the verge and jump over the fence. The grass is yellow and tired, trampled into the mud. I scout around until I find the place I used to hide, the hollow of a bush. A lair me and Ray constructed, camouflaged with a sheet of plastic to keep the rain out, and furnished with a candle and a scrap of carpet from a skip.

I'm too big now and it doesn't look as inviting as it once did. To get comfortable now I'd have to fill it with a mattress, 200 fags, some booze, crisps, a TV, a stereo and power it with a line from one of the old prefabs they used as classrooms. Suddenly I feel old. I remember Ray getting pulled out of there by his legs, while I sprinted through the trees carrying nothing but a couple of books covered in thick cream wallpaper and enough cash for some Bensons and a bottle of Coke. That used to do me all right for a whole day. Then the only important marriage criterion was not to have an ugly wife. Now, ten years later, I'm going to have a beautiful wife and I don't think I ever asked myself why. I can't help but think I made the decision with the mindset of an eleven-year-old boy who was just doing what he was told.

Back home there's a note on the mat saying Sarah called and she'll try my mobile. Since the ear tumour frenzy in the papers I've taken to using my mobile as a pocket answering machine. Calling people back from landlines like a blackmailer. The last four days without sleep are starting to tell. I know I'll get some rest at the end of tomorrow, that I'm coming to the end of it now. I'll have a long sleep and Sarah will lie next to me and stroke my hair.

It's 11 p.m. She'll be getting ready for bed. I grab the cordless and make for the spare room. The suit is hanging on the wardrobe door. A tightly stitched seam, penny-cut corners and loud St Martin's lining.

'Hello? It's Charlie.'

'Couldn't you have called earlier?' hisses the woman I won't be calling Mother. 'She's in bed now.'

'Sorry, I went for a walk. So could I speak to her please?' Nearly adding ma'am.

'I'll have to wake her up.'

Yes, yes, nice try. Guilt? Yes. Go through the first set of doors, second left, left again and join the back of the queue.

'Charlie?'

'Sorry to wake you up.'

'You didn't. I was reading. I told her I was going to sleep so she'd stop bothering me. She's been a fucking nightmare.'

I love it when well-educated women swear – the words regain their original power and meaning when delivered unexpectedly with so much poise.

'I'm sorry I didn't ring. I haven't done this before.'

'Neither have I, Charlie. It would have helped if you'd at least tried to make yourself available.'

'I know.'

'You scared me, Charlie.'

'Sorry.'

'How was the flight?'

'Six, seven hours, I don't know, eat, movie, sleep.'

'Were there strippers?'

'No. Please. Strippers are a waste of money, we stuck to hookers.'

'Don't, Charlie. I'm not in the mood.'

'Look. Tomorrow. Tomorrow will be good, I promise. I'll make you proud and you'll be so beautiful. Everyone will be so jealous of me. I'm lucky to have you.'

'I do love you, Charlie.'

'I know. I love you back. I'm sorry I make it difficult. I get confused, people take advantage of my kind spirit.'

'I know.'

'Really?'

'Really. I love you. You're the kindest, stupidest man I've ever met. OK, that's your lot. I'm going now.'

'Now?'

'Yes.'

'I love you too, babe. I love you, too.'

☐

If you know you're not going to sleep, the night is less terrifying. When you stop resisting, the terrible becomes merely boring.

The hours pass, and I rehash the future over and over. My arm is now bandaged. I dissolved the cast in the bath. I had to claw the mess out of the plughole and then run another just to get clean and remove the evidence of the last few days. Underneath, my arm had turned white and tender. I washed it and wrapped it tightly. I'll take the bandage off for the ceremony and the pictures, and have a good day, give a funny speech, cut the cake and dance with the bride. And we won't stop dancing. Ever.

**4**

You change, and then you know that nothing is going to be the same again. I need a cold towel for my face, need to rub it round the back of my neck and place it over my eyes so I can't see. So people can't see me, see my eyes, see what I'm thinking, understand what I've done, why I've done it, why I'm here now. If they could see what I've seen, if they could stand where I stood, half an hour ago, they'd have an answer, they'd have it in spades, maybe someone should tell them.

Here I am, more fat than thin, angry skin, my neck red and hot like a stop light. The room, big and square, lit by a ludicrous chandelier the size of a transit van which is flushing all its poisonous yellow light through my eyelids. Each way I turn, into every face I look, I can see a reflection of myself and my life. Especially the old people. My family, the cheap suits, tired wives, lazily shaven chins and the tie knots that look like the work of a knackered hangman. A family do. All here for me. On the other side, the bride's family, confident and minds made up, facing me like a firing squad. They all know we shouldn't be here, that I'm wrong. Looking at my family, maybe I was born wrong. Watching TV has told me that this is the only excuse left for my generation. Bad genes, a catch-all for every social dysfunction from being unable to spell to indiscriminate murder.

Am I hyperventilating? I don't even know if I'm breathing. What is hyperventilating? Is breath supposed to be so hot coming in and so cold coming out or is it the reverse? Needle-pricks around my eyes, hands and feet, shaking. Shut my eyes and stare down at the carpet again, concentrate on the pattern, very biological, like millions of interconnected sets of ovaries. A tangle of ovaries. Try to fight this, take one long breath, stay with it. Can see the registrar so clearly, the skinny-fingered government vicar, beaming God and law at me over a collapsible catering table. Waiting.

Behind door number one, which might as well be a hospital waiting room, is the happiest woman in the world this minute, this second. Sarah Cane. And all that happiness boils down to words I can't even remember saying. What does that make me? Four words and her eyes opened wide and I kissed her softly and it was done, like that, no going back. 'Will you marry me?'

I can remember the week I decided to propose, when I must have realized that she was the one. We were in Vegas, so I was happy anyway. She didn't want to do it there; she wanted to come home and do it properly, responsibly. I'd bought the ring in a jeweller's in one of the newer casinos on the strip. I used the money that I had been going to spend on the world's largest TV, but by then Sarah looked like a better, longer-term investment in home entertainment. That tiny sacrifice made things better in a way – my kind of sacrifice, one that walks and talks like a sacrifice but hasn't got the shoes for denial. I'd put the ring in the breast pocket of a well cut royal-blue Aquascutum suit (which made me look, for better or for worse, like Roger Moore) and booked a table in the Buccaneer Bay Club at the Treasure Island Casino because I wanted to be near the live sea battle while we ate dinner. This wasn't the most romantic set-up, especially as they repeat the battle every half-hour, with explosions. But what did she care? She must have felt she was a long time waiting, and I knew she wanted me to ask her. That still confuses me. Why? Why choose me? I was not, am so not, in her league. She looked older than me – incredible, sophisticated and did not belong in Vegas. Every dolly bird and pig-skinned Iowan housewife in the room knew this. She came over like European royalty, I came over like a bloke with a bucketful of stems and twenty quid in shrapnel in his pockets. A rose for the lady?

She was confident of what was happening between us, this thing that had developed, alive and unassisted. I wasn't. It was too much for me, the ring in the pocket and the uncontrollable smell of ripening nuptials in the air. And then some time later, near the end of the menu, I stopped thinking and it came. I must have swallowed my fear with the whisky and asked her and she said, 'Yes, I will, I do, for ever . . .'

Over my left shoulder are Mum and Dad. Proud words coming from the East End's finest. Then Nan my dad's mum, and her best friend Mary. Nan is the special one, she looks out for me. She knows I'm shaking like a refugee under this suit. She's never said anything to me about this, I never asked her what she thought, but then I don't suppose she even gave an opinion when my old man got married. Best thing for him? Best thing for me? Fidgeting to my right is Ray, wearing a proper smile and crumpled grey suit, double-breasted and straight out of *Minder*. He looks like shit as usual, but carries his confidence like a hod of gold bricks. Why isn't he the one getting married? Tugging on his lairy Versace tie and flirting with the old girls. He's having a good time, good booze, good laugh. Where does that leave me? Mum's out of her seat.

'We're so proud of you, you know that don't you? I don't have to say it, I know I don't, but we are, both of us. Have you eaten? Did you eat breakfast this morning? Ray, did he eat anything? He looks so pale.'

Eat what? I haven't eaten for days, my stomach's been on fire ever since I realized. Have you ever made a decision you couldn't back out of? Ever made a mistake that was bigger than you?

'What?'

'Nothing, Mum. I'll be fine. I, it's so hot in here, that's all.'

The music starts. Don't go, Mum, slow down and we'll just walk out of here slowly, me and you and make like nothing ever happened. Mum? Help me out here. Responsibility. I can't be responsible for her happiness, the expectation of everyone in the room. Don't they understand that there is more at stake here? Just another invite on the fridge door for this lot. One more do at the tail end of a long summer of weddings. Some people with big families will average up to nine or ten of these weddings a year. No wonder their clothes look so shapeless and worn. They turn out of bed, sit in a hotel they couldn't afford to buy a dessert in, eat the weight of their own heads in prawns and carefully drive home smashed. I have to stand here, swear to a love that I haven't given, pledge a commitment to a life I haven't lived, to a woman I don't know, because I don't even know myself. Muttering now.

'Ray, I can't . . .'

Bile in my mouth, mixing with my words, keeping me quiet.

'Don't be daft. She's coming, mate. Wait till you get a look at her, she's fucking beautiful. Shh. Big smile now, big smile.'

The music stops and she's standing beside me. Sarah. Black hair, beautiful and kind and I'm going to pull her life out from under her because I never thought it would get this far. Just being here, I'm telling everyone in this room, half of whom look like they just left the job club with a handful of free stamps, that I'm going to spend the rest of my life with a woman I can't even look at.

'Charlie? What's wrong?'

Don't. Can't look at her. She'll see straight through me.

'I'm here, I don't feel too good, be OK just got to . . .'

Hold it together. If I move my head up a slow inch, just a little, I can see the registrar's mouth moving, video cameras rolling on either side of him. His bottom lip is swimming with spit.

'I'm overjoyed to see so many people here at the wedding of Sarah and Charlie.'

You don't know me.

'You may not realize this but you're here today not merely as guests but as witnesses.'

I needed witnesses when I crashed my car. Does watching me go through this make them feel like they did the right thing? No eyes filled with tears, remembering their big day, just grey faces. Join us, join us, get married. Want a Merc and a baby seat with a microchip that switches off the air bags? Here's a space-age rucksack rigged up with poles to carry babies and an iPension with iFixed fluctuators and a regular return and fifty pounds a week to die on. Loan rates, Labour's back in again, how's the dollar? ECUs, interested?

Rates? Another penny in the pound and the weather to follow the news. Then death, mate . . .

'Charlie?'

Ray. Whispering during the service. Inappropriate, rude.

'Leave it.'

She knows.

'Charlie?'

Leave me alone, leave me alone. I'll be fine, fine, fine. I'm on my knees. No music playing now. I can feel a cool breeze. You don't have to worry about me, I'll stay still, speaking in whispers now, slowly mouthing every syllable. I'll be here. Lie on my back for a bit.

'Get off my elbow.'

'Mum, get a doctor! Something's wrong with Charlie!'

I'm not collapsing, I just don't know how to say what I want to say and now I can't say anything.

'Get him on his side for God's sake!'

Cold floor.

'I'm not doing this, I can't.'

Sarah crying. This couldn't possibly look worse than it is.

'What's wrong with you? Why are you doing this? I don't understand.'

Her dad's with her now. Look after her. Important man.

'I love you, I'm sorry. I'm sorry. Don't cry.'

Sobbing now. Sobbing because I can't stop the bad thoughts coming that say this is all we have. This life that she wants me to live.

'I don't understand, Charlie. Why?'

'I didn't want this. It isn't your fault, you just believed me when I believed myself when I asked you to marry me . . .'

When is the right time to say, I don't? It isn't during the service. I knew that then, I know that now. The first time you think, I can't do this, you think I better not say anything, it'll pass, I'll get over it. Then two, three months down the line you're lying awake all night pushing your doubts around your mind like golf balls in a can till it's too late. Someone pays the hotel, it's too late. Pays the caterers, it's too late. I'm not hungry and the salmon's dead anyway. Who'd pay twenty grand for dead salmon? I wouldn't. I'd want them alive. Too much pressure. Not a good time to say, 'Like your dead fish, Mister Cane, but I can't do this any more. I was wrong about your beautiful daughter.' Then there's the DJ and the band. All this happens because of something you said on a cold night in the desert to the applause of a bunch of waiters dressed as pirates. At what point does anyone turn round and say to you, 'Oh by the way, when you said that you wanted to get married, do you still feel the same way? Because we can call it off if you like, no harm done.' You really have to be sure about what you're doing. I'm going to do that if I ever have a son. I'll ask him every day. I'll ask him every day, long after the wedding.

This woman. Another couple of minutes and she would have been my mother-in-law. Family. What kind of mother allows her daughter to repeat the mistake she herself made and regretted every day of her married life? Statistically speaking, all of them, I think. Bent and bitter, though I know that on the outside she passes for well kept and moneyed and sometimes wise. But right now our little secret looks like it's about to bounce out into the open. Her eyes are indicators, flashing with hate. She gets her daughter back again sooner than she had thought. The centre of attention. The rich are born for disasters like this. She should be grateful that I've given her the opportunity to shine, to be so right in front of so many people. Mum's pushing her out of the way.

They talk, they both look angry, with each other, maybe not me. My mum's warm hand on my face.

'Can you move darlin', can you get up?'

I'm all right as I am thanks. You see I'm still a baby, Mum. I can't get out of bed in the morning, I've been throwing my job away, I can't pick my own clothes off the floor, I hurt myself on the corners of tables, I drink too much whisky – any whisky – and I won't ever change.

'Please, baby, take a sip of water. Lift your head up. Harold, please . . . for God's sakes.'

'I'll take him to the car, love.'

If you want to know the problem, Dad, it's that I couldn't look her in the eye and see all that love because there was no place in me for it to go. Dad, are you listening? Because you're not going to be here for ever and this has got to be said. There was no place in me for it to go. Did you ever feel like that with Mum? And now I've hurt her. The only woman I think I've loved in twenty-five quick years.

'Grab his legs, we'll carry him out.'

Through the brown window I can see the white speck that is Sarah, ringed by her family, as we pull away from the kerb. You know something's changed and you know that nothing is going to be the same again.

5

'Oh my God!'

Inside the car our tears have turned the air clammy and damp. Mum is crying with her face turned away from me, gulping and honking like an injured seal, face stuck to the passenger-seat window, scaring pedestrians.

'Oh God. Oh God. Oh God . . .'

And I'm rolled up on the back seat wishing the old man would stop the car and make her walk home. That or buy her a fish.

*Shut-up-please-shut-up-please-shut-up-please-shut-up.*

This is like in the old days when they'd drag me out of Ray's house, hysterical. I'd have wanted to stay for dinner and play late and I'd have disgraced them with a bit of early, formative swearing. Maybe asked for a cunting sandwich or pulled down the curtains or annoyed Ray's dog, Lady, so much she'd been sick, again.

I'd be, I am, an embarrassment. I wanted to ask Dad if everything was going to be all right, but that has to be the stupidest question in the entire world right now. And then I see him look at me, see how he looks at me, and my tears stop, dry up.

*I let him see me cry . . . Jesus.*

Why can't he speak to me? What? He can't turn around,

he can't even pull the car over? Stop, lean round and just put a hand on me? Why?

Back at the house everything is so small. It's like looking inside one of those dual-purpose hollow plastic fun trees they stick in pub gardens. The ones that the kids are supposed to play in while everyone gets wasted – and where you always find used condoms and old syringes. That says a lot about smack heads. Injecting themselves in fantasy trees. Mum is crying. Dennis is pulling packets out of the freezer, assembling a patchwork slop of dinner. Dad has both his hands on the sink, staring into the garden. Smash robots without the mirth.

Really the only reason to be here is the bathroom cabinet. Six Nurofen, a couple of sleeping tabs and twenty milligrams of Valium. To take the edge off. Mum's got these pills backed up in that cupboard like beans in Tesco.

Twenty minutes later I'm hunched over on the edge of the bed in the dark waiting for the mixture to have the Ready Brek effect, get down and glow, when Dad knocks on the door. I'm happy that he's here. He walks over to the bed and gives me a body-temperature Scotch in a tall thin glass – the kind you used to get free if you collected six tiger tokens and were too impatient to wait around for the combination clock radio/ear strimmer. This feels like the kindest thing he has ever done for me and I want to smile. We don't speak much ever, and we haven't had the practice for a conversation this big. Even though I don't know what to say, I could really do with a hug right now, but he leaves straight away. No words, nothing. Then the door closes, and left inside this room, inside me, the pain erupts, so much that I'm bent over clawing at the walls and the floors. An open, endless scream of pain that won't sound, won't stop, that can't go anywhere but around the inside of my head, never escaping, trapped like an underground blast. Double-glazed with pills, I can't be hurt, and I should feel all of this. I want to drown for what I've done. I'm sitting here watching, doing nothing, exploding.

Don't get me wrong, the drugs do work. Whatever quiet, calm normality I have now comes like an advertising break during a lurid Channel 5 special about my life. Distracted, I can operate. Moving radio switches. Bedding. Loosening my tie. Taking off my shoes. Slowly the numbness finds its way across my body until I am upright, by the edge of the bed, rubbing my head, sipping whisky. Feeling shapeless and indifferent.

I go downstairs for dinner; the house remains silent as Mum serves up the food. I suppose I would have liked everyone to change out of their wedding clothes. If Sarah was here in her dress, crying a river, we'd have made the effort then. Stumbling round the house dressed like we are, we could have spent the day at a funeral.

Dennis drops into the chair next to me like a spider monkey reversing cack-handedly out of a tree. He smells like coal tar soap and Persil. You can read Dennis like the order of service. His whole life story could be sung in order. Regular, righteous, monotonous. Slightly repelled by my new misfortune, Dennis is careful not to touch me in case I jinx him on his long on-going quest to dredge up a woman. I know he had a girlfriend once and we've seen pictures which he put before us like a defence lawyer.

From the hollow 'Jesus Fills This Space' expression on her face, you could tell she was too much even for Dennis. You could tell she lived in her walking boots. That they never really had any fun together. That their relationship was probably nothing more than an extended geography field trip. One picture sealed it. It was of her in her bedroom. She was wearing a thick fleece and rugby shirt. For decoration: three scented candles and, most important of all, an impassable pile of teddy bears arranged over the head of the bed, which positively screamed 'I don't fuck here! You have no chance! Back away from the bed with your hands behind your head!'

I remember then that I almost felt sorry for him. He probably didn't ask much of her and treated her well, with respect. I don't know why they split up. I didn't care enough to ask. We never really know why people split up, but if we are honest the reasons are often a lot darker, more unpalatable than we are ever ready or willing to let on.

You know what I mean. Take a moment.

Dennis brushes against me, manoeuvring himself into the small awkward spaces left by the bulbous faux-ornate table legs. We touch thighs, some warmth is exchanged and he pulls himself back, shocked and disturbed, like the soap on a rope he just grabbed in the showers wasn't a soap on a rope but a very thick, very soapy penis.

'I'm sorry,' he says officiously.

'Don't worry, Dennis,' I say, 'I don't think I'm pregnant.'

Despite Mum's desire that we chew food and engage in clever discourse like Oxford dons, mewing over each other's ripe wit, dinner in this house has always been about getting your head down and finishing first. With Dennis still in the grip of a cold homophobic/anxious fear, Mum starts assembling the peas and carrots in silence. Her movements are methodical and definite. As if to say, I can do this. I can serve vegetables like the Queen of England. No one can say I'm a bad mother.

Our heads are bowed, looking down at the food, untouched. We could almost be saying grace, but it would have to be: 'For what we are about to receive may the Lord make us truly suspicious.'

It smells of toe jam and dairy fats and is orange. It is suffocating under a gleaming white emulsion that is itself speckled with red-and-grey vegetable fragments. To be honest it looks like it fell out of a pipe, exhausted, a mile offshore of Margate. Dennis tucks in first. Having had the privilege of reading the packet before he heated it up, he will at least be able to tell the doctor what it was we ate when we get to the hospital. Over and over again it keeps sliding off his fork before it reaches his mouth. It resists even in death. I feel drawn to watch him like I am to an emailed MPEG of a skateboarder shattering his hip.

Mum finally brings herself to look at me. She is shaking, her eyes ringed black and red, mascara and anger.

'I'm sorry, Mum. I—'

Immediately she heaves and begins to sob again, pushing her plate forward and crying into the palms of her hands.

Dad turns on her.

'For God's sakes will you stop now?'

Then he turns to me.

'What did you set her off for?'

'I wanted to say sorry.'

She is still crying. She is becoming hysterical, banging and knocking the table.

'What about Sarah? What about that beautiful girl whose life you've ruined? You've ruined everything, your life, her life, everything. You stupid bastard, you stupid bastard, you've ruined your life. You've ruined your life.'

I start crying now. I didn't realize that she might love

Sarah or want her too. I thought this was my choice, my life, that this was exclusive to me.

'I'm sorry, I'm sorry, I'm sorry, I'm sorry.'

My heart breaking in a thousand different ways, my stomach folding in on itself. 'I never wanted to hurt you and—' Can't say this, why can't I say her name out loud now? Say it. But I'm interrupted by the cheap invasive trilling of the phone in the hallway.

No one moves, hoping it might ring, ring so loud and so long that the plaster falls off the walls and Dennis's teeth explode in a crimson cloud. But Dad wants to leave it be. No one, thinks my old man, is picking up that phone. We might all go crazy waiting it out. Mum keeps looking forlornly out into the hallway, while Dad attempts the kind of telepathy usually employed by senior X-Men, trying to block her desire to pick it up.

Dennis attempts to put the same forkful of thing back into his mouth.

Mum has secured her hands in her lap, she throws her head back. 'Harold!'

'No, leave it!'

Dennis looses a slither of thing from his fork. It drops onto the edge of the plate, sliding onto the table like a wounded Slinky bleeding cream sauce.

Harold loses his patience.

'June, Will You Please Take The Phone Off The Hook.'

'But Harold,' she sniffles, 'it might be someone important.'

'Now, June!'

She pulls herself arthritically out of her chair and stands guard by the phone like a half-starved, hypothermic sentry. On the next ring she yanks the handset off the cradle.

'Yes?'

Dad leans forward, wraps his arm round his plate prison-style and angrily chews away while she talks.

'Hello, Nan. He's been in his room. No. No. He's not been well for a long time.'

One call is followed by another, then another. Are they going to set another date? Is he in hospital? Is it meningitis?

Does your mother ever stop making excuses for you? Three hundred people asking why? Three hundred. On the phone, eating their Marks and Spencer microwave broccoli: 'Do you know so and so's boy? . . . I heard . . . you won't believe . . . never seen anything like it . . .' Everyone I know, don't know but was expected to know.

That's what happens when you fuck with responsibility. Questions. You owe everybody. Owe money, owe time, emotions, answers, explanations . . .

Then another and this time she is silent and then her voice morphs into Mary Poppins's. 'Yes, speaking. Oh, hello . . .'

This is not good. This is the kind of voice she used when someone's mother phoned up from school about broken windows, broken noses or a missing bike. Mum would say indignantly, 'My little Charlie just isn't like that, Mrs Thurstings.' Even if she'd just seen me park the kid's bike in the garden and the old man was turning purple because I'm refusing to give it back.

Flushing cold, I can only think of one person with anything to demand of my mother right now.

'Yes, no, you're welcome to. Really it's only right. No. No. We all are. No. I know. Yes. About an hour? Yes. I understand she must be. I'll tell him. I'm sure, OK, goodbye then.'

Red-faced and panicked, she pops her head around the

doorway and calls Harold out to the hall. Harold returns to the dining room, puts his hand on my shoulder.

'Go and get cleaned up. Sarah's coming round in an hour.'

*What?*

I'm out of my seat.

'What did you do that for?'

'You owe her.' He puts his other hand on my shoulder to steady me from bolting out of the room.

'You've got to talk to her. She needs to know what happened, don't you think?'

'I can't.'

'Well, she's coming now,' says Mum.

'Cheers.'

What do I say? How many times can you say sorry to someone before they realize that it's actually insulting. Once? Most times not even that.

There is no one word I can use to get out of this. There is no hole I can fall down, no emergency hatch. Time can't go backwards only forwards, and waiting in my old room lying on this tiny single bed with brown cotton sheets, worn smooth, I feel as inept and as stupid as I ever did as a teenager – when I prayed I'd get out of this house, be with a good woman who loved me, and I'd be strong and rich, because that is what happens. Because I believed that there was someone for me somewhere and that they would actually come along at the right time and nothing would ever get in the way of that. Yeah, right.

I hear a car pull up in the street and three doors slam, Kerchunk. The satisfying sound of German engineering. Footsteps on the stairs and then my door opens.

My thin curtains have no lining and can only sieve the light from the street lamp outside my window. She is standing in the corner of the room, I can still barely see her. Partly because from here she seems to have been swallowed by the orange shadows that cross the ceiling. Instinctively I press the soft underside of my arm against the cold woodchip on the wall and cool the blood that runs in mass under the surface of my skin. She sets herself at the edge of the bed, starts crying, sobbing. Proper wrenching. Crying openly, freely because she can, because it's only us now.

'I don't know what to do . . . I . . . don't . . . know . . . what . . . to . . . do . . .'

*It wasn't my fault.*

My stomach instantly seizes and my bowels seem to fill with hot tea.

Strands of smooth rich black hair are stuck to her damp skin. Her lips and eyes swollen. She has been crying for hours. It strikes me that I might look like her now if I hadn't taken those pills. I look dead instead. I don't get up.

The air has turned perfume-counter sweet. Her scent, her mother's, their car, her father, their house fills the small room. I always noticed as a kid that every family had its own smell. I used to check out the smells of other people's houses and remember them, like a dog nosing around the park. The wrong kind of smell; the unfamiliar, like spiced cabbage, or the overwhelming, like fried fish, and I'd feel wrong-footed, unwelcome.

She speaks.

'If you didn't want to marry me you should have said.'

*I know. But it wasn't my fault, I didn't know what to do.*

'Can't you even look at me?'

*It wasn't my fault.*

'Why, Charlie, why? Don't you have any respect for me?

How could you break your arm? How could you be drinking for five days? You were going to stop, and cut down and get fit for the wedding and you didn't. You were in New York and now I don't know where you've been or who you've been with or what you've done. Why? Why now, why couldn't you wait? Got through today? We could have.'

'I couldn't do it.'

'What do you mean?'

'I couldn't do it. I realized I couldn't do it and it was too late to stop. Stop me, stop you. Stop anything. I couldn't tell you.'

'You fucker. What do you mean you couldn't do it? What does that mean? You couldn't tell me. What?'

'The pressure. I can't. I'm not right enough for this kind of pressure, not now.'

*We should do this another time.*

'Please.'

Slowly I bring up my knees, curling away from her like those stupid Christmas-cracker fish you place in the palm of your hand.

'What are you fucking doing? What are you doing to me! Don't turn away!'

'You shouldn't be here. I couldn't do it. That's all.' Facing the wall now. Hands covering my ears.

'I'll never be able to face anyone ever again. Why, why now? Why now, Charlie? You were going to stop drinking. You were going to be there. For us!'

She is on top of me, hitting me. Her fists drumming on my back.

'Look at me when I'm talking to you. LOOK AT ME. Look at me. Look at what you've done.'

I put my hands over my head, to protect my face, my ears.

Not from her punches but from her voice. The sharpness. I can't bear it cutting me, a storm that rattles and shakes the windows and doors. 'Why couldn't you have told me?'

'I couldn't, there wasn't time.'

*How could I have told her?*

'But we are meant to be married. This morning you told me you loved me, Charlie.'

'I'm confused, there wasn't time.'

'What? Stop saying that.'

'It's better we stop now.'

'Don't you love me?'

'I do love you. I love you more than you know. I'm scared. I can't see you now. I'm scared, I don't know what to do. You should go because I can't.'

She cries for another five minutes, maybe more. I think about her and the way I thought she'd solve all my problems. Now, I have no memory of her leaving the room. When she is gone my room kind of smells like *our* house might have smelled. Our family. And later I realize that I have no memory of whatever it was that ever kept me upright. Helped me walk, fight. Get up from defeat and carry on. I can't do that any more. I can't love her any more. I can't be with her. Because I'll be unhappy. Because, then my life will be her life. I don't want to be what I'll be if I'm married to her.

**6**

The next day I can't look in the mirror. I just try to remember to have a bath, eat whatever gets put in front of me and deal with it. Even growing up in this house I felt like Terry Waite chained up to a radiator. I realize there is no place for me. No place I can exist. I'll never be happy anywhere, because I'm not that type of person. I'm a freak, an uncomfortable combination of the Incredible Hulk and Morrisey – destined to roam the world friendless. Also what I really need is to get my hair cut.

I've been going to the Greek barber's on the roundabout since the day I was born. For a fiver and a small piece of ear cartilage you'll walk out the shop looking like Tom Cruise in *Top Gun*. This is a way better cut than the one you get at the unisex place on the parade where they make you look like Tom Cruise in *Risky Business*.

I get halfway there and I seize up. I'm standing outside a Wetherspoon pub, opening and shutting my mouth. I look like a snake swallowing lizard eggs. There are people walking by, staring, and there's me and my floppy jaw. I've lost it, I'm one of them: mental, homeless, a day-release screamer, care in the community. I just wear better clothes maybe, got a bit of fat on my bones.

I'm frozen in space. I can't move and it's like my heart is

wide open in my chest and anyone can take a piece of it. I am vulnerable and weak, my expression set and vacant. The computer has crashed and the monitor has frozen. Right now, no sound penetrates this bubble. Inside, I can hear the electricity snapping around my brain. Snap, crackle, pop.

I am descending into hell as, garden gate by garden gate, palms speckled with grey paint and dirt from grasping at lamp posts, leaning, stumbling, falling, I crawl my way back home. Oxygen flashing around my worthless plastic lungs.

Mum is at the front door and Nan is telling her to be quiet, that I need hot sweet tea, and then she sticks a little bottle of evil salts under my nose. Her sleeves are packed with rolled balls of pink tissue. A flame of ammonia blooms in my sinuses. When the mug of tea plays across my front teeth I start to wonder whether I was actually safer on the street.

In a kind of medieval way, the agony and burning liquid return the colour to my cheeks, convincing the well-meaning fishwives that I'm in better health and in no more need of bleeding or rigorous purgatives. I nod, smile and blink rhythmically – mimicking the intake of deep restorative breaths, the universal silent code for 'I'm all better, please stare at somebody else now.'

'He needs a doctor,' says Nan.

'He needs a bath. He's got a hangover, what a bloody fuss over nothing.'

I try to tell them that I haven't been drinking, but I'm not sure if I have or haven't. Getting into bed, I remember that me and Sarah were at a dinner once when she asked the same question. I said no, honestly, I hadn't drunk anything at all that day. She said I was acting a little strangely, which was true. I was talking 'hep' like Snagglepuss and repeatedly grooming myself – picking small pieces of fluff off my sleeves and paying close attention to my nails. I was in the process of smoothing out my eyebrows when it occurred to me that I actually had been drinking since before lunch, and I'd probably downed about fifteen doubles. I'd just blanked out, forgotten, lost the whole session. I was fuming drunk, but believed myself to be sober, perfect and attentive. Sarah never mentioned it again so I guess the evening ended OK and no one got hurt.

The old man walks in the front door, and shouts up the stairs, do I want to share a curry?

In the lounge Dennis is watching TV and eating mutter paneer. The only seat left is between him and my mum. The air reeks of Dennis and his curried cheese. I have to forcibly close my swollen eyes with my fingertips, jamming my thumbs in my ears. The realization that my mother is going to fuck Dennis is crushing. I walk out of the room blind, like my father.

On my knees halfway up the stairs I know there is no blood in my face and that I'm not strong enough to push Dennis away from my family. He belongs here more than I do because at least my mother wants him. From here I can see into the kitchen. Dad is opening and shutting cupboards, scratching various parts of himself, just being human, flesh and blood, and hopeless, and so close to being hurt. How, after thirty years, can you be dropped as fast as a teenager on the end of a phone line. Doesn't life get safer, fairer? Is that how close we are to losing what we have? Later he drives me to casualty. We sit there in silence for six hours. My arm is X-rayed and recast. The doctor tells me that I have been a fool and that he might have to re-break my arm.

☐

Back at home the wounded soldier is in his bedroom. Messing with everything. Rearranging the two wooden chairs, taking down posters and putting them back up again, sniffing and shouting involuntarily and doing a pretty fair impression of Al Pacino at the Ideal Homes show. All I can see is a wish made three decades ago unfolding and revealing its true worth. Can only see that marriage is just a promise, no more than an elaborate handshake. It has no value, no weight, no miraculous adhesive qualities. It's nothing more than an envelope that, depending on how two people feel, can hold a million dollars or a worthless wad of newspaper.

I'm sitting up in bed, staring at nothing in particular and thinking that leaving Sarah was the right thing to do. I have to keep hold of this, I can't let my mind be in all those places. I have to stand by what I have done.

It's dark when I go down to the garage and dig out a couple of bottles of home-brewed red wine which is bloody and thick, the sediment turning my teeth red. In a brief moment of satisfied, drunken amusement I smile at myself in the mirror. I look like I fell asleep eating a live rabbit. Attractive.

The wine is finished, and at 7 a.m. the front door slams shut and Dennis is out of the gate, galloping down the road like a giraffe. The noise is a signal for everyone else to rise. I can hear the old man blowing out a loud fart in anticipation of his entrance to the toilet.

He always gets up earlier than he has to, listens to the radio and takes some time for himself. Last night in the kitchen, when I could see him, really see him, I thought we had something in common. It would be nice if we could leave for work about the same time, walk down to the station together. Talk about work. We've never done that, it would be cool.

I pull on my dressing gown and go downstairs and watch TV. Some weather presenter praying for a slot on *Watchdog* says it's going to rain. I've got to eat, wash, dress and be back down here in half an hour to catch the old man by the door. The thing is, I've never managed to maintain a state of alertness through an entire weather broadcast. By the time they get round to 'the weather in your region' bit my breathing is often dangerously shallow and I'm dribbling like Uncle Clive when they turned the machine off.

Mum sits down beside me eating something called a toaster pocket, which is filled with jam. She looks at me as if I've chewed my ropes, outwitted the dogs and escaped from my cage in the cellar. Scowling, she puts one on a plate for me but it tastes like something you might eat at the fair.

'What? I'm watching telly,' I say.

'What are you doing out of bed?'

This confounds me. She looks back at the TV. I can tell I've got in her way. I'm in her space. I blush with embarrassment.

Dad stands in the doorway and stares at us in our dressing gowns.

'I'll be late . . . Architects.'

Mum doesn't even register his presence. I blush again, this time for both of us. He leaves without me.

I get it in my head that I'm needed at work, that I've got a job to do. Something I haven't really cared about in a year. I mean, I'm on my last legs, I can't use a toothbrush and now it's suddenly important I get to work? Straighten up and fly right. Build bridges, get on board, do the right thing. I think, Fuck Sean with his burnt head. Fuck all of them, I can make things right, they hate me but they need me, I can live with that. I also need a smoke – grass, or heroin if anyone has it.

I'll need something, and self-medication is better than no medication. You see there's not much difference between getting your drugs from a dealer or a doctor. It's all about money at the end of the day. Rasta or Pfizer, makes no difference, and no one ever gets the doses right anyway. The one singular difference is that when you pick up your prescription from the chemist you don't have to sit around for three hours sharing your Anusol with him and helping apply it to a couple of old girls while listening to Armand Van Helden. Not much of a scene that.

I decide that I'm going to use the last three hundred in the bank to buy enough little bags to get me through the next couple of weeks, maybe longer. Get the train in, be there for 10.45 to clear the desk. I'll go through the back door, wait around, obscured by the partition surrounding the fashion editor's desk, and arrange things on the sly from my remote command post . . .

This train. I can't not look at the people in the carriage. There is a part of me in all of them. All their thoughts, frustrations, anger and failures. I am the old, the young. I am the dirt on the floor, the bad suit with the scuffed shoes, I am the hopeless vanity of the designer jacket, the gel on the hair meant to impress, a Belisha beacon of failure. I belong nowhere, they belong nowhere, only they don't realize it and I can't help them because I can't help myself.

I start gripping my head. And the more I try to stop the more the thoughts become bigger, more painful, faster. I start talking, people move away from me, and now they're watching. I roll into a ball, while they sit there reading the

*Daily Mail.* They couldn't possibly understand that while they're looking at a picture of a badger with its leg wrapped up in plaster because it's fallen off some council-house balcony and saying ahhh I am less than that badger.

All sound is amplified ten, twenty times in a huge rush of fear. Heat. Anything moves and I know it, feel the air move. I am four steps back from the real world with the panicked panoramic vision of an injured animal, waiting.

The world is moving faster than I can possibly imagine, one mouth holds a thousand conversations and individual cheek hairs stand on end, scaled and broken – and I'm moving further and further away from the fight, there is too much information coming in, too much danger, I have to shut it down, I have to stop thinking and then I remember what I've done.

SARAH, AGAIN, AGAIN, AGAIN.

My insides twisting and I flash hot and then cold and people are backing away from me and I'm being sick over shoes and legs, rolling on the carriage floor.

What I thought was pressure has become something else. I have become something else. I can't even ride a train. I can't not be sick on people. I black out.

I'm drinking a Coke, sitting on a chair on the platform, wondering how I'm going to get home, when this old lady stops to drop a pound coin into the can.

Ray says he'll come and get me. It takes about ten minutes for me to find an exit and a street name and a place he'll see me. No cab is going to pick me up covered in sick. I sit in a charity shop doorway where no one seems to mind that I went wrong today. Where was I going? For the life of me I don't know. Was I going to see Sarah?

A white van pulls over across the road and Ray runs through the traffic. He looks indestructible.

'Now, mate, I'm on a double red.'

All right. He pulls me across the road, sticking his arm out to hold up the traffic, me scuffing and tripping behind him.

'Jesus. You ain't sitting in the van like that. You stink of sick.'

It's on my hands where I wiped my chin.

'You need clean clothes.'

'I've got no money. I need a bank.'

'I don't mean a fuckin' shopping trip, Charlie.'

He pulls open the van door and roots around in the back.

'What happened? Drinking with the boys again?'

He tries to make this sound empathetic, matey.

'I had a drink last night, on my own. Nothing. Something else. Flu, something. I've had a sore throat for weeks.'

'Yeah.'

'Look, an old lady gave me a quid,' I rattle the can at him, 'but it's in this can.'

'I hope you didn't have to do anything serious for it.'

He looks at me, we both laugh and he grabs a greasy plastic zippersuit, the kind you use when you're crawling around in dirty places and you need to keep your normal working rags decent. As I start stripping down I want the laughing to hide the shame, but it doesn't. Throwing my clothes in the back I'm blushing again, face hidden. I want Ray to drive, watch the road, say nothing and forget everything.

If anyone actually noticed me getting home in a synthetic white boilersuit they didn't mention it. I don't bother to get changed. After days and hours playing the same worn loop, my head pops like the bulb in an overheating projector. The two sides of my brain, bound to the time Sarah left the room, push away from each other like disgusted lovers. One side, the sweating, screaming animal me wants to live. The smaller quieter half wants to die. I don't know which one suffocates my shouts with my pillow or hides my growls from the outside. But now my mind is made up.

The last time I thought about suicide was as a teenager. I'm not saying I stood at the top of the stairs and shouted that I'd kill myself if I didn't get my own pony or anything like that, but sometimes I'd dwell on it for a while, wondering who might be tortured by my death, before having a look in the cupboard to see if there were any crisps left.

No, this is the first time I've come close to being serious. That's if serious means standing over a sink, turning purple, holding a razor. You ask yourself one question. It all hangs on this. Do you really want to stop being, now?

And then for want of a better word, you bottle it, you cower before the blade and life comes back in a rush of pain and you evacuate the scene as fast as you can because you don't really want to die, in shame.

It's the first time I've even been aware of myself, my body, for a long time. I can feel, see everything. My colour, the shape of my limbs, my teeth, my hair – how big my ears are. There's a mirror opposite my bed, nothing kinky. I've never spent any time lying here applying lipstick like Dennis Nielson or talking to myself provocatively in French or anything. It's just a mirror. I realize that I am overweight. I have love handles. I am all new to me. I am new tonight.

The small half might want to die but the big half wants to live. The big half still cares. Cares about everything. That's me. I'm not about dying. The little half sounds full retreat, suicide banners disappearing over the hill in clouds of gun smoke. The big half wants to see how it ends. Wants to see the sun come up, wants to see what's for dinner, wants to know if Charlie should have got married, and wants to know why this is happening. Maybe just wants to know what's going to happen next.

# 7

I had a moment of clarity. The kind geniuses have on TV when they solve a big problem scrawled across a blackboard. Where every point of the mind joins instantaneously, and a bolt of nano-lightning fires along an exact synaptic route from ear to ear and you say, 'Bingo.'

I am slapped sideways by my own brain, and before I know it I'm dressed in the wedding suit, wearing a fine pair of gold-framed Cutler and Gross sunglasses and slamming the door behind me – and I'm not frightened this time. I'm churning up the road, and I mean truckin'. I'm unstoppable, the pavement's disappearing under my feet. I'm thinking I can walk like this for ever, walk all the way. 'Hello, baby, I'm home. Did you wait up?'

I catch my reflection in the minicab office window and strike a pose. I look pretty fucking dandy. Then I get hungry and realize I can't remember where her parents live. I know it's a place where all the houses are big and you can't see into the front gardens because of the big black gates and police-approved anti-burglar shrubs. I also realize that it's bad manners to turn up without a gift basket or something for her mother. So I look around for a shop, and before I know it I'm standing in front of the pub where I bought my first pint. Within seconds I'm through that door and propping

up the bar like nothing ever changed. I've got my pint and
my short and my money and my fags arranged around me
like guard dogs, and I'm having a big smile at everybody. No
one passes me without getting flashed the full beam. I'm
spinning around on that bar stool like Liberace taking
requests. I'm buying rounds and talking people out of halves
and shaking hands and chucking over crisps for the kids.
Then I realize half my cash is gone – I must have dropped it
or something. So out goes the gift basket, and instead I get
a bucket of chicken, choccies, a bottle of brandy and some
vino. I can hardly walk with all this and the taxi driver
doesn't like it either, he won't shut up:

'You ain't eatin' that in the car.'

And I'm like, 'Kentucky Fried Chicken Party Bucket Cole-
slaw and Beans? Small chips? Why not?'

'You ain't gonna eat that in the car.'

'Why?'

'Chicken grease on the seats, man, shit.'

'Small fries?'

'What?'

'Small fries?'

'Man, you getting chips on the floor. Put the lid on it or
you gettin' out.'

'I got more chips than I need. Don't kiss your teeth. I'm
offering you free chips. If you don't want 'em I'll throw 'em
out of the window.'

'Man, not on the seat. Where you say again?'

'North, just keep going north.'

'North?'

'Can you hold this bottle for me?'

'Shit.'

□

'Charlie, what are you doing here? Is this a joke?'

'Sarah, who is it?'

'Charlie, my mum's coming, just go!'

Her face seems drawn and hospital white. Hair pulled back tight over her skull into a sickly looking ponytail. She must have a cold because she's wrapped a blanket round her shoulders. She needs me to look after her. Sort things.

'Sarah, please, baby. You don't look well.'

'What! Charlie? Are you surprised? Three days ago you ruined my life. You were on drugs at our wedding, Charlie. Fucking drugs at our wedding. Why should I talk to you? When I came to see you, you said that was it. Well fuck you, what do you want from me?'

'Just to talk for a minute. Look I've brought dinner with me . . . it's getting cold.'

I hold up the bucket of chicken so she can see it clearly from her bedroom window.

'Oh God, Charlie. Look at yourself! Can't you see what you've done? Why can't you understand?'

Her mother opens the front door and rolls forward. She dominates the porch like a cashmere tank.

'Hello, Mrs Cane. I forgot what a nice house you have.'

'Stay away from my daughter.'

'I've brought dinner.'

'What? What's that?'

'Chicken.'

'No one wants anything from you.'

'Mum, please let me talk to him alone.'

'He's drunk.'

'He's not well, Mum.'

'Look at him.'

She turns on me. Her face begins to rearrange, drawstring

eye sockets, top lip curling under her nose, baring her slab teeth.

'How dare you come here after what you've done? Go away. You're not welcome. Get out of my pond or I will call the police.'

Sausages, you old dog.

'Mum, please, go inside, let me talk to him.'

'I've come a long way, Mrs Cane, Andrea. I got all dressed up, and I've brought some brandy and some chocolates for you.'

'Go away!'

Woof, woof.

'You go away!'

'Mum, you're making things worse!'

I try to move. I didn't intend to stand in the pond; I sort of fell into it sideways. I'm up to my knees in mud. It's a serious miniature lake, with sloping banks and fat orange and white fish that look as if they could see off a fox.

'Don't come near me. You're a disgrace!'

'I can't. I don't want to.' I offer her the chocolates.

'I'm here to say sorry to Sarah. Don't get in my way. Please let me say sorry properly. I've done a lot of thinking.'

Sarah leans further out of her window.

'And what do you think I've been doing, Charlie? I've been thinking too. What you did to me was disgusting. Look at me.'

'I told you, I didn't know what was happening.'

'You did. You don't think you do but you did. We were meant to be on our honeymoon now, Charlie!'

That last bit comes out as a scream.

'And look at you!'

Andrea now stands between the two ornamental Roman pillars, hands on hips.

'Stay away from this house!' she booms with lungs resonating like bass bins.

I can't climb out of the pond holding all this gift food, so I start throwing it – the wine, the chicken and the chocolates – onto the grass bank.

Andrea starts screaming, 'Sarah!'

'He's not throwing them at you. Charlie stop! You're frightening us.'

'I can't get out of this fucking pond! I want to talk to you, I really do.'

'Please go away. Maybe you can come back when you feel better.'

'For God's sake shut up, Sarah.' Andrea dry heaves, her anger must be taxing that underused leathery heart of hers. 'Right. I'm calling the police.'

'Mum, don't. I'll call Ray.'

I can't believe this is happening. I've got no energy left, crawling up the bank. I'm stuck halfway out of the water. It's like I've swum thousands of miles to bury my eggs on her lawn.

'Mum, let me help him.'

'No!'

Why can't she just come down here and speak to me? I can't do this on my own; my lungs are burning and I'm cold and tired. Most of the chicken is now floating around behind me. The fingers on my busted arm are numb and I smell. And I think I might have fallen from the top of the gate. The last time I was here it opened by remote control. I spin around and sit on the bank, knocking the top off the brandy bottle. I've got my back to the front of the house. This way they won't see me. It burns a cyclone down my gullet to the pit of my stomach making me cough and retch.

'Charlie, please don't drink any more.'

I'm choking in the fumes, gasping for air that is already thick with evaporating alcohol. I need some of that chicken.

'Let him do what he wants. Your father will be home soon. He can drown for all I care.'

'Great,' says Sarah.

One of the fish rises to have a go at the batter and I notice that I've ripped the left trouser leg of my wedding suit. I sit there dazed until the arrival of Sarah's father.

'Wake up, you stupid bastard, get up.' Sarah's father's long girlish fingernails rake my neck as he pulls impotently on my collar. 'Get up. Get out of here, get out of here, move, go on.'

'Please let me help him.'

'No!'

Someone's got hold of my wrist, dragging me.

'Fuck off, fuck off, fuck off.'

I snatch my arm back and turn myself over onto my knees. Grabbing my brandy and my chocolates, I run towards the big grey Jaguar parked on the circular gravel drive. Her old man is behind me. Shouting and showing off, making a load of noise like he's trying to scare a bear away from the family picnic. He's five foot tall and about as dangerous as a cheese plant. I don't know what he thinks he's going to do when he catches me. Am I going to get an audit? I'm not a bank. He can't scare me. I jump on the car bonnet, then scramble onto the roof.

Sarah runs out of the house with the blanket around her shoulders.

'Why are you doing this? I can't believe you're actually making things worse!'

'Sarah, please. We can go for a walk. C'mon, Sarah, just me and you.'

A man in a suit is leaning on the fence next door.

'Is he going to jump?'

'Oh fuck off, John.'

'Harvey!'

'Sorry, Andrea.'

Christ, they're all turning on each other.

'I only wanted everyone to have a drink with me, Mr Cane, and now your fish are eating my chicken.'

'Why don't you use the power hose on him?'

'What! Mum. Dad, you can't!'

He already has the garage door open, pulling out the hose like a giant tapeworm.

'No, Dad, you'll hurt him. Ray, stop him! Dad, no! Charlie, get down.'

The water hits me right in the chest, I drop the brandy bottle through the windscreen. I'm on my knees. Screaming, 'Don't tread on me! You can't stop the music!'

Ray comes out of nowhere. He gets a good hold and pulls one of my legs out from under me, spinning me onto my back and dragging me off the roof. I need to be on the car, they listen when I'm on the car.

'Aaargh. Fuck off, Ray! Ray, please, fuck off!'

He puts me in a headlock and drags me away from the house. He's breaking my neck and I have to run to keep from choking. My flimsy wedding shoes can't get any purchase on the gravel. I hear the motorized gates opening, chank, chank, chank.

Ray pulls me into the road, tripping me onto my knees while he unlocks the doors.

'You fucking traitor.'

'Shut up.'

'Traitor!'

He grabs me round the collar and leans right into my face. 'Now you've lost it. You've fucked that bloke's Jag. Can you hear me? Do you know how much shit you're in now? *I'm* a fucking traitor? I'm the only mate you've got left, pal. You're mental. Shut the fuck up!'

He drags me to my feet, throws me in the back of the van and shuts the doors. It's only then that I realize and I start laughing, because this is very funny. They've come to take me away. It's really happening. The white van, the screaming, the doors slamming. They've come to take me away.

My eyes open and I remember shouting through the gate at Sarah while being dragged to the van by Ray, then the tape runs to an anaesthetic blank. Your brain logs every instance of you clicking your jaw or asking for more butter in restaurants but the real glory times – the ones that had you jumping up and down like Japanese air command after Pearl Harbor – are lost for ever like so many sunken battleships.

It's something I've got used to. I've had blackouts before. Strange sharp attacking pains and waking up in beds full of dirt are usually all that remain of the experience. Then, six months down the line, you're walking through the park and you stare at a flower bed and feel a sensation – as Dr Jekyll might of Mr Hyde – and shiver, as your subconscious recalls you rolling around in the muck, oink oinking like a prize hog with a bellyful of old eggshells and cheese rind.

Lying in bed now the first thing I do is run a mobility test on my fingers and toes. Drunks in films always wake up rubbing their head and reluctantly brew a pot of coffee. Real people drink water out of stolen pint glasses while trying not to vomit. I prod myself under the covers. I've got the typical blackout bruises (around the tops of my legs and pelvis from catching myself on door handles and the edges of tables). My hands are covered in cuts and scratches. There is grit inside my cast which is already in need of some mending. Tiny dark crystals of stone stud my palms which means I've fallen onto tarmac. I've also got green stuff inside my ears, indicating that I must have been fully submerged at one point. Which is quite cool. I start trying to piece it all together. Clues like 'arm smells of brandy' are of little use. Slowly, however, fragments of evidence will combine to create an image similar to the mural in the kids' section of McDonald's.

My old man marches into the bedroom, slams a mug of tea down on the side cabinet, and tells me the whole story in that official 'we regret to inform you' manner. That I've lost everyone's trust. That my wedding suit is now outside the kitchen door in a bin bag, and that my mother has been crying. His retelling is heavy with woe. I'd swear the pond thing was a lie if the proof wasn't silting up my ears. He punctuates his speech with long silences and an even longer face. I know this is why I moved out of home. It's not because I needed space or wanted to have sex in private. It's because hearing the phrase 'your mother and I are very disappointed' makes me feel explosively violent. They are the wrong words to be using right now. I can smell them coming like the stink from a burger trolley.

'Your mother and I are extremely disappointed,' he says.

I feel like smashing every window in the house.

Well of course you're disappointed, Papa! Things just haven't been working out as planned. Please pass my regrets on to Mother and tell her I will not be joining the family this year at Château d'Oex but instead will be wintering, alone, in a chalet in Canvey.

Christ.

'Harvey and Andrea will say no more about the damage

if you get help. Your mother and I also think you should stay away from Sarah for a while.'

Being slumped in bed with twigs stuck to my face doesn't exactly elevate my bargaining position either. 'I appear to have mislaid my drinks' might as well be tattooed on my forehead. Sometimes you've just got to know when to shut up, say nothing and follow orders.

'They want you to go to a doctor. Sort yourself out.'

'What about you and Mum?'

'We said we'd make sure you went. So I've booked you an appointment an hour from now. And you're going.'

He throws a towel at me.

'Don't I get a say?'

'It's the doctor or you can find ten grand to fix his car.'

'That's it?'

'That's it? Sort yourself out. I'll drive you there and back. Not another word.'

I know this has come from Sarah. No one in my family would suggest seeing a doctor about head trouble. I call her mobile. I want to tell her I can ride this out, that I don't need a doctor.

'I can't talk to you,' she says.

'What, you can't or you don't want to?'

Silence.

'What, because your mother told you not to?'

She cuts me off.

And again.

'Is this your mother's idea?'

'What?'

'The doctor.'

'Yes. No, I don't know.'

'And I need this?'

'You're ill. You need help. It's time you got help. I want you to.'

'And then what?'

'What do you mean?'

'Us. After I get help, when I get better.'

Sarah hangs up.

☐

Trusting the NHS the way it is, I know I can bounce out of the surgery with a tidy little prescription, but it pays to be careful. I've managed to clip someone going to Mexico, to bring me back some Xanax and Rohypnol. So, in two weeks I'll have something, whatever the weather. If I can get good drugs, things can go back to the way they were – but the more I think about it the harder it is to pin down a time that's right to go back to.

With GPs there is no real point in telling the truth unless you don't actually care what drugs you get. They have ten minutes to decide if you are ill or not. Most of that is gone by the time you get from the waiting room to the examination room, sit down and wait while they flick through the record. You have to help them a little. Don't go too wide on the preamble and the symptoms, just point at your head and the doctor should have no trouble in finding an appropriate salve. It's all paracetamol and booze anyway. I remember talking to a private doctor once about the drugs; he just told me to stop mixing amyl nitrate with cocaine and Es 'because it's dangerous'. I thought he was a good sport, but then I wasn't crying in front of him. I wasn't sitting on a plastic chair with Lanacane written on it, wearing my father's clothes and a dog-blanket fleece. I've known this GP my whole life and I can't lie to him or pretend. He's kind and reminds me of antibiotics that taste of overripe bananas. The last time I sat in front of him was because of a twisted bollock. That was seven years ago and I was wearing a blazer with the school badge stapled to the front pocket. I thought *that* was humiliating. I tell him what I think has happened to me. I've never spoken about it aloud. It streams out of me, unedited.

'. . . I crashed. I never realized what the expression meant until now. It's like I've hit a wall and I'm still running. I'm everyone, everything and nothing, I can't rest or sleep or think without getting angry or upset. And I'm drinking quite a lot.'

Silence.

'How many units of alcohol do you consume a day?'

'I don't know.'

What's a unit? You only ever see drinks in units on the news. Three quarters or a half of this, an eighth of Cinzano, two fingers off the top of a glass of wine. I mean, speak to me in English.

'Tell me how much you drink in a day.'

'Which day? Tell me a day and I'll tell you how much I drink and what I do.'

'Well, on a Monday.'

'Well . . . say at work, lunchtime, I'll have a couple of pints and some whiskies, then in the afternoon I'll have some beers, maybe some more whiskies – it's OK to have some booze in your desk – then in the evening I'll have a bottle of wine, then maybe another bottle and if there isn't another bottle I'll have some whiskies, to finish it off.'

'How long have you been drinking like this?'

'Four or five years,' I say. I knew it was bad when I got halfway down the list. I thought, this is taking me long enough to reel off, how much time is it taking out of my life to actually drink it?

'So in your opinion, Charlie, how many drinks is too many?'

This is a good one. I'm quiet for a minute, thinking if I say two it'll sound stupid. Say the drink-drive limit is two, I don't drink and drive so I'll double that. And I can hold my booze. Realistically I'm always at my best, most entertaining, on my ninth drink.

'Eight?'

'No,' he says. 'One drink is too many. When you're an alcoholic, one drink is too many.'

This is when I feel my chest fall and the tears start to come again. But not out of fear. Out of loathing that I should sit there and hear that and not walk out telling him and the world and anyone else listening that he's a fucking nut. I'm not an alcoholic, I'm twenty-five years old. How can you be an alcoholic at twenty-five years old? There are a million like me. Alcoholics drink vodka in the morning, pour it on the cornflakes, hide bottles in hedgerows like Cheggers, and bust up late-night intellectual debates on abortion while attacking feminists. I just shout a lot.

'I'm going to give you six sessions with our counsellor. You'll have those sessions here. You can make the first appointment at reception. Please consider attending Alcoholics Anonymous. Now, do you have private medical insurance?'

'What?'

'BUPA?'

'Yeah, I got something like that with work.'

'Good, that means you can see someone straight away. You'll do six sessions with a counsellor here, then I'm going to refer you to a psychiatrist, I know him very well. He'll decide what medication you might need and take care of things from here.'

'OK.'

This is bad.

'In the meantime, I'm going to prescribe you diazepam which is a form of Valium, and propranolol which is a beta blocker. They'll help with your anxiety and panic attacks. OK?'

'Yes.'

'It's up to you from here. But you shouldn't drink any alcohol.'

'How long for?'

'For ever if possible.'

I walk around the block before going back to the car – I don't want the old man to see tears. I can't even work out if I believe the doctor or not. I always wanted to be a drinker, I was always proud of it, but an alcoholic? I always thought an alcoholic was a big drinker with no mates. I know there have been nights when I couldn't see a way out of the drinking, especially when Sarah was angry with me for being pissed again. Then I could never imagine a time in my life when I wouldn't need to be numb and drunk, falling asleep at night, rolling up warm and anaesthetized. How can you not love that? I don't want any more people sadly informing me of anything else for at least a week. I can't handle it.

Back in the car the old man folds up the *Mirror* and drives me straight to the chemist. He stands behind me to make sure I pick up the prescription. He's behaving like a screw and I'm on remand. Everyone in the chemist is unsettled that I'm not actually handcuffed to him. Later he'll watch me take them. He's got the wrong end of the stick.

# charlie big potatoes

It's my enjoyment of any sort of pill, even strange ones picked off the floor, that put us in this line in the first place.

Mum is watching me closely. Her head is tilted to the left like a cockatoo waiting for a cracker. She knows this is the correct look because she has an intimate unspoken relationship with Dr Hilary on GMTV, who has been training her in low-level medical procedure and diagnosis for about five years. Lesson one in TV doctoring is head position/tilt.

'And?'

'I've also got to see the local counsellor before I can get a referral from the doctor to someone better. Harley Street, something like that.'

'And what else did he say?'

'Nothing much.'

'What else?'

'He said that I was an alcoholic.'

Mum covers her mouth.

'What? That's not possible. Harold?'

Dad says nothing.

'Harold, our son is not an alcoholic.'

*My dog did not shit on your lawn.*

*But I saw it.*

*Not this dog, mister.*

'Harold, it's not true, is it?'

'Well, maybe he should stop drinking at least while he's on the pills. That'd be best.'

'Well, you heard him. No drinking.'

'Jesus. OK.'

*You are an alcoholic.* That's a benchmark moment in life. Right up there with losing a friend.

'And stay out of the garage,' says Dad.

◻

Initially, I find following the doctor's orders liberating as I can no longer effectively make my own decisions without descending into a mire of self-hatred. Still, three sessions with the counsellor and I'm crying about everything from my grandmother to not taking my old man to the football and being bad at adding up. I work out that a counsellor is someone who keeps asking if you're going to kill yourself, smiles too much and incites you to fill silences with gibberish. We began with one point, now we have a thousand.

Slowly she's filling up my head with an old syrup of irrelevant painful memories and humiliations. Pouring in my ear a milky succession of 'let's think about thats', 'mmms' and 'aaahs'. The next feasible progression would be for her to physically break my spirit using starvation and forced marches around the car park.

She's annoying me so much I've already secretly sworn that if I do decide to kill myself it'll be in front of her and I'll make it spectacular. I answer no to the suicide question, even though I suppose the answer is yes. I think they only really care about those of us who want to take a bunch of civilians along with them. They must have an agreement with the police – possibly with some kind of commission involved – to weed out the people-worriers who are most likely to walk into B&Q with heavy weapons.

I've thought about it, we all have, but only special people act on that thought. The pills keep me level now, my fear and emotion contained and chained in a little white room. I can visit but nothing ever comes of the noise. It's something else when even you can't hear your own screaming.

I try to get the appointment with the psychiatrist in town over with as quickly as possible. I barge into the consulting room expecting to railroad myself another load of pills but he's not the usual golf club jolly boy. He gives me forms to fill in. Written quizzes with deceptive questions about feeling punished, putting on weight, sex and sleeping. And asks about me wanting to kill myself again. I still don't want to, but it's always nice to be asked.

'I think you'll benefit from a course of CBT, cognitive behavioural therapy. You'll need to go to hospital, a private hospital.'

'Really? Hospital.'

'Yes.'

'Do I have to stay overnight?'

'Not if you don't want to. Some people prefer it.'

'Not me.'

'Fine.'

'You'll come back to see me to change your medication. I'll monitor that, and change the dosage when required.'

'Sweet,' I say.

Hospital. Sounds like no responsibility, which is what I need. Hospitals also cure people and I need to get better, or at least act like I'm making the effort. I want to get better, I do. I just don't believe I will.

I call Sarah at work.

'Sarah? It's me.'

'Oh.'

'I did it. I went to the doctor and saw the counsellor.'

'Good.'

*Hello?*

'You did want me to go, right? Are you busy or something, do you want me to call back?'

'No, no. I'm busy but now is good. What did he say?'

*Do you care?*

'I'll make it quick.' *Jesus.* 'He said I might be an alcoholic.

I'm not sure though, I think he went a bit over the top, trying to scare me.'

'Maybe. Maybe you should listen to him.'

'You think he's right?'

'Maybe.'

'Maybe?'

'You're ill, Charlie.'

'Could you be a little more specific?'

'Alcoholic is a start. When you know how something got broke, you know how to fix it.'

'A bird in the hand is worth three eggs in the same basket.'

'Charlie . . .'

'I know, it's a game of two halves. There are teams losing every week and I'm pleased to have an excuse for my behaviour.'

'What do you want me to say? You got some help? Do you want me to jump up and down? What do you want from me? You've got some pills. You feel good. That's great. I don't feel good, Charlie. You have a long way to go yet.'

'I'm sorry. Maybe you could get help as well.'

'For what? I don't need help.'

'Shit. To help get over the thing, you know. The wedding. I'm just thinking of you.'

'Really.'

'Look, I wanted to tell you that I went to see a man up in town. He said I should do a course of therapy in hospital, a month.'

Silence.

'I expected you to be pleased.'

'Pleased? How? Why? You've not even done one day there.'

'But I'm going. I mean, that could really sort me out. I really want us . . .'

'Look, this is great, Charlie. Take a month off. I have to work. Next time why don't I call you.'

**9**

Have you ever felt like your minutes are longer than hours and your days are longer than your weeks? It is only two weeks since the wedding, but now each second is like a prison in which all my thoughts turn on me like twisted screws. These new seconds are like weeks.

I'm looking at this woman in a nurse's outfit wondering how truthful I could ever be with her. How honest I can really be with anyone. I want to ask her which big miracle cure is going to sort me out. Switch my life back the way it was, forgiven? Or make me forget? Will she just neutralize my mind? Can she feed me pills and slip me gently into a rut that I won't even notice?

'What do we do now?'

'Well, do you want to talk about Sarah?'

*No.*

'I miss her.'

She's kind and she trusted me, and right now that just makes me sad.

The hospital is nothing more than a big old house and the garden is a mess of people that look like a continuation of the kitchen refuse. Twisted alcoholic faces, and shiny hands smudged with DIY tattoos pass around low-brand fags like Rothmans, and Lambert and Butler. I've always thought that the cancer you get off these fags must be particularly nasty and painful, involving a long and drawn-out death. I smoke Marlboro Lights, so I know from the adverts that when it's my time to go I'll be wearing a cowboy hat, bearing my pain in silence like a real man, before shuffling off for an eternity in Marlboro Country. I don't think they'll let me take a horse into hospital though.

Except for the fag hags – the odd one or two who just prefer the company of smokers – everyone in the garden smokes. There are no pipes or cigars, just people with fast-delivery nicotine tubes pegged to their faces, taking long, lung-cleansing drags of smoke, chasing away that sick hospital air. One woman, beautiful and definitely rich, is sat on her own, smoking one of those long thin black numbers that sways in her hand like a conductor's baton. That or a monkey's erect penis. You should really only smoke those in casinos, in the dark. Next to her are a couple of jabbering younger alcos wearing shelly bottoms. The skinny one's got something to prove – dancing around in a pair of old grey Reeboks, punching the air, hooks and jabs.

'Ah go' 'im reet. Na roun is ne', bam, bam is head fook, fook, fook ye bassard!'

Hack, hack, laugh coughs his round-faced mate.

The wealthy woman exhales a rain cloud.

It's cold. The rat-a-tat of cutlery on crockery peppers the air around the garden.

I thought I'd stay out here smoking until the rush died down in the canteen, then I'd find somewhere quiet to sit.

'Have you eaten yet?'

Sorry?

There's a girl standing in front of me, my height, red hair, jerky.

I used to have a real problem with redheads.

'I saw you this morning,' she says. 'You were signing into CBT.'

'What?'

'Cognitive behavioural therapy. Do you want to come and eat with us?'

I can't speak and see and listen at the same time. Parts of me are now shut down, overstretched and undermanned. You only have so much blood and it can't be everywhere at once. My ears and eyes might function but nothing happens around my mouth. I have to nod my agreement.

'Er, yeah, OK,' she says.

'Cool,' I manage to say. Standing up, gathering my moving mess of matches, minidisc, phone, fags, stuffing papers back into pockets. My voice sounds unattached and could have emerged from the end of a snorkel. I join her at the back of a group walking in through a side door. A tall man in a stained shirt and black jacket slips into our midst, talking nonsense. He smells like the back seat of a minicab. He grabs my meal ticket from my hand.

'Oi! Give that back!'

'No, it's OK,' she says. 'He's the restaurant manager.'

'Oh. Right. I'm not that mental, I promise you. My name's Charlie.'

*All I need is my mum to show up and say: 'You know, Charlie finds making friends so difficult.'*

'Celeste.'

She extends a long floating hand; it seems unattached to her body. I think that I already know what her problem is.

Inside the dining room are thirty-odd tables. Of those lunching here, some are just plain frightening, others are too soaked to eat, their eyes wander over the room on invisible stems.

I fork a bit of salad and a vegetable cutlet onto my plate and pull in a chair. I don't really feel like talking, like I'm part of this, like I belong here. Though I have got lots of questions, like, just how mental do you have to be to need that much medication? Do they put people who bite on a separate table? What happens if one starts biting you? Does it make things worse if you shout? Celeste starts telling me the names of the other people sitting at the table. So fast I know I will forget. But I remember a girl called Lisa but not the name of a second girl who looks at me so severely that my brain freezes on hearing her name. Then she starts speaking and all I can fix on is that she's severe-looking for a girl and she seems to be fixated with desserts and sugar. Both girls eat like horses and mostly the conversation swings from a kind of wistful politeness to caustic foul-mouthed rambling.

'You must have the pudding, it's custard apple.'

'No, no, I can't. I'll have to fucking chuck it up.'

Or they talk about shrinks they don't like:

'He's weird sticky-looking and he wants it.'

'She's a useless bitch. She singles you out? She singles me out! The whore.'

I thought I could just hide here, listening to them, but that seems impossible. They all have specific problems, all know how severely depressed they are or how many panic attacks they have when they leave the house and what they obsess about. They rank each other. Kind of like Mental Health Top Trumps, breaking one another down into categories. Depression: 10 years. Crazy Eyes: 2. Nervous Tics: 45 twitches per minute.

Two tables away a young blond man picks his plate up and smashes it hard down on the table.

'Why do you pick on me? Why make all the words against me? Is it because I am different to you?'

'Don't worry about him,' says Celeste. 'That's Heinrich, he's from Düsseldorf and he has anger problems. He doesn't feel like anyone understands him. He'll stop in a minute and run out, he always does.'

'No one understands him?' I say. 'Even in here?'

Lisa leans in between me and Celeste. 'The sooner he comes to terms with the fact that no one fucking cares or understands him anywhere and kills himself the better.'

'That's right, keep up the group spirit, Lisa. You keep it up like that and we'll all get through.'

For a moment I think I am safe because everyone at this table is female. Then I remember how I got here, and all the women in my life and I start to hyperventilate. The big girl leans forwards again. 'Has anyone got something for paper-bag boy to suck on?'

'Make a face like this,' says Celeste, puckering up her lips. 'Breathe through the gap, that's it, nice and slowly.'

I nod in appreciation, my eyeballs filling up with what feels like fruit cocktail syrup.

When Lisa leaves to go to the bathroom the severe-looking girl grabs me on the arm.

'Both of you listen, quickly while she's gone. Lisa told me what it is today, she told me why she's here this time. She gets drunk and does hideous things in front of men.'

'Where?' says Celeste. 'What things?'

'At home in their houses. With things!' she rasps.

'What things?' says Celeste. 'Rodents? Wooden spoons? Carrots?'

The severe-looking girl grips my arm tighter and says, 'Toys and probably carrots too!'

'Ssssh, kids' toys? What kind of toys?'

'Celeste, don't tease! Cock toys! Dildos!'

Lisa walks back into the cafeteria. She certainly looks lighter on her feet after a visit to the loo.

'I'm sure she meant all that to be private, maybe until the day she died,' I say.

They both smile at my ignorance. Lisa pulls out a chair while severe-looking girl mugs innocence. Celeste and SLG grin at her. I hide my face.

'What?' says Lisa. 'What did you do to my food?'

'Nothing,' says Celeste. 'In fact we were just asking our new group member why he's joined up for the four-week stretch. It's not just for the broken wrist.'

'I could have broken it by repeatedly batting myself over the head.'

'True, but we like to look to the core of that anger. So again. What's wrong with you?'

They chew their food, rationalizing, staring. Waiting.

'What's wrong with me? I don't know. I messed up.'

'Right,' she says.

'I have anxiety attacks,' I say, embarrassed, because I really don't know what an anxiety attack is. 'Panic attacks or something like that.'

'Everyone in here has panic attacks,' says Lisa scornfully, 'six-year-olds have panic attacks. Haven't you got anything better than that?'

I look at Lisa and smile. Then think of her parading around her front room in front of a drunk man, belching Drambuie with *Brookside* credits rolling, ticklers and the dragonfly hum of a ten-inch black dominator with variable speed dial. I have a pang of empathy for the ridiculousness of it. I ought to tell her about the wedding, so she could see the fool that exists in me, but I'll save that for later. It will be the firework in my back pocket that I've saved for the summer.

'What do you do for a living?' says severe-looking girl.

'I'm a journalist.'

'Who for?' she says.

I'm embarrassed that I have forgotten her name already.

'Magazines and some papers, but not really much with the papers, I'm too lazy.'

'That makes you the closest thing we've got in here to a celebrity,' says Lisa. I have to close my eyes and try not to think of her eating sausage.

She turns to severe-looking girl.

'I thought there'd be loads in here but there haven't been any. I was at least expecting someone from *Hollyoaks*.'

'A sports presenter would have been nice,' says SLG. 'One of the best things about being an anchorwoman would be getting to fuck sports presenters.'

'Someone famous, and seriously depressed yet too poor to go exclusive.'

'*Blue Peter* presenters?' says severe-looking girl.

'No. Not that bunch of vicar's kids.' Celeste places a long menthol in her mouth and pushes the food into the centre of the table.

'I can't eat this. Does anyone want to come to the garden and look for a footballer?'

'Get some coffee first,' says severe-looking girl.

The others are already out of their seats, ferreting for smokes. I get up to leave. I'm not going to join them.

Celeste has one foot out of the door.

'Are you coming to group later?'

'I'm supposed to.'

'But you're not coming?'

'No. I only wanted to get a handle on things today. Find my way around.'

'So you're not coming?'

'I don't want to start yet.'

'Well, I wouldn't worry. The woman talks shit anyway. Are you a day patient?'

'What?'

'Do you sleep here?'

'No,' I say, trying to hide my relief.

'Well, I'll see you tomorrow then.'

'I look forward to it,' I say, sounding like a man with a pair of pliers in his mouth.

Ray is waiting for me outside the hospital. He hands me a plastic carrier bag from a petrol station.

'What's this?

'Biscuits, nuts and fags.'

'I'm not in fucking prison, Ray.'

'I thought you were staying in. June made it sound . . . I didn't know you were going to be coming back.'

'I'm not staying nights. If you stay nights you have to do yoga; nutters in underpants touching their toes.'

'I don't reckon much on that,' he says.

I keep rooting down the bag. 'No way am I going to be staying nights. I don't need looking after that much. Being watched. Where are the jazz mags?'

I grab the fags out of the bag and throw the rest of it back at him.

'No tiny escape shovel? Don't ever bring me anything ever again.'

'I won't.'

'Don't.'

'Where do you want to go then? I've got a couple of hours free, juicer is it?'

'I can't.'

'What?'

'I can't, I can't drink for a while. The main doctor told me I shouldn't.'

'Do what? For how long?'

'Maybe for ever.'

'Shit. What are you, AA now?'

'The doctor reckons I should be.'

'Are you?'

'No, not until I've failed once or twice on my own, if I can sort myself out. Anyway they're all Scottish in there, it's like fucking Hogmanay. I don't think I'd fit in AA, they're serious drinkers, I'm not one of them yet . . . I can sort myself out.'

'Can you?'

'Well, I don't know, mate. It's easier for me to do what they say than make my own choices. They say I can get better. That's good. They've given me pills, but they don't stop me feeling sick. I think I went through the worst of it a week ago. Paranoia and all that, now I just feel . . .'

I spread my fingers out in front of me, shaking. I am frightened, I really am. I get that bolt again. That feeling you get when you wake up in the morning and everything is different yet familiar and frightening at the same time.

*Severe. No booze.*

Through the dryness in my mouth I can just about form the words. It comes out more a plea than an explanation.

98

'You know when you're a kid and you go to the fair and you've only got so many tickets for the rides.'

'Yeah.'

'Well, I blew all mine, no spliff either.'

'I can't have a spliff while I drive?'

'Not when I'm in the van, no. No pubs, no clubs, no discos, not even drinking orange juice, no restaurants, offies, licensed cafés, licensed premises of any kind, The Spar, your house, garage forecourts . . .'

'NO SPLIFF!'

'C'mon, Ray, help me out. Here, eat a fucking biscuit and drive, you'll get used to it.'

I know it's the right thing, and in a way I want the punishment. I'll suffer a bit. Already I've had some quiet moments in my head, when I work out how to put everything back together. Then I write it down on a piece of paper, call it a sanity list. So when things start falling apart again I can read it back to myself. Except that then the list doesn't make any sense because I've got no memory of myself. Who I am. What I want. I know what I'm not, I think. But I can't remember what I was when Sarah found me in the first place. Did I have something special that I've lost? Something she wanted? Was it a physical thing or something I said? How can I get it back if I don't remember me?

'So are you going to see the blokes from work then? The ones who got you in this shit in the first place?'

Ray cuts a route through the city, rolling a ciggy with his free hand.

'I'll see.' His fingers turn white on the steering wheel. What's really shocking is that he has both hands on the wheel at the same time, he never does that. Not even when he has to swerve. 'Don't try and tell me who I should and shouldn't see; they're just mates.'

'Mates? I don't see 'em here now, do you? They filled you full of shit, not just the drugs, but everything. You're a different person, you, you've turned into a cunt.'

'Nice, Ray. I really need this now. Christ.'

'They won't tell you. They're happy you being like them, they want you to be like them. Fucked up.'

'You want me to be boring? A nice boring life?'

'Did I say that? Oh that one's for me, is it?'

'You sound like my fucking mother.'

'At least I can get up in the morning without a load of pills, I don't get into fights and break my arm. I don't need to go to New York to have a good time. I'm not in hospital.'

'You don't know about me. What do you know about my life? When did you ever say anything?'

'I did, Charlie. I did, but you didn't hear me. Because you weren't listening. It all got said, but you never listened. You only hear what you want to hear, mate. Why don't *you* have a fucking biscuit.'

Back home Ray doesn't stop. I want to run down the street after the van kicking it. Inside, on the doormat, is a letter, an invitation to a wedding – Sam's. An old girlfriend. I didn't think it was serious. The news goes straight to my stomach.

'Sam's getting married, Mum.'

My voice is broken and weak. I'm swallowing incessantly.

'Ooooh, you liked her didn't you?'

'We went out for a bit.'

Mum walks into the hallway rubbing her hands with a tea towel, like she's even been near the sink and not sitting in front of the TV, half reading a magazine, her hand suffocating in a barrel of Weight Watcher's chocolates.

'I'm in the middle of dinner, it's vegetable lasagne. Dennis likes that.'

'Don't you want to know where I've been?'

'I know where you've been. I just hope it's going to do you some good.'

She turns around and goes back to her magazine. She is chewing her lips, waiting for me to leave, get out.

After today I know I can show Sarah I'm changing. I can even say I've stopped the drink and drugs. I can tell her that I went to hospital, that there is something wrong with me, and when I find out what, I can fix it. Then maybe she'll understand why it all went wrong. I decide to ring Sarah again.

'Hello, Mrs Cane.'

'Yes.'

'It's Charlie.'

*Keep it nice and polite.*

'Oh, Charlie. Today was your first day at the hospital wasn't it? Do you plan to go back?'

'Yes, tomorrow. If you don't they come after you with a big butterfly net. Would it be possible to speak to Sarah please.' *Smiling through my teeth now.*

'. . . No. I'm afraid it wouldn't, she's not here.'

'Right. When will she be back?'

'I think it's best you don't call again, Charlie.'

'When will she be back?'

'She's gone away.'

'Away? Where?'

'She's taken the honeymoon.'

'I thought it was cancelled.'

'No, she's taken it.'

'What do you mean she's taken it? That's our honeymoon.'

'She's gone. She went yesterday.'

'On her own? Hello? On her own?'

Mrs Cane puts the phone down.

**10**

I've had this palsied feeling all morning. I had it coming here in the taxi. I've got it now, walking on the thin green carpet, floorboards undulating sickeningly beneath my feet. Long corridors empty into stairwells into corridors. Fibre by fibre, square by square it runs beneath my feet until it becomes one fast-flowing river. This is the life of a vacuum cleaner.

I spent last night at home thinking about Sarah, phoning her friends to find out who she went away with. A process of elimination. I didn't ever think she'd go without me. I thought she'd wait. I thought that would be my prize for getting straight. I called a lot of people, I took a lot of pills.

The nerve that runs across my shoulder is shot because I threw away my sling, and my cast is pulling me down like a concrete boot. I keep needing to readjust to maintain a decent impression of a straight line.

Yesterday morning when the nurse showed me the schedule of all the sessions I would be required to attend I felt ashamed. Art, Yoga, REBT, What is anxiety? What is depression? What am I doing here? I'll probably go to half of them. What is absenteeism? When I saw this other one, down for twice a week, I bit a small hole in my cheek. Alcoholics Anonymous.

The room I am looking for is empty except for that uriney

chemical smell of old cigarettes. I'm early; I didn't want to wait around in the common room where you can get picked up by a passing nurse. I can't take another mother. I spend a bit of time wafting around and fidgeting, performing various hygiene tests to see if the smell is coming from me. Then I'm testing the seat with the back of my hand. I can't tell if it's damp or just cold. Sniffing it very carefully (making sure I don't touch the end of my nose) I realize that the smell is everywhere. Even in my clothes.

There are two giant boards each bearing six statements. The twelve steps of Alcoholics Anonymous. God is mentioned directly or otherwise nine times. Other words include:

Sanity
Fearless
Restore
Moral
Wrongs
Defects
Character
Persons
Amends
Meditation

These words are for the desperate. I am not one of them. On my way out I pass the alcoholics on the way in.

Watching for nurses I slip into the garden where Celeste is creeping around after a patch of sunlight, smoking one of her menthol cigarettes. She is wearing some kind of black shawl that makes her arms appear deformed, attached to her back with a bat-wing membrane. She doesn't look surprised to see me. I get a light off her.

'You know that the co-founder of AA was a chain-smoker who died of emphysema?'

'No.'

'And that if you smoke two or more packs a day you're more likely to be an alcoholic?'

'What would that make the Marlboro Man?'

'Pissed with a death wish,' she says.

'I always liked the Marlboro man. He made me want to smoke. I always saw cigarettes as the little present you could unwrap for yourself every day.'

'He probably hit his wife.'

She lights up another superking-size cigarette. I can't remember what they are called. I don't read the right advertising to know this. Mores or something.

'Why do you smoke such stupid fags?'

'My mother smoked these.'

Smoked as in used to smoke as in can't smoke any more.

'Oh.'

'So you just bunked AA?' she says.

'It made me feel ill.'

Celeste's lips pinch at the end of the filter; she listens as I go on.

'Religion . . . AA . . . has got nothing to do with my drinking.'

'You're supposed to feel ill. That's what makes you stop drinking.' She is confusing me, making me feel drunk. 'It's already annoyed you. Think how much more annoyed you'll be in a month. You could be so annoyed by AA you quit the drink.'

'I didn't come here to sing hymns. I want blood tests, fucking state-of-the-art space shuttle technology. I'm not paying for monks. There's a thing on the wall in there about letting God take charge. I mean that's not science. That's fucking mumbo-jumbo. I don't want to spend the rest of my life closing my eyes and humming "Michael, Row the Boat Ashore" when I walk past pubs. You start letting God take over, it's a short step from that to standing by a burnt-out building telling the firemen that Jesus told you to do it.'

She curls up into the corner of the bench and wraps her shawl round her head.

'You know if you continue to be this unreceptive to treatment they may not be able to save you.'

'Fuck it.'

'Thinking about that gin and tonic? Cracked ice, slice of lime?'

'Not my drink.'

'What is?'

'Whisky and Coke.'

She unravels herself, pulls her red hair from inside her shawl and stretches out her legs.

'So if you weren't planning to go to lessons, what were you going to do today?'

She is behaving like a secretary in a porn film. She turns so both her knees are pointing at me. Eyes wet, skin powdered and dusty.

'Why do you want to know?'

'I'm just curious.'

She is lethal.

But I know she is just playing games. At any other time I'd have loved to have played at being her window cleaner. Except she is damaged. I'd like to ask her what she is in here for and I get the feeling she wants me to ask her outright so she can shock me. Whatever, I don't want to take the risk. No one wants a conversation to stop midway because the other person has run away crying. In this case that person might be me.

Alex and Doyle call my mobile to see if I want to meet them in the boozer. I say yes and they send an account car to pick me up from the hospital. I haven't seen them since the wedding. I'm thinking, impulse reaction, it'll be good to have a drink, sup a pint, be normal for a while. Then I remember that I can't have one. I forgot. By the time we pull up outside the Cat and Badge I realize why they encourage you to stay overnight in the clinic. The world is a dangerous place and I have certainly found more things to be frightened of since I started talking to doctors. I know now that I have to become someone else. Live another person's life.

Last night I ended up thinking about all the things I could do to utilize the time I'll no longer spend drinking. According to a pamphlet the hospital gave me on depression, I could go for a walk. Exercise. There is a picture on the front of a man playing tennis and another of a woman on a horse. I wonder if the horse is depressed as well? According to a second pamphlet I should also reduce caffeine and sugar. I could also try evening primrose oil and milkthistle to help repair damage to my liver. I could take nutritional supplements and eat more salad, as diets loaded with junk food have been found to increase alcohol intake in animals. There must be a laboratory somewhere littered with burger wrappers and some very loud rabbits.

The truth is, I am more likely to start a gift shop called All Things Clowns, stocking only models and pictures of clowns, than change my life on the advice of a pamphlet. I have never completed one serious lifestyle change. Who does? Yet now, according to the people at the hospital and the twelve steps on the wall, I will at some future point become a walking medieval fire bishop, shaking hands with all the nice people I've wronged. Whacked up on God, therapy and righteousness.

I sign off the cab receipt with the name of the managing director's daughter and walk through the front door of the pub, straight to the men's toilets, and retch into one of the stainless steel bowls. Why do they have to meet me here? Why do we have to be in a pub? The diazepam does nothing for the pain in my stomach which seems umbilically linked to the pain in my heart. I'm throwing up so much I don't even know if I'm digesting my pills. I should tell a doctor. A drink would stop the argument. I need a drink. A nice fucking ice-cold triple Jack Daniels and diet Coke would be fucking brilliant right now. I push open the toilet door and walk into the bar. The smell of slops and cigars cuts into my empty belly. I recognize all the grotesque faces but now they look so much sicker. Everyone putting aside that time each day to get a bit more fucked up. Five seconds and I'm back in the toilet being sick again.

The private bar on the first floor is nothing more than a converted bedroom with a small counter and pump, serving warm house doubles and peanuts. The walls are panelled with wood recovered from old wardrobe doors. Sometimes, to lift the damp ambience and reward the stalwart customers, they put out a roasting dish piled high with piping-hot sausages – the smell of burning pan fat making us mad as dachshunds. I've lost count of the times I've had furry tongue burns off those sausages after drunkenly sticking one in my mouth like a lollipop.

Alex and Doyle are sat in one dark corner, pale skin and dark glasses, like a couple of subversive mushrooms.

'Hey, Charlie, how's tricks?'

Doyle flicks out his hand and makes a fist by the side of mine. It's dipping up and down and side to side knocking my knuckles.

I exhale, puffing out my cheeks.

His hand performs some final flourish, up then downwards in a hammer-type strike. I'm supposed to remember where to put my hand. This end portion changes whenever someone gets back from LA, and I can't keep up with it. I throw my hands above my head like an old man surrendering a game of chess, mumble 'Fuckit' and sit down in the corner. From here I get an almost convex view of the small bar room, ceiling to floor. A mouse in the bottom of a jam jar. I can tell the couple on the table next to us don't have much money. I don't want them to overhear anything we say. I already feel ashamed by what doesn't need to be said.

I stake a cigarette straight into what's left of my smile. I know Alex and Doyle are shocked by my appearance. Give me a pink wig, I look like Mollie Sugden.

'Yeah, nice to see you,' says Doyle. Doyle's jeans are hanging down around his arse, like a four-year-old who doesn't want to put his trousers on. He looks stupid. Why does he dress like that?

'Your jeans don't fit.'

'What?'

'Nothing.'

He's now clicking his fingers and thumbs to some imaginary beat, created in a basement – probably by the same corporation who made the jeans – for people just like him.

'. . . Shaking a little bit there, Charlie?'

'Yeah, little bit.'

I put my hands flat on the table. Keep 'em out of trouble

as my Nan would say. She'd also say Doyle looked like a sack of shit tied up round the middle. But then she's not here.

Alex is also bored of Doyle's energy.

'Oi, tubby, are you going to get the drinks in?'

'Tsssh,' says Doyle, trying to kiss his teeth, but instead making a sound like an old man losing suction on a beaker.

'No drink for me, Alex.'

'What?'

'Don't get me a drink. I'll have a Coke or something, get me a Coke.'

Doyle turns around halfway to the bar.

'You not want one?'

'No. I can't . . .'

Silence. The happy pretence peeling from their faces like the paper on the wall. I am the damp now.

'. . . Medication.'

'Fuck that.' Alex turns back to Doyle to send him on his way.

'No, seriously, I can't.'

My stomach aches, my teeth hurt and I imagine that drink will soothe me like calomine lotion on a chicken pox blister. I can recall every lager advertisement I've ever seen, the glass tilted under the tap, and the beer swirling and kicking upwards, alive, sharp from the bottom of the glass. Amber-extra, ice-cold frozen triple brewed better than before. Bright white foam, and gas stinging the tip of my tongue. Sunshine = friends = drink = drinking = friends = sunshine.

'So what do you want then?'

Doyle waggles his hand in front of his mouth in a drinking motion.

Alex is impatient at my silence.

'Coke.'

'Behave.' Doyle squints in disbelief.

'OK. Cokey Cola. Do you want a straw with that?'

'Yes please.'

I retreat so far inside myself that I almost feel comfortable. I can shout from here but by the time the shout reaches my mouth and passes my lips it has become a barely audible whisper. I can hear the echo of the outside world like an emergency radio signal. Roger. Over. Dustbins fall down in the middle of the night and you go back to sleep again. The conversation has turned cold.

Alex: 'Sean wants to know when you're coming back to work.'

Me: 'I don't know, they want me in for a month.'

Alex: 'Sean wants to see a letter from your doctor.'

Me: 'My dad is sending one, I think. And I've got lots of doctors. Can he be more specific?'

Alex: 'What's wrong with you anyway?'

Me: 'I don't know yet, I've had some kind of breakdown.'

Alex: 'What from?'

*Fuck you.*

Me: 'They don't know, might be stress, drink, drugs. I don't know. They said I might be an alcoholic.'

Alex: 'Fuck off.'

Me: 'I know.'

Alex: 'You don't drink enough.'

Me: 'I know, that's just what I said.'

Alex: 'You just need to get away. Getting married, that whole thing, what was that?'

Me: 'I'm still getting married.'

Alex is silent. Doyle comes back with the drinks.

Alex: 'The doctors reckon he's an alcoholic.'

Doyle: 'That's bollocks. If you're an alcoholic then so is everyone else. They tell you that to fucking scare you.'

Alex: 'He's right. It means nothing. You don't drink any more than me, we're all the same.'

Doyle: 'Shit. You could be worse. Fuck. Sean's worse than you; look at him, he's been doing this shit for years.'

Alex: 'Since I first met him.'

Doyle: 'Fuck it.'

Alex: 'How are you meant to get better if you can't even relax? Look at the state of you. You need a weekend away. Me and Doyle will sort it.'

Doyle: 'We can use the caravan.'

Alex: 'Skill.'

The craven. I hate the craven. Shitting and eating in that little tin box. The drugs craven. We've been there a few times and gotten out of control. My face is split in a forced grin. Alex takes a deep breath and leans forward, as if taking me into his confidence.

'Look, Sean really wanted us to meet you today. He's all right about the hair thing.'

I know that's a lie.

'Is he?' I say.

'Well he's fucked off, but not about that. He thinks that you should maybe go freelance.'

I can't stop my face turning bright red. I can feel the pills in me fighting a panic attack as I resurface. Kicking. 'Resign?'

'Give yourself time to get over Sarah.'

'Right.'

How will having no job, no money, no life help me get over Sarah? My hands are shaking. Ray, and Sarah gone and my mum and dad and hospital and now Sean. I can't breathe.

'Sean thinks it might be better for you and the magazine.'

'Alex . . . I need the money.' I look for some help from Doyle, but he's gulping from his pint.

'Listen. You know Sean. You know what he's like, you know him. You think you can work with him again?'

Alex is fierce now, like I've done wrong, like I should make amends.

'Do you think anyone wants to work with you now? There's only so much me and Doyle can say to anyone. Think about it.'

I've got a tear on the end of my nose.

Doyle says: 'You haven't touched your drink.' I sip it; it tastes like Coke, but then I can't remember what Coke tastes like without bourbon in it. Chocolate and coconuts? I check my breath. Booze.

'I told you . . . you wank—'

I run for the toilet and try to throw up but there is nothing there. I'm out into the street and into the park. Running again.

**11**

I met Sarah Cane in a bowling alley in Brighton. That fact alone, when repeated aloud, should have set alarm bells ringing in her head.

'Where did you meet him, darling?'

'In a bowling alley, Mother!'

'In a bowling alley? How delightful!'

Now be Sarah's mother for a moment. Put yourself in Mrs Cane's shoes. Where have you gone wrong? Your daughter has been picked up in a bowling alley. This man is probably a chronic alcoholic with baldness and crabs. He probably hits on the weekend girls who wipe the dried cola syrup and chip grease from the keyboards. The big leech will still be doing the same thing thirty years from now! He probably doesn't even have savings!

In certain circles, you don't ever recover from a first impression like that. I mean, she should have told her mother that we met in a supermarket or something – both reaching for the oyster sauce. It would have pleased her mother for me to have emerged from this sanitized environment half-alive, harmless and building a stir-fry. But that was never going to be me. As Ben once said, 'Trolley equals pram equals trolley.' Brief, but he had a point. He knew I would never be a supermarket kind of 'guy' even if Sarah didn't. To Sarah's mother it was just the first sign of chronic criteria failure. Still, whatever her mother's personal or sexual requirements might be, Sarah didn't fall in love with me because I appealed to a rational side. She came to me and fell in love with me because I made her laugh and taught her how to bowl at the work's outing to Brighton.

That day I was on fire. Literally. Doyle had poured lighter fluid all over my legs and set me alight. It was something we were doing a lot of, mostly in pubs. It really isn't as serious as it sounds as long as you remember the three steps of dealing with a fire on your person: Stop, Drop and Roll.

You see, Doyle was jealous because I'd discovered the secret and I wouldn't tell him what it was. I was bowling strikes on strikes on strikes, taking applause and bowing to the audience. It was like I'd been touched on the forehead by a saint or something. I may be delusional – actually, technically speaking I am delusional – but I made this look attractive. My secret, of course, was a woman, and she made me a one-man strike-making machine, a preacher speaking the gospel of the gutter putter. Man, I had everyone bowling like they truly belonged, and I mean everyone. Just watch me, it's easy. BOOM! CRASH!

I stared down that lane, exhaled and watched those pins disintegrate like atomic test dummies. I even thought about spending £200 I didn't have on the little number in the display case by the arcade – the Brunswick Command Zone in Plum Pearl – a ball that has excellent high-track flare potential. An excellent piece of sporting paraphernalia. Steeeeeeryyyyyke!

All night I was bowling like a god and focusing my power on this one girl – this woman, and I say woman because she was definitely a woman. Up till then every woman I'd been with – college, before and since – was a girl pretending. By the way, if you've still got one of those picture frames on the wall of your bedroom or maybe your kitchen – a collage of happy snaps of all your friends, maybe including a couple of shots of your first serious boyfriend – then . . . well, I wouldn't be surprised if you still want a pony for Christmas, if you know what I mean.

Just being near her seemed to make my power grow. I knew if she was to turn and walk away, leave me, my strength would go with her.

From the clothes she wore and even the way she'd learnt to sit I guessed that she was older than me. She was definably, empirically, quantitatively more beautiful than anyone I'd ever seen. It amazes me how people can appear in your neat little bubble. That day a new person existed. She was born for me right there on the edge of the booth. I knew she worked in the marketing department. I'd never spoken to her before. She'd been out with a couple of people I knew but was part of another group. Everyone she seemed to hang out with drove Range Rovers to work. My mates were lucky if they got a lift in on the back of a milk float. There I was, a young staff writer, didn't mean anything to anybody; there was a pecking order to follow – a sexual hierarchy being broken here – so forgive me if it took a while for me to catch on.

I was thinking, Why is this beautiful woman hanging around me? Does she think I've stolen something from her handbag? It helped that she was laughing. I mean I've always liked people laughing – with me, at me. I don't even mind being ridiculed since there is nothing anyone can say to me that I haven't said to myself, better and nastier a thousand times.

Crash!

But she was kind.

Steeeeeeryyyyyke!

She could have come over and talked to me, she could pretty much have demanded I buy her a drink or hit me over the head with a stick if she really wanted. I couldn't understand how she could be nervous. What for? I needed her to make the first move because I didn't have the blood pressure to bowl well and play it cool at the same time.

Fainting is no good. Women don't like to date a fainter.

'Do you want to learn how to bowl?' I said.

'OK,' she said.

It was that easy.

For the next couple of hours we were like two people in the dark, shining torchlight into each other's faces. We were all we could see. She was excited, curious, confident. I was bombastic, juvenile, charismatic and I began to show her how.

Crash!

Steeeeeeryyyyyke!

Soon we stopped keeping score, except that with every strike and every ball bowled it seemed more likely that we were going to have sex.

Does that sound stupid to you? We took over the lane, and the next time I looked we were the only people bowling. Freeze that picture right there. Sarah sitting, sipping a beer, laughing, me bowling. I want to stay like that for ever.

I was still conscious that she was older than me, but she found me in a place where I wouldn't run away – where I could be someone other than me. She was so confident, she just let me ride out whatever wave I was on. I mean, I was making no sense whatsoever. I was refusing to speak to her about anything other than her bowling technique – and when it became too obvious, reprimanding her for flirtatiousness. I mean I stamped it right out – maybe because it made me nervous. But she just loved coming on stronger and stronger until it wasn't just obvious, it was painful. I mean we had to sort it out or otherwise require hospitalization, rubber gloves and some magazines about the tiling industry.

Later, after the bus got back to town she drunkenly pushed me straight over a wall into someone's front garden. Lying there in the dirt and the flowers, I thought OK, OK, this is proper. This is serious. I think at that point I would have done anything that she asked me to. I was in love.

Now, outside my window, down in the street the dustcart idles. Through the dim light I recognize one of the blokes in my garden as a cleaner at my old school. He looks up at me staring from behind my net curtains like Mr Strangeboy waiting for his dog to come home. This is the third time in so many weeks that the dustmen have caught me ogling them out of the window. It only adds to my general feeling of dislocation. I'm not sure where I am any more. I don't exist in a time frame; I exist in fits and spurts, in reverse. I'm seeing a whole other side of the world. It's not something I can ever see myself correcting. Once you start living on the wrong side of the day, the other side, how do you ever get back?

□

The light on top of Canary Wharf blinks off and on and off again, fading as the morning light diminishes its reach.

I think about not having her and what life would be like with another woman. Maybe Celeste. This fantasizing feels deceitful. Dishonest. I haven't left her, not really. I don't want another woman or other women. But I know there are types who fit into my lifestyle. Does anyone know what type they are? Because we are so sure about other people. People we don't really know. What type are you? Frightening isn't it? I know there are women who drink as much as me and act and talk like me. Who will love all the same things I love, and we'll have private jokes and not rush. I'll want what they want. What everyone wants. We won't go to supermarkets or cook and push prams and 'garden'. Maybe if there was some way of asking Sarah to come back in five, ten years time we could do this all over again and do it properly. I know I'll never find a woman as beautiful and clever as her. I know I'm wrong for her and it hurts, but I probably did the right thing. Because what I've done hurts me the most, and no decision can be bad when it causes you so much pain. Can it?

# 12

Heinrich Arzberger screams obscenities at me in guttural German. I am Heinrich's father and Heinrich wants to kill me, he really wants to kill me. If I hadn't been watching him closely from the very beginning, he would have smashed my head in with that chair. Now I'm holding him down on the floor.

'Do him, fucking do him!' shouts Celeste.

'Shut up!' I shout back at her. 'You're making him worse!'

I'm ear to ear with Heinrich, pressing his head to the floor so he can't bite me. I can smell the bitter sweat, see red contusions daubed on his pimpled white neck.

'Stop it!' screams severe-looking girl.

'Do him!' shouts Celeste. 'This is like prison! Shank him!'

'Shut up, Celeste. I fucking promise . . .'

'I kill you!'

He bulls his chest and arches upwards, deep-mouthing a cry of violent frustration.

'Killlll you!'

'You can't kill me,' I shout back. 'I've paid for three weeks.'

Dr Arthur Sklansky makes for the door.

'Stop, everyone sit down, please sit down. You are breaking the rules of this hospital. Stop now.'

□

At the risk of sounding like an eight-year-old with a portion of his friend's eyeball on the end of a particularly sharp stick, I did not start this. Heinrich and the doctor did. I can explain everything.

I was first in the room because it was my first session and I wanted to make a good impression. The room must have been cleaned last night because the slight breeze that drifts in from the garden is swiftly deodorized. On the dirty vanilla walls there are no twelve-stepper joy placards. No 'YOU CAN DO IT' inspirationals illustrated with sea lions outwitting killer whales, or ships battered by a hellish squall. Nothing. I think an oil painting of a matador, in callipers, sidestepping a giant bull would be an appropriate metaphor for mental illness. Maybe I'll paint one. That dark bull, never tiring.

On my lap I have a pile of paper – lists, forms, handouts and notes that I have to pass between my two doctors. Every sheet is documented proof that I'm actually here, evidence of my arriving and getting better. I have noticed from other people that the closer you get to leaving this place the bigger the pile gets – so you can imagine how much better off I feel than someone who doesn't have any paper at all.

It was when the room had half filled up and I finished reading that I noticed Heinrich Arzberger was waiting for me to make eye contact. As I look up his eyes widen and my body tenses – his face is stuck somewhere between a gibber and a howl. Fresh hot blood flumes through the capillaries in his cheeks. His Aryan skin is the perfect canvas for anger.

I must have already rung some kind of bell in his head. He is upset. He must have looked at me and seen someone else, someone who hurt him. Deep breath out. Now I have to think about him coming at me, if he's going to come at me. Do people hit each other in here? Haven't they got security? I think I should at least be prepared. I break off eye contact and begin by methodically putting all my papers and books back in my bag. I move my keys and my telephone out of my jeans pockets, rub my stiff legs. When he comes he'll come straight at me. Maybe I could hit him round the side of his face with my cast? How much does he weigh? How much of that is muscle? I see a neatly broken nose and a lush pink scar running underneath his left jowl, note the long fingernails. I'll watch his fingernails, watch his hands.

The room begins to fill up. Celeste, Lisa, severe-looking girl and an older woman file in, each taking a chair in the circle. The older woman sits on my left, Celeste to my right. Three flies circle in a holding pattern underneath the chandelier.

Outside in the garden is a group I saw yesterday. They are spread out and seem more heavily medicated. They have their heads down, some like monks in contemplation, some rubbing their scalps as if attempting to nurse the blood and the sense back. Two large male nurses stand together smoking, watching.

Dr Sklansky barges into the room in a hurry and has everyone sign a piece of paper. No notes, not a bag, nothing. We are that easy. He scans the room and says:

'Small group.'

If I were the only one here I'd ask him for ID. He doesn't look like a venerable Dr Arthur Sklansky Ph.D. He looks like a fat man who cheats at cards.

With no time to spare, he scrawls on the whiteboard, in the laziest manner possible, the word 'Anger'.

Celeste, desperate for nicotine, complains that she's done this group before and doesn't see why she should do it again. Can she go outside?

I look out to the garden again. The heavily medicated group has gone. I notice the rain tapping against the window panes.

'Fucking rain,' says Celeste.

Thunder claps like a gunshot in Harvey Nichols.

'Forget that, Arthur,' says Celeste. 'I'll stay. Will you be getting out the toys?'

The middle-aged woman in the chair next to me writes 'Brenda' on the piece of paper and hands it to me to sign. More paper, more evidence.

'No toys, Celeste, but I'll buy you a cup of coffee if you can tell me the difference between assertion and anger?'

Blank faces.

'Ask someone else,' she says.

'OK, can anyone tell me what the two types of anger are? Healthy and . . .?'

He looks at his piece of paper, then looks at me.

'Charlie?'

*No speaky*, Doctor.

'Unhealthy anger?'

'Yes, there are two types of anger, Charlie. Healthy and unhealthy anger. Healthy anger is based on rational beliefs. Unhealthy anger is anger nobody needs.'

'Ha!' says Heinrich.

*No, I'm not getting any of this.*

'When do we need anger?'

'Always. For life!' says Heinrich looking at me.

Heinrich needs his anger. I feel like the mirror in Heinrich's bedroom as I see Heinrich gazing intently at me.

'OK, give me one activating event. What pushes your button?'

Like the selection arm of a jukebox Sklansky pans around the room looking for a record. He stalls on Brenda. It's her last day today and she must be looking for value for money. Some extra bang for her buck.

'I get angry when my son won't listen to me.'

For the next ten minutes she rambles incoherently about her son and her husband. Brenda says she gets angry all the time and Sklansky confirms her fear, suggesting that she is angry because she is not asserting herself effectively and that this is unhealthy. No one has anything to say. Sklansky makes her go on and she tells us everything about her impossibly miserable job in an office full of young people who exclude her. Again she looks at us apologetically.

'Who else has problems with anger when trying to assert themselves?'

Other hands creep up. I think they are lying to make Brenda feel better. On it goes. The Sklansky jukebox provides no new selections. Backwards and forwards he spins, playing the same responses from broken and scratched records.

'So does anyone here feel they have problems in dealing with their anger?'

Severe-looking girl and Lisa put their hands up quickly; so do I in a kind of bad-tempered angry way. Everyone puts his or her hands up except Celeste

'I'm not putting my hand up any more,' she says. 'Just take it as read that I agree with whatever you say, you genius.'

Sklansky laughs. 'Celeste, my dear, I will give you special dispensation to nod, OK?'

I smile, look up and see Heinrich looking at me with big wet eyeballs, and feel at risk again, wishing I was full of my booze and my old-fashioned drugs. Not the shitty blister-packed tenth-generation Prozac that I took delivery of this morning.

'Right, now we role-play,' he says. 'Two volunteers?'

'Can't we, sorry, can't you, just talk about it?' says Celeste.

'I'm not doing anything. I feel sick,' says Lisa. 'They changed my pills, and they don't work. They make me want to throw up.'

Sklansky ignores all of this.

'Right, who wants to go first? I want you to all think of a situation outside of here where you need to assert yourself. Where you often feel anger. Then pick someone to play that out with.'

For some reason Brenda picks Heinrich.

Heinrich is supposed to be pretending to be Brenda's teenage son and Brenda has become Heinrich's mother. I don't know what he thinks Brenda does to her son but he's making like it involves a vice and a bag of nails. He's hollering at her and pointing at her face. Understandably, Brenda is crying. Heinrich starts screaming German. This is his panic language. Everyone has a panic language, the language of your insides. It's the language you would scream at the bull. The language of your childhood. Fear is regressive.

Dr Sklansky pulls Brenda out. Heinrich is told to stay where he is, as it will be his turn next. Sklansky asks Brenda how she feels it went and what she was feeling. She says she was embarrassed, scared, upset. Like she was actually talking to her son. If Sklansky had a third arm he'd be using it to whack himself on the back. In shrink land, upsetting people for a reason is like scoring with a supermodel.

'Heinrich, what situation would you like to role-play?'

'When my father was angry at me for leaving Germany.'

*I'm* angry with him for leaving Germany.

'Who do you want to play your father?'

'I want him.'

'Chatty Charlie?' says Sklansky.

'Chatty Charlie,' says Heinrich.

'Chatty Charlie, please take a seat opposite our friend here.'

Around about now things start to go a little pear-shaped/blurry/arse-up for Chatty Charlie as Heinrich tries to hit him with the chair.

Celeste leaps up but Sklansky shouts, 'Celeste, get back in your seat!'

Celeste says, 'But they're fighting, they're really fighting!'

I try to sit on Heinrich, hoping he'll calm down.

Heinrich starts yelling, 'I kill . . . I kill you!'

I want to tell Heinrich that he is being hysterical but I also want to thank him. He's doing more damage to me than I am to him. As he claws at my shirt and hammers his fist against my head I begin to enjoy the thump, thump, thump. His fingernails run down my cheek. I feel cleansed. My eyes shut. I sigh. My head under the cold tap of his agony. I have been numb for so long. I lie on Heinrich like a hearthrug. His hatred is a fire. As long as he wants his father dead I'll be here for him. He can attack me as much as he likes, as long as he makes me feel great. Effective anger, said Dr Sklansky, is good for both parties.

As Heinrich kicks away, I slide my bicep and forearm around his throat firmly, using my cast as a bar across the back of his neck. I go up on one knee and trip the vagus nerve, which sits in his carotid sinus. The vagus nerve sends an alarm to his brain indicating a massive rise in blood pressure. But there is no real rise in blood pressure thanks to the vertebral arteries, which I haven't touched. His brain sends a message to his heart, which switches blood flow from gush to dribble and Heinrich begins to go to sleep.

It looks unsavoury and you can kill people if you do it too quickly. Everybody thinks I've broken his neck. I slowly stand up on the other leg, squeezing firmly, pulling him backwards. After fifteen seconds he goes limp. Lights out. Good night. Don't let the bedbugs bite.

I want to march around the room clapping and shouting, 'EASY, EASY, EASY!'

But even I know this is not a good beginning to my therapy. I don't want to get labelled as a hooligan.

'Do him, fucking do him,' shouts Celeste.

'Get a nurse,' says Sklansky.

'He said I was his father, then he swung the chair at me. He went for me.'

'OK, OK,' says Sklansky. 'Please sit down.'

Celeste is leaning over Heinrich, exuberantly slapping his face.

'He's fucking dead, you killed him.'

SLAP, SLAP, SLAP.

'He's not dead,' I say, 'but he will be if you keep doing that.'

I can't focus. I feel sick. Nausea. Sklansky is in front of me. Heinrich is now sitting upright, shouting at a nurse who is taking his pulse. Maybe it would have been better if I let him attack me. If you lie back and let people do what they want no one cares. I try to think about what have I learnt today. That anger is bad? I can only think of two clear examples of people using anger to the benefit of others.

1. The Incredible Hulk on occasions too numerous to mention.
2. Jesus at the moneylenders who set up shop in a temple, when he kicked over their tables.

Grrrrrr. You won't like me when I'm angry. Anger alienates you. Angry people don't have many friends. Angry people are just alone. The Incredible Hulk, hampered by his poor temper and swollen green fits, was doomed to walk the earth alone. Christ tried to assert himself with the Romans and was crucified. Anger and assertion only work when you have the numbers on your side. The rest of us, we have to take the middle way.

'Charlie, I need you to slow your breathing down.'

'This one's fine,' says the nurse, disinfecting my face.

'What should you have done differently?' asks Sklansky. 'We aren't leaving till this is resolved,' he adds when people start trying to leave the room.

Heinrich is shouting about suing me and the hospital, and the cycle begins again.

When your traffic lights are on green, someone else's have to be on red. It's just the way it is. This mass righteous anger could gridlock the entire world.

Proof of this lies at home. When I get back from the hospital Dennis is on green. My father is on red.

'If you don't mind, Harold,' says Dennis, 'as your mother is here I'd like to say grace tonight.'

'I wasn't planning to say grace, Dennis.'

'Don't say grace on my part,' says Nan. 'Not just because of me; I don't want the fuss.'

'Sorry,' I say, 'but when did we ever say grace?' This is unbelievable.

'I think it would be nice to say grace,' says Mum. 'We always said grace in the old days. What a lovely gesture, Dennis.'

I let out this low growl. Snarling now. Green light for Dennis. If he says 'Will you please bow your heads' he'll find himself floating face down in the canal.

'Dear Lord Jesus . . .'

*You're closer to him than you know.*

I'm holding on too tight. My mother pours me a glass of wine.

'So we can toast Dennis. He's just been promoted,'

I don't even see a drink. I see a dose of alcohol. I only need 11.5 per cent of it; the other – 88.5 per cent – is just padding.

'Cheers over there,' says Nan raising her glass.

'I am so pleased for you, Dennis,' says my mother.

No one notices when I don't pick up my glass.

If you didn't want the dog to lick the scratch then you shouldn't cover that scratch in liver paste. Drink it. Lick the scratch. Bad dog.

'Cheers!' he says.

We eat and Dennis tells us how his new promotion is unheard-of for someone with his level of experience. My mother is amazed. Dennis is a real fuckin' go-getter.

So I hate to spoil the party.

'Mum. My doctor wants to see you and Dad.'

'What's that?'

'The doctor at the hospital wants us all to have a session together.'

Dad looks directly at me.

'It's just a talk at the hospital.'

He puts a tongue over one of his teeth to try and push out a piece of stuck food.

'What for?' asks Mum.

'I don't know. I think they need other people to come in to give them an idea of what I'm like at home.'

'Why?'

'So they can see if I'm lying. I don't know. Can you come in?'

'I'm not sure.'

My mum looks at Dennis, who lifts his eyebrows. My father is still kissing the meat out of his teeth.

'Tsch. Tsch. What would we have to talk about? Tsch.'

'I told you that already. Me.'

Deep suspicion and paranoia are now airborne contaminants and beyond containment.

*Do I want their help? Look at them eating away at themselves.*

'You come or Sarah comes. Someone has to come. Sarah's not even in the country. That leaves you. One time only. Yes or no?'

'Stop pressuring me!'

'June, it's the least we—'

'No, Harold. No. They say he's an alcoholic, he's an addict. Is that our fault? Did we give him the drugs? Did we bring him up to abuse people?'

This is a woman whose sweat has to be 80 per cent Solpadeine.

'We'll think about it,' says Harold.

'Well, I'll tell the doctor that, shall I? That my parents aren't quite sure they want to come up the hospital? That'll sound just fucking right!'

Nan puts her hand on my arm while my father blushes. Mum is out of her seat. Where's that bald bloke off Jerry Springer when you need him?

'You've got no right to speak to us like that after you've put us through so much. You owe us an apology. Do we complain? Do I complain? What do I ask of you? Twenty-five years old and we're still looking after you, a roof over your head, food on the table. You have no right. You have no idea how much we do for you. How much you take out of us!'

I've heard this before. Nan's smooth dry fingertips grip my wrist.

'Me and Charlie'll clear the dishes, won't we, Charlie?'

Now I owe them large. Now I know. The hospital, the food, the hot water, the attention, it's all on the slate. Everything, everything is on the slate.

Nan dries, I wash. Well, to put it more accurately I mash the plates around in a puddle of cold water while she smokes.

She draws a Beaumont XL out of the pack, this takes a while. They are horrible cheap cigarettes, as long as your arm, that she buys from two Moroccan blokes who stand outside her supermarket. She places the tip in her mouth, the lighter appearing from the same hand, sparks, the cigarette end glows and is jammed into the ashtray before she's even exhaled. If David Blaine was here he'd be asking her if she could do that again.

Mum puts her head round the kitchen door, bottle-green eyeshadow. She and Dennis are going for a walk. He's bought himself a new leather jacket. He's wearing it over his work trousers. The sort of look Ron Atkinson might sport walking down the petrol station for some milk. Nan shuffles a newspaper around, finding the letters page. No one asks where my mum and Dennis actually walk to. When I used to go out after dinner it was with a whole gang, robbing, up to no good. I hope Mum and Dennis aren't getting in over their heads. I can just see Dennis pushing Mum's big butt through the back window of a newsagent's.

'My cab'll be here soon.'

I want to be in it with her.

*Don't leave me here.*

'Right. Sure. Do you think they're looking at houses, Nan?'

*Don't go.*

She looks up from her paper.

'Your father still lives in this house.'

'Yeah? For how long?'

I watch her. How can I say 'Please rescue me' to an old lady.

I start crying. She comes over and gives me a hug. I am twice as big as she is but she is worth ten of me.

# 13

I try to say 'Hello, Mr Pigeon.'

I can hardly speak straight from the Valium. I realize I'm slurring. Then, that I'm hanging halfway out of my bedroom window, saying good morning to the ungrateful pigeon, who sits in a tree adjacent to my window. I bet he comes from a nice village. He's always talking, telling the world about himself, the big wannabe. Always one eye on me, one on the big city. The tart. He knows how easy pigeons have got it here. There aren't exactly a lot of golden eagles to worry about. And how much better off we'd all be if we could hide in trees and on chimney pots from nothing in particular.

Breathing hard I wriggle back inside the house, dragging my cast after me, and drop onto the carpet. I realize my co-ordination is shot.

SHUFFLE, HOP, SLAP.

To get comfortable I have to move around like a seal. I am beached and hopeless but I am warm. I can almost feel the sun on my face.

SHUFFLE, HOP, SLAP.

I bask underneath the clock radio which reads, in vibrant red matchsticks, 4.20 a.m. I've been drinking tea and smoking cigarettes all night. Ten three-bag servings drunk out of an old milk jug slosh around my insides. I've got a loose memory of offsetting the caffeine with more of my new pills. Then with Valiums washed down with ice-cold glasses of Solpadeine. I look at the little brown bottles and feel the ruptured empty pocks in the blister packs. I finger the foil wrappers and try and work out what I've taken. I can't.

SHUFFLE, HOP, SLAP.

The tannin and tar have lined my throat. If I move my tongue I make noises like a startled hen. I need water, but it will have to be water without pills in it because I've had too many already. I will have to be careful to stay away from the windows. I don't want to get myself some kind of strange reputation.

SHUFFLE, HOP.

Carpet, what an invention. Socks for floorboards.

SHUFFLE.

Somewhere on the wrong side of my mind a film is running about me building the perfect shed. Slowly I become more involved and take over the building process. I sleep.

□

A bright, shining light.

In the garden at the hospital a man on his knees breaks off a piece of banana and places it on the ground, for the ants.

'It's too heavy for them,' he says.

'Give them a smaller bit,' I say. 'They don't care how big it is.'

'OK.'

'Tell me more about ants.'

'The worker ants are female,' he says, his mouth working amidst a mess of patchy whiskers, rotten pores and cuts.

'And they have no wings and can't lay eggs. These ants collect food, clean and guard the nest and dig new tunnels.'

This could keep him occupied for hours. I've seen him a few times in the garden but this is the first time that he's actually come over to me. I think he needed to see me a few times before he could trust me. Likewise, I suppose. I call him Banana Man because whenever I see him he's holding a banana – either eating it, or trying to give it away. We should all be able to make friends like that.

'Underneath there,' he points at the paving slabs, 'is a labyrinth of tunnels, with a queen ant at the bottom. Sometimes there is more than one queen. They all have to look after her.'

A cold wind rushes through the trees and bursts over the clinic, filling my shirt like a balloon. It's going to be a wet summer. I grit my teeth and feel the cold in the sodden marrow of my bones. That's the trouble with sleeping on the floor: no matter how right it feels at the time, you'll always wake up roughly the same temperature as a piece of skinless chicken. I realize that I put myself at risk last night. That I'll have to watch the painkillers, not so much for the codeine, but the paracetamol and delayed renal failure. They put paracetamol in everything now. One day it'll be in apples and carrots.

Between gusts, the sun gathers up a heat, reflecting off the whitewashed walls. It momentarily warms us but it gives as much heat as a child's light-bulb oven. Banana Man doesn't seem to feel the cold, or any change in this world for that matter. He has almost curled himself into a ball. He has his ants.

'The male ants don't work. Some ants die after mating.

The queen ant then tears off her wings and starts to look for somewhere to build a new nest.'

'New nest?'

The ants have collected on the same piece of banana. It's like a VIP section. For insects.

'You want to give them slightly smaller pieces. Then they can all have some.'

He tries to break the banana into smaller pieces but mashes the ants up with it. George Clooney couldn't save those ants right now.

'Oh no,' he says. Greasy fingertips covered in spots of white and black flesh.

He starts to lick them clean. Where's my camera? KFC moment.

'Nooo! Don't do that! Go to the toilet and wash it off.'

'Oh no. Ants in my mouth. Oh no.'

'It's OK.'

He opens his mouth for me to look in.

'That's all right, there's only a couple in there. There are more ants, thousands, millions of ants where those came from. They've got their own ant planet and everything.'

'Yeah?'

'Yeah.'

He smiles. Looking at his hands he could be anywhere between thirty and forty years old. His teeth are broken and the bottom row are mostly recessed and green. Maybe no one ever told him or even taught him how to brush. His face is defined not by bone but by clusters of pocks. Scars, some no more than deep scratches – the kind you could make with a blunt razor – decorate the left side of his face. He puts a hand onto the arm of the bench to pull himself off the floor.

His fingers are inked with tattoos: a crucifix, a swallow and a thoracic blob with antennae. A queen ant.

'You go wash your hands while I go get another banana from the canteen.'

The food in the canteen is already in an advanced state of brown. Einstein searched his whole life for the universal theory that would link all things. But I already know it. It is this: If you leave anything long enough it turns brown. Anything. And things turn brown in this canteen faster than anywhere else in the world. I hate it. I hate the brown custard puddings, the twenty grams of pustular fat in the brown vegetable cutlets, the pasta bakes, which are filled with cream to wind up the anorexics. Each cut of meat comes with a glistening lobe of white fat attached. All this food seems designed to plump up skeletal girls and people too stoned to eat more than four mouthfuls of anything.

The cook definitely knows the theory. Everything – us, trees, cars and potatoes – we all turn brown in the end. Everything rots. Except the brown cake in the rejuvenating cake cabinet at the end of the display. That is the exception to the rule. That self-replenishing fucking gateau with its stinking cherry jam was born brown and as such will not die. It is the Bruce Willis of cakes. I hate that gateau.

Checking out the fruit bowl, I can't clearly recall the last time I ate a banana. I think I was at primary school. I remember that it was hard and watery. With a cyst-like brown lump at the very bottom end of it, I thought it was a spider's egg sack. I was sick on the carpet. That was the end of that.

It is only when I go to break off a couple more speckled fingers that I realize that I'm not alone. In the corner of the dining room a nurse is watching another patient eat. I haven't seen this girl eat before. The nurse is paying close attention to everything she does – repeating something to her, over and over again. In the darkest places of the jungle, orchids grow. Her hair is long and golden brown, and pushed back behind her ears. The rest falls forward over her eyes. She holds her fork like a fountain pen and twirls it across the surface of her plate in a calligraphy of boredom. She senses my presence and with her chin still resting on her hand she stares directly at me. Accusing and challenging. She is beauty shaken. Her eyes arrest me for everything I've ever wanted, needed and stolen. By looking, by feeling, I am guilty. Immediately I have to leave her alone, get away. My ugly, stupid face, wanting, staring.

How can something, someone, so beautiful be damaged? Be here?

Back in the garden the name on the display of my mobile reads 'OhNoSam'. Beep. I am still thinking about the girl. Beep. Be upbeat. Beep. Sound normal. Beep.

I throw Banana Man his ant food and press the green OK button.

'You're getting married in the morning, ding dong the bells are gonna chime.'

Sam is Sarah's best friend and has officially been so for a year, ever since we got engaged around the same time as Sam and Darren. I know this because Sarah made a point of telling me. She made a point of telling me because Sam was the first girlfriend I had when I started at the magazine. I think she'd previously been the girlfriend of everyone there. It was just my turn. Now she's getting married to a record producer called Darren the Elephant. I want her and Darren the Elephant to be happy, but I think he is wrong for her. Producers are merely fat DJs. All DJs are in the process of becoming fat and/or producers. She needs someone who is going to be more stable and eat less peanuts.

'Fuck off, Charlie. Did you call me at 4 a.m. this morning?'

'No.'

*Yes. Probably. Shit. Who else did I call?*

'Why would I do that?'

'Because you were drinking with Alex and Doyle.'

'No, I wasn't drunk, not last night.'

*I did get a little fucked up though. Still got carp mouth.*

'Your number is on my phone. Stop lying.'

'I'm not, I just . . . You know me, I would never phone you intentionally. I probably only rolled over on my phone or something.

'You woke Darren up. He'd just got in.'

'I'm so sorry. Did you have to give him a sticky bun? Did he get back to sleep all right?'

'Charlie.'

'Do you ever have to wash him down with a hosepipe and big broom?'

'You haven't RSVPd the wedding.'

'. . . Sorry, I was going to.'

'Oh.'

'Good luck and everything else.'

'That sounded enthusiastic.'

'I try my best. I'm coming, swear to God.'

'Where are you now?'

'In the hospital garden. Playing with a bald man and some ants.'

'Cool. You're obviously well, so I'm going to put the phone down now.'

'Hold up, Sam . . .'

There is something very wrong. I know I'm being slow. I know these new pills, the ones that give me carp mouth, have boiled my brain to pudding. That these all-new thoughts from the last couple of days, hours, minutes have to be added to the mix.

'Charlie? Are you there?'

'Yeah.'

'Quickly.'

'Sam. If you're on the phone to me now and you're Sarah's best friend. Who is Sarah in Africa with?'

'Um. What? Shit.'

'Who is Sarah in Africa with?'

'Shit, shit, shit.'

'A name. She didn't tell you? You don't know?'

'No. She didn't think to mention it.'

'Sam, give me a name.'

'She didn't tell me.'

'It's not a problem. Only, if she's not with you, I just want to know who. That's all. It was half my honeymoon.'

'What?'

'Sam?'

'This is . . . you're cutting out. We can't have this conversation on a mobile. I mean, maybe I should come and see you. Look, you're cutting out. I mean it. I promise you really are cutting out. If you can hear me you've got it all wrong.'

'Sam? Sam? What have I got wrong? What's going on?'

□

I call a taxi to take me to the office. My gut, that mother of all senses, says that Sarah doesn't want to see me because I fucked up her life. The evidence? Collapsing groom, masses of uneaten pink fish. A succession of unconnected thoughts muddle through my mind. Why would Sarah go away with someone other than Sam and not tell me? Has Sarah had a row with Sam? Probably. Sam annoys everyone and we're all pretty emotional at the moment. I started this. Sarah can go away with whoever she wants.

A police car pulls alongside the cab. The policeman is shouting at the driver. The driver winds his window down.

'What colour was that light?'

The driver immediately buckles under the policeman's anger.

Games master to confused schoolboy.

'What colour was that light?'

'Yellow.'

'That's right, it was fucking yellow. What do you do at yellows?'

'Stop.'

'That's right.'

He is shouting but my mind is racing ahead, rolling over the white line, pushing till I can't see red any more. I always want to be the first one across. Have all the answers.

So how do you kill the paranoid thought? You can't. How do you stop it? You don't. You make friends with it. You treat it like a daft uncle – keep it pissed up in the corner of the room with a plate of peanuts on its lap. Hang on, that's not right.

Sam, I loved Sam. I loved Sarah. Are they fighting or hiding something? Think about this. It's very hard to fight or understand what you can't see. Like tickly coughs. Like oestrogen in the tap water, electromagnetic waves from phone masts. Do the peculiarities in your house wiring mean you are part of a government experiment on the effect of electromagnetism on fertility in obese people? My boss doesn't like me. The tap water is filled with larvae. HAS MY FIANCÉE GONE ON MY HONEYMOON WITH ANOTHER MAN? These are all common paranoias which are all mere stepping stones to the inevitable and calamitous, bomb on chest in a shopping mall, 'I KNOW WHO THE LEADER IS,' law enforcement showdown.

Is your pulse racing a little faster today, could it be the potassium in your lungs, or just the monoxide in your brain making you think it's so? The effects of too much and too little oxygen are virtually identical. I grab my mobile and dial.

'What?'

Doyle's breath distorts.

'Doyle, listen to me. I'm in traffic. Sarah's gone away with someone. I thought you could go up to her office and see if you can find out who she's gone with?'

'What? No. Why should I?' He shout-whispers.

'Because they know you. They won't speak to me, not now. They're not going to tell me who she's gone with. They never liked me anyway. They think I'm mental.'

He coughs.

'Doyle, sort me out, please. I need to know who she's with.'

'Leave her alone, forget it.'

'I can't; I need to know she's all right.'

'So call the hotel.'

'They won't put me through to her room.'

'You haven't tried.'

'I don't want her thinking I'm suspicious, creeping around phoning her up like a freak.'

'Shouldn't you be playing fucking Scrabble or something.'

'What about Alex or Ben, is Ben in?'

'No, he's not. Alex is in with Sean doing the award nominations. Ben is—'

'What nominations?'

'The PPA.'

*The awards, the awards. It's my turn.*

'Am I being nominated?'

'How should I know?'

'Sean owes me it. I need that nomination. I need an award, it'll get me back on track. Come on, sort me out, Doyle, what's going on? Why didn't anyone call me? It's like I've disappeared or something. HELLO! HELLO, DOYLE! DO YOU REMEMBER ME?'

'I'm going, I'm going.'

'Good, put Sean on the phone.'

I hear a clink as swearing Doyle throws the handset onto the desk.

'He's in with Alex.'

'I'm coming in, then.'

'What?'

'I'm on my way now.'

◻

Inside Sean's office. He sits well back in the stupid oversized director's chair he bought out of his own pocket to make himself look more important. He has a book on his desk about the – I can't read it clearly from here, but I imagine something like the hygiene of successful people. Last month he was reading one about power desks, which examined the desk habits of creative people and how their desks are an important conduit for the lightning of their genius. It's a little-known fact that the desk was invented for no other reason than to stop your tea and your pens from falling into your lap.

Alex is sitting between us. Ben's being out of the office has liberated Alex – giving him the chance to sit right up next to Sean. Sean's red hair is cut short and he has chosen to cover the scab with a baseball cap. You wouldn't even know it was there. My mouth feels like a vacuum attachment, rigid and coated with dust.

He looks like Roy Castle's last month.

'Are you nominating me for an award then?'

'What?'

'Are you nominating me?'

'Why should I?'

'We,' says Alex, drawing a pattern on a polystyrene coffee cup. 'We aren't putting in an application for you.'

'Why not?'

'Because.'

'Why do you think, Charlie?' says Sean.

'I don't know.'

'Well, what shall I forward to the PPA? What shall I nominate you for? Let's see.' He leafs through a pile of magazines. He picks one up like a dead seagull and throws it at me.

'Do I put in this shit? Tell me one thing you've done this year that's worth an award, I'll put it in.'

'Alex?' I say. It's all good. Why doesn't Alex tell him?

'Find one good fucking story then you can read it aloud.' Sean doesn't let Alex answer.

Alex is uncomfortable, punching holes in the coffee cup with his biro.

'Sean, c'mon.'

Alex is trying to hold Sean back, but Ben is the only one who can do that.

'Sean.'

'Shut up, Alex. Go on, pick a story out. How are things going by the way? I hope things are going well.'

'I can find one in no time,' I say.

Sean is laughing. This is funny.

'Go on. How's your treatment? Did they find a cure for you yet?'

'Please, Sean,' says Alex.

On my hands and knees. Trying to find one that the judges would like. Thinking that I can't use anything which starts with swearing or is maybe too subversive.

'Get off the floor.' Alex is pulling my shirt. 'Charlie, get up.'

'Leave him,' says Sean, cracking a big smile. 'This is funny. Look at him.'

I remember the first time I saw my byline. I thought I was finally worth something. Every time I saw someone reading the magazine I'd hover around like an insecure pickpocket waiting for them to turn to my page. I felt like shouting out, 'See that, see that! That's me! Then I remember what it was like before I was in the magazine, before Sarah, before I wrote. If I'm not in a magazine, if I'm not here, then I'm invisible. Another body, nowhere. That thought is like a bucket of cold water.

'Can't find anything, can you? Because it's all shit.'

I can just about make it to my feet, dehydration making my head swell and thump.

'Why are you even here? No one wants you here. Do you think you have a job here, is that it? You're finished.'

'Alex,' I say, 'you'll have to get Doyle to help. I'm sure you can pick something appropriate out, something broad.'

'Gimme that fucking magazine back,' says Sean.

'Sure,' I say.

'Where's Sarah by the way? Do give her my best wishes if you ever see her again.'

'I have to go now,' I say. 'I have an appointment.'

I am the only one in the room who even tries to sound quiet and kind.

Doyle is waiting in reception.

'No one knows who she went with. I asked everyone. The company let her rearrange and take it later. That's it. Extenuating circumstances. That's all I know.'

'OK.'

'What are you going to do now?'

'Bell me if you find out anything. I'm going to go see her. You couldn't lend me five hundred pounds, could you?'

I have made one deep scratch, a scar if you like, on the underside of my cast. This is all very unexpected. As much as she could still be away with a friend I'm thinking that whatever stupid game she is playing she should play it carefully because she doesn't know how much is at stake.

See, now I think she wants me to pay. This shocks me. This means I don't know her as well as I thought I did. I didn't think she was that kind of woman. If I did, I wouldn't have tried to marry her.

You see, there were two directions in which she could have taken this.

1. She could have taken the sainthood. She could have made me suffer quietly in the long term through a

146

painstaking programme of gentle passive–aggressive, 'thank you for showing me such mercy' retribution.

2. Or revenged herself via a self-esteem-boosting, one off, sport fuck.

Me, I'd always accept the sainthood and wait it out. But then I have never been wronged like that. Like she has. Hurt like I hurt her. I wouldn't know what goes through her mind. Does she really believe that I set out to hurt her? With malice?

**14**

'Yes, but everyone else who gets escorted around by a nurse looks like they spent last year cuffed to the wall of a Russian police cell. She looks like Natalie Portman.' We're about halfway through a group session on anxiety. The shrink is at the whiteboard covering it in thick black circles. She looks like she's been dragged backwards through Whistles. She is ineffectual, liberal and way too touchy.

'Portman?' says SLG. 'Was she the one in *Star Wars*?'

'Fine looking,' I say.

Celeste raises her eyebrows.

'You make her sound like a greyhound. I'm not sure whether you want to fuck her or brush her.'

'She is a dog?' says Heinrich.

'She's not all that,' says Lisa. 'I saw her today at breakfast; she's nothing special, another little princess.'

'I just want to know her name,' I say.

What I don't say is that I can't look at this girl I saw in the canteen or even look at Celeste without going to a place I can't be right now. To a place where I'm alone, where I have no one. In that place Sarah is crying again and everyone can see me for what I really am. A hoaxer. Now, wanting this girl makes me ask the question, Would that thing, over there, be better than what I have now?

We are all too scared to jump the fence. If I'm with Sarah will I be asking that question every day of my life? Without her there is no order in my life, no signs to follow. For years everything I have done has been subject to planning or consideration by committee. Life is now what I make it. As I walk each leg extends into thin air waiting for the pavement to appear beneath my feet. I am blushing a hot flush, sick.

'Listen to yourselves,' says Celeste. 'You're talking about hitting on a woman in a mental hospital. That is extremely suspect.'

'Eeeeeurgh', belches SLG in agreement.

'It's obviously not cool,' says Celeste.

'It's all right when *you* do it.' Lisa rounds on Celeste. 'No, really Celeste, are you telling me that just because you're in hospital you don't want sex?'

'Right.' She gets up and walks over to the exit. Lisa must be thinking she's found Celeste's mark.

'Celeste, you flirt more than anyone in here.'

'I only flirt with doctors because it's safer.'

'Bullshit.'

Having pushed open the fire door Celeste lights up a state-of-the-art defence cigarette. 'Doctors are fair game; they can get struck off if they try and fuck you back.' The small commotion draws Whistles lady away from the whiteboard.

'Ah, Celeste, you will remember that in the conduct session we all agreed to no smoking in the group rooms. I think you were part of that discussion.'

Celeste isn't finished.

'You're supposed to want to fuck doctors.'

'I watch *ER* and *Casualty*,' says SLG on the verge of admitting something frisky. 'And just because I'm on medication doesn't mean I don't want sexual attention.' She positively swells with cheekiness.

'Put that on a T-shirt,' I say.

'I couldn't!'

'Yes,' says Celeste, 'in hospitals you only fuck the men with stethoscopes and white coats. Even Lisa will agree with me that they are far more fuckable than the ones on the trolleys with gunshot wounds.'

'Eeeeurgh,' gurns SLG.

Celeste told me yesterday that flirting with the doctors causes boundary issues, even with the women doctors. That it was harmless and statistically more likely to put her at risk of sexual exploitation than anyone else. 'You shouldn't, if you're strong, exploit other exploited people.'

'So weak people can't ask for sex?'

'Weak people get fucked every day.'

Whistles perks up: 'Perhaps we can turn this into a discussion.'

'It already is,' says Lisa.

'I suppose you feel like some right now?' Celeste infers.

'I feel sexy. Who else feels sexy?'

I can't stand that word. 'Don't say "sexy",' I say.

'Sexy, fucking, nasty!'

'Eeeeurgh,' gurns SLG again. 'That's why you're in here Lisa, for sex things. I saw it on your form. Because you show off for men!'

'So. I could have some right now!' Lisa bursts out laughing. 'Everyone wants it! Even Heinrich!'

'Who says I want to do it with you anyway?' says Heinrich.

'I've seen you looking!' screams Lisa.

'So have I,' says Celeste.

'Liars!'

'Celeste, would you please put the cigarette out and return to your seat.'

'Does anyone actually know her name?' I try and steer the conversation back to the girl.

'Who, the shrink?'

'No, the girl with the nurse.'

I can't help myself. Did you ever do something you shouldn't just because you could? Is that amoral?

Lisa leans forward conspiratorially. 'I don't know her name but I can go over and ask her. I can ask her if she fancies you. Just like in a disco. We're all on pills anyway.'

'I wouldn't know. I've never taken pills in a disco,' says SLG.

'Fucking hell. I'm not opening my mouth in here again. I only want to know what her name is.'

Until I came here I never really believed that ugly people thought much about sex. Had needs. Personally, I only ever credit attractive, tanned people with thinking about sex. I forget that the pasty walking corpses who make up 99 per cent of the population tend to breed as well. I now know mentally ill people think about it too. Maybe everyone here is obsessed with doing it because if you put seven neurotic people in a circle for two hours with no cigarettes or TV the mind will turn to rutting. We think our darkest thoughts, sometimes bring them into the open. We listen to each other – sometimes with voyeuristic interest, sometimes bored but always affected. That is a kind of sex, a power. Understanding is sex, listening is sex. Feelings. Desire. All that you reveal in here, everything that is and was secret, becomes sex.

Nan's invited everyone to dinner at her house and Ray said he'd give me a lift.

'You still going?' Ray asks, kicking the passenger side of the door open.

I get the full Ray experience: fags, Wotsits packets and unwashed jeans. Lucky they haven't invented the smellophone or he'd be out of business.

'How are you?' I say, ignoring him.

'I'm fine,' he says.

'Good,' I say. I refuse to be one of those people who start a conversation with how bad things are.

'Well, are you still going?' he asks.

I called him yesterday to get his credit card number to pay for the flight.

'Yes, I'm still going, Ray. I've already booked. I'm going to pick up the tickets at the airport.'

'Have you asked people at work?'

Ray's got a compilation-tape problem. He's got compilation tapes on the floor, in the doors, falling out of his sleeves. It's not that Ray actually makes compilation tapes, it's that he steals them from other people. This means that Ray possesses one of the most eclectic chart-funk-speed-goth-easy-metal-softbag-rock-hip-hop crossover vans in the city.

Musically, Ray is a machine-gun firing wildly. None of his tapes is marked. Some of them are frightening summer holiday of '94 collections. We go from 'I Should Coco' to 'Groovy Kind of Love' in a beat.

'Why don't you wait a week. She'll come back; you'll be fine.'

'No, I can't do that. This honeymoon is the only chance we've got to get things right. It was scheduled in as happy time. Everything we had was scheduled and this is the last on the list. We never planned anything beyond it, and when it's gone we'll have nothing left. I have to be there.'

'I am telling you, it's not a good idea.'

'Ray, even if this is the end, I have to be there. I'm not running away now. It's like she wants me there. She wants to play a game, I'll play. She wants to see me make the effort, Ray; that's what women want. You have to guess how much they think they are worth then slightly exceed that expectation. More or less than that expectation and you're dead in the water. Right now I know she needs to see a big sign. It'll be just like in films, not real life. Which makes it romantic. I know what I've been and I've got no regrets any more and I've been anything but romantic.'

'Stalking is a crime.'

'Shut up. When I first went into hospital I couldn't move, right? I couldn't handle anything, right? I mean you picked me off the floor a couple of times yourself. Right. Look at me now. I stop the drinking and the drugs. BANG! Just like that! For her! And I start taking these pills to keep my brain nice and neat. Now I've been dry for two weeks and I have all these things I want to tell her. I'm actually straight and I can look her in the eye and listen to everything she has to say.'

'Slow down.'

'I know her, Ray. I know what she likes – this is what she wants from me. She needs me there.'

'Be serious.'

'I can pay you back very soon. I only need another two hundred quid.'

He goes silent and I look out of the van window, taking in the run-down shops and urban squalor.

I don't think that my Nan's council house will ever sell

for three hundred and fifty thousand notes, get decked out in repro Eames chairs and lived in by young media professionals. It's too horrible even for them. Too post-war. This whole ugly area was built on the rubble of Hermann Goering's extensive demolition work – and its ugliness is the wire mesh, the canopy, that protects its inhabitants like rare birds. It is one of the few parts of London you can still live in if you're poor. The shops are a disgrace. All the best stuff is out the front rotting on the pavement or going pale grey in the window. Discount baby clothes, funny-looking turnip melons, broken toys, rusty tools and furniture from skips. There is no must-see lamp shop, no Sunday market, no tube access. It's the closest thing that this city has to South Central. You don't come here unless you have to be here. There is no reason to even pass through.

In the shadow of a ten-floor block is a square of houses set around a patch of grass which helps to concentrate the dog mess in one place. If the sulphate rankness of the bins under the giant rubbish chutes doesn't get you then the fact that you have to enter the houses through a shared dark archway will. The family who Nan shares her entrance with has a wolfhound that Nan swears is harmless. The kids on the estate ride around on it like a horse. I once watched it race against another kid on a black Labrador. The wolfhound's longer stride saw it through. And because the dog is too big for the house, it virtually lives in that tunnel. That's good for Nan or anyone else whose smell it recognizes. Bad news for the rest of the world. This donkey-lion will faze even the most seasoned smack-head burglar.

I note that my mum and dad came in separate cars. Both are newer and cleaner than the rest of the cars parked in front of the houses. Both took the metallic paint option.

Ray's van fits in just fine, though he makes a show of checking the padlock on the back doors and removing the stereo – which he then waves around over his head like a white flag.

Nan opens the door and I give her a big hug. She smells of some proper old cologne that she keeps in the cupboard over the sink. Inside, the gloom of the hallway is exacerbated by the lazy tock of a cheap old grandfather clock. A multi-coloured blown-glass clown, frozen mid-slapstick, sits on a glass shelf over a radiator. That clown has been there for fifty-odd years and never got a single laugh.

'What's for tea then?'

She smiles uncomfortably.

'Chops.'

When I see everyone sitting round the table I see what's going on. They must have all looked so aimless sitting there before I walk in. I've given them a purpose. A pot of tea is set in the centre of the table. A visual stink ball bounces backwards and forwards, between my mother and father. Dennis is also sitting there.

My mother begins speaking before I can turn and leave. She uses her words as a lasso.

'Ray told us what you are planning today.'

'Thanks, Ray. That was quick. What, twelve hours you held out on that?'

'Sorry, but you won't listen to me. It's for the best.'

My mum holds her mug with both hands.

'We thought we should tell you that we think you're making a mistake. That you should stay here, in your hos-pital, and leave that poor girl Sarah alone. That what you're doing is wrong.'

Er, they must be confused. Had a bad journey, eaten something funny and not had enough sleep. Got out of the wrong side of bed. Because they can't be feeling themselves. Now isn't the time to start all this caring – might go and pull muscles they didn't even know they had. Always ask a doctor before beginning a new programme of strenuous mental exercise.

'Mum, is this an intervention? You've been watching too much telly. And what the fuck is Roger the Lodger doing here? This is family business.'

'Well, Ray is here.'

'Ray is obviously part of it and Ray is my family. Dennis, go and play by the canal.'

'I'd just like—'

'Dennis, would you like to accompany me the next time I go to the doctor? Perhaps he will let you look up my arse!'

'I came to lend support to June. I happen to agree with her.'

Dennis is sitting closer to my mother than my old man is. The lodger and the father are becoming interchangeable.

'It's a bad idea, son,' says Dad.

'It's true, mate,' says Ray. 'It is a bad idea.'

'Jesus, Ray, shut up, you've already agreed to lend me two hundred quid.'

'Ray!'

Mum makes a face like a partridge hit with a cattle prod.

'Sorry, Mrs Marshall, you know what he's like.'

'Where are you going to get the money to pay him back from? I'm not lending you any more.'

Blah, blah, blah.

'It's bad enough that we have to try and find money for the hospital.'

'What?'

She raises one finger to smooth over her left eyebrow. She

is being manipulative. People often try to cover their face or disguise their voice when they are trying it on.

'The medical insurance doesn't cover everything.'

'June, please, there's no need.'

'What about the bills, Harold?'

'We'll talk about it later.'

*Not in front of Dennis, he thinks.*

Dennis isn't finished. He should know that when it's my old man's turn he should shut up.

'You should listen to your parents and Ray. It's obvious to me that Sarah needs some time alone, time to think.'

'Dennis, you are such a bitch master. I didn't know this about you. In fact if she was thirty years older I'd even consider your advice.'

I want to bash him, but Ray grabs the back of my collar. He's stronger than I am. I can't fight everyone.

'I hope you're glad you started this, Ray.'

'Charlie, I don't like Dennis either, but he's half right. She's back in a week. One of us can call her out there and check she's all right.'

'It's also a waste of money,' says Dennis.

'Dennis, know when to shut up! Open your mouth again and I'll throw you in the fucking canal. You all settle for nothing because you're too frightened. That's not me. This is none of your business. I got here by myself, I'll get myself out of it.'

'You are going to make a fool of yourself.' Mum's back in the fight.

'I'm out of here tomorrow morning. I already booked the flight last night. It goes tomorrow morning.'

'You're having a laugh. You think you can fix this by getting on a plane? Don't be stupid.'

'You aren't fit to travel. How are you going to lift a bag with a broken arm? Harold, say something.'

'If he wants to do it, let him do it.'

I'm leaving the kitchen.

'Sorry about ruining dinner, Nan.'

This is how it is. I have no secrets left, only shame. If I could hide under a drain cover right now I would. I have had no privacy since the wedding, and over the last couple of weeks I have been stripped and cleaned. I am told how to speak, where to sit, where to be. I am a baby again. I want out. Tomorrow.

The night before my first date with Sarah it was so hot I could hardly take a breath. I had my bedroom window wide open, and the grey net curtains pulled back so I could feel every little disturbance in the air. The heat was keeping the thieves and drunks up later than normal. A police helicopter agitated the air overhead, its searchlight strafing gardens and rooftops. Sirens screamed and faded left and right.

☐

I am trying to lie as still as possible, glass coffee pot full of ice by my head and a bottle of Famous Grouse. It feels like a night in New Orleans, except that on the stereo Steven Morrissey is singing sweetly to his mother about the soil falling over his head, anchoring the room firmly in England. It is one of those nights when you want to revisit every record you ever loved. Take full inventory. Read every diary, pull out every box. I would do if it wasn't too hot to move. I've had sleepless nights before and I'll have sleepless nights again. Some based on fear and terror, some on excitement. Nights when I know I am in trouble, when I know my life is about to change.

Sarah scared me because she took me for a man rather than a boy and I believed that even speaking to her again under this obvious pretence meant carrying off a colossal, impossible lie. Can you imagine that? You'd have thought I was trying to make initial contact with an alien spacecraft, not a woman. I'd have been better off trying to communicate with her using flashing multicoloured lights, a team of French love scientists and Rick Wakeman on keyboards. I even thought about getting out of bed, going down to the petrol station and getting a magazine with women in it to remind me of what they actually looked like. Then I realize that the likelihood of me going into a petrol station and coming out with anything but *Razzle* is very slim. Sarah isn't at all like the women in *Razzle*. This would not help one bit.

Guilty people sleep soundly because it might be their last chance. The innocent stay awake. They panic. They plan, they plead. I take whatever time I feel I have before the world begins revolving in the opposite direction to empty out the junk-filled wallet of my life. By rights every contact, every scrap of information I hold on women, should come into play right now. It doesn't. Nothing I know is applicable. My mind is blank.

I see my future on the horizon and she is still the most perfect woman I will ever meet.

A panzer on the brow of the hill, beginning its descent.

I am there waiting, a kamikaze bomb dog with a grenade strapped to its head.

Life has not equipped me for this challenge.

Is she lying on a bed in another part of town thinking the same thoughts? Thinking I hope that he doesn't think I'm too beautiful or too clever or anything like that.

I doubt it.

Women I've been out with. All sorts. From non-discriminating drunks met in twenty-four-hour takeaways to the popular, the promising and intelligent. Regardless of shape or size I could always find a reason for them being interested in me or being with me.

1. I was more attractive than they were.
2. They had low self-esteem.

The thought crosses my mind that I might be charming company. I like this odd positive thought. It is ZANY. See you the same time next month.

Most of the women I have known from school onwards have come and gone with the minimum of fuss, maybe a couple of weeks of agony here or there. I always thought I was either too young for a serious relationship or never going to be anyone's ideal of a perfect partner. Not anyone I'd want anyway.

Minimum, you want someone who can give you what you need, when you need it. Maximum, that person has to be someone who completes you. This person is 'the one'. Some people use this dream of 'the one' and completion to torture themselves day and night. I avoid thinking about 'the one'. I am only thinking about it now because Steven is on my stereo and he doesn't ever seem to think he'll find anyone, really, ever. Thoughts like this scare people like me. How can I possibly complete anyone? Compared to Steven we are all mutants. He is beautiful. Why would anyone settle for me? And when I find that perfect person I have to wonder whether I'll actually be happy. When I've finally got that someone I've been missing my whole life, do I really think I'll be relaxed enough to smile? From the beginning I have believed that Sarah is the best thing to have ever entered my life, yet by the pained expression on my face you'd have thought she was working on me with a set of wrenches. I wanted her to be this perfect person who completed me. I wanted to be that perfect person for her. I'll change. I'll do this. I'll do that. I'll do anything she wants. We had only spoken once.

Nothing that I'd thought about so far was of any use for impressing girls. I didn't need to know or care what women wanted or thought. What I really needed was a load of money and a tan. Having confirmed that, I fell asleep with a smile on my face.

Someone should have spent the next couple of days walking ahead of me waving a red flag, clearing the street. I was that dangerous.

At work the morning after we'd met at the bowling alley I asked everyone I walked into if they could tell me the name of a good restaurant. Most people told me that I should have booked weeks ago for the really good places. I'd turned pale. I'd had no experience of restaurants. I mean nothing. White to jaundiced yellow and I still couldn't remember being in a restaurant that wasn't on closer inspection a canteen or café, didn't have a salad bar, six types of chilli sauce or free extra toppings.

I was, am not, a sophisticated person. I mean most of us know this about ourselves, it's just we don't make it obvious by picking nits out of our arses like chimpanzees and eating packs of biscuits in the middle of shopping centres with our mouths open.

'I'll have the celery.'

In my mind, I imagined that her expectation of dinner was: A man playing the piano in the corner of a large white room. Large potted palm in the corner. Me wearing a dinner jacket, her wearing a dress with pearls, waiters either side of the table removing those great silver covers with a flourish, '*Voilà!*'

My expectation of dinner was: An overpowering smell of ammonia wafting over from the toilets. My cowl finally slips off completely, revealing to everyone that I'm the Elephant Man. She freaks. People pelt me with food. I wheeze, 'Ghi promissss ghi gan eksthphlain efferythingh!'

She is embarrassed. We leave the restaurant and she complains about the smell of chip fat in her clothes.

I began to believe that she had only agreed to go out to dinner with me because at the time she was hungry and drunk. At times like this we never say no to food, even if it was promised weeks ahead of the moment. This evening was looking more and more calamitous. People were laughing behind my back. I was thinking that I should have settled down with that girl who used to pinch my arse when I was packing bags in the supermarket. I was hoping she didn't marry one of the day managers and have bags of oven chips with him. I was thinking I should have been bouncing around on top of her tonight, rattling with frozen peas, cheap steaks, Es and booze.

Then this skinny bloke from marketing, looking like a cross between Michael J. Fox and Joseph Goebbels, came up to me and told me that he knew a great restaurant – it was even supposed to be cool. He knew the name of the place, what street it was down and even the phone number. It was written in his book. The man had a book! I didn't know anyone with a book! I'd just had a piece of paper! I was getting me a book tomorrow!

In hindsight, Sarah worked in marketing; I think she sent him down to help me. Still, in my ignorance I phoned her. I was filled with a kind of relief that this whole aim-high thing was paying off. It could be done. I didn't have to stick to my own kind! The bearded lady could take a rain check! At least for now!

I telephoned the restaurant and told them it was a special night. They said they'd sort me out. I called Sarah and without breathing I told her to meet me at 8.30 p.m. at the restaurant. She asked me what kind of food; I said, 'Sort of French.'

She said, 'Great.'

I thought what she really meant by 'great' was: 'This is a surprise. I thought you knew someone at Ocelot Burger who was going to give us a bag of squirrel rings.'

I'm thinking: Oh shit, oh shit, I hope she doesn't think it's better than it is.

I was also surprised that she didn't have me on speaker-phone and surround it with a load of people standing around her giggling 'Ha ha, what a retard' while I make a 'huich huich' noise like Elephant Man's sinuses discharging into his malformed windpipe.

The small Bohemian restaurant was full and noisy, with people at each table taking turns to chew and shout and be heard.

The staff walked me straight though the restaurant, and up a flight of old wooden stairs that twisted sideways to a door that didn't even seem to be in the same building. It was dark inside and lit by a single candle; the walls appeared purple and flashed with flecks of gold. Instinct told me this was already good because it was like no other place I'd ever been before. It was magical.

I sat on the bench and asked for a drink while I waited. I'd have liked to have been able to ask for something sophisti-cated or at least respectable as the only drinks I knew – Pernod, tequila and vodka – all made me aggressive, rowdy and flap my gums like a foul-mouthed baby clam. I decided on whisky. A double Jack and diet Coke, truly the drink for any occasion. I thought it was the waiter coming back with the order when I looked up and saw her walk into the room.

*She turned up.*

Two words described my state of mind at this point: Blank and Dangerous.

My mouth was ajar. I got up to greet her without allowing any sweaty part of me loose. A peck on the cheek, linger slightly. I wanted to be sophisticated but felt an excitement-related emotional Tourette's developing from this over-stimulation. I was thinking too hard and felt so tense, waiting to say something stupid.

All I knew was: DON'T RUSH THINGS.

I wanted to tell her she was amazing but I knew she would hate me for it.

One bloke I knew. He was so eager to impress a girl that he gave her jewellery on the first date. He is no different from another man who tells his girl, 'Look, I've been collecting your hair.'

I was still sitting there in silence when she laughed and said, 'Say something.'

'Oh,' I said. 'You look lovely.'

'Thanks,' she said, 'you look lovely too.'

I blushed. I couldn't believe she said it to me. She looked like someone off the telly.

We had nothing in common but that was a good thing. That meant we had more to talk about. The food, a daft vegetable stew, arrived in a large steel pot and was doled out with catering ladles. We ate, drank and talked – mostly about how different we were. The difference being our backgrounds, histories. I told her about my manor and she told me about growing up in one. I knew at some point that this was going to come up. That we had to get it out of the way. I was embarrassed about my life, about my family, about the house I'd grown up in. I was already thinking, How am I going to avoid her seeing where I live? I asked her about where she'd grown up, how she'd got here, now.

She said, 'It's embarrassing. I can't talk about it, you'll hate me.'

I said, 'No I won't.'

She said, 'I'm not exactly out of the ghetto.'

I said, 'Neither am I. I think.'

She said, 'I didn't mean that.'

I said, 'I know. So . . .'

'I was born in Hertfordshire,' she said. 'I went to school in London, I studied art at Oxford. I wanted to work at an auction house but I ended up at a magazine company.'

She made going to school in London actually sound good. My turn.

'How did you get here?' she asked me. 'How did you end up working for a men's magazine?'

'By mistake,' I replied. 'Everything I've ever achieved has either come to me by mistake or as a surprise. I went to a school with two good teachers and then to a college that was nothing more than a mobile library parked next to a pub. That's where I started writing, when there was no money for the beer or the bookies. But don't take that at face value,' I said, 'because I am pure class. And the only reason I asked you out in the first place is because you're pure class too.'

She said, 'I've never been called pure class before.'

I said she'd obviously been hanging out with the wrong sort of people.

In that room alone with her I could be just who I wanted

to be. She wasn't a monster, she didn't loathe me. I didn't feel clumsy and she didn't make me feel stupid or common. I felt right, and there was no one else looking, no one saying I was wrong. No one standing up and shouting, 'You wanna know the real him! I'll tell you the real him!'

All of life should be like this, I think. Unobserved except by one other. I was owed this moment. I was owed the chance of her. Why shouldn't I take what was mine. What was coming to me? She was my miracle, and the light that she had shone into my life made me strong.

Then, as sure as if I got down on my knees and started to pray, chant and slap and pound on my own dumb head, I started to worship her.

# 16

The single green leaf weaves a path though the leopard spots of sunlight on the ground. Where I sit waiting, by the lagoon, I can feel the last of the day's heat in the dry wooden decking beneath my feet. As the light begins to flatten and the shadows smear, a group of grey monkeys creep towards the shoreline and begin to feed on shellfish. I let the scene wash over me. A single cold breaking wave. I remember why I'm here and my mind burns.

Epaulettes, gold braid, peaked cap. The security guard waves the taxi through the gate. For the moment it takes us to pass he stands alert, watching the area around us like a cat. Before going back to sleep he is determined to be a crime-fighting animal.

The reception area is open so the wind and anyone else can blow straight through. I don't want to go anywhere near the front desk and concierge. I march up to a bellboy who is standing by a large book eating a star fruit out of sodden tissue. He looks a bit stupid. You shouldn't eat while you're on duty. You don't get staff walking round the Dorchester eating burger and fries. I tell him imperiously to hustle up a golf cart and take me straight to Miss Cane's room. He gets a twenty-dollar bill.

This is way more than he earns in a week so he looks in

his big book and says Villa 29. I really thought it would be a bit more difficult than this. I was just going to jump the fence, but then that's virtually B & E. So I maintain the front that I'm just visiting a friend who doesn't know I'm visiting. No harm. He waves at a mate who rolls a golf cart alongside me long enough for me to climb in before he rips away from reception. The motor seems to have been tweaked. Rich people obviously don't like to hang about. The car bounces downhill, gathering momentum as it speeds through the narrow lanes of jungle towards the beach.

Once I get a hang of the room numbers I get him to stop. He doesn't understand why I don't want him to take me all the way to Villa 29. He looks at me suspiciously He gets a ten-dollar bill to say thank you and move on. This is more discreet than ordering a bunch of cakes on room service and following them to the room. That would only have embarrassed her. At least I am using my head.

It's late afternoon, and the thick air under the jungle canopy is making me tired. She'll probably be sleeping. I decide that, as I've come all this way, I might as well go and sit on the beach and smoke some fags. I'll come back later when I've worked out what I'm going to say to her; everything I say has to be exactly right. Too much or too little will make her despise me. Women really don't like too much or too little.

The beach restaurant begins to fill, bustle. There is some kind of theme buffet with chefs dumping large slippery hand-fuls of grey shrimp into karahis. There is a band parked in a hut somewhere down the beach, the drummer doing that jazz brush, shuffle, shuffle. Men wearing slacks, boat shoes, holding a jumper for the lady because it might get cold later on. They are well fed and of good stock. They belong in a place like this. I'm sure a couple of centuries ago these men would have beaten the likes of me for asking for more potatoes. They walk the crescent of the shoreline as surely as they've walked through life. It bores them confident. They have nothing to fear. Every now and then I catch someone's eye. In the moonlight my English whiteness must give me an owl-like appearance. They obviously don't expect to see you in a place like this without *someone*.

The restaurant begins to empty, and as the lights die around the extremes of the compound the jungle begins to come alive again. I can't face her until I know what to say. If I knock on her door and say, 'Hello it's me,' will she just scream? Will she even open her door? What do I say? 'Tra-la!' I have to calm down. I have no idea where my pills are. I have nowhere to sleep tonight.

Piano music drifts down from the lobby bar. The bar is neutral ground. The bar is breathing space. I know this. There are old couples in here working their way through the cocktail list right now.

Nothing to say to each other like every year.

*We should have gone away with friends.*

Avoiding going back to their rooms.

*One more drink.*

Looking at other couples, other women.

*If I was him I wouldn't be sat here drinking.*

Avoid sex, avoid confrontation, avoid life.

*One more drink?*

I don't want that to be me.

Outside Villa 29 the insects vibrate and click and shake in the trees and the undergrowth. Four times I walk up to the front door and try to knock on it, to just come right out and do it, but each time I retreat and end up back on the path. This was supposed to be inevitable but I haven't got the guts to go through with it.

A room-service cart spins by for the second time, metal hot box clattering and clanking.

The driver gives me the once-over. 'Hello, Meester Cane! How are you tonight?'

'Hot.'

I try and make it look like I'm out here having a cigarette. I can't stand around here all night; sooner or later someone is going to pass by and start asking questions. It is still humid and my shirt sticks to my back, my collar rubs my neck sore. I need a shower after that flight. I can't let her see me like this, I decide to pick a flower and write a note. I'll write down in the most businesslike way possible that I came out to see her, and take control of the situation. I'll come back tomorrow, we can meet for drinks in the bar. I walk back and stand under the porch light for another ten minutes, dive-bombed by fat moths with wings as wide as dinner plates.

Hack. Cough. Nice.

The darkness can play tricks on your hearing so I concentrate. It's coming from behind the door.

Another. Cigarettes.

Hack, hack, hack.

A man.

Meester Cane.

I'm standing by a red T-bar fire alarm. If I pull this my best guess is that everyone will assemble down on the beach. I'll walk down there slowly and see them. I'll be able to get a good look. In the confusion maybe they'll see me, maybe they won't. Then I'll leave. It only matters that I bear witness to her moment. That I catch her. Make sure I feel something of what she felt. She needs me to hurt as much. To be sorry as much as she feels I need to be. This is her pay-out. Why do I find this so hard? This is fair. What is my problem?

Pulling the fire alarm in a major hotel or shopping centre isn't that different a rush to jumping out of an aeroplane.

I count two beats and then the bell begins to sound.

Slowly the bungalows start to empty out. People plod down the long pathways complaining about the insects and the late hour. I am pulled with them towards the beach. I hear two arguments spat out through grinding teeth. I don't look anyone in the eye. I walk back past Villa 29 and see that it is empty.

There is a crowd of 150 people around the beach bar. Staff in white uniforms run backwards and forwards attempting to count everybody. Some guests are complaining, asking for drinks. Complimentary half-bottles of champagne are given out to all. I sidestep into the darkness, over some windsurfs, into what must be the doorway of the water-sports hut. The bay isn't tidal so you can hear almost every word spoken.

A female, in a don't-waste-my-time-I'm-rich voice, says, 'The only thing worse than a fire alarm is not seeing a fire.'

There is no smoke; there is no comforting orange glow. There is no crackle of tinder, wood or screaming. I'm sorry to disappoint everyone. Welcome to my new theme buffet, attendance is mandatory. I'm calling it False Alarm Night.

So many identical bodies and faces half hidden in the dark. Many are wearing the dressing gowns that obviously get freshly laundered and hung every night by his 'n' hers showers. I know I'd have liked it here and those dressing gowns would have looked great in my suitcase.

The last to join the crowd are the no-wanna-go-homes

from the lobby bar who have all walked down with their drinks.

'There is no bloody fire.'

'Will the cocktails be on the management?'

The crowd starts to break up.

I see her.

Two or three deep, waiting to be counted. Shoulder-length black hair snared in the fat diamanté clip I bought her. She is looking around for the fire. Looking at the buildings, looking around the beach. Looking at me. I stop breathing. I look at my feet and realize that emergency lighting has come on. Come on all over the compound. The klaxon is turned off. All of a sudden I am bathed in the terrible and fearsome orange glow. I am the fire she is looking for. Sarah stares at me. Next to her a man turns around. My friend Ben.

# 17

I was asleep on the table for four hours. Banana Man woke me up, prowling round my head like five foot of shaven house cat. The sun a bright yellow alarm. 'Are you sleeping? Why are you sleeping?'

'I'm tired. Go away.'

'Why are you tired?'

The why game. My mouth is too parched to play the why game. I believe I can taste the heat of the sun. When I lay down on the table top the sky almost looked like it was going to rain; now I've got a thumping ache in my forehead and maybe sunstroke. I pinch the end of my nose to see if I've been burnt. Yes. The skin feels sharp and wrinkles like an old squeeze box. Banana Man sits down and begins to eat his lunch by my head. I smell bean juice and hash browns.

'Seriously, move that away from my head; I'm going to be sick.'

'Why are you tired?'

'I don't go to bed any more.'

'Why?'

'Because I'm a chicken.'

Because when I had the chance to say something I turned and ran all the way home. Because I should have grabbed him by the throat and thrown him in the sea. I think I deserved that. This strikes me as being something of a loser's mantra, so I simply try to stop thinking it.

I cannot, however, escape the overwhelming paranoid conviction that everyone knew about this except me. Imagine them talking, saying, 'Yeah, and they're fucking now; that idiot, he's still in hospital.'

People probably found out in small groups. This has probably been a long and gradual humiliation. It is far from over. What did they think? That I would just go away. I realize that as much as I underestimated her pain, she has overestimated her pay-out. We are finished now, we have to be. I don't want to be with someone who is capable of doing this to me again. Ever. This is the thought, rerun over and over, that kept me awake until I got back to hospital and crawled onto the table top.

That sleep was my first serious brown-out in forty-eight hours.

It would be frightening if I wasn't already living life in reverse – sleep/eat/work – I'd probably be in real trouble. Instead I have this permanent feeling of evaporation. There is less and less of me every day. It's not that I'm losing weight. The human body is designed to conserve weight, not lose it. This evaporation is simply energy. I expend more than I put in. I'm like a chicken whacked on bennies. Bolt upright in my cage, eyes bulging, pushing out eggs and losing handfuls of feathers. Yes, Masser!

SQUARK!

If I had some decent chlorpromazine like Banana Man I'd probably sleep like a baby. I fantasize about decent pills. Fat horse biscuits of ketamine and even roofies. Over the far side of the garden the restaurant manager is clearing away the lunch slops. He looks over to see our little picnic. One lump spreadeagled on the table accompanied by that other freak who steals all the bananas. He bolts over. I have to shield my eyes from the sun to actually see him.

'Get off the table,' he spits.

Frayed grey-oiled cuffs, shirt falling over the front of his shiny black slacks. A forty-year-old man in school trousers telling me what to do.

'What?'

'Get off the table.'

*When you're tired the first thing to go is your breath, which is immediately followed by your temper.*

'I was trying to be polite. Who the fuck are you?'

He jumps back alarmed.

'What! What!' He runs to the kitchen door to put his plates down and comes tearing back out. 'Say that again! What did you say to me?'

Banana Man thinks he's come back for him and panics. 'What! What did I do!'

I'm still lying on the table. I've managed to start all this fuss while remaining horizontal. I have a gift for this.

'What did you say to me?'

What does he want me to do – apologize for cussing? I scream so loud my voice fragments.

'GO AWAY!'

He grabs at my sleeve. 'Fuck you!' Trying to drag me off the table top.

'MOLESTER! MOLESTER!' I shout, pulling my arm away. He darts backwards. I pick up Banana Man's plate and throw it at the manager artlessly. That sends him running. The adrenaline feels good, a surge from the mains.

'PEST! MOLESTER! EAT SHIT!'

He fakes a right which telegraphs his intention to do just that. I throw one to meet him there.

Banana Man screams and runs for the other plates. He thinks it's a game and lets one go hard left like a frisbee. That fifty-pence dinner plate explodes by the manager's head like a hand grenade. He tries to get some bite out of the soles of his slip-ons but they slide out from beneath him. He panics and crabs backwards, belly in the air. Banana Man lets a cup rip. It smashes by his hand. That could have been messy, jammy red knuckles.

'MOLESTER!' shouts Banana Man.

Getting fragged by shards of porcelain while being accused of sex crimes can destroy anyone's nerves.

'Sssh. OK, OK.'

'SEXUAL PERVERT!'

I haven't called anyone that since school.

He scuttles towards the kitchen door. 'Right!' he shouts through an extractor fan. 'You fucking cunts are dead!'

'You. You're the cunt,' I shout back.

Sit down Oscar Wilde.

☐

In group I experience the kind of exhausted serenity that only comes after sex or violence. I understand that the only other time I feel this good is when I take drugs. Booze, I realize, only dilutes the quality of all three.

'Involve yourself in the therapeutic process,' says Sklansky. 'You have to be ready to step inside yourself. Healing can be painful. You have to want to find the source of your anger, your depression. Are you ready?'

Dr Sklansky spins around and points right at me. His 'praise the Lord' inner vicar is really operating today.

'I don't know. What? Now? Yeah, why not? Heal me, baby!'

He advances.

*If he doesn't stop pointing at me, I'll bite his finger.*

'Charlie, do you want to get well?'

'Yes, boss, but only if it doesn't involve that finger.'

'Excellent.'

I might as well try. Tiny grains of sand remain in my shoe.

Obstacles to getting better. I have to accept that some kind of fuss will be made about the incident in the garden. I know this can't carry on. I know I have to try and reverse the process. If I don't fight it I may as well surrender. I know that if you look at anything long enough, you see patterns emerging. But every piece of rubbish that comes my way hits me in the centre of the forehead with the force of a tin of peas travelling at about seventy miles an hour.

If I don't do something to protect myself, duck the next can of peas or whatever, I'll end up looking like those people on *Surprise Surprise* being reunited with their families. Big greasy Ted, lychee skin, thin lips, panda eyes, still smoking. Hands cuffed to the rear fender of the out-of-control articulated lorry that is life.

Weeping, 'I haven't seen Barry in fifty years.'

'Well, this is going to come as a shock, Lorraine, but we have your brother, Barry. Here in the studio. You thought he drowned in the Mersey but he's not dead yet! Barry!'

TV studio explodes in applause, Day-Glo pink glitter strips, cardboard sofas. Potato-shaped Scouser.

'Barry, what would you like to say?'

Barry says, 'Well, I'd just like to say that it's a wonderful thing to be back with my family.'

Wait till Christmas, Barry; you'll wish you were still missing.

Sklansky is at the whiteboard again. IRRATIONAL/RATIONAL BELIEFS.

I have two scratches in my cast now. One for the wedding, one for the honeymoon. I'm going to add one each time I mess up. Keep score.

I try to pick the grains out of my shoe. But for each one I find, two or three appear in its place.

'What are you doing?' says Celeste.

I'm holding one of my shoes up to my face.

'Well, everyone is just full of questions today. I'm getting rid of the sand from my shoe.'

'There's nothing there.'

'No, because I'm getting rid of it.'

'Where did you get sand from?'

'Africa.'

'Africa?'

'Yep.'

'Africa?'

'That's what I said.'

She looks at me, deciding whether to say it or not.

'Don't bother,' I say.

'You loon.'

'Yeah, yeah.'

I could get into that whole was-I-really-there thing. But it would have to have been an hallucination, indicating a brain tumour like a clenched fist. Plus I can quite clearly see sand in my shoe.

There is a reluctant knock at the door. Through the window I see the girl from the canteen standing there with her nurse. As she pushes the door open Sklansky is instantly on the attack.

'It's clearly written in the rules, young lady, that if you are more than five minutes late to a session then you may not enter.'

She looks bewildered, colourless, and takes a step back.

'Jesus, Sklansky, you're the only one who gives a shit.'

'Thank you, Charlie . . . It is also disrespectful to everyone who has made the effort to get here on time.'

The nurse's look alone says: I don't give a monkey's what you think, it was hard enough to get her here in the first place without your showboating.

'Well, is it all right if we sit down and promise to be on time tomorrow?' the nurse says.

More hot air in the centre of the room.

Lisa closes her bag, leans over and whispers, 'Sticking up for your girlfriend.'

'Blow it out your arse, wing nut.'

The girl moves towards the door but only finds the nurse's outstretched arm. He can't be serious.

'Argh, let them sit down, PLEASE!'

'Thank you, Charlie. OK, this once, yes, sit down. Name?'

'Constance,' she says.

She takes the seat next to Heinrich, who is slumped, incapable. His stoned blond head turns and slowly grins.

'I'm sorry about him. We had a party once and he's been here ever since. Go on, Heinrich, show her what a charismatic fucker you are.'

She smiles and her cheeks flush pink.

'Again, Charlie, please respect the rules of the group. OK?'

'Yes, boss.'

Constance's nurse takes a chair from the stack and sits by the door.

'Parasuicide,' whispers Celeste.

'What's that?' I hiss back.

'Constance, she cuts herself.'

'She was fine when I saw her the other day.'

'Maybe she cuts where you can't see?'

'Maybe.'

Look closer and you can see Constance try to hide the scratches on her neck and plasters on her arm. I have a cast; we already have something in common.

Celeste arcs an eyebrow, 'The nurse is watching for sharps. She makes me feel positively mundane.'

'Yeah. I bet she's got everything wrong with her,' says Lisa. 'I want to know if Charlie still wants to fuck her.'

'Jesus, Lisa.'

'She is very fuckable even if you take into account the bandages, but I bet you like that.'

'Say that again,' I say, 'and I'll push you through the window.'

'Touchy.'

I look at Constance staring blankly at her first-ever form. I've been here two weeks and I have to ask myself if I'm any better off than before. Around me: chewed nails, clenched biros, complaining, gale-force sighs. Am I really one of these people? Severely depressed, no. Cut and broken, a little. I can't say my wife beats me or my parents abused me or I never got that pony. So what do I write on the piece of paper? All I have to do is find one incident that I can remember disturbing me and I'm on my way. We can work backwards from there, back past every pizza I've eaten, maybe even past what Big Ted said to Jemima, until we find out the one bad thought that made me worry in the first place. Then all we do is get hold of that thought and replace it with a shiny new one. A cinch. 'That's right, people. We'll take your old thoughts and replace them with brand-new, tried and tested happy thoughts for only £1,000 per week! Price excludes potent childhood memories of the circus. Recovery is subject to full background check and financial status!' All your old beliefs, the thoughts that you hold dear, everything that underpins your whole being, out of the window they go. You are in the process of being reformatted, initialized, please back-up any data you do not wish to be erased. That's the idea anyway. But I've tried and I don't know my good or bad thoughts from a lorry-load of cabbage. Everything I think seems to serve a purpose. Sklansky hands me the forms, I punch them and clip them in my folder. And that's that. I don't want to be rewritten. I look at the blank form and I want to drink. Get out of it, laugh a lot and fall asleep with a fag in my mouth.

Identify a situation in which you felt disturbed.

I had a dream about Pat Butcher getting out of the bath.

No. Be a man. Do it. That won't do. I know I have to start answering these questions sooner or later. The nib of the pen begins to drag and carve a trough in the paper. The black scrawl seems to have added ten or fifteen pounds to the weight on my lap.

I write: *Seeing my fiancée with another man made me feel extremely upset and anxious.*

That's a start right there. I've done my therapy, can I have my drink now?

'Charlie, are you OK?'

'What?'

'You were groaning?'

'Groaning?'

'Yeah, like oooarggh ooooarggh. You—'

'Please, Celeste, don't fucking say it.'

☐

In the canteen SLG dabs her fork into a bowl of cake while the nurse reads a copy of *Woman*. This I can't work out: Lisa sitting talking with Celeste. I thought they hated each other. Constance is obviously some kind of star. She has managed to unite the ranks of lunacy. I mean, she looks the part. She can't be older than twenty, twenty-one, but her eyes already say that she has seen enough. The cuts on her arms say. Bring the curtain down, performance over, the audience feels sick.

Three tables away Celeste's chin scrapes against the Formica. 'That's the whole problem with group therapy,' she says. 'It's all tell and no show. A lot of bullshit attention-getting.' She pokes at the air in front of us. She makes SLG nervous. 'Yeah, yeah, right. You yucked the pills up at the last minute, you had the belt round your neck? Really? Next time you're going to do it? Sure. You actually picked up the bread knife? Ooooh, I know! Bullshit, bullshit, bullshit. I mean the good thing about parasuicide is that it really gives you something you can take to the bank.'

I slide off and get my food while shooting looks at the kitchen door expecting that angry idiot of a restaurant manager to come out any second. I want to talk to Constance but I know if I go anywhere near the table that Lisa will blow her mouth off.

'Sloppy,' says Celeste. 'I'm glad we've got a cutter. OCDs are such a fucking bore . . .'

She aims that at Lisa who has OCD traits.

'Watch this.' Celeste shouts across two tables and a man blowing on a spoon of hot banana pudding. 'Constance, is it? Would you like to join us for coffee? You do drink coffee, don't you?'

Constance looks up, then at her nurse, who nods and returns to her magazine.

Constance gets up, walks over to where we are sitting. 'The last time I was here I thought people were poisoning me,' she says to Celeste.

Then, turning, she looks directly at me.

'My name is Charlie, pleased to meet you.'

'I'm Constance.'

'Yeah. I know.' She smiles sweetly.

Celeste snaps, 'Do you mind, we're having a conversation.'

I say, 'Who is poisoning you?'

'The kitchen,' says Constance. 'Don't laugh.'

'I'm not laughing, I agree with you,' I say.

'Charlie, shut up, this is important.' Celeste rocks forwards. Constance is fuel, pure energy. In centuries past I imagine that Celeste would have drained her blood for food.

'How long have you been doing it? Cutting yourself?' asks Celeste.

I cough, embarrassed. It's like that in here: people always expect too much too soon.

'Subtle,' I say, glaring at Celeste. Celeste can hardly keep her fingers off the bandages.

'Years.'

'Why do you do it? What's the point?' says Lisa.

'What's the point of what?'

'Cutting yourself up.'

'It's obvious,' says Celeste royally.

Constance stares at her nurse.

'Not to me it isn't.'

'You make new pain instead of dealing with the old pain. The cut gives you something ... shit. I think we all get pain, life is pain. I, you can control a cut you make yourself, right? You can't control one from another person. Other people hurt you more.'

Constance is still looking at her nurse.

'You can't control the pain you feel inside, can you?'

'I couldn't cut myself,' says Lisa. 'I hate blood. Blood makes me sick.'

'You hurt yourself in other ways,' says Celeste.

I look at Constance and see a fresh reason to come in tomorrow. I want to help her. I don't want her to hurt herself. She doesn't deserve it.

'I don't think you should cut yourself any more,' I say.

She looks at me, frustrated. 'I need it. Now, now it hurts.'

'I think if you have the strength to cut yourself you have the strength to get better.'

'I doubt it.'

'You're no more fucked than anyone else.'

'I know what I am.'

Her head sags, because when you speak it out loud it feels like shit. Every time. Lisa butts in.

'We all start off bad. When I got here three weeks ago everyone wanted to kill themselves.'

'God, that was boring,' says Celeste. 'I mean, put up or shut up.'

'Celeste wanted to do a dead pool. We all put a tenner in and pick a name out of the hat so if anyone tops themselves there'd be something to show for it. Except no one wants to be on Celeste's ticket because she could talk you to death.'

'I wouldn't. Any tampering would void the ticket.'

'We should do it,' says Constance.

'Yeah, that'll lighten things up,' I say.

'Put my name down first,' says Constance.

Everyone is in for ten quid. Celeste begins ripping up a hospital schedule.

'I'll hold the cash. As I am least likely to die.'

'I hope I get you, Constance,' says Lisa. 'No offence.'

'None taken,' she says.

Constance writes her own name on a scrap of paper. We all do.

**18**

They want me to apologize to the restaurant manager. I have to start behaving normally. Think pitiful, non-threatening.

'What day is it? Wednesday? Shit, fucking Wednesday already,' I say.

'Do you need some time alone, Charlie?'

This is an evaluation. Almost halfway though the treatment. It just happens to coincide with my poor behaviour.

I like this nurse, but then I never met a nurse I didn't like and psych nurses are the best of the lot. They live alongside people whose lives balance on the edge of a knife. So they know how to watch and listen. Do you know how refreshing that is? To be spoken to like a child holding a fully automatic rifle. It's pure sulphate. Outside we get used to people not asking, not caring what we think, what we do, or if we even live or die. In here you get heard. In the beginning, the difference in tone makes it hard to adjust. How can these people care for me when I am nothing, scrap. Then you realize that knowing you are mental, that behaving strangely while being surrounded by people desperately trying to be nice, is the norm. In fact you could say this is just what it's like to be a major celebrity.

'I need this treatment. It was my idea to do this, no one else. The first time, I came in because I was told to. I didn't care. But now I know I need it more. So I'll fill in any form you want and I never thought I'd say that, ever. I promise I'll work harder in groups, play the game. I'll get up to date on my work, everything.'

'Well, that's good to hear, Charlie. So, how are you feeling this morning?'

'I'm racing this morning, but good, you know?'

See? I could get addicted to that. It makes you wonder what you'll do when the nurse isn't there any more – when you don't have someone checking on you like an ever-present thought butler. The nurses are the one constant here. I mean you've got to love the doctors – the glory boys with fresh legs who roll onto the pitch in the dying minutes of the game to stick in the easy match-winner against a well-battered opposition. The first session I ever had with Sklansky reflected that. He played us all, one by one, like a junior chess champion; challenge, move, cure, challenge, move, cure.

Flash-bangs, shock and revelation that ten minutes later felt as meaningful as two nipple clamps, a vial of amyl and a game of Find the Lady. It doesn't take long to realize that nurses who ask kind questions and then wait around for answers before firing a statement into your ear are actually precious to your recovery. I really wouldn't ever give lip to a nurse.

'Will the insurance cover this?'

'Yes, well, that's what we're checking now, but you should be all right.'

She gives me the weekly questionnaire. These want to know exactly how much more frustrated and angry I am than the last time I filled one in. You tick a box indicating less, more or the same amount of pain, and eventually all the measurements are collated into a pleasant line graph that neatly displays your madness/depression/eccentricity as it leaps and plunges. It would make an excellent tattoo. Other questionnaires are more entertaining and actually leave spaces for you to fill in names and locations. Here's a classic: 'Do I feel frustrated when people refuse to do my bidding?' Some ask who I blame or if I feel much hate. Mostly these seem to be questions asking: 'Do you feel like committing suicide?'

Between the lines you read: 'Do you want to do it?'

Yes, much more than I used to.

'Are you going to do it?'

Maybe.

'Do you want to tell us how?'

No.

The nurse comes back with some tea and wants to know if I have been using drugs since I came to the hospital and whether I feel my depression is worse.

'No and yes.'

'It will get worse before it gets better,' she says.

Mostly she wants to know why I'm checking in as a night patient. We'll go to my room later and she'll search my things. I haven't got anything to hide. I don't want to mention the thoughts of suicide playing noisily around my mind. I don't want to be watched day and night. I can't say it's because of my parents or Sarah and Ben, because that all sounds so common, so worthless. There are people in here nursing holes and welts where tumours grew. People carrying real scars.

'I need time to focus,' I say.

'Focus? Focus on . . .'

'I mean, even if I don't get radically better I could still

just sit in the garden. Like today, if it was sunny, I would probably be just as well-off sleeping in the garden as I would be in group. We used to sleep on the grass when I was at school, sometimes through the afternoon. I mean that's how you spend a day.'

'We'd all like that.'

'You know, what if I tell you the truth? Come right out with everything I know and someone says, "Christ, boy! Can't function? That's not a problem, take two of these and go work in Starbucks for the next five years." '

'That's not going to happen, is it?'

'I'm rambling. I never used to ramble. I don't think I did anyway.'

'Look, Charlie, how we, how you go on with your treatment from here is up to you. There are certain considerations we have to . . . Your behaviour over the last two weeks, your acting out, your absences. You have to take responsibility for getting well.'

'I know that now.'

'I have complaints from staff and other patients about your behaviour. And I see in reports that you've broken group rules on a number of occasions and even damaged hospital property.'

'I'm . . . That's in the past. I swear that's why I'm doing this now. I know what's been going on up here. You don't have to tell me I'm out of control; I'm sitting here aren't I? That whole thing with the kitchen.'

'I have a record of four incidents. And six complaints in total. Four from kitchen staff. This is a verbal warning, Charlie.'

'You're talking about the plates thing, right, a couple of days ago?'

'Yes.'

'He was trying to fiddle with me. That was assault.'

'That's a very serious allegation. And the waiter you chased out of the men's toilet?'

'He was going to jump me! I get nervous, you know, and when I get nervous I get paranoid. And I can't control myself and I go on the defence. Which is natural, right? It's like my brain goes a million miles an hour. Fight or flight, all that. I don't mean to scare anyone.'

'So, if you have a genuine problem then bring it to the attention of the appropriate member of staff. When we have a problem we talk it through. You have to promise me that you won't cause any more trouble in the canteen and the garden and, really, I mean this, you have to promise not to tell other patients that their food is poisoned.'

'Shit, I'm sorry. Jesus, that was just a joke.'

'Yes, I understand that but many of the patients are not so able to discern what may or may not be a joke. Do you understand that, Charlie? We have to think about other patients. We have to balance our desire to help you with the health and progress of the other patients. Do you understand? Are you OK with these points so far?'

'Yeah, sure.'

'Is there anything you'd like to say?'

'No, no, you're right. I'm ready to try now, I really am.'

'Now, I've also got in your notes that your parents are coming in for family therapy today. With Dr Sklansky.'

'Yeah, right.'

'Is there a problem?'

'I left home five, six days ago to go abroad and they didn't want me to go. I had to go to Africa.'

'Africa?'

'Africa, yeah. I left the airport and came straight to hospital. I don't want them here.'

'It sounds as though you have a lot you can talk about.'

'They don't buy into this. I was living with this woman I was supposed to marry, but I crashed, whack, during the service; it's in my notes.' I reach over and flick the bundle. 'She's the one who should be here, but she's with someone else now. I mean that's the reason I'm here. I think.'

'Why not go through with it all the same, Charlie? You've got an hour till the session, maybe you can think about what you'd like to say to them?'

'Yeah, sure, they won't even show.'

☐

In the hospital reception my mother is bent forward in a small purple armchair. Think airsick passenger in economy class. Hugging herself around the stomach, hair pulled back into a tight knot. Rocking backwards and forwards, washed-out jeans and well-worn flats crumpling up her toes. He, the old man, is trying to ignore her and read the *Daily Express*, but he can't help twitching in her direction all the same. I walk over and take a seat on the other side of the beech veneer coffee table.

'All right?' I ask.

She looks up, eyes floating.

'Where the hell have you been?'

'Ray's.'

'You know where he's been, June.'

'Africa. Selfish. Selfish.'

Eyelids are mallard-green scales – flick, flick.

'Ray called us last night, said you'd been sleeping on his

floor since you got back. We're a bit unclear on what's been going on.'

'I don't even know why I'm here,' Mum begins to wail. 'I can't believe I'm here. Harold, why did you make me do this? I didn't want to do this.'

'June, it's just the once.'

'It's all because of you; why did you have to do this to me?' She turns on me now.

'To you? I ask you to come in one time.'

*Useless bitch.*

'June, please.'

'No, Harold.'

She stands up grabbing her bag to her chest.

'I shouldn't have come. I told you I couldn't do it. I told you, Harold.'

'Mum, what are you doing?'

'June.'

'Mum, please, it's nothing. It's just talking, please.'

Dad does that X-Men thing again. Silent screwed-up forehead, trying to control her without speaking. I look at Mum, trying to discern if it's having an effect. Nothing appears to have happened here, but there might be a load of penguins floating upside down at Colchester zoo.

'I'm going.'

He puts an arm out to stop her. The strain flashes across his face.

'Don't touch me,' she says, swerving past him. 'I told you never to touch me, never again.'

'Shit, Dad, let her go.'

She crashes through the door. He covers his eyes with his hand.

I've never seen him cry, but I'm sure he must do it somewhere.

'You shouldn't have to see that. The way you are now. Things haven't been . . . We didn't want you to know until you got better. I should go after her.'

'Don't worry about me, Dad.'

'I brought your wedding suit. It needs dry cleaning.'

'Thanks.'

'Well, be careful.'

'Dad . . .'

'I should go.'

He turns and walks out of the door. I don't go after them. I'm glad they are gone. Glad we had the chance to do this. I needed to see them like that. I know I need them both, but if they're falling apart they're going to have to do it without me. I won't stand in the middle. For the first time I see that I really can't help them. They should have had the sense not to come in here like that. So selfish and petty. It will be better for all concerned if we just leave each other alone. I should go my own way. They can't help me with what I have to do now.

Ray arrives an hour later. Mentally I would say I'm in a destructive place. In my mind people are dying and cities are turning to dust. Everyone who ever relied on me or demanded anything is choking to death. Ray, however, is pissed off because there's a new sticker on the back of the van that says, in thick black letters, 'If you see this vehicle on the road between the hours of 9 p.m. and 5 a.m. please dial 999 as the vehicle has been stolen.' This has upset him even more than the old '0898 – How's my driving?' sticker which he claimed people actually used to pay him compliments. Now he can't even use the van to go down to the petrol station to buy microwave burgers. He makes me stand there and read it in silence. I can't possibly imagine what he's thinking right now. I mean that.

'I'm not buying a car. I'm not buying a car. I'll buy another van probably.'

'You can buy my car.'

'That piece of shit?'

'Sure,' I tell him. 'Now are you going to take me to the juicer or what?'

'What for?' he says.

'What do you think?'

I feel the lag from the last forty-eight hours, the rough sleep. I need a shave, some fresh cigarettes and Ray's company, at least for the first smoke anyway. We'll have a laugh – after that I don't think I'll care one way or the other.

'Go on, buy my car. You can't drive a fucking van your whole life.'

'You drive a Nova. It's a piece of shit.'

'Sell it for me then; you can have ten per cent of whatever you get.'

'That's ten per cent of fuck all.'

'Done.'

'Need money in a hurry?'

Suspicious.

'Whoa there, Jessica Fletcher, don't be so suspicious. I'm going liquid. I've got to start paying people back sooner or later. I owe you enough, why don't you take fifty per cent of the car?'

'That's OK.'

'No, really.'

'It's OK.'

On the way to the boozer he asks me a load of questions

about hospital – decent ones like what did I do today and what are the people like. I tell him about Celeste and Lisa and Banana Man but not Constance though. I want to keep her to myself. I don't even know why. I haven't got an evil plan, she's just my secret, my pleasure. I don't want him to think I'm two seconds out of the fat farm and already I've got my arm stuck in the biscuit barrel.

He slides the van around the back of the Woodcutter. A borderline country pub that looks like a Tudor mansion. I can smell tropical fizz and sense the Pink Panther fruit machines from here. He's on the handbrake.

'Well?' he says.

But I've already got my leg out of the door thinking about a quadruple Jack and Coke and crunching on some of those half-melted cocktail-onion-sized ice cubes. I can't remember if I first wanted this drink two weeks, two hours or two minutes ago. At some point I promised myself if the wanting got too strong – if I started to jump about – I wouldn't fuck around whining, I'd just take the drink. Now, since I've been clear for two weeks, I know I can get in and out of this booze thing when I like. Ray calls me a prick and drags me back to the van.

'I can't do this. I want a drink with you but not like this. You've got to get better first.'

'What do you want? A note from my doctor.'

'I didn't think you were fucking serious.'

'I wasn't joking. I want a drink.'

'Well, not on me you're not. We could go in there and get fucked up for no reason or we can be sensible, do something else.'

'What?'

'Let's go back to mine, watch some telly. Cheese on toast,

all that. You can tell me what happened in Africa and then after all that if you still want a drink then we'll see.'

'We could be in there now, two pints, ice-cold, chicken Kiev. Fuck the cheese on toast.'

'You want chicken Kevin, we can get it on the way home. It'll have to be from the Spar though.'

'I hate Spar Kevin.'

'It's exactly the same,' he says. 'It's all made in the same place.'

□

You know when you're in a Chinese restaurant and you have to walk down a long damp corridor, maybe a mile, mile and a half, before you finally get to a bathroom? Well, that's Ray's bathroom. All restaurant corridors lead here. Ray likes to joke that his bathroom is so dirty that the sink calls itself Derek and likes to be taken to nightclubs.

'Not too much tea. I don't want to spend any more time in your bathroom than I have to.'

Just lying on the sofa and dozing is good all the same. He brings in a big tray and sticks it down on the brown table top that reminds me of thick Iranian sunglasses. There's a pot of tea and two steaming VHS-sized pasties. He bites into his, unleashing the armpit smell of mechanically recovered meat paste.

'I'm not eating that.'

'You can have toast, just let me do half of this bastard.'

A ribbon of fatty meat liquor rolls down his chin.

'You know that they take all the chicken, pig and cow spines, send them to special plants where they have the technology to produce economy burgers and shit like that.'

'Tasty.'

'Then they strip the carcasses with machines and rinse the remains with high-pressure steam so it runs into giant vats.'

'Yeah, that's how you get brain disease and meet people off TV in the hospital. The steam is making my nose wet.'

'It's making my clothes smell.'

A lump of hard shiny potato drops onto his leg, and sits there like a pebble glistening on the shoreline.

'You know it got fucked up in Africa.'

'Yeah, I know, mate. I'm sorry. Sarah phoned me up to tell me. If you can believe it, she was worried. She said she wasn't sure it was you though.'

'Yeah?'

'Don't worry, I told her it was you.'

'Shit.'

'Well, who else is that fucking stupid?'

'When did she ring?'

'Yesterday, before you got home.'

'She tell you who she was there with?'

'Yeah.'

'Ben.'

'I know.'

'I saw him, Ray. I saw him with her, on my honeymoon. I can't get it out of my head over and over, Ray. This fucking . . .'

I start hyperventilating again. It's the first time I've spoken it out loud to anyone. I'm crying again.

Hysteria pours over me like a cold shower. The initial shock of the experience is everything. A blast of a cold wet reality that leaves me trembling like a stray dog. Ray brings me a couple of blankets and wraps them round my shoulders. We sit in silence for a while.

'I saw him with her; they were together. They were together, Ray. They're my friends. He's my friend. My friends. What am I going to do?'

He wipes fragments of pastry from his fingers onto the plate and puts his arm around me.

'Come on,' he says.

'I wish . . .'

'I know,' he says. 'I know, mate. We'll sort this, I promise.'

I wish a lot of things. I wish Sarah wasn't in my head fucking Ben. I wish I had a place I could hide. But, most of all, I wish I had my mum here. I wish I could lay my head down in her lap and we could go back to when she could tell me not to worry, and I used to believe her. That will never happen again. That time is gone.

'Do you still want to kill yourself?'

Pause. I shake my head. I don't know.

'How did she sound when you spoke to her?' I say.

'Worried.'

He sparks up two fags and passes me one.

'She was fucking disturbed, Charlie. She got caught; no one wants to get caught.'

'Right.'

'I told you not to go.'

'Yeah.'

'I knew this would end in bollocks.'

My face is still hot from the crying, from embarrassment.

'If you want you can kip on the sofa.'

'Thanks . . . I always thought if I ever caught her cheating or whatever, found her with someone, that it'd be worth doing time over.'

'I know that.'

'But when it came down to it I stood there and I looked at them together and swallowed it. I sucked it up.'

'Shock.'

'No, no you see I can't do anything to him. What can I do? I can't challenge him. He's got my whole life, my job and my woman. He's got it worked out. If I move on him, then I'm fucked and he wins.'

'He treats you like shit. He doesn't fucking care about anyone but himself. They're all the same. That fuck Doyle and his albino mate.'

'Ray . . .'

'Now you walk away, get a job at another place with some grown-ups.'

'I can't do that. That's not what I am.'

'What are you then, Charlie? Fucking hell, they're both the same as Ben.'

'They're my mates.'

He stands up.

'You call me up to take you drinking. You say you want to kill yourself. You don't fucking listen to me. I'm banging my head against the wall. What's it going to take? It's over, mate, that life. It never existed.'

'What are you talking about?'

'You get paid fuck all, you walk around like you own the fucking world. Walk in here with models demanding money for drugs. You get on a plane and go to Africa at the drop of a hat. You have your stag night in New York. You think you're in fucking Guns 'n' fucking Roses and you haven't even got a Blockbuster card. Is all this shit really you? Because you can have it if you want. This is a warning, Charlie. You'll drink and pill your whole life away if you want it enough.'

'Look, tomorrow I'm going to check into hospital, I promise. Jesus. Sell my car. Take the money. As soon as they can get me a room I'll be in there. I'll see my doctor in the morning. I'll be a night patient, the yoga, all that. I'm going to do it properly, Ray. Then, couple of days' time, I'm going to Sam's wedding.'

'Don't be stupid. Leave it. Do what you said: go to hospital, take your pills, read books.'

'She'll be there, Ray. How can I not go?'

'Are you stupid?'

'No. I can't get better with this over my head. I'll see her on her own; we got invited together. Ben won't go to a wedding. I'll see her. I'll put a cap on it, there and then, end it my way, properly. I'm going to sort myself out. I know what I've got to do.'

# 19

It was the first night we ever spent together and same as always I needed to be on the road by 3 a.m., embarrassed and done with it all. Not because I had somewhere better to be. I wasn't pretending to be a bit of a boy, jumping out of bed and disappearing to knacker out some other tart – 'Sorry darlin', can't hang about. Have you seen where I left my kids?' I'm talking about gathering everything I have in my arms and actually needing to hide. I don't know why. Go home or wait out the rest of the night watching TV, wrapped in a blanket, suffocating in stupid dirty guilt. Like a doctor trying to sleep after a botched operation. To me, to stay would be unthinkable. Breakfast, not so much the first meal of the day as a painful and argumentative diagnostic session.

I know sex was a) supposed to be fun, but b) mostly wasn't – because like surgery the whole exercise is dependent on skilful finger work, good hygiene and when possible a minimum of two nurses. What are the chances?

Worse than slim.

So you go do it. You get to press up against someone naked. You expect very little, you get less. Then when you can, you go home.

So what if she is beautiful? So what if I care? Well, if the sex is good, easy and not over quickly then I feel that as the booze wears off, so will her memory of wanting me. The more I ever found myself caring and needing that body next to me, the quicker I had to find the door. I couldn't even remember the last time I wanted to be there to see a woman wake up. I was always sure I was doing everybody a favour by getting lost. I knew there was a world of good mornings, hugs, touching, kindness. But in my mind it could only go two ways. She could:

1. Open her eyes, and remember me and smile.
2. Dress rapidly and self-consciously, saying, 'Shit, shit, shit.'

Both of these had happened to me. As much as I enjoyed the first, I'll never forget the second. The brain mostly recalls that which is important or dangerous. Danger is replayed.

That first night with Sarah I thought I was going to die. I was sitting up in bed, with her sleeping next to me, my mind calculating every single twist and turn I'd made to get to that point. Pinching the bridge of my pink nose making it turn red and gritting my teeth. Thickly remembering her stripping me down in the lobby of her building and walking me through her front door naked. Still grinding my teeth, smelling the six-pound drinks and the smoke on her clothes, thinking how easy that part was. I remember how she finally dropped everything in the bedroom and I jumped on her like a cowboy on calf sprinting and we thrashed and wrestled and dug our heels in until she was taken care of and wanted to hold me. I was quiet after but she was kind and she talked about my 'great shoulders'. I remember my mind bursting with her drunken flattery and the pleasure of it.

She said, 'You were great.'

I was great.

She was great.

'You were great.'

There were so few coins in the charity box at the time you could really hear those fuckers landing. It was enough to carry me this far.

So I was thinking that this was the be-all and end-all. In bed with a beautiful naked woman, the kind of woman you see in adverts for deodorants. TV quality. Did I do good? Yes. Did I feel cocky? Fucking right. I astound myself. Am I staying? I didn't know. I knew I couldn't avoid the virulent infection of positivity spreading through me. Fishing around under the bed, I found some cigarettes and foolishly tried to anchor the moment, which never works. By the time you've recognized it, it's already gone. This one time, I wanted things to stay just the way they were. Her breathing built into a steady even rhythm and I lay there listening, too scared to breathe lest I woke her up.

I watched the clock turn 4.00 a.m. She wanted me, but I wondered if she would still feel the same when she woke up. I wouldn't want to wake up to me and she looked so happy sleeping. I covered my eyes in shame remembering my bleached-white body framed stark against the yellow hall walls, the sickly pot plants and reproduction art. What could happen that is so bad? If I walked out now, all that pain and worry, getting this far, would be for nothing. We had a good time. We could have a good time again. Why do I have to ruin it? Why do I have to run? Would anyone else be stupid enough to care this much or am I the only one? Shit.

Another hour and any glory I felt had passed by in the darkness. The urge to back up and run grew stronger but it was too late to make a move by then. I had to trust that she'd know how to handle it. I thought when she wakes up she can just give me the number for a cab. I stayed calm, watched the ceiling and ignored the clock. She's done this before. It'll be easy; she won't embarrass me; she's too kind for that. Crick, crick, crick. That fucking clock sounded like a giant woodworm eating the wardrobe.

I remember the dehydration became almost exquisite. I was desperate not to wake her and the discomfort served as some kind of penance. Even if I could get to a tap I wouldn't be able to drink anyway. I'd have to start by moistening my lips with a sponge, maybe by dripping some liquid into my cracked and swollen mouth.

Too late I actually remembered that sleep is a basic human necessity. When I was little my nan used to say that the best way of getting to sleep was by trying to stay up all night. I let my eyelids close, out-argued and without defence, feeling the onset of a cold dawn.

I fell about 200 feet, my body slamming into the concrete. My body rigid, I push out as I land and find her.

She put her lips to my ear. 'It's all right.' Then gently placed her hand on my forehead, drew it back and then leaned forward and kissed the spot softly.

'I think you've got a temperature.'

'I . . .'

'I'll get you some water and some aspirin.'

'That's OK.'

'No it's not OK. Stay in bed,' she said.

She pulled on a pair of knickers and a vest and ran out to the kitchen. This was not what I expected. This was worse. This was humiliating.

She returned with the glass and gave it to me. She lay back on the bed.

'How sick are you?'

'I'm not sure,' I said and took the glass and the pill.

She pressed her body onto me like the lightest quilt.

'I should go,' I said.

'Will you stop it. You're starting to make me nervous. You don't have to go anywhere. I'll look after you.'

I feel her pressed against me and I can't work out where in the world she came from. I close my arms around her and pull her in to make sure she stays where I can find her. I want to thank her for being kind, for making me feel welcome. One heart to another. She squeezed back as hard, and exhaled, long and easy. This is what you stay for. She isn't saying, 'Shit, shit, shit.' She isn't making for the door. I haven't got a plan for this. Maybe I should still get going as fast as I can.

'Coffee?'

'You don't have to. I can . . .'

I don't want to tell her that I'm not sure. That I'm worried that I'll never be able to let go of her now. That if she pushes me away I'll kill myself in the street, on her doorstep. I wanted to say instead that I could always go home to my mother's house if she wants.

'You were funny last night.'

I *blush*.

'I could forget how young you are, you know that? What are you, really?'

'Twenty-three.'

'Really?'

Did I make a mistake telling her?

'That's young.'

'I know. I still get nightmares if I sleep in strange beds.'

'Ah, baby, you got scared!'

She curled up closer and kissed me once on each cheek.

'I was scared of you, I think.'

'Why? How could you be scared of me?' she whispered.

Her experience overwhelmed me. I felt then as close as I ever had to being a man. I realized that if I ever lost her I would go back to being nothing again. How did she scare me? What had changed? I didn't know where to start.

**20**

Sarah used to have this book about weddings. She told me once that at Ukrainian weddings a mock capture of the bride is staged at the reception to remind guests of the many times their homeland has been invaded.

She was always trying to read me stuff from that book, but I never wanted to listen. It seemed to be everywhere I looked. In the toilet, by the bed, on the table in the kitchen. I couldn't get away from its 'jolly yet informative mix of fact and trivia that could keep the pair of you giggling and pleased with yourselves right the way up to the big day'. There was only one other entry that I liked in that whole dumb book. It was about Armenia, where small coins may be thrown at the bride. Coins, not confetti, coins. Imagine how hard Armenian women are, that on their wedding day, carried away with the romance of it all, playing princess for a day, they also have to watch out for twisted bridesmaids with sharpened fifty-pence pieces. Now that's a proper wedding. Don't like the service? Just go for the head shot.

Sarah sits on her own. Her hair is scraped back tight and her eyes hidden behind Gucci wraparounds. The look is male. More *ID* than I've ever seen her. This would be Ben's influence. I know that coming to the wedding on her own must be hard for her, though she has already secured herself

a high-profile aisle seat so she can dutifully beam while Sam
floats back and forth.

She turns and looks in my direction. Scanning the crowd
at the back. I'm skulking around with a couple of forgotten
second cousins. The kind that wear shiny suits, who look so
lost and anonymous that each side always attributes their
presence to the other. I couldn't be more invisible.

The interior of the church smells of dry-cleaning fluid,
perfume and decomposing tapestries. Darren is blocking up
the end of the aisle like something that would show up early
on radar in an old horror flick.

Beside him is Sam, dressed like the good witch of the
west. The vicar refers to his little black book to get the names
right then begins. Now the game starts. You tune in, you
tune out. You stare at the walls. Read the names of the
valiant dead. Try to work out what's in the stained glass and
think about two thousand years from now, when Princess Di
and Elvis will be up there in red and green and yellow, their
crazy antics and good deeds unchallenged scripture. Listen
to the tuneless hymns and try not to laugh. Elvis singing
'How Great Thou Art' could save us all. In the same future
vicars could be made redundant. Thousands of them milling
around parks and shopping centres causing trouble, looking
for Catholics, Muslims, Sikhs, anyone they can start a theo-
logical argument with. Maybe it will be safer to keep them
inside churches. Then wake up, tune back in, catch some
static on the dial, and back comes the vicar's voice: Africa
is starving, we can help . . . So many young people here . . .
Falling church attendance . . . Marriage is about more than
just children. It's about sharing . . . Who is he kidding?
Everyone in this room is looking at Sam and Darren now,
imagining them having a giant row and maybe fucking a bit.

Looking at the size of Darren, I bet he comes like a Mr Whippy machine with a broken lever.

During the vows I get so agitated that I might start breaking my own bones. I slip quietly out the back and make for the reception hall where I steal a bottle of white wine and a glass and make for the car. I do know what I'm doing. I am hopeless, I am lost, I need this drink and nobody cares but me. I am certain of one thing though. If I'm going to have a drink, it's going to be from a nice glass, with some style. I am glad I am not going to have to resort to drinking something tramp-like and regrettable like VP sherry or White Diamond or in fact anything worse than a sub-standard bulk-bought Riesling.

I sit inside my car and allow the weight and momentum of this do-bad impulse to carry me through.

When your throat is all cut up from cigarettes it's hard to know you're drinking at the best of times so the room-temperature white booze goes down like flat lemonade. Regardless of taste it works quickly, pushing its fingertips through my forehead and twisting my attitude a good ninety degrees south of normal.

Everything you do inside a car is subject to exaggeration. Smoking drugs, farting, sex, choking, drinking, aggression. The tiny space increases the potency of the action, intensifies experience. You can be as rude as you like in your armoured womb. The trouble comes when you climb out of it. Stoned, drunk or baring your teeth ready to bat someone. You drag the fantasy of your own meanness alongside you. This is why I have to give this car to Ray. Ray only has the van and he'll drive me anywhere I need to go anyway.

Stumbling from the car to the hall I am sorry that I am drunk; I blame other people and whoever decided to portion booze out in such large bottles. The old barn is cold. What a shame no one could anticipate the weather. Potted mini-trees are decked in pinpricks of light and cream ribbons. The theme is Gibb/Streisand/Pastoral.

I examine the seating plan, barely able to make out my table's location. When I get to my seat Sarah is standing behind my chair, pushing and pulling a steady flow of smoke in and out, searching the room. I wouldn't want to be her right now. I move up from the side and pull the chair away from her.

'Hello.'

She jumps back in shock. Maybe expecting me to hit her.

'Shit.'

'Yeah, same to you.'

I drop into the chair.

'I didn't think you'd be here,' she says.

'Yes, you did. I saw you watching out for me in the church.'

'I was going to come and see you,' she says.

'No, you weren't,' I say.

'Don't tell me what I was going to do.'

'You're right, I couldn't hope to fucking guess.'

I lean back smoking. She looks thin. Already the other guests seated at our table are watching us intently. I don't mean to intimidate her, them, but it is inevitable. Unfamiliar faces surround the table. People filing in in twos and threes, the odd single clutching her bag too tightly to appear at ease, casual, confident. One couple I see look fresh and still into each other; the rest are merely a mismatched bunch of scrubbed-up Daves and plain Janes. Usually at this point we would be introducing ourselves. Offering details like name, which side we are affiliated to, how we met either the bride or groom. Blaaah, blaaah, blaaah. Where you sit is so important. You want to be far enough away from the family to drink and swear, but not so far away that you're on a table with a couple the B and G met on holiday. Put me on that table and I really am insulted. I know that I'm only one unexpected RSVP away from eating with the waiters. All of your worst fears are compounded in these first few minutes. Everyone knows that the guarantee of a hot meal, free booze and the chance of screwing a loose bridesmaid, or bride, is what keeps people coming back for more. Because two out of three is the best you can hope for, what you really want is WCS – Wedding Conversation Syndrome – a severe cognitive reaction to trauma-level boredom.

With WCS you shut down so many of your enjoyment valves you become convinced that you've actually had a 'great' time, that the person you spoke to was really rather interesting. You could have spent the last wedding you attended with an expression on your face like a lone ambulance man at a motorway pile-up and you wouldn't know a thing about it.

I take a bottle of white from the table and fill my glass.

Sarah jumps again.

'Jesus, will you stop flinching; it's not like I'm going to hit you.'

One of the men to Sarah's left blows his chest out when I say 'hit you'. I want to tell them that this is only an argument, and arguments happen – even at fairy-tale weddings with little lace bags of sweets and trees you couldn't tie a My Little Pony to.

So for the benefit of the whole table, as well as Sarah, I say, 'I'm not going to start anything now.'

She moves her face straight in front of mine, close enough

that I can smell Bubblicious, and growls through gritted teeth, 'Go. Home. Then.'

'No,' I say, upbeat, righteous. 'You go.'

'You know,' she says. 'I really didn't think you'd come. I thought you'd have more class than to make a scene. So did Sam.'

'If you were both so worried, she could have told me not to come.'

'She wouldn't do that.'

'So you asked her to un-invite me?'

'No, I said she wouldn't do that.'

'So you asked her. And she didn't. That's awkward, isn't it?'

On the table is a rock with my name written on. Sarah has one. We all have one. This is a twist on the traditional calligraphized cardboard. I can't remember what we decided to have at our wedding.

'Did we have these at our wedding?'

'No.'

Rocks with our names written on, strange glass pearls and an instant camera so we can take pictures of our new friends.

'Why are you even here? You hate weddings.'

'You're right; weddings fucking suck.'

The table gasps.

'I love honeymoons though. I love honeymoons. Doesn't everyone love a honeymoon? The holiday of a lifetime. All inclusive? Free water sports? What about you, Sarah? Don't you just love a honeymoon?'

'I had a great honeymoon, Charlie. How did you find it?'

'Well, I'm not sure if I really enjoyed it, as my wife had

another man's dick stuck in her.' Fore. Straight down the middle. 'What's wrong, nothing to say?'

Her hand swings hard into my jaw. It's nothing; I do worse to myself when I get angry.

The table is looking a little concerned.

'We're on the bride's side,' I say.

Arguments. Only scum argue at weddings. Fully ripening domestics must be compartmentalized, saved for the car ride home. Shut those doors, throw a you-know-what's-coming look, pull out of the gate and really start spitting it out. FUCK YOU, NO FUCK YOU! The truth, the dark realities of life, must be hidden. Obviously this deceit is practised nowhere more than at weddings.

'Sugared almond anyone?'

'Shut up, Charlie. You're making a fool of yourself.'

'Where were we?'

'Please, Charlie.'

'That's right. Ben had his dick in you? Sorry if that's made me a little cranky, dear. You know how it is with him being my best friend.'

'You have no right to say this. You're a liar. I know about you.'

'What?'

'What right do you have to judge me after what you did?'

'What? After what I did? I was ill, am ill. I did what I did with a clean conscience. I wasn't fucking anyone!'

'You fucked me, you fucked yourself, you fucked that whore at the festival, a week before we were supposed to get married. I even found out her name.'

That. Now they're looking.

'Did you think I was stupid, that I wouldn't find out? We've got the same fucking friends, you idiot.'

The bread arrives.

'Did you think I was stupid?'

We can all pick what bread we like out of a large wicker tray. Olive, cumin, sun-dried tomato. This do must be about £40–50 a head easy.

'We've got the same fucking friends. How long did you think it would take before I found out? A week?'

It's very hard not to follow the tray around the table and see what everyone chooses. Jesus, I have to say something now. I've got no stomach left for this fight. Ben told her about the girl. He was there; he must have seen something. Who else?

'I didn't do anything. I swear I was so fucked.'

'Is that supposed to make me feel better?'

'No. Because it's not even on the same fucking scale as what you did to me. What you did involves new maths. Different, bigger equations. Pages of algebra. Work it out. You fucked my friend behind my back while I was in hospital.'

'It's the same thing.'

'Why?'

'Because it hurts the same. Do you really think it's any different, you fool? Do you think that matters?'

'It matters to me.'

She goes cold. 'I thought you'd stopped drinking.'

'I did.'

'When did you start again?'

'An hour ago.'

One of the Daves leans across the table and says, 'Perhaps you should go outside.'

'I'd like to, Dave,' I say, 'but it's raining.'

Sarah gets up from the table.

'I can't stay here with you.'

She runs around the table bumping chairs and people on the way out. The whole room is alert to this now. I hope no one here was at our wedding as well. How would that look? I follow her outside where the light is harsh and white, irradiating us through a filter of high cloud. The rain when it does come is cold and thick.

'We can sit in my car.'

'No.'

'Please.'

'Leave me alone.'

'Get in the car.'

'I'm not getting in a car with you, you're drunk.'

'We're not going anywhere.' I open the passenger door and she gets in.

I walk round to the other side and climb in. I notice the plastic dog with butterfly wings which hangs from the rear-view mirror and brings me good luck. I notice that a kind of dirt, resembling breadcrumbs and grey feathers, has collected in the crevices of the cheap plastic dashboard. Breadcrumbs and feathers. I collect some on the tips of my fingers. It's like I work for Bernard Matthews.

'We've got to talk about this,' she says, waving her arms around.

'About Ben,' I say.

'Not about Ben.'

'I want to; we have to,' I say.

'No.'

'Are you ashamed?'

'No. Ben isn't the issue here.'

'Yes, he is. Why doesn't what you did make us equal?' I think I am being fair.

'Where do you get this from? This is not about being equal. This is beyond that. You are behaving like a child.'

'I know how this works.'

'Here we go.'

She flips down the make-up mirror, and starts rooting through her clutch bag.

'When did you start with him?'

'Not now.'

'When?'

'I'm not talking about him now. He's not important.'

'He is to me.'

Water drums on the roof. Drap, drap, drap. Over the other side of the courtyard, blocked guttering empties into a wide slick of ice-cold water. Through the gaps in the doors the wind is harsh and cold. They put fairy lights on trees and decorate cakes and dance in an attempt to make at least one day out of your whole life different.

'This is not about Ben. Not about you fucking around. It's about what has happened between us. It's about what you did to me before. You never being there, not loving me.'

'I was ill. How many times do you want me to tell you? Why can't you see that? I don't want to keep making this same excuse. What do I need, a bandage on my head? Would that make it easier for you? What if I had a load of nice cuts to look at? Or measles? Would you believe me then? Would that be more convincing? There's always the chance that I'm making all this up. That I'm hiding in hospital because it's fun and I hate you. Why can't you see that there was more to this than just me being drunk and selfish? If you can't even believe that I loved you, then you never loved me either.'

'Don't turn this around.' Crying. 'Like I could have

known what was wrong with you when you were never there? Don't think I didn't care. Don't you think sleeping with that girl changed anything?'

'That's a lie! That's all shit!' I shout.

'Why don't I believe you? It was all a lie. The wedding, everything.'

I want to scream. Tell her that she has no excuse for what she did. What she did with Ben was about spite, that's all.

'I was ill in the head.'

'No, I don't believe you. I wanted to marry you, Charlie. I thought you were serious about marrying me, but it was a lie. I had the dress on. I walked down the aisle for you. Remember that? You. No one else. But you had already broken your promise. You broke down in front of all those people because you couldn't keep lying. Because you felt guilty.'

We have collided. My head is thudding. We are breaking up on impact. Separating. Not admitting responsibility. Not offering closure. Not conceding. Textbook bad. I know I could explain myself in time. That we have been stretched so far, that whatever joined us gave like silly putty. Now she needs to hate me to make this easy. There was, there is, guilt in me. But it's not related to some girl, in a field somewhere. I don't know where that guilt is from. It's guilt; it's just there. It exists, it's horrible and you hide from it. I could tell her all this, but some things really shouldn't be explained while you can smell drink on your own breath.

'Sam's pregnant,' she says.

'I bet big Darren comes like a Mr Whippy machine.'

'Shut up, Charlie.'

'Do you want a lift back to town?' I say.

'No,' she says, getting out of the car. 'Leave me alone.'
She runs back into the wedding through the rain.

☐

3 a.m. is a lonely time, on the motorway, drunk. You push
on but you know that there is just no way that you, in
this state, can deal with this amount of relentless visual
stimulation. Instead of a brain you have an old Play Station
scrolling through the giant bit-mapped chunks of reality. This
is about as existential as the uninitiated can get – watching
that light as it sweeps the road in front. Seeing your whole
world appear and disappear along with the rain on the blades
of the windscreen wipers.

Accidents always happen at the end of the journey
watching for coppers, watching your speed. The calorie-
burning alertness begins to nag and tell on your faculties.
Near misses become frequent, you start jumping at nothing
in particular. Traffic cones, reflective strips, lights on skips,
animals, people's eyes. Accidents that never happen. I get to
Nan's house at 4 a.m.

Her dressing gown is shiny and quilted with decorative
diagonal stitches She puts a kettle on the hob, takes a single
match in her shiny fingers and strikes it with one single econ-
omical touch – lighting a small blue flame underneath the
kettle. That inconsequential blue flame is the only source of
heat or colour in the room. Nan brings me one of Granddad's
old jumpers and lets me sit by the radiator which she swears
she is going to switch on.

'I hope you didn't have anyone else in the car.'

'Ah not now, Nan. I'll just have the tea thanks . . . if you
don't mind.'

She looks at me, a sideways look, bristling.

'So how long have you been like this?'

'I shouldn't have come here.'

'You went to Africa, did you like what you found?'

'No.'

'You weren't likely to either, were you?'

'What?'

'Like what you found there?'

'No.'

'So why did you go then? That's what I don't understand.'

'It seemed right at the time. Can I have my tea in a mug?'

'Do you want something to eat?'

'No, it's too early for me.'

'You should have something for your stomach.'

'Whatever.'

'Are you back in hospital now?'

'Supposed to be.'

I'm shivering.

'Well, why aren't you in there now?'

'Because I went to a wedding.'

'Well, that explains the drink then.'

She gets up and lights the grill. Throwing a slice of white under the bubbling flame. 'I never liked weddings myself.'

'Did you not enjoy my dad's?'

'Not especially.'

'You're using a lot of energy up on one piece of toast. What's wrong with a toaster?'

'Toasters make soggy bread.' I can hear the clock on the wall.

'It's freezing in here. Does this radiator work?'

She turns the bread.

'You've got cold bones. Come and stand by the cooker. I'll put the fire on in the front room.'

'Sarah was at the wedding.'

'I liked Sarah.'

'Everyone likes Sarah.'

The kettle begins to boil.

'She bought me a lovely pair of slippers.'

'Those slippers?'

'No, I keep hers upstairs.'

'What? For special? For visiting?'

Nan always takes her slippers when she visits someone's house. According to Mum, she used to make my old man do the same when he was young.

'I'm not going to ruin them walking around here, am I? What a waste. Is she well?'

'She looked thin.'

Nan has been thin her whole life.

'I suppose you caused another scene then? Embarrassed yourself?'

'No. Probably. We're finished. I think.'

'I thought that was long over.'

'Not to me. To her it was. I deserved it though.'

'That's the first sensible thing I've heard out of you.'

'I know what I've done.'

'Do you now? You keep making the same mistakes. If I didn't know you I'd think you were stupid. It's sad, but now you can both get on.'

'I don't know. I don't know if I can keep on like this. I'm lonely, going mad. I can't have people around me because I'm rude and I hurt them. I say stupid things. I get angry, paranoid.'

'You don't look too good on it. I can't imagine it was doing much good for Sarah either.'

'She can look after herself.'

'We all need to be looked after, Charlie. Did you ever ask her what she wanted?'

'Yes, of course I did. We wanted the same thing once. If I could change things back to how they were then and go from scratch I know we'd be good, but something went missing along the way. I need to put all the pieces back in place.'

'It doesn't work like that.'

'I'm the same person I was when we met. I'm no different now. I don't think she knew what she was taking on.'

'Did she tell you that?'

'No.'

'Well, I wouldn't try to guess what she thinks.'

'Why not? I can put it right. I haven't changed.'

'That's a lie. We all change, sometimes for the worse, and this is not the Charlie boy I remember. When did you get like this?'

'Get like what?'

'When did you start taking drugs, stop caring about people, stop listening to what people who care about you say?'

'I listen to myself. I can trust that. You can't live your life for other people, Nan. But that's exactly what you do when you get married. Which is why I'm not married.'

'So why are you sitting in an old woman's kitchen at five in the morning pissed out of your head?'

'I haven't got anywhere else to go.'

'You can start anew.'

'Yeah, right.'

'That's your problem. You are twenty-five years old. Do you want to be treated like a baby, lean on everyone? Or stand up on your own? You want this life. I think you're welcome to it. I don't think anyone will want to share it with you. I can't think of one woman in the world who would. Maybe you should marry your friends.'

She gets up.

'I'll make up the bed in the spare room. You can sleep here, then back to hospital you go.'

**21**

In the taxi to the hospital something Nan said just before I got in the car is jammed in my mind.

'It doesn't matter what other people think about you.'

My self-esteem has always been governed by what other people are thinking about me.

From a philosophical standpoint, you could argue the absolute necessity of people thinking about you, because, if no one thought about you at all, then on a theoretical level at least, you might actually cease to exist.

I think the majority of us feel that we actually vanish now and again. You are walking around your flat alone, and you stop thinking, you zone out. Alone and out of sight, out of mind, you cease to exist. You have so little impact on the rest of society, that the memory of you just times out. You lose your connection.

'Sorry, I zoned out for a moment there.'

Yeah, I stopped being. Everyone forgot about me. My parents closed the bedroom door and I disappeared like a white blip dropping off a radar screen.

I always get like this when I've done a handful of pills. Sorry for myself, wrong-footed and slightly frightened, like Obelix after an illicit sip of the magic potion. Usually just before I begin thinking about walking up to outpatients. I took a couple of days' worth of Propain this morning and piggybacked those with some Valiums, a sleeping tablet and all my antidepressants. I could have taken the black pills I got from Mexico but I now want those for emergencies, civil disturbances and/or a breakdown in satellite TV services. Any subsequent overdose would be a long zone-out. A giant loss of reception. The final failure to connect.

Consequently, you are never more alive than when your fate is on *their* minds. When your ears are burning and you are more than likely about to be rationalized, unemployed, disenfranchised. Because people only ever talk about others when those people are being mocked, envied or loathed. Right now I can feel the vibrations. Ben and Sarah talking. Ben asking Sarah about me; Sarah telling Ben, Sam, her mother; tearful confessions of this and that. That I am a pig, a liar, a cheat, a drunk, a drug abuser. Yes. Yes, yes, yes. At some time or another I have been all these things. If I didn't mostly believe everything I thought they were saying about me, know most of it to be true – if I thought everyone was just spreading lies – I could feel injured or even maligned. That would be bliss. I would love to be maligned. Maligned would change everything. Maligned would give me some focus. I could move into revenge then. I only imagine the worst. I am powerless, no outs or options, or recourse. I start groaning and hugging my stomach as I think of Sarah telling Ben that I am a bad lover. This is so ignoble, pathetic and maudlin. But the groaning is self-perpetuating and I can't stop twisting their words around my head.

Sarah: 'I always found Charlie asexual and robotic.'

Ben: 'I thought you said he was clumsy and inept?'

Sarah: 'Did I say that? Did I say he was clumsy and

inept? I meant to say that having sex with Charlie was like being groped up by my little cousin.'

Help me, help me, help me.

They think, therefore I am.

I could spend the whole day actively being punished by this invisible conspiracy. Sarah telling Ben that he makes her feel like a real woman, implying that I didn't. And Ben laughing, and asking for more sex, more stories.

Ben: 'What else, what else!'

Sarah: 'Did I tell you about when he came to Sam's wedding, got drunk and tried to sort things out?'

Ben: 'No, don't tell me now, save it for later. Let's have more sex. Pull my handsome cock!'

This is a thought-wall that I can really bang my head against. Really draw blood. Really destroy myself against. I imagine these two people conspiring to propagate the ruin of my life, stop me living, stop me escaping, starting fresh. I want to punch this thought-wall and leave Steve Austin-sized fist dents in it.

Today we have a general group session. This is much like the Monday morning meeting that occurs in every office in the country, except here if you sent anyone out for bagels they wouldn't come back. I have to decide whether I want to talk about the wedding. I would be making a serious mistake telling anyone I'd had a drink. While this might suck up at least twenty aimless minutes of I-know-why-he-did-that debate, I'm not drunk now and I don't plan on having another. And I'll never be able to say anything self-righteous again. As no one really knows the real reason they are in here, you can make a cosmetic decision about what you declare and what you hide. Your real stink is academic and is only for your own shrink to hack away at, energetically, outside hospital hours for a hundred quid a throw. I mean you sit there crying on your first day thinking you're in here because of your girlfriend. You think that your girlfriend is to blame for everything. She ate your early twenties, chewed up your friendships, made a paste of your self-esteem and swallowed your hope. NO! Wrong! They tell you that you're actually in here because you consider yourself to be worthless and your circumstances unacceptable. They tell you that you've taken all this loose, existential pain and fixed it on something, anything close and easy. Like your job. Which, even though it is truly bad, isn't as bad as you think. Unless you work in a cheese factory, dealing with Brie all day. I knew someone who did that; after one week staring at all that Brie he thought he was Jesus. I think they promoted him. That your job is the root of all your pain is acceptable to you. It is confusing why it has you on the brink of suicide, but it is acceptable all the same. Everyone hates their job, everyone is tormented at work.

Like any hospital you come in for one thing and leave with another. You go from A, your original assumption, to B, the real pain, as quickly as you can. Four to six weeks is preferable with most insurance companies. Anything longer than that and you'll have exceeded the time insurance company accountants feel it should take you to make a real therapeutic progression and shrug off all that profit-sapping pain.

I have a lot of nervous energy.

I think that group therapy should naturally reveal some evil problems, horrible memories that will make mine dim by comparison. Cancers in the family, exploding boats and hard-core sex husbands who don't wash. After two hours of other people's problems, any anxiety I feel about Sarah/Ben enjoying each other physically will bleed away quietly like acid from an old car battery.

That's before I get pushed into a corner with Constance. When I took those pills this morning I needed to dim the lights a little. Pull the curtains. So Constance, with a bandage just visible under her sleeve, is the first and the last person I wanted to see today. She makes me think inappropriate uncomfortable thoughts. About sex. Makes me remember that I like doing it. That I feel like the only person I know who isn't doing it with someone. The codeine and Valium, which usually kick in around an hour after the ingestion, start to loosen me up. I know this is the wrong place to get aroused, the wrong time. I'm wrong. She's wrong, she's vulnerable, I'm vulnerable. But I look at her and I begin to send out invisible sex rockets. I can see them exploding all over her. I am your dentist dancing towards you at Stringfellow's clutching a Harvey Wallbanger. I am that bad. I am naughty strawberries and cream tonight baby. I am the centre of your universe. Experiencing this in a room full of sick people is so far beyond ordinary morality it is actually suburban. It must be something to do with the thin blue curtains and the film the Ajax deposits on the surfaces. Pineapple and cheese on sticks: 'Gillian, have you met Bob? Jenny, Bob's wife, just left him so Bob's a little tender right now. Bob, Gillian's husband Glen is presently on the oil rigs. He never does it with her. Have you got johnnies? Would you like me to change the music?'

The alarm, the buzz of being bad is so right. It's so three up two down. I'm all jacked on being naughty. I am your father bogalling with the woman next door.

I look at her and she looks at me. That look is everything I need now. I feel sunshine. I feel the cool water on my toes. For someone who could be in an emergency room I am doing an excellent impression of being alive, which is good – and believe me this sounds more joyful than it is – but any feeling I can get today, anything that surfaces and tells me that I'm still functioning is good.

Constance is dressed in jeans. I love women in jeans. Why doesn't Sarah ever wear jeans? Sklansky is at the whiteboard drawing the outline of an 'I' and filling it with a load of smaller 'I's. Constance is also wearing a tight-fitting sweat-shirt and a beaten-up pair of trainers, Green Flash or something like that. I think that I want to pull her jeans off her while she laughs. Sklansky writes 'part whole' next to the big 'I' and I see me and Constance naked.

The big 'I' is you. The smaller 'I's are incalculable. Hobbies, your relationships with other dog owners in the park, the way you hide your face when you cry in the cinema. They make up the big 'I'. Sklansky says, 'That one small "I" does not have the power to make the big "I" and all the other little "I"s bad. This is the part/whole error.'

I want to suck her toes.

Casual sex is still teenage to me. When a situation actually arises where clean, free sex is offered I get the urge to stick on soft rock and run around in Speedos. Is it possible to conceal this kind of excitement? No. We have evolved to give away and retrieve this information with one glance. You may choose to ignore it, but it's all there any time your eyes meet with another human. The only thing in my favour – weakened in this heightened state – is that most people don't believe they can make other people this excited.

We take our chairs to the corner of the room. I carry hers for her and place them so we'll be facing each other. This preparation builds anticipation. Anticipation is sex. Constance, slim but untoned, speaks first:

'You're supposed to challenge me then I'm supposed to come up with a positive statement to defend myself. It's embarrassing. Have you ever done this before?'

'No.'

She leans in close and whispers, 'Do you give a shit about this?'

I have to take advantage of this. I'm going to do it. I'm going to breathe in the smell of her hair like a man in an advert.

'No,' I whisper back, sniffing the area around her ear. 'I get embarrassed. I don't think my problems are equal to yours. Though I'm not saying you're worse than me or anything like that. I don't see why you'd want to listen to my shit.'

'Right.'

'But I didn't mean it the way you think. Like that you're worse than me or anything.'

'Well, look at it this way. If it's not important to you then you're probably not ill; you shouldn't even be here because you're just wasting everyone's time.'

'What?' I say.

'I said,' she shouts, 'that there is nothing wrong with you. You're imagining it. Go back to work!'

The whole group including Sklansky looks up.

'Shhhhh,' I say. 'Shhh, shhh, shh, sh, shhhhhhh. What are you doing?'

'I want you to refute it,' she says.

'I thought you were having a go at me.' I lean forward to whisper in her ear, 'Can't you be more discreet?'

'You're meant to defend yourself. You know, be positive. You're worse than me. And did you just sniff my ear again?'

'Yes.'

'Why?'

'Because it's impossible to whisper something in anyone's ear without smelling their head.'

'Are you a dog?' she says.

I have to think about that.

It's harder than you'd think to balance sex and therapy. I like irresponsible shouting. I like sitting next to her. I want to find a cupboard somewhere and do it with her.

'You go while I think of something. You can talk shit and I'll try not to agree with it for a while or until I can come up with a reason why I should even be here. Now, how do you feel about yourself today?'

'Today,' she says, 'today I don't like myself.'

'OK,' I say. 'That's good.'

'Yes,' she says, 'it is, isn't it?'

'I didn't mean that.'

What could she possibly hate about herself that would make her cut herself? What could have happened to make her like this?

'So, when you say you don't like yourself, what of the many things about you, that are bad, come to mind, in particular?'

She smiles. 'You are so shit at this.'

I want to ask her if I can I smell her hair again.

Without the cuts she would be flawless. Not too tall, about five foot six. Brown hair, a couple of bleached streaks. Soft slender arms, neatly tied little bandages and . . . I can't even check out her breasts. If I get any more obvious, I'll be better off handing her an explanatory drawing.

'Do I have to be more specific?' I say

'It would help,' she says leaning forwards, propping her head, bored, in the palm of her hand.

'I'd rather not be specific.'

'Then it won't work.'

'OK. You're, er, not a nice person.'

My brain seems to be hanging out of my mouth on the end of my tongue.

She smiles. She is beautiful. Sex in an institution might seem like rock bottom to you, but I used to think like that myself once.

'Look at my arms,' she says. 'You know what to say!'

'You think I've already worked you out.'

'I know what you're thinking,' she says.

'Believe me you don't.'

'Believe me I do,' she says.

Long pause.

'Well, haven't you?'

'What?' I say.

Got you undressed, completely, talking nonsense . . .

'Got me all worked out?'

'What? No, why would I?' I say.

'People usually think they have. Everyone thinks they know. They think I made this choice. That embarrasses me. I didn't make these marks on myself so I could come here and get attention.'

'I didn't think that. You seem genuine enough to me.'

'You don't know me.'

'Well, call it trust. Can I smell your hair?'

'You shouldn't trust people you don't know, you could get really hurt.'

She stops speaking and stares at me. And I swear I wasn't

thinking about sex. She says, 'I've never really met anyone. People are mostly hostile to me.'

I take one more sniff.

She laughs and puts her hand over her mouth. She laughs, Sarah laughs. For a moment their faces become one and in her I see Sarah. Sarah when we met.

'The cuts freak me out but I know they aren't you. Ask me a question.'

'So what did you do to get here then? Did you try to sniff someone important?'

Sarah without complications. Sarah without anger.

'I was meant to get married,' I say, one part of me still falling backwards, 'but I collapsed in the hotel. During the service. It was a conflicting lifestyles thing.'

Honesty?

'What happened to her?'

'I'll tell you later.'

'Great, we can watch TV together.'

'Are you allowed? Haven't you, like, got a nurse?'

'I'm losing her soon. And we're only watching TV.'

'Right.'

*What music do you like?*

*What places have you been?*

*What have you done?*

*Can I buy you a drink?*

*You should wear more pink.*

*I like your hair like that.*

'So?'

I don't notice Sklansky standing by the side of us, stomach hanging over his grey pleated slacks like it wants to be stroked.

'What are you supposed to be doing?'

'The challenging game,' she says.

'We can't do it,' I say. 'It's shit.'

'I'll pick a subject,' he says. He puts his hand on my shoulder and begins to ramble.

Constance smiles at me.

SHE KNOWS.

Sklanksy rambles.

'Focus on that,' he says.

'I want to,' I say, and I make sure, when I say it, that she knows exactly what I mean.

☐

When I get back to my room all I can think about is her. I sit on the edge of the bed with my head in my hands and try to think how I have to be better, and help more than I hurt. Give more than I take. It was good laughing with her. When I was busy cutting another notch in my cast this morning, she was cutting her arm. When I was swallowing pills and thinking about the wedding, the car and the rain, she was still bleeding. Yet she got to the session. She lives. She laughs. I can be like that. Her drive infects me. It is a part of myself that I have forgotten. That I liked in me. Sarah has that. She didn't wait for me. She could have. We could have made things right. She must be strong to move on like she has, and I feel like I am being shown up a little. I must appear so weak in contrast to her. She's already back at work, already seeing other people, already making a new life. Her survival without my help is the final heel stomp at the end of a long beating. I have to realize that I am that easy to get over. My absence from her life has not been crippling, but emancipating. I obviously loved her a whole lot more than she ever loved me. And how embarrassing is that? In the battle to appear to care less I am quite clearly the loser. She has shown everyone we know that I am nothing more than a fault to her. A mistake easily rectified, the glitch in the mainframe. Nothing.

I decide I'll cash in a PEP I got when my granddad died. Then I can put a cheque in an envelope and courier it to Andrea, Sarah's mother. To take care of the dead salmon, and maybe it'll go some way to helping her see that I wasn't such a lost cause after all. I'll move on. If Sarah can do it, surely I can too. I will be careful, cautious even. I'll watch TV with Constance, see how the situation develops and, continuously and with a clear head, assess its effect on my behaviour. I'll watch for signs of the erratic, the irresponsible, the destructive Charlie. If I start to weaken, act like a fool, hurt myself, I will burn it off. Constance might be dangerous for me but it is important to remember that as much as we can hate the world – blame it and a multitude of individuals for what has been done to us – all the bolts on all the doors in the world will only ever make it harder to save us from the real danger. Ourselves.

**22**

Andrea has got a council-house face, a touch of the Doris about her. I never saw it before. She is standing in front of me in the hospital reception holding my cheque in her outstretched hand. And I can see her Doris face. It's so plain. She has spent her whole life trying to look like another woman. As she says my name, I realize how hard it must be for her to rearrange that simple face and make it stun. To look like money in every sweep of her make-up brush, application of eye pencil, achieving class by plucking, peeling, cutting and bleaching. Birth-Andrea ceased to be years ago. What you see now is a projection. She has been moulded, wrapped, draped, tailored, manufactured. Her clothes are expensive and designed by men and women skilled in selling the concealment of age to the rich but who can do nothing about her hardened Doris face. Her crude bones. Her thin lips, nothing more than a sharp little ripping. I wonder if her mother was poor and struck lucky, or if Andrea was the first to pull herself off the estate? Maybe that's what scares her about me. Maybe that's what makes her so worried for her daughter. She wanted someone better. I know, we all know, what she'd rather have had for Sarah. Maybe the man she'd rather have had for herself. I'm guessing a foot taller than Harvey, drives a Boxster, something mediocre in the City, 120k, no love, no time, no life.

'What do you want me to do with this?' I say.

She continues holding the cheque out in front of her. I wonder how long she was thinking about this moment and how it would look. The muscles strapped over her harsh bones constrict, and she becomes a screaming skull. 'Take it back, we don't want it.' She grabs at my hand.

'No,' I say, knocking it away. 'I gave it to you for a reason. Have the courtesy to accept it. There's a couple of grand in there. I owe you that much. I can't understand you. It's yours. I explained all of this in the letter.'

'What do you think we're going to do with this? Do you think we need your money?'

She brushes her thick hair back behind an ear showing me a pearl earring. I see the gold rings on her fingers, and as for the rest of her, I imagine if I turned her upside down in a pawn shop I could walk straight out of there with a flying V and at the very least a pig nose and a couple of crap pedals.

'I know what you're worth but you paid for a wedding that never happened. That was my fault and there's some of the money back.'

'Do you think you can buy your way back?'

'No.'

'I told you to stay away from us!'

The cheque is screwed up in her fist, fingernails like polished cockroaches.

'I swear I don't want anything from you. I want to move on. That's just to pay back some of the money that I cost you. I know it was my fault.'

'Well, you can keep it. God knows your family needs the money.'

'I meant no offence to you.'

She looks and sounds like some hard old cow whose debit card is being rejected in Victoria Wines.

'Take it, spend it on drugs.'

She is pushing it into my hand.

'Get off me.'

'Buy some drugs, go and wreck someone else's life. Sarah is well rid of you. Don't you know she's happy now?'

'Me . . . Sarah and I have already sorted this out.'

'She told me that you followed her to Sam's wedding.'

She is bent over. She has bad posture and needs to breathe properly. She probably has a lot of headaches in the afternoon. A good excuse to plonk her fat arse in bed, I imagine.

'We were both invited to that wedding,' I say. 'I didn't follow her anywhere.'

'She told me. Stay away from her.'

'She told you what? We spent half an hour together then she walked away and I let her. I got the message. She's with Ben.'

'What?'

She doesn't know. When she hears this she'll really flip. I'll ask Matron if they've got a room free. We can watch Catchphrase together, snort her Thorazine and take turns regurgitating food.

'I saw her. With Ben, on the honeymoon. Don't you know who Ben is?'

Andrea's face contorts. 'Ben?'

'Yeah, Ben.'

Hello.

'You don't know who Ben is, do you? So she doesn't tell

you everything, good for her. Maybe you should let her speak for herself.'

Andrea begins to vibrate, left and right.

'You're sick, you're a liar. Sick. Sick. You need help.'

'Look where you are! I'm getting help! You're in my hospital! I'm doing something about it. I'm being straight with you. I don't have anything to lie about. I'm trying to give back whatever I wasted, can't you see that? This is me being straight with you. Why do you think I gave up? She's with someone else now. You should meet him. His name is Ben. If you think I'm a piece of shit then I can't wait for you to meet him.'

'Stay away from us.'

'You're not listening,' I say. 'Look around you. You're in my hospital. And, get this! You came to see me. You didn't even bring anything nice!'

It's like I reached down to her stomach, caught hold of the barbed wire of her anger and wrenched it straight out. 'She doesn't want you, she doesn't want your money. It means nothing to us.'

She is now hyperventilating. I keep my hands outstretched to keep her at a distance. If she doesn't drop dead of a stroke right now, I swear she's going to try and hit me.

'I really think you should sit down, Andrea.'

'This is what you understand, isn't it?'

'What?'

She pulls herself upright with one deep breath. Her whole flabby offal-like body swinging from her shoulders.

'You're scum and your family's scum. Always were. She knows that. I told her, but she can see it for herself now. Stay out of her life. Do you hear me? Scum. That's what you are, you and your family.'

She staggers.

'OK, that's it, you've said enough.'

'She's better than you.'

I don't want to physically intimidate her, but the only way she is going to leave is if she gets a little of what she expects. I walk towards her, my arms spread wide.

'She's better than you.'

'Go home, Andrea.'

'You're scum to us, scum.'

She takes the door handle and pushes it open. She stops to turn around and lay into me again but I grab under her elbow and tilt her out of the door onto the driveway.

'Get your hands off me.'

'Start walking. Go on.'

She stumbles across the tarmac. Now I know why she hates me.

'Look at you, you're an embarrassment,' I shout. 'You're making us all look bad. This is all you know.'

As soon as she is gone I call home. My mum picks up the telephone. She is crying, dribbling wet sniffs. I haven't got time for this. I need her to back me up, not require instant sympathy from me. It isn't there. I don't want her manipulating me into aiding the destruction of her marriage. I hate the way she is going about this.

'This isn't a good time to call,' she says.

'When is?'

Mothers are meant to hold us all together.

'I wanted to tell you that Andrea—'

'Why? What have you done?'

'Why are you so quick to jump to conclusions about me? I've done nothing. She's just been here. Screaming at me and everything.'

'Well, she must have had her reasons.'

Like you did?

'You know, I had to push her out of the door? I wanted you to hear it from me first. I knew you wouldn't fucking believe me.'

'What did you say to her?'

'I sent her a cheque to sort things. It wasn't anything to do with me. I had to walk her out of the building. She was calling us names.'

'I hope you apologized. They've been very kind to us.'

'What? You're not listening to me. Don't you want to know what names she was calling us?'

She sniffs.

'She said you and Dad are scum. That we are all scum.'

'What did you say to her? Why did you make her angry?'

'I didn't do anything. I told you. I tried to pay back some of the money I owed them for the wedding.'

'And they're such good people too.'

I let the silence widen and then let her go. Sitting there picking lumps off my cast in this bare little room, going fucking nowhere. My fingers are bitten red raw and the skin around the side of my thumbnail is bleeding slowly. Why is it every time a part of me begins to heal, another piece of me gets damaged again. I stay perched on the edge of my bed rubbing my forehead with the palm of my hand. No one listens to me. I want to pack myself into five separate suitcases on five different planes and explode simultaneously.

You don't give a box of matches to a man who has already doused himself in petrol.

When I walk into the room Constance was already sat in one of the two prize chairs, directly in front of the TV. She has her legs stretched out onto the rattan coffee table.

This is how it starts.

'You see our parents are children,' she says. 'I see that already. They are hopeless and each of us, their children, is a failed experiment. That's what we've become. We're conceived and incubated by science, and raised according to textbooks and schedules, then they turn around and scream and shout when so many of us fail. I mean I could only have ever turned out like this. There are only two real outcomes to any experiment. Success or failure.'

I say, 'I don't think you turned out so bad.'

Which is a lot better than, 'Did you do science at school?' I guess that I am trying to deliver this line like Richard Gere would, though realistically I sound like a game-show host getting ready to move on to the next contestant.

'Yeah?' She smiles. 'Do you think so?'

'Yeah, I think you turned out fine,' I say.

'Thanks, Charlie.'

She is wearing pyjamas and drinking coffee. She draws

her knees up carefully, setting the raised edge of the table into the arches of her feet. Why are you staring, Charlie?

Where do you think you are?

This isn't some drunken chance meeting in a booth at the back of a nightclub. This is fluorescent light and staffroom chairs. Cheese plants and perseverance posters. No dry ice, cologne, designer labels and stomach punches of heavy bass. No simulated euphoria. No waking up halfway through a pill with a woman attached to your face. Mouth filled with thick flavourless saliva. No drunken confusion. It is stark and cold and it is new to me. I use my thumb to rub the varnish from the arm of the chair. Flecks of smashed amber. I watch her toes ball up when she moves her body. Her feet still soft. I am here for sex. She turns to look at me again and starts talking. We know we are up to something.

'You know, some of my friends think that the cuts are cool. Like I'm accessorizing. Or they think that it's an attention thing. You're one of the first who doesn't think I'm doing this . . . I don't know—' She breaks off, unable to find the words.

'For kicks and sympathy?'

'Yes,' she says, 'for kicks.'

She asks me how I have my tea and leaves for the kitchen.

I remember going to meet this girl when I was at college. I'd asked her out the night before and I'd been replaying this meeting over and over in my mind. I had a lot of doubts and was well past remembering why I'd even asked her out in the first place. It's like every time I wanted someone I fell to pieces. I could do the flirtation, the sex, but I couldn't, still can't, go through to the end or rather a beginning, the start of a relationship. The second time we met I got this pain. This anxiety so severe that I got twenty paces out of my house and was sick into a bush. I stuck my head in that tree like a fucking partridge. Vomiting. The same feeling I had after my first time with Sarah. The same feeling I had at the wedding.

What if something happens with Constance? Will I have the same feeling tomorrow? Why do I bring this on myself when I'm supposed to be using my time to get better? Why do I have to go and complicate my life? I could have played ignorant, simple and comfortable and slept on Ray's floor. Eating toast and watching *TenPin Masters* on Sports 3. She puts a cup of tea down in front of me and I am looking up at her and smiling. I have déjà-vu for every bad night or morning after.

'Thanks,' I say.

People think that confidence is what enables you to have sex with strangers. But this is a simplification. To manufacture even the poorest level of confidence (enough to get you laid in most situations) you only need to be good at just one thing. It doesn't matter what. The only requirement after this is that you are psychotic enough to believe that this skill is of world-humbling importance and vital to humanity's survival. You don't have to tell anyone what it is out loud; you just have to believe it yourself. Whatever you do that sets you on fire, use it.

She drinks from the cup then clasps it between her knees. Maybe having less blood makes you cold. 'So,' I say, 'do your parents think you're doing it for kicks?'

'I don't know,' she says. 'I can't talk to them. Nothing I say is valid or right and they don't believe that I'm capable of telling the truth.'

'That's no then,' I say.

'I could be on fire in the kitchen and they'd say, "No

you're not on fire, you're exaggerating." I'd say, "No, look, really, there are orange flames coming out of my ears." They'd say, "Oh, so you think you're the only one with orange flames coming out of your ears? What makes you so special?"'

'Sounds bad,' I say.

'Sometimes I think that things have been good. But if that was true, if we'd ever talked, communicated, whatever, I wouldn't have started cutting myself. I wouldn't have become this.'

Is what I am doing bad? Am I misrepresenting myself to her? I believe that you have to at least attempt to reveal a true part of yourself to the person you want to become intimate with. Why pretend to be a stuntman or a fireman? Have a bath, put on your best clothes and smile but why tell lies? It's not clever. It doesn't exactly make you Face from the *A Team*. I'd much rather use some pathetic part of myself to build fraudulent confidence than pretend to be a navy diver or an astronaut. Worse still is the little-boy-lost act. I view this as a form of mental and, if it works, sexual assault. That whole Waterboys, floppy-haired, I play the fucking mandolin and read Keats, look-at-me-while-I-stare-into-the-corner thing makes me ill. I have never been able to work out how that actually translates into good sex. How do you go from that introspective helplessness to bouncing your-selves off the bed and into the wardrobe? What do you say afterwards? Do you thank her for helping you out of your shell? Do you phone Dial-a-Ride for a lift home? You freaks.

'Brothers and sisters?'

'There used to be four of us, all girls, now there are three. I'm the little doll of the family.'

'Used to be four. What happened to the other one?'

'She killed herself. My oldest sister, she got married first. She killed herself five years ago. I was the last one to leave home and I've come straight to hospital. The rest are all married. Babies everywhere.'

'I'm sorry.'

'I was already doing self-injuring behaviour before that.'

'What?'

'Self-injuring.'

'I don't really understand it. It's a coping mechanism, right?'

'I think so. Something like that. It helps me. To, you know, to cope with pain.'

'So why are you here now?'

'Long story.'

'Cut it short then, so I can tell you all about me.'

The best thing you can do when a woman shows interest in you is to shut up and let her talk herself out. Like any negotiation, the less you open your noisy mouth the better. I don't mean you should be silent. Don't just stand there like a seventeen-year-old squaddie on ketamine. Conversational gambits will be required, but not yet. Don't get greedy and ask for too much too soon.

'Thanks,' she says.

'I hate long stories.'

Does this sound cynical? It isn't supposed to be. You can't make an instant connection with every woman you meet, clip together like two pieces of Lego. Not all women are Sarah.

'I met a boy . . .'

'What happened?'

'You know?'

She looks at me like I know. What do I know? The only

thing I am sure of right now is her. Constantly revealing her intentions like a revolving billboard.

'What?' I say.

'You know what I'm talking about.'

'No, I don't.' I love this. 'What? Sex?'

'You do, OK,' she says.

'Not recently,' I say, truthfully. 'Tell the story. What happened?'

I hope she never asks me again about any of this because I won't remember anything.

'He was a couple of years older than me, fit and strong, good-looking, all that embarrassing shit.'

'Like me.' I can't help it. 'Keep going.'

'I can't.'

'I don't care, I've heard worse.'

'He was seventeen. He just wants to get laid, right? He didn't understand. I know he didn't care really, that he just wanted to fuck. I mean it was easy. I'm attractive right?'

'Stop fishing,' I say.

'OK, I can try, can't I?'

'Yeah, you slid that one in like a professional.'

'You caught it like one.'

'*Bitte schön.*'

'So we go through this process of pretending we have a relationship, you know, acting out the whole thing. Thinking we were in love. I got pregnant.'

'Pregnant?'

So, what do you say to a woman if they've chosen to tell the truth? There does come a point when you will have to open your mouth. You'd like to be funny, proactive and engaging, but you don't know how to without telling lies. If she has nice breasts don't mention them. Don't even look at them. Look in her eyes. Study her. Don't get overwhelmed; if you have to say something tell her that she's funny. If you catch yourself thinking that she's perfect, incredible, excuse yourself and come back to the conversation when you're prepared to behave sensibly. She is not perfect. Better to work that out now than tomorrow or two years down the line. Think. What is she trying to achieve with her look? What could she be paranoid about? Examine the clues and tell her what she wants to hear, not what she already knows.

'The baby wasn't expected,' she says. 'The baby was terminated.'

'Shit, that's terrible,' I say.

'Aborted, I mean to say aborted. I keep saying terminated like I'm Arnold Schwarzenegger or something. They tried to make it clear that it was my decision but in reality there were only two options – I do it for me, or I do it for them. There was no third way. I was in hospital pregnant, but the baby was being killed, not delivered.'

Keep quiet.

'So I got a lot worse after that. That was the first time anyone medical saw the cuts. Then two days later my mum barges into my room carrying a load of linen, like that's some kind of warrant or something.'

'Open up, it's the cops; we've got clean pillowcases!'

'Yeah, like that. I think they found out at the hospital, so Mum comes in and I'd just got out of the shower and I'm sitting there, haven't got time to cover myself. She sees the red marks and pulls at my arm, screaming for my dad. "What are these? What are these?" My dad runs into the room. I shout at him, "This is my fucking space!" They think these are track marks and I'm doing smack. Look at the evidence: I've been quiet for a couple of years, my posters are gone from the walls, I'm wearing more black these days and I'm listening to non-chart music. It's obvious . . .'

'What is?'

'That I'm on smack!'

Her face is flushed red, excited. Revelation. Dumping emotion equals narcotic rush.

'Excellent,' I say.

'So they start searching for drugs.'

'We do that in my house,' I say, 'except everyone gets to keep what they find.'

She smiles. 'See, that's civilized.'

I hand her a cigarette. Her soft body relaxes under her clothes. Everyone has a weakness. With most people it is just to be understood.

'Anyway, my mum pulls my bedside drawer open and finds the razor blades and the TCP and a couple of towels.'

'You wanted them to find that stuff.'

'No, I didn't, I needed it too much. I didn't want to stop. And being found out just made it worse. You can hurt yourself with anything, anyway. The shame I felt from their disgust. I knew I was messed up and that only made the pain worse, so I cut myself again, I went too far. I didn't intend to, but I couldn't feel *enough* pain. I couldn't get enough and I ended up in casualty.'

'So what now?'

'I don't know. They want me to come out of here cured. Buffed and polished. They really do. But the longer I spend in therapy, in hospital trapped like this, the worse my situation is going to get. I thought that was what they wanted. My parents. You know. For me to be like my sister. Take her place. What about you? Where is your fiancée now?'

'She's not my fiancée any more.'

'Oh right. Is there a ceremony for that?'

'No. Just a buffet and a lot of crying.'

I remember my weaknesses. Sarah. Honesty. Anxiety.

'So where is she now?'

'With someone else.'

'She left you?'

'Something like that.'

'How long ago?'

'A couple of days, a month. It depends on your perspective, who you know – that kind of thing.'

'While you were in here, though? That's cold.'

'I don't want to blame her. I'm the one in here. Not her.'

'Do you still care about her?'

'I care about her more than I've cared about anything in my life ever but it's over now.'

I am stopping myself as I say it, but the response is innocent, straight up. Pure and fast. It's over now. How deeply is she buried in me? How can she have betrayed someone who loved her with this much intensity and passion? What does that make her? Why didn't I see that before?

Constance's expression is a book all about wanting. She tries to maintain eye contact, but can't. She looks away. This game is over.

'What about you?' I say.

'When I do get asked out I just want to show them my arms and maybe even my stomach and then look in their eyes and see what they really want.'

'Your cuts don't define you. If you keep people away it's because you want it like that.'

'That's the only way I can protect myself.'

'You're scared now but you won't always be.'

'I should be. If I know what's good. I want to remember what it felt like, all of it.'

If you're so fragile, what are you doing here, in this room with me? I think. She is showing me her arms.

'Is this too much for you?' she says.

I hold the silence.

'What do you think is going on here? Don't embarrass me.'

People can't wait to find out if their shit is really working.

'I don't want to embarrass you. I don't want to get in trouble either.'

'So what do you suppose we do then?' she says.

'I don't know,' I say. 'How much trouble can we get in watching TV?'

# 24

Sarah had told me, sitting in the car outside her parents' house, in the sweetest possible way, that nearly all the boys she'd taken home had complained about her mother. I was holding a box of chocolates and a small bunch of flowers. Right then, what I wanted to hear was, 'My mother's great; you'll love her and she'll love you.' I wanted her to tell me that her mother ran an open house with a disorganized life-filled Disney kitchen, shelves stacked high with mismatched plates and hearty-looking pies cooling on the sills. I wanted to hear about the bubbling cauldrons of pasta sauce, cook-books, kittens curled up in shoeboxes and wounded foxes drinking milk from saucers by the hearth.

What I got was a pre-warning. That her mother always asked a lot of questions, and that some of the boys Sarah had taken home had found her to be aggressive, intrusive and hypercritical.

'Sometimes,' said Sarah, 'boys can be such girls. It's almost impossible to hold a conversation with her without being insulted, but once you get used to it you hardly notice.'

I said I could empathize with her parents. 'I understand their disgust,' I said. 'They must be sickened. How many times have they had to go through this? How many hundreds of men have you dragged up there? How many times have they finished a meal and thought fucking hell I hope this deadbeat little insect crawls back under the rock he came from. How many can one woman screw!'

'Shut up!' she said.

'They must be pretty bored by this old horse-and-pony show,' I told her. 'Let's just get it over with for their sakes so we can all go home and breathe again.'

When her mother opened the front door I handed her the small bunch of flowers that I'd hand-picked from the plastic bins at the florist. She looked unsure whether to take them, give me a tip or show me where the electricity meter was. We stared at one another. I waited, unwilling to move towards her in case she hit a panic alarm or Maced me. After a moment of awkwardness she beckoned us both inside.

I toyed with the idea of shouting out, 'Where's the safe?' but decided I'd save that for Christmas or some other special occasion.

We followed her into the kitchen where she dropped the flowers onto the counter. 'I'll have to find a vase,' Andrea said. I got the impression that the vase she thought was appropriate for the flowers I'd given her existed elsewhere, perhaps in someone else's house.

She smiled, face aching, and Sarah said that dinner smelt lovely. I agreed, mostly concentrating on standing still and not smashing anything. I was struck by the pale enormity of the room and felt that I was somehow being decontaminated in the shower of halogen downlights. Bacteria, mitochondria breaking down. Why, I thought, was I doing this when Alex, Ben and Doyle were out getting fucked up? Why had I chosen to go through all this? Why was I standing rigid, smiling, waiting to meet her father when I could have been out sucking on ice cubes and laughing? What was wrong with

the way my life was going? Was any of this absolutely necessary? The answer was yes if I wanted to keep Sarah. Or at
least that's what I thought. I, we, could have kept the relationship more casual and never met the other person's parents.
But she needed their approval, and I suppose I did too. For
me.

To help stem the fear and give us some time to adjust
before dinner Sarah offered to give me a brief tour of the
other public rooms. This was good because if I stood in that
kitchen any longer I was going to start getting my picture
taken by tourists.

The rest of the house was the same. Rinsed clean and
shock-lit. Brushed and rubbed and polished to keep it looking
brand new. Cleaning was a daily occurrence and this was a
house at war with dirt. I reckon if they'd had a horse standing
in the middle of the front room you could have eaten your
dinner off it. There was no paint missing from the skirting
board, no black marks on the walls from grimy hands and
shoulders. In fact nothing was identifiably soiled or broken.
It was like they didn't actively live in the house – at odds
with the doors and the walls like the rest of us – so much as
pass through it like ghosts.

Back in the kitchen I was dazzled by my distorted fun-
house reflection in the chrome splashback and the marble
floor. Did they have one of those gyratory cleaners you get
in museums? Could you get miniaturized motorized floor
buffers from Argos?

Impatiently her mother asked if I'd like something to
drink. I didn't hear the first time.

'What? Sorry, I mean.'

I'd seen houses like this before, mostly from the road. I'd
never been inside one. I always thought my parents would

love to live somewhere like this because all the space would be like living in separate houses – but they'd make such horrible neighbours that it would never work.

'Whisky and Coke please.'

It was about then that I realized she had a big nose.

At dinner I should have asked for a glass of water apparently. Booze was already becoming a problem although I didn't know it at the time. When I started drinking I didn't like to stop. I didn't have a convenient, easy-to-reach off switch. That's all. That didn't make me a wino. I stopped when there was no more money or booze or I browned out. I didn't have that internal voice that says 'too much'. When I sucked down my first glass of white like a Formula One car refuelling, Sarah kicked me under the table. She told me later that at dinner it is only good manners to eat and drink at the same pace as your host. At least I hadn't belched and dumped the glass on the table upside down. I said that I knew a little bit about etiquette myself. My dad had told me a million times not to treat dinner like a race. Or that I didn't have to eat so fast because no one was going to steal my food. This wasn't prison, he'd say.

Sarah kicked me again when I emptied the last of the bottle into my glass. She told me to pace myself. Later I saw a TV programme which claimed that clearing up everything on the table like a large seabird indicates that the hostess has failed in her duty to meet your modest requirements. Likewise, the programme suggested that you should leave a little food on your plate or in the serving dishes. This was logical but also contrary to everything I had ever been told. I still think you should eat as much as you can and then claim on finishing that if you were forced to take one more mouthful you'd need to take a back-breaking shit.

One thing that became clear to me was the logic of the comically large dining table – her father at one end, Sarah directly opposite me, her mother at the other end. I know that the whole 'We're miles apart, can you pass the pepper' routine is a subject of ridicule, but in my opinion you can never have enough distance between you and strange people, in case they turn funny. Big tables also allow the rich the privilege of flapping their elbows and splashing their food around while they eat. This is never a bad thing.

The food itself had been prepared in strict and austere measures. There was no mess, no oversized spoons dumped in dishes of potatoes and no sticky pots of vegetables in cheese sauce. They had all this money and time and they ate boring food. Airline rations.

'Two of those, take one of those and three of those,' said her mother, who made no attempt to cover the fact that she had been through this a thousand times before. It was obvious that this was a defiantly low-effort menu for people they knew they would hate.

'Oh, and one of these.'

My mother would die. Would cut off her own head before she told anyone how much food they should take.

I watch Sarah, see what she does, hoping they use tonight as an opportunity to catch up with their daughter and find out how her job is going.

'So . . . Charlie . . .' Andrea said, like she'd read my name from a bowl on the kitchen floor, 'you work at the same company as Sarah?'

'Yes.'

How else could a person like her have met a person like me?

'What is it that you do at your magazine?'

She put her knife and fork down.

'A bit of everything,' I said, 'but mostly writing.'

'Is that full-time work?'

'Yes,' I said.

'And what do you write about?'

Sarah is quiet, watching her mother.

'I write interviews mostly.'

'Interviews.'

There was something wrong. There was something rough and brassy about her face.

'Oh,' she perked up, 'interviews, how interesting. Anyone we would know?'

'I wouldn't have thought so,' I said.

'Oh,' she said.

I couldn't work out if I should be evasive and vague or truthful and give painfully detailed responses. I mean, until you know someone well you should always be vague, surely? It's the job of the liaising family member to translate and amplify in the right places. If I don't make enough of the fact that I have an extensive collection of pottery ballerinas, it's Sarah's job to pick up on this and relate my love of collectables to her father who has a recreation of a small Cornish village in the loft. That way we have something to hit on – and we don't have to sit here suffering.

Intermittently, her father would wander disinterestedly into the conversation. He'd watch me struggling away – we'd make eye contact and I would try to look a little humble and at least try to appear as though I hadn't put out my back bouncing up and down on his daughter. He didn't seem like the sort of old geezer I was used to. I was sure he'd never been to a driving range in his life, a bowling alley, or even a nightclub. I doubt he knew any Elvis. He looked like he'd been born fifty-one years old, plagued his whole life with an unimpressive build, maggot-thin little fingers and soft white nails. Even the hairs on his arms were smoothed and flattened, curiously straight. There was nothing rough or even vaguely male about him.

'Where do your parents live?' he said.

Regretfully, I told him where.

'There are some nice houses there,' he said, 'and a beautiful old train station.' He smiled at his wife who was by now unable to smile back.

'Is that where you were born?' said his wife.

'What? In the station? No. I was born in a hospital.'

'I meant to say, were you brought up there? In that area.'

'Oh, yes I was, sorry.'

You'd think I'd asked her to pull my finger or something. I was trying to lighten things up. Sarah looked at her mother looking at her father. Who in turn went back to his food. Maybe he was worldly enough to stay out of this. Interfering in matters of the heart, especially the love lives of your own children, is probably as unpredictable and as dangerous as waking someone up when they are sleepwalking. I think he could see that as much as Sarah was willing to kowtow to her mother, she had brought me here for dinner and was not ashamed of me. And she really wasn't either. She wore her feelings so openly that I often got embarrassed. Sometimes, when we walked down the street together and she'd grab my arm, I'd catch women looking at me, then at her, then back at me. Thinking, What is *she* doing with *him*? I didn't want us to be one of those freak couples whose very existence together was a cause of confusion and disbelief in other people.

*Please do not stare at the animal.*

I couldn't explain what she saw in me to anyone.

*Sarah has sponsored my feeding programme at the zoo.*

I could find no reason to support her infatuation; it was her word against physical science.

And of all people, her parents were not going to understand.

I'd already got the impression from Sarah that if it was up to her mother she'd just peg her down outside a large broker's and sell her to the highest bidder.

The men Sarah had brought to them previously were serious candidates for seats on any Bond villain's space shuttle to repopulate the earth after biological warfare. Seriously. The list included all the major professions. No media, a couple of lawyers, an accountant, a historian and, best of all, an accident and emergency doctor. That's some treat for Mother. I mean, what a touch – a real-life action doctor. Beeper goes at the dinner table. 'Sorry, Mrs Cane, I'll have to skip your wonderful dessert; it seems that a child has come in with a saucepan stuck on his head. Goodnight, Sarah, my love. You take the car, I'll run. It'll be faster.'

In contrast I offer what? 'I'm glad you like my suit, Mrs Cane. No, I don't wear a suit to work because it's my only one and I wouldn't want to get stains on it. No, it's funny but I don't even own a pair of slacks. I had to buy this for my granddad's funeral. What's that? You wouldn't say it's appropriate for anything other than work experience in the back office of a small northern spoon factory? Oh. Well, now you say that, I picked it out in about twenty minutes, and I'm not even sure that the trousers match the jacket because they had to get them out of the window and the sun had bleached them a little lighter. Nice drop of wine this, are you going to finish yours? Cheers.'

'So have your family lived there long?'

I should have said that they hadn't always lived somewhere that nice.

'Yes.'

Another neat smile.

'What does your father do?'

'He's a builder. He runs a building firm.'

'Oh,' she said.

'Yes,' I said, 'he runs his own firm.'

'Builders are very important,' she said.

'Yes. That's right.'

I wanted to say, 'And what do you do, you lazy big-arsed, big-nostrilled cow? Fuck all, that's what.' All she wanted to know is were my parents like them? Did they aspire to be like them? She had already formulated any answer she required. I sat there fuming. So much unsaid already.

'We're going to go on holiday soon,' said Sarah.

'Where?' said her mother.

'We haven't really decided yet. I want to go somewhere tropical,' she said. 'I saw this place in a brochure called San Salvador. In the Caribbean.'

'Isn't there a war there?'

'That's El Salvador,' said Sarah.

'What's wrong with France?' said her mother. 'You always go to France, don't you, Sarah? Go to France every year?'

'But I'm bored of France.'

'But we all go to France together,' says her mother.

'But me and Charlie want to go away together, Mum.'

'You could have mentioned that you didn't want to come away this year.'

'Well, maybe we can do both.'

'No, that's all right, we'll go on our own.'

'No. We'll work something out, maybe we can go to the Caribbean later in the year, or . . .'

We can't bear to hurt their feelings and this is why they win. When someone traps you on a guilt bluff like this you should always call them on it. You can always reverse your position later if that person then doubles up on you and attempts suicide. While her mother was getting dessert I whispered to Sarah that she needed to stand up for herself.

She told me that she thought I had upset her mother. 'You were rude to her; that didn't help. I wouldn't be rude to your mother,' she said.

'You haven't met my mother,' I said.

'Charlie, you could have been friendlier.'

'No way,' I said. 'She thinks I'm a piece of dog shit.'

'No, Charlie, she doesn't. That's what you think. You need to have more faith in yourself.'

'Shit,' I said, 'I'm trying, I really am. I'll make a special effort over dessert.'

Later, when dessert was passed around, her mother looked at me as though she wished my head would slam down on the dinner table and snakes slither out of my nose. I was taking her daughter away from her and I was all wrong. The best that she could hope for was that I would get bored or drunk or do something dumb like cheat on her. In short, the best that could happen is that I be everything she expected.

# 25

'You know that my bed is supposed to be my safety zone.'

'Well, that's that fucked.'

Constance lies pink and naked, covered in hot sweat turning cold.

'Was that sleazy?' she says.

'That was a little sleazy,' I say, 'but sometimes sleazy can be good.'

'Institution sex rocks,' she says.

I think I saw something like this on *Panorama*. I feel like a documentary crew is going to jump out of the wardrobe.

'Have we broken lots of rules?' she says.

'A couple,' I say.

She spreads her arms out, Christ-like. I move back on top of her and kiss each wet salty breast. We are both safe in the darkness, hiding together.

'The last time I felt this . . .'

'Don't say normal.'

'They treat me like a baby. It's hard for me to find the space to do this.'

'Do what?'

'You know?' she whispers. 'Be normal. With a man.'

Oh Jesus, what have I done?

'How long have we got till your nurse comes back?' I

say, then wonder how many times I'm going to have to ask
that after sex.

'Maybe another hour. She usually sleeps a couple of
hours. Sometimes longer if she can get the TV room to
herself.'

I want to ask her if she's OK. But this question is such a
fake. It really means, ask me if I'm OK.

'You don't feel bad, do you?' she says.

'No, no way,' I say.

'You don't look at all happy.'

'I'm being treated for severe depression and anxiety dis-
orders in a mental hospital, of course I don't look happy.'

'So you want to go again?'

'Ah. Wait a little while.' I pull at the sheets. I feel like a
fish, drowning on air.

'What's wrong?'

'I'm getting a little spooked.'

'Spooked?'

'Spooked – that's all.'

'Why?'

'It's part of my condition. Sometimes I need time to adjust
to stuff. You know when you get ahead of your own brain,
you haven't thought something through and you find yourself
standing there and you get this first-day-of-school feeling.
Like you find yourself in the middle of something that you
have no real understanding of.'

'I know that feeling.'

'Of course you do. That's why we're on similar pills.'

'We have so much in common.'

'Darling, shall we take our medication together?'

'Yes, but not all at once; we'll save that for our anni-
versary.'

She cups the back of my head and pulls me towards her. I go along to prove I have balance, to prove I have control, to prove I am a man, but inside I am twisting away, revolting myself. I am corrupt. My whole life is a frayed rope, hanging me. I could never let her know. If there was ever a time to be stable for someone, that time is now. When you make a decision you should stand by it, no matter what the consequences.

'I want to stay like this,' she says.

That's bad.

We are cheek to nose. She begins to feel harsh underneath me and I am tired of supporting my weight. I move downwards, kissing around the top of her stomach and move down, thinking, buying time, my hands planted either side of her hips.

'Do you think two people like us could ever, you know?'

'What?' I say.

'I thought you weren't ever going to be in a relationship?'

I push my tongue in her belly button.

'Eeek!'

'Be quiet.'

'Well don't do that.'

'I thought you didn't do relationships?' I say.

'I don't know. I was just thinking.'

I stop kissing and lay my head between her legs, my hands behind her hips.

'We could both hurt each other. In a relationship.'

I am dead.

'I know, I know about getting hurt,' she says.

'Don't get attached to me,' I say. 'The only reason I

understand you is that I'm like you. I'm not clever, I don't have answers, I'm just equally fucked.'

'What are you doing down there anyway?'

I lick her and she yelps.

'You know, if I was bigger I'd kick everyone's head in, every night.'

'What, even mine?' I say.

'I'd kick your head in first for being annoying.'

She slaps me hard round the face. The pain is enough that I have to take a sharp breath. The contact makes me feel more alive than ever.

'Don't fucking hit me again. I mean it.' Now I am freaked out. She grips my head tight between her thighs.

'If you're going to do it, just do it,' she growls.

She throws her head back as I begin, looking at the ceiling.

'And you think I don't know you already,' she says, pushing herself into my mouth. I grab her hips tighter and suck. On reflex her knees come together, her thighs clamped over my ears. I don't know what I am. I know I am supposed to have boundaries. I know that these boundaries are built on the Ten Commandments, and that they govern and underpin all interaction, protect us from gross errors and reinforce our fundamental do-right instincts. When you have to ask a question, like, Am I doing wrong? you already know the answer.

'How bad am I?'

You know how bad.

I let the *idea* of Sarah back inside for one second, and with it the thought of Ben performing this same act on her.

It hurts me that I am so lonely, so weak, that I have done this. Why? Because a woman I took for granted, thought would always be there, has gone? Has moved on and chosen not to be with me because I was unable to be the man she wanted. If this is what my new life is supposed to feel like, if this is moving on, then I hate it.

**26**

A British tan will always be uneven and patchy, branding our pale wind-battered skin. We sit in small fenced-off areas and stare at the clouds, not so much alternating angles and factors as various layers of clothing, umbrellas and wind breaks. If that cloud isn't black and bubbling with fire like the gates of hell; if there aren't crows falling frozen from gateposts, church roofs disintegrating, dogs stiffening and howling at the horizon – then we eat ice cream and drag the TV into the garden. One small break in the thick cloud can cause joy and misery in equal measure.

Even the smack heads, with bellies full of food and minds filled with grand notions of wellness, have begun to turn a comfortable pink. Contrast this with the smack head's more common colouring, which is porcelain going blue (OD, dead five days), and you have a holiday atmosphere. The kind of fun you can only have when you haven't fallen down the stairs recently or poured boiling water over yourself. Bare arms and legs flash around the garden like fluorescent light bulbs. Figures – blurred, reddening – divert and diffuse the light until there is no place left to hide. In the heat I am dizzy. I can no longer look.

I am tired. My eyeballs stick and are slow to move; they feel like they are coated in Vaseline. They are hidden behind dark glasses. I also have a large white bath towel wrapped round my head. Both towel and glasses seem to help me with the continuous panic attacks that have been dogging me following the sex I had with Constance three days ago. Since the only place I could hide was the garden, I got badly burned on day one of this cancer-fest heatwave. That night I stood in my room and lit it up like a two-bar electric fire. Day two, the only way I could protect my red head was the bath towel. No one mentioned it. Today I'm still hurting. My cheeks, nose, forehead have been burnt raw. I let the towel down a little lower until it rests on my mirrored aviators. I'm thinking that I can't live without this towel. It has enabled me to become immersed in my world. I see only what is directly ahead and hear only the wallowing sub-aqua thump of my own pulse and the long parade of clicks and snaps that come from my locked neck. As long as I keep drinking water to replace the fluids that I'm losing from dehydration I will keep myself out of the emergency ward.

'They tickle,' says Banana Man.

He has stolen twenty-odd individual portions of red jam from the canteen and stuffed them jealously in his pockets. He is crouched, head burning, about a metre away from my feet. One at a time he rips at the lids with his stumpy fingers and pushes the contents into the cracks in the paving stones like a midget grouting a giant's shower. He wants to tease the ants out of the ground and let them on his hands.

The trouble is that while jam is a potent ant bait, it's also an extremely difficult medium to work with in the sunshine. It begins to clump on his fingers in sticky globules. It looks how my blood feels. His hands have become disabled by it; his fingers stick together making them into flippers. He has even more jam in his hair and on his face and he is under constant attack from wasps. The smell is enough to make you faint. I let some of the ants that aren't stuck in the jam crawl over my hands while he watches, impotent.

When Constance sits down beside me I catch myself flinching but remain firmly planted on the bench. I've been avoiding her for three messy days so my hysterical lurching is the inevitable consequence of being found. If you don't jump like this, then you probably shouldn't have been hiding in the first place.

As she fishes around in her bag for a cigarette I realize that no matter how disturbed I am about sleeping with her, I still want to have sex with her. This turns me on, exaggerates the feeling in the same way that panic can beget more panic. For three days I have felt burnt and dead and alone and now I want to fuck someone's brains out in a patch of sunlight I've seen at the bottom of the garden. This is a pocket of oxygen in an upturned, sinking ship. I could open my mouth and inhale but this prolonging of my life would be worse luck for me. How great would this feel if I didn't need a towel wrapped round my head, and she wasn't covered in cuts and scratches? If we weren't drowning. If this wasn't a hospital and she didn't have the nurse – with one eye on her and the other on the hexagonal jumbo crossword in *My Statutory Tea Break* magazine.

Maybe I could work for them when I get out of here doing puzzles, or writing the captions on double-page spreads of celebrities with cancer leaving nightclubs: 'Looking smooth, Hugh Grant with his tumour removed.'

I act like I am pleased to see her and brush the ants off my hands – as you should always do when you begin a conversation with any beautiful woman. I turn to look at her and still see the only good thing in here. The only other three women that I know anything about, Celeste, Lisa, SLG, are twisted and, in comparison, not worth saving.

'I got a cigarette,' I say, not knowing what to say.

'Charlie, it is you! I wasn't sure. You look like the invisible man.'

There are a lot of reasons – mental instability, sleeping sicknesses, depression, medication – why we might not have bumped into each other over the last couple of days. So many that she might not even suspect I've been avoiding her.

'So why have you been avoiding me and why are you wearing a towel on your head?'

'Do you know that you're the third person to ask me that today?' I bite my thumbnail.

'Did it occur to you that everyone else's towels have been confiscated?'

'No. Have you got a light?'

This I think is mainly for the benefit of her nurse. It is well known among non-smokers that people who smoke can always find something in common with each other. There can therefore be no suspicion in her mind that there is anything between us.

'I was worried when I didn't hear from you at all for the last two days. I thought you might have left the hospital or the country. And if I sound a little bit insecure that's because I am.'

I smile at her. The kind of smile that says, 'I am still your friend.' She continues: 'I even thought that you might be hiding from me.'

She looks at her feet. As if she is ashamed at the thought. How stupid of her. This should have been the first thing that she presumed.

'How are you?' I say. She looks back at me and takes a

deep breath. How are you? is the greatest delaying question of our time. The only drawback is that it can be a real lucky dip. Its success depends very much on the assumption that the subject will forget the initial purpose of the conversation. Even if someone really wants to punish and torment you they can rarely brush aside an opportunity to tell you how great they are.

She readies herself to answer like she really wants to tell me something. Wants me to hear her. I feel terrible. Not only for her, but also because I am a miserable failure with a towel wrapped round his head.

'You know,' she says. 'I've been hanging around; I've been all over the place. I did my last few general psych groups. Yesterday everyone sat there, no one said a thing. The doctor, therapist, counsellor, whatever she was, she actually shouted at us and walked out of the room. She said we had ten minutes to think of something we wanted to talk about.'

'Yeah?'

'No one could think of anything. The group was abandoned. She left.'

'Cool,' I say. And keep smiling because I'm not listening. I want to think that I saw her troubles as evidence of a knowing, stronger mind. Her maturity was caked on like bad make-up. I was fooled into believing she was older, harder than she seemed. She's young, I'm stupid. Together we have the power to make medical insurance companies tremble.

'I'll be back in the grown-up therapy tomorrow,' she says.

'What, my group?'

'Yeah,' she says.

'Cool,' I say, not meaning it.

'Are you all right? You look . . . twitchy.'

She is trying to find my eyes through the dark lenses.

'Is there a problem?'

She fixes on me, and hooks her hair back from her face. Of course there is a problem. A catastrophic problem. I can't imagine two worse people to have had hard-core emotional sex together, ever. Sensible people only do emotional inside the framework of a successful relationship. But then most sensible people never try to have sport sex in a mental institution. A record-breaking half an hour after we finished I already knew we'd done a bad thing. That we were fucking deluded. That we couldn't be together even in a perfect world, because in that perfect world she'd have better chances, good relationships and access to honest men. She would have seen my understanding and pursuance of her as a sign of huge weakness in me and walked away. Wisely, she would not have wished to be a member of a club that would so easily have her.

In capsule form I try to explain it to her like this: 'We're a bit like two pissed people who've had their licences taken away, stealing a car to drive to Spain. Do you know what I mean?'

'Not really,' she says, looking over at her nurse.

'Well, don't you think that what happened the other night was a little bit advanced if you take into consideration our combined state of mind, poor health, that sort of thing?'

'No, not really. I didn't think of it like that.' She folds her arms and wrinkles her forehead. She is a cross child. 'That's how everyone else thinks.'

'I've been worried about you.'

'Why would you be worrying about me unless you were going to do something horrible?'

Good point. How do I tell her that by having sex with her I managed to double the load on my shoulders? How can I say in the nicest possible way that I momentarily confused this place with a disco?

'Can you take off your glasses; I can't talk to you wearing those glasses.'

I take off the aviators. She is more attacking than defensive.

'Well, imagine,' I say, 'that those two drunks in the car on the way to Spain had their licences taken away. Maybe because one was a bad driver and maybe the other one was fucking reckless. And what if they never should have been going to Spain in the first place because they both had to be in other places, that they should really be in, that were better than Spain, and were more important, but they decided to go to Spain all the same, fuck the consequences.'

'And?'

'And on the way, even though they were laughing and having a lot of fun and forgetting all their troubles, they were really bad drivers and they crashed on the motorway and died.'

'That's nice.'

'Yeah.'

'Oh, I get it,' she says sarcastically. 'We're the drivers of the car. You and me.'

'Exactly,' I say. 'And I mean it in the nicest possible way.'

'And Spain is what?'

'Spain is whatever idea we have, had, then or now, wherever we think we might be going together.'

'Right.'

'What I'm trying to say is that the idea of us being together might be nicer than the reality.'

'But I didn't ask you for anything.'

'I know that.'

'Interesting. What's the car supposed to be?'

'The car. I think the car is like a late model Vauxhall Cavalier, but I don't think that means anything.'

'I see. So you think we're going to kill each other.'

'In time we will. But faster than most.'

'Don't you think all this is a little extreme? The dark glasses, the towel.'

'Yes and no. It's cautionary. I just wanted to cool things off for a bit. Just so no one gets any ideas. People see us together, they put one and one together, you know. And I don't want either of us to get carried away and make a mistake. We need to think about what we are doing much more than other people.'

'So we can't be happy or have fun then?'

'Can I put my glasses back on?'

'No.'

'The sun's getting in my eyes,' I say.

'It does that.'

She sits back on the bench with her hands in her lap.

'I wanted to leave you alone for a while. I wanted things to cool off. These things have a dangerous momentum of their own. It was intense the other night. I don't know any better words than that, or I can't think of any. I was unprepared for it. I wasn't expecting to feel so much. I don't want you hurt. I don't want you to get hurt in any way, even so much as shake over this. No more people are getting hurt. I can't take that.'

'But no one is going to be hurt.'

'That's why I have to be responsible about this. Because we both have a fuck that, fuck this attitude that gets people in trouble.'

'And that's the way we should be. You can't take responsibility for this anyway. No wonder you're so fucking wired. Trust me. I can look after myself.'

I've heard this mantra spoken by the doctors: that you can't be responsible, psychologically, for other people. I think it's bullshit. If you're strong, if you even have dreams of being strong, then you have to take a little responsibility. Our lives are composed from the consequences of our own actions. Even people who win the lottery have to buy a ticket first. Life is not completely random. Life is not someone else's mistake.

'So that's it,' she says. 'We stop because of what might happen? What kind of way is that to live?'

'The clever, untroubled way.'

'You're backing away from me.'

'Don't say that. It's easy to think bad shit like that. This is not one of those situations where I had my cake, you know it's not like that. I swear everything I've told you is true.'

'Then it's about Sarah, isn't it?' She goes to a mean whisper. 'You fucked me even though you still love her. Unbelievable. No, very believable.'

'No, that's not true. I swear.'

'Then why are you backing out?'

'Out of what? There is nothing to back out of. Listen to me. You are too much for me; you make me remember things that are painful. Believe me, I want you again and again and again and then more but I should never have dragged you into my life.'

'You didn't drag me anywhere. I wanted it too. You—'

'Don't say it, because whatever it is isn't true.' Suddenly I want this conversation over. I'll do anything to make her go away. Say anything she wants to hear. Whatever it is. 'Look, you got me on a bad day; I'm all over the place.

Maybe I'm being too dramatic. Just give me some time and I'll sort my head out.'

She leans over and kisses me on the cheek.

'You're fucking mad,' she says. 'You need to focus.'

She didn't listen to me.

'Thanks for the fag,' she shouts, her nurse looks up, 'and the light.'

I don't say anything else to her. I'm glad when she gets up and leaves. I was stupid to think that she didn't want a relationship. That she wouldn't become dependent. I should have asked her outright. Now both our lives can only get more fucking complicated. I can feel this new strain starting to attack my organs, drain into my muscles like resin. My neck is, click, click, click. Ants swarm over my hands and I realize that they were never really gone.

**27**

Sklansky closes each group session with his thought for the day. He smiles conceitedly. No progress we have made so far is deserving of his effort and genius. There must be something we as a group can do to accommodate him further. Perhaps his laundry, or clean his car.

'You need to push it,' he says, 'try harder, chutzpah.'

I'm rubbing my chin, giving him my you're-really-making-me-think face. This is my special face. It's a deeply disturbing face. I like to think it's the kind of face someone might give you over a dinner table in prison. Sexually predatory towards the subject, yet submissive, grateful and receptive to the casual observer. To do it properly you have to stroke your chin while communicating this exact thought telepathically:

'Look at me, look at me while I'm fucking with you. Yeah I'm fucking you now! Think about me fucking you!'

Make sure you don't move your lips and your eyes will be unable to hide the message. We can never conceal what we are thinking and Sklansky is so open to signals. It's his job to translate this nonsense into hard cash. Of course the mixed message is confusing, annoying and maybe even makes him regretful that he hasn't 'reached me' yet. But it is my only way of resisting the heavy measure of superiority that he projects. I'm sure he's got a fat old manual somewhere where this behaviour is categorized. Maybe under 'Unnecessary Teasing, Homosexual'. Obviously we are dysfunctional while he is at pains to appear highly functional. So heavily mentally endowed that he can hold the whip and train these seven very disparate, unruly minds. I feel this is the equivalent of a surgeon skipping through a radiology department singing, 'I don't have cancer, I don't have cancer!'

Most of all I don't like the way he makes each piece of advice sound like the last ounce of sense he'll ever throw at us mongrels. We've already paid for it, but we'll only have sanity on his terms, from the scraps off his table. He might be rude, arrogant and mildly repellent but he is right.

The conventional belief is that I am ruining my life. I believe this; most people I know believe this. I've got witnesses to say that I and no one else has screwed up. Sklansky says that I'm comfortable with this belief and use it to support and nourish my other negative self-beliefs. Like I should never again be allowed to have a relationship because I'm not so much a human being as a harmful substance that should be hammered into an old oil drum and left to break down harmlessly at the bottom of a quarry. What else can I say? Shall I blame the town I grew up in? Women? My parents? What's the point? Some people in here blame everyone but themselves. It's always other people – people at work, friends, lovers. But no one has ever stood in my way. Only me. I think of all the people I have hated and how they seemed to cast such long shadows over my life and my thoughts. I think how I could be a long time in darkness obsessed by the effect of some of these people. But they are gone. Andrea, Sean, now Ben. I think of all the bad times. Times, like now, where I have been trapped, but see no real reason why. Where are the ropes, the tall figures in black? The more I look, the more I see nothing. Just empty space. I used to believe other people made the hurt but it's always been me. Standing there, pushing, striking wildly against nothing. Angry only at myself.

Today Constance gave the group our first lesson in the elegant communication of pain. Looking us in the eye she told us each a piece of the story, allowing us one by one to experience the richness of her suffering. Teeth were chewed, dead skin was eaten. The room was noisy with the cacophonous symphony of unpractised concentration. Heinrich appeared to have concussion, kept his jaw wide open and his hands in his lap. Celeste also listened intently, perhaps for lies, while stabbing at her own leg with a biro. It was a story people were waiting to hear. No one made the customary cross-eyed 'loony' face, or fattened their tongue like a scopey. Hardly anyone does this any more. Except behind Sklansky's back.

When the group finishes I presume that I'm going to get clear away because Constance has new friends now. She can roll into the cafeteria with an entourage like J-Lo but she doesn't move from the room. Instead she waits, looking for a chance to get to me. My mobile rings and I stare at the name blinking on the screen. Sarah. I look over at Constance who mouths that she wants to speak to me. I could tell her I'll see her later. Bring her the comfort of believing that we can still have something. My plan was to let this relationship die silently of starvation. I hope she will see that there is no way she can expect Big Love to come out of a place like this. When she sees me I'll try to act a little lobotomized and distant but well-meaning. Hopefully, after a while, she'll come to think of me like this. I will be the boy who can only

stare at the other children and their curious ball games from
behind a heavy curtain. It's sick, but then so am I.

Sarah's name still flashes black in the bright blue display.
Constance starts speaking; I have to take this call.

'Can I see you later?' she says.

'Constance, about the other day, I meant what I said.'

'I know, but can I see you later?'

'I have to get this,' I say.

I hold my mobile up in front of her so she can see the
display.

Clearly.

She stands with her back to the wall, insolent.

'So?' she says.

She refuses to move. This is like being back at school.
Don't worry, go wait by my locker. I'll see you at afternoon
break. Everyone else in our year knows that it's finished
except her. I'll be long gone. Arm in arm down the shops
with another girl.

'Hello, Charlie?'

'Yeah, I'm here.'

'I thought I'd come by today.'

'Why would you want to come and see me?'

'I've got some things I should say.'

'Oh. Does that mean you really want to say them or that
you're coming here because you think you have to?'

'Can I come or not?'

'Of course. Yes. When?'

'Now?' she says.

'Now? Really now? There's stuff I have to do.'

'Well, can it wait?'

'I suppose.'

Constance is making faces, still leaning against the wall widening her eyes and puffing her cheeks.

'Hang on.'

I have to make Constance scram. If my life continues in this manner I may well have to consider carrying a gun for my own protection.

'Look, fuck off, Constance,' I say. 'I'll see you later.'

Into the phone: 'How long are you going to be getting here?'

'Five minutes.'

'What? Shit.'

'Shit you,' says Constance.

I have to get rid of her. I cover the mouthpiece.

'Look, seriously. Constance, fuck off, I've got to do a bit of business. I'll see you later; where are you going to be exactly?'

'Why?'

This can't sound too suspicious.

'So I can find you if it ends early,' I say.

'I might go and sit in the garden. I don't know.'

She tries to communicate some extra promise with her eyes.

'Well, I might see you there.'

At least if I say I'll meet her there I know where she'll be.

☐

This is not good. Sarah is standing by her car at the front of the building. I walk towards her with an expression I could have borrowed from a pall-bearer. I just want to get this over and done with. I can't look her in the eye; I don't want to find out anything new. I might see something that I don't want to. We are no kisses, no hugs, only business.

'This is nice,' she says, motioning at the old house. She is wearing a serious work suit with a light summer blouse. I'd ask how the office is but I don't want to know.

'It's OK,' I say. 'You good?'

I mean to say 'I miss you.'

'Yeah. Good,' she says.

'I'm glad,' I say. Then she looks at me as if to say, I said good, not great. Then I think, Well, fuck you, I can't forget what you did with Ben. I don't care *how* unhappy you are. You were happy enough then. Happy enough on fucking holiday. Was Constance right? Are you cold? Is that true?

I think I'm muttering again.

'So how are you?' she says, moving her bag strap from one shoulder to another.

'I'm here,' I say as kindly as possible. I have to acknowledge the weirdness of this situation. Our meeting in these circumstances was not part of the plan. 'We should go and speak in the TV room,' I say.

'Indoors?' she says. 'Can't we walk in the garden? I've been stuck in the car.'

'It's the only place we'll get any privacy. The staff are all over the garden; no one stays inside when the weather is like this.'

'Except you,' she says.

We are walking without touching. Cold, alone. We should have a mortgage and maybe even be thinking about a kid. Isn't that why you get married? Because you want a kid. A home. A family. I never thought of that. Can't you get married just because you want to be together? Because you want to show someone how much you love them, are devoted to them. These are choices I could have made. That I can no longer make. The thought of my life, scythed apart, causes the constant ache. All of a sudden I want to bend over, drop down on the floor and cry for everything I have cut away. The giant part of myself that lies abandoned. Now my should-have-been wife visiting me. My ex-fiancée arriving to see how I'm doing. I stop walking momentarily and let out a small groan. I don't know if this is something that I've always done or it's a recent thing – or even if other people can hear me – but I'm sure they're at a low enough frequency to annoy moles and other underground mammals. They specifically occur whenever my mind stops moving forward. When my painful memories surface from the bang and clatter of daily life.

'What was that?' she says. 'Are you sure you're all right?'

'It's nothing,' I say. 'Something I forgot, is all.'

We walk down a long lime corridor, up the first flight of maroon stairs, then across a landing, along a corridor to another flight and another landing. Every now and then I turn around to see her walking behind me. I'm glad she is seeing all this. Maybe she might understand more. See that this isn't just some kind of hotel, that I'm not hiding here.

I absent-mindedly kick open the TV room door

'Are you finished already?' Constance looks up, surprised.

'I thought you were in the garden?' I say.

'I thought I'd stay in here.'

'Constance, I told you . . .'

It strikes me that this is the first time I've seen them in the same room together. Sarah is standing behind me. The TV is switched on in the corner with the sound turned down. A controversial stand-up comedian is selling washing powder.

Constance places her can of Diet Coke on the coffee table and stands up.

'Constance, this is Sarah. Sarah, meet Constance.'

Constance's face is a cloud-covered lake.

Damage.

She is pushing past us, heading for her room.

I want to grab her before she runs and tell her that I am honest, but all I can think about is her hurting herself and it being my fault.

Sarah pulls her bag close into her stomach. 'Did I upset her? I don't want to disturb anyone.'

'No, don't worry about that. There are a lot of fragile people in here. If she needed privacy that bad she should have gone to her room or something.'

'Well, she didn't like me.'

She hates you.

'I should see if she's all right.' I can't make this obvious. 'I mean if she's upset I might have to tell someone. Do you mind if . . .' I motion to the door.

'No, you better go. Can I do anything to help?' She touches my arm.

'No, nothing. Just stay in here, and don't talk to anyone.'

I find Constance's room and tap on the door. 'Constance?'

I can hear her crying.

'Can I come in?'

'Leave me alone.'

Her voice is muffled. I guess that the bed is between her and the door. She is probably on the floor in the corner of her room.

'Constance. Don't cut anything. Where's your nurse?'

'I'm here, what's wrong?'

I turn around and she's standing there holding a plastic cup of coffee.

'Jesus, you want to creep around a bit more?'

'What's happened?'

'She got upset,' I say.

'Constance, dear?' She speaks firmly through the door. 'Constance it's me. I'm coming in, OK?'

'Leave me alone. Please.'

The nurse holds the door handle and turns to me.

'Do you know what happened?' The subtext of her question is obvious: Did you do this?

'I walked into the TV room with a visitor and she freaked out.'

'I'll take it from here.' She waits for me to stand back then slides in, careful to obscure anything untoward from my view. Still with one large octopus eye on me she pulls the door shut with a snap. I go back to the TV room and find Sarah.

'Is she going to be all right?'

'She'll be fine.'

'Do you know her?'

God.

'I need to sit down. And I need a drink. Not *drink* drink. Tea or something. I should get something.'

'She looks young.'

'She's older than she looks. Early twenties.'

'Are you friends?'

We have just lost the back tyres at ninety miles an hour. We are facing rapid disintegration.

'Yeah,' I say.

'Oh.'

A stumble. I try to look offended by the insinuation.

'Not friends like that,' I lie. The words fall awkwardly over my cardboard tongue. If I was clever enough or had the strength to stop the lies, I would. 'I never expected to see you again.'

'Can I smoke in here?'

'Not officially,' I say.

'I didn't think you'd want to see me,' she says, a small gas light briefly and expertly flicking at the end of her cigarette. 'That's why I drove here. I knew if we tried to set something up we'd never have got anywhere.'

She's smoking Superlights again. Not a good sign. Only unhappy people smoke Superlights.

'I'm sorry about Sam's wedding,' I say. 'Did I ruin your day?'

'No, you didn't. I was horrible to you, you know? I should have been kinder.'

We both have to back off a little.

'I found the cheque you gave my mother.'

'It wasn't for you to see.'

'I phoned Ray to see if you were OK, but he didn't know anything. We had a chat. He said coming in here must have been a big decision because you didn't like it. And he said you were really trying. I needed to hear that. I asked my mum about the cheque and she said she'd been here . . . Then I spoke to your mother about it.'

'Shit. You speak to a lot of people. What did she say?'

'It took me half an hour to get her to admit that she was even on the telephone. You know what your mother's like. She said that my mum had been here and said some things. I'm so sorry, Charlie.'

'Don't be,' I say, 'you're not responsible for her.'

'I know you're trying so hard. My mother, you know

she's under so much pressure. At the moment Daddy's business isn't doing so well, and she thinks they might have to sell the house.'

She appears to be genuinely ashamed of this failure.

'That's annoying,' I say. 'I always wanted to live in that house when they died.'

'Charlie.'

'I mean it,' I say. 'I was going to fit it out with a snooker room and everything.'

'Seriously?'

'Tasteful. With their ashes in a trophy cabinet. Framed picture of your dad behind the cocktail bar. Plastic fruit, the works.'

'Don't ruin this. I thought that your cheque was a sweet gesture.'

'Sweet?'

The end of her cigarette throbs.

'I mean good.' She takes another drag. 'I can't find the words.'

'I hoped she would be more discreet. I didn't send that cheque to get you to come here.'

'I know; it came from the heart.'

'That's the truth. I expected her to cash the cheque, I really did. And quickly.'

'She doesn't want your money.'

'Maybe I could do a bit of work in her garden then. I know she'd like that. Odd jobs. If I was smaller I could get up her chimney. Though not in a rude way. Look, she should get the money while it's there anyway, because it won't be there for long.'

'Aren't you getting paid still?'

'Well, I don't think I'm going to have that job for much

longer. Not after . . . I think Sean and Ben are going to get rid of me when I get out of here.'

'Charlie, about Ben.'

I keep speaking. I don't even want her to say his name.

'They wouldn't put me in for an award – I don't blame them – but they won't have to fire me. I'm going.'

'Charlie, I want to talk to you about Ben.'

I won't look at her. My eyes will betray my childish jealousy.

'I don't want to hear it.'

She gets out of her chair and walks over to me, dropping down on her knees. 'You don't know everything, Charlie.'

'I don't want to know everything.'

She reaches out and holds both my hands. I feel dirty. Too dirty to be touched by her.

'Don't. Please.'

She grips tighter.

'We were on and off when I met you. We used to see each other.'

'No.'

I shake my head. I don't want to think of them fucking, casually meeting and being that comfortable with one another they could just fall back into that kind of intimacy.

'Please. I want to tell you that I made a mistake. I was going mad.'

'Right.'

'I wanted you to know because I want you to know how little it meant because I don't want it to get in the way of you getting better.'

'Are you still seeing him?'

'No. Not ever again. It was just a physical thing . . .'

Physical? I search her face for any sign of pleasure at the

memory of him. She is divine in expression. Calm. Direct. Honest. I am bad-tempered, exploding. I do not want to hear the word 'physical'. Physical is her pleasure. Physical is a better man than me.

'It was physical. It's important to me that you know that.'

'What do you want me to say? That it's OK? I can't, because it isn't.' She glares at me. 'Sorry,' I say. 'I don't want us to be at war again and that was fucking conceited. That's no good, is it? There is stuff I haven't worked out yet. I better shut up.'

'Yes. I'm not apologizing to you, Charlie. You started this.'

My medication washes away under a crystal tide of adrenaline. I am mad. I am arguing with the only person in the whole world who I have ever cared about. Who has ever claimed to care about me. Who was even willing to marry me once. Who tried to understand me. Am I going to push her away again? Lose her friendship? For the sake of what? Regret? Guilt?

'I haven't even offered you tea.'

'I'm fine.'

'Will you come and see me again?'

How bad does a relationship have to be for you to be on 'visiting only' terms? I am the type of person who gets visited. This is off the chart.

'Will you come and see me again? Please?'

'I don't know. Maybe.'

I blow out air like a punctured lilo.

'I'd like you to.'

'Do you mean that?'

'Yes, I do. I wish you didn't have to visit me, but I wish a lot of things were different.'

'So do I.'

'And I want you to come back. I've had a bad couple of days. Maybe when you come to see me again I'll be over this, thing.'

'Thing' meaning Ben. Meaning my bleeding pride.

'Sure, soon. But let me decide when, OK?'

'OK.'

We are so close we could . . . And then she stands, she smiles and I stand too. What is she thinking? Maybe she needed to know what it is like to be apart? Maybe we'll come back together when we have proven to each other that we are what we want. Maybe she is waiting for me to change, to see that I am all right again. She takes a ghost step forward to kiss me goodbye and then thinks better of it, turning to take the door handle. Suddenly I feel like I have some chance at a life outside when my time here ends. As she closes the door behind her I remember that I believed myself when I told Constance that this woman was out of my life. Now I know that she was never out of my life at all. And if I am honest with myself, I know that I never want her to be.

That night in the hospital I got so hot I thought I would melt my cast from the inside out. The sheets on the bed shrank back revealing the gross purple mattress. For an hour I lay there, soaking up the old sweat and urine through my bare skin, unable to move. I wanted to stay in bed staring at the dark sky, thinking I'm here to get better, I'm here to get better, I'm here to get better.

I watch my skin for the scabies rash until I can't take it any more, imagining the thousands of microscopic spiders scuttling around my body as uncomfortable as a tight shirt on a hot afternoon. By the time I decide to remake the bed the spiders have grown into translucent millipedes with horns and legs. By now I am scratching and slapping myself like a tramp in a ditch. Properly awake, I stare at the mattress thinking about maybe putting it on a bonfire and then urinating on it – but looking closely I soon realize that it's probably been subjected to both of those actions before.

Down in the canteen I pick up my sausages with one hand while I scrape around for eggs in my hair with the other. It doesn't bother me that I'm infested and I'm rooting over the food in the buffet, my spare hand inside my shirt, in my armpit. Other people have been here already, doing the same, scrounging around themselves, flaking over the food, and it doesn't worry me one bit.

Celeste doesn't take any food. She doesn't even take much coffee. Not like the rest of us with our Starbucks-learned behaviour. Celeste has obviously never been inside one of these fabricated modern coffee boutiques. She refuses to see the mmm goodness, or the comfort that can be had from a hot drink. The message has passed over her head like a drunk sleeping through Mass. Her cup is half full of black coffee and gripped carelessly like it used to be when it meant nothing to most people. When it was taken only in swigs by stressed old men in bad jobs who needed to stay awake. Now we walk into work holding foot-high beakers of hot dairy fat, sugar and burnt beans. We all grind our teeth more. This new kind of smug but pained oral consumption could be called grinking.

'Stop staring,' she says.

'You look like you were plucked out of a field last night and partially digested by an owl.'

She has wrapped herself in her black shawl. I'm wearing an old Diesel sweatshirt with a tea stain under the chin.

'Yeah, this place is no fashion parade,' she says.

'Do you have any lighter fluid?' I say.

'What for?' she says. 'A fire?'

She has the seat next to mine, back to the wall, facing the rest of the canteen.

'Don't tell anyone,' I say. 'I want to rub it on myself; I think I've got bed spiders.'

'Lighter fluid and bed spiders? I can see where this is going. What's wrong with TCP?'

'I don't like the smell.'

She drops her cup onto the table, letting off that

municipal gunshot of porcelain on Formica. Black coffee, nothing on the side. I feel hungry and fat by proximity.

'You pour yourself a coffee like that you just want people to say, "Ooh Celeste, you're so skinny. Why don't you eat a real breakfast? Why don't you eat something proper?" It's the worst kind of attention-getting.'

She picks at the filter of her unlit cigarette.

'And could you try and eat something while you're waiting for that smoke; you're making me feel like a pig here.'

'That isn't as difficult as you might think.'

I look down at my full plate. Whenever I try to cut one thing, something else, a sausage or a fried slice, falls off the side.

'Why do you put so much on there? It's not like anyone is going to stop you eating. Do you think people are going to steal your food? Is that it?'

'I don't know. Maybe; that's what my dad always says.'

I like Celeste because she was the first person who was nice to me in here. I do feel bound over to display an unswerving loyalty to her for fear of seeming ungrateful.

'What can you do?' I say. 'It's free. When someone offers you a free meal you take it.'

'What, all of it?'

She puts her cigarette back in the pack. It's raining outside so she has nowhere to go.

'I meant to tell you this sooner but I haven't had the chance. It's something I noticed the other day, weird as it may sound, but I suddenly realized what a sick freak you are. When I saw them, one after the other. They look kind of similar, don't you think?'

'Who?'

'The cutter.'

'Her name is Constance.'

'Constance. And that woman who was here yesterday. Your other one. Your old one. So many you get confused.'

'You mean Sarah?'

'Yes, Sarah and Constance, don't you think they look, well, the same? I mean you must really go in for that Slim-Fast Pre-Raphaelite look.'

'What's one got to do with the other?'

'You know.'

'I know what?'

'You know.'

'What do I know? What do you think I must know?'

'Charlie, close your eyes for a second. Try to quieten that slide show of horror you call a brain and picture each woman's face. Ex on the left, Constance on the right.'

'Sarah on the left. Constance on the right.'

I cannot imagine them both whole, only parts of both their faces. I mean, you see only what you want to see, what you need to take in. People are too complex. We compress and simplify everything we see. I don't have to stare at a table for four hours to know it's a table. It just is. I don't need to stare at Sarah for four hours to realize that she is Sarah. I looked hard once, when I had to, when her face was all I knew.

'Jesus,' I say.

'Yeah. Now add ten years to Constance.'

Constance looks like a younger version of Sarah.

'Shocking, isn't it. Sisters? Cousins? Which is more disgusting? The old and the young, Dr Sex and his bed spiders.'

'Where did you get this from?'

'Charlie, absolutely everyone knows that you and Constance have—'

'What?'

'Everyone knows. Even if you haven't, it doesn't matter. Because everyone thinks you have! And I mean everyone!'

☐

The group session is an angry and unfocused argument about responsibility and honesty. Sklansky admits that he wants us to be honest to our partners and families, but at the same time states that there is no law that says that we have to be honest one hundred per cent of the time.

'Truth and honesty are irrelevant,' says Celeste 'People lie to us; we lie to them.' She maintains eye contact with me. 'We are never honest. Yet society requires us to feel bad for being dishonest, and pay these little penances for things we've done.'

'What's your point, Celeste?'

I start thinking about the most pointless place I could find to set myself on fire.

'It's her dad,' says Lisa. 'She hates her father. Up the revolution, says Celeste, but only after I've moved my trust fund into gold.'

'You don't know me,' says Celeste.

'I can imagine. I doubt you've worked a day in your life,' says Lisa.

'Guns,' says Heinrich.

'You know nothing about me. Don't even think you can imagine my life.'

'Why don't you both shut up,' I say. 'I'm not paying to hear you bitch.'

Celeste continues, 'There is a hierarchy of success and

failure and in between there is punishment. We are all being punished, by degree. And that begins with other people's expectations.' She looks directly at me. I stare back at her, and then scratch my head like a chimp.

'What people?' says Sklanksy, pressing his fingertips together. 'Where do these expectations that we perceive originate from?'

'I don't perceive, I know,' says Celeste. 'I wasn't born with these expectations. They belong to other people.'

'This is trite shit,' says Lisa.

'No one is listening to me!' shouts Heinrich. 'I am speaking as well but no one listens.'

'You must try to speak in turn, Heinrich,' says Sklansky. 'Your turn will come.'

'It won't. It never does. I will never be heard in here.'

'He's right,' I say, before turning to Heinrich. 'You're right, Heinrich.' I give him a big smile and two thumbs up. 'You're the original invisible fucking man.'

Lisa moves her chair one space away.

'Calm down, Lisa,' I say, 'no one's fighting.'

'See this!' Heinrich shouts, indicating nothing in particular. 'This is my life!'

As Heinrich sets about angrily grinding his own bones to dust and Lisa retreats across the room I realize that the most pointless place to set yourself on fire is a field where no one can see you.

'Let's extend that. Charlie, can you suggest to Heinrich a better way of bringing his concerns to the group?'

'Maybe he could get a tattoo. I need a glass of water.'

'You can wait. I know that you ask for water, then you go outside and smoke.'

Lisa picks her folder off the floor and stands up.

'We've had this discussion before. This session has nothing to do with me or why I'm here. I should be doing my forms; you're wasting my time.'

'I didn't want to start a revolution,' I say. 'I only wanted a glass of water.'

'This is disruptive behaviour, Charlie.'

'Someone write that down.'

'Remember your promise.'

'What? I just want to work hard and get a drink of nice ice-cold water when I need it.'

This is the thing. I need to smoke a cigarette. Importantly, I need to smoke it on my own, now. No one is going to let me get out of this room for a cigarette, especially if I ask outright, but they will if I keep complaining of serious headaches and dehydration. No one wants to stand before an internal inquiry and say, 'He was complaining that his saliva was like peanut butter. I thought he was lying. I thought it was a trick to get outside so he could smoke. I didn't think he meant it. I didn't think he really needed water. That one glass of water I denied him, that could have saved his life.'

'We have discussed this,' says Sklansky.

'But my pills make me dehydrated. Peanut mouth. Look it up.'

'You only need to drink three litres of water a day. Drinking more water will not help you.'

I look around trying to find other people with peanut mouth.

Lisa stands up again.

'I've been here nearly four weeks. I've had this stress session twice already.'

'It's not working very well, is it?' I say.

She is nervous about returning to the real world. She

could get an extension if she wanted, but she might have to pay out of her own pocket. Only special cases stay here longer if they haven't progressed or responded to treatment. Severe-looking girl told me that after four weeks institutionalization becomes a bona fide risk, that you begin to change. She looked very concerned, but I told her that I couldn't see how it could be any worse than having a chromosome missing or working for a big company like Sainsbury's or IBM. At least this way we don't need a home help or have to commute.

Lisa maintains her petulance. 'I need to get my forms finished, all right?'

Sklansky is petulant back. 'You can take the forms that you haven't completed with you when you leave, fill them in and come into the weekly drop-in sessions.'

'That's great,' she says sarcastically.

'How long have you been depressed?' says Sklanksy, right back at her.

'Eight years.'

'Eight years!' he cries. 'Eight years! How can you expect to write off eight years of depression in four weeks? This is not an instant fix; you have to keep working!'

'I don't. I just want to get on with this. I don't want to come back.'

Me neither. If it meant I could go home early I'd open up my head, remove my brain, wriggling live in my hands, and tack it to a table with guide ropes while it hisses. Then douse it in ether and bright lights and make it talk. We all have $x$ amount of time to acquire the truth about ourselves. Time in here is not the same as time on the outside. Truly. You can accomplish more here in one week than you could in a year on the outside; outside people have no time for your introspection and depression. They say that one in six of the population is depressed. It doesn't please me that other people feel like me. Am I supposed to be glad that I'm like Heinrich, or compatible with severe-looking girl? I have found no real comfort in this room, these groups. Like a passenger going down in a flaming 747, I don't feel happier because the man in the next seat is burning too. Other people's pain belongs to them. They own it. The people who find salvation in these groups could have found the same thing in a church congregation twenty years ago. Community.

Think like a vicar. Your soul is a Swiss army knife, and it comes with all the tools you'll ever need. Fix your own problems as quietly as possible. Function. That is all society requires of you.

SLG hands me a folded piece of paper like a flaming bag of turd. Her I'm-being-buried-alive expression doesn't lend itself well to poker-faced small-time espionage such as this. I take it warily in case it's from Heinrich. I'm looking for a greasy film, any kind of slick of stickiness, bloodstains, saliva or brown marks. Inside are the following words, heavily carved in a rounded print. I realize it's from Constance.

Q. What was she doing here?

A? YOU LIED!

It is not like I've been ignoring Constance so much as moving and smiling and miming, like an estate agent showing himself around his own dream home. I have tried to make myself look busy, grown-up and unflustered. I fold the note and put it deep in my pocket. She's chewing gum like she doesn't care, watching everything I do, interpreting it.

I have two weeks to go and still I find that the honesty required is too painful. When I fill in the forms that ask me to record what I believe, how I have acted and how I feel, I lie. Not intentionally, but because the alternative is a blank space where the truth might be. Instead I fill the gaps in with logical rational reactions to my own disturbed thoughts. Most of my forms are crammed with these lies. They are a dream of the me I'd like to be.

Heinrich crossing and uncrossing his legs as if he is trying to untie his pelvis. I waste my time.

Celeste glares at me. She must have seen me put the note in my pocket and wants to get involved. I write the following, mark it for Celeste and pass it around.

FUCK OFF.

Celeste scrawls something back. Constance watches her hand the note around the room to me. I get Celeste's reply. It reads:

My desperately sick friend fancies you.

I raise my eyebrows and wrinkle my mouth in disdain. I fold it neatly in half, sharpen the crease with my nail and slip it into my pocket, businesslike. Celeste laughs out loud.

Sklansky tours the room. He stops at the pen suckers, helping them through. In case he stops by me I actually have a form half done, entitled 'Why I don't like being told off' that I can use as a decoy. I need my privacy. I have a thousand forms half completed like this. I use them to make my stack look bigger.

I get out of my seat and walk over to the table where Sklansky keeps all the blanks. He looks over suspiciously. I gather a mess of them for later. Celeste laughs again. I'm going to fill them out in my room. I swear to myself that I'm going to catch up on the last two weeks' homework, I don't care how much it hurts or makes me itch. Back in my chair, SLG passes me another note, smiling this time. I open the note thinking about everyone's faces tomorrow when I

come in with a pile of these babies all completed and combined with my already impressive stack of duff ones. The
note is from Constance, it says:

You are laughing at me.

I turn to Constance and see she's in tears.

'I'm not; I'm not laughing at you.'

Sklansky steps forward – frayed, hostile.

'What is going on here?'

'It's all right.'

'You're laughing at me,' says Constance. 'Why are you
laughing at me?'

'I'm not. I'll show you. Celeste, give me that piece of
paper.'

'No.'

'I need it, now. Give me the piece of paper.'

'What piece of paper?'

I move towards her.

'What have I done to you?' says Constance.

'Charlie, please take your seat.'

'Charlie, sit down.'

'NO.'

Constance vanishes through the door, running down the
corridor.

'Now please sit down,' says Sklansky.

'Oh, when Charlie does it you care,' says Heinrich.
'Everybody stand up when Charlie wants to talk. What does
Charlie say that is special? More than me? Well fucking shut
up, Charlie!'

'I'm going.'

'Heinrich is right. Charlie, I think you owe the group an
explanation.'

'I'm sorry. We were sending each other these daft notes.'

'Don't you think your time here would be better spent focusing on your therapy rather than writing childish notes?'

'Yes. I'm going to work very hard tonight.'

'The group would benefit from your working hard now, Charlie. But I'll see those forms tomorrow all the same.'

'Yeah. First thing.'

'Does anyone have anything they'd like to say to Charlie?'

I twitch, rat-like.

'No?' says Sklansky. 'No one has anything to say?'

I'm here to get better.

I keep saying that over and over.

I'm here to get better. I'm here to get better.

I need to get out of here; I need to know if Sarah is coming back and any time soon. I need to make Constance think I've left the hospital. Calm her down. Not seeing me might help. We file out of the room and I call Ray's mobile and tell him that we're going fishing this weekend. I've never been fishing before except on a canal by school, and that was with a shrimp net and an air rifle. I tell Ray to get some worms and a rod and a line, the whole lot, by Saturday.

'The whole lot? Where am I going to get that from?'

'Your old man.'

'My old man doesn't fish. He doesn't do anything. Do you know how much shit you need to go fishing? You need boxes of it. I've seen it on TV.'

'So, what about your uncle with the shotgun? He does pole fishing.'

'No, he doesn't.'

'One of them does. The one we got the rifle from. The fifteen-foot carbon poles. But I don't want a pole, I want a proper rod and line. Oh, mate, I can see myself there now in the sunshine, under a tree.'

'But you need boxes of shit – worms, hooks, Spam, pliers, nets, scales, all that.'

'That's a scam,' I tell him. 'All you need is some ciggies, a tree to lean on and a brolly in case it rains. It's not like the fish knows if you've only spent twenty quid, is it? I don't care if I have to tie a bit of string to my toe. What about it?'

'But aren't you supposed to be in hospital?'

'Ray, it's a bank holiday. Nothing happens here; they won't care if I go missing. I'm serious. It'll be like old times.'

'But we've never been fishing before, how can it be like old times?'

'Fuck it, Ray. It'll be like someone else's old times. What do you want to do? Spend the weekend vandalizing cars?'

'No.'

'Right then, let's get out of town.'

I think it'll look good if I phone Sam and ask how Sarah is. Maybe we can set visits up through her. I am surprised when she picks up the phone. I really wanted to speak to the answer machine where I could have dropped this on her quietly.

'I thought you'd be on your honeymoon,' I say.

'No, we can't go because Darren is working in New York. When he's finished we'll probably go to the Catskills or something.'

'Somewhere romantic?'

I can see Darren, in a drive-thru car park, loose meat sandwich falling into his lap, licking his chops like a raccoon.

'What do you want?'

'I wanted to ask you about Sarah.'

'What about her? You know I can't say anything to you.'

'I know.'

'I heard you made a real scene at your table. That was

my wedding, you loser. I was very pissed off. I still am. You didn't even say hello.'

'It was nice of you to keep a place open for me.'

'I didn't think you'd come.'

'It's like you had faith when no one else did.'

'Please.'

'I won't forget that, Sam. That means a lot to me. And I wanted to say sorry for any damage I did.'

'Darren is still angry.'

'He has every right to be. I'd like to get him a present. A gift. A big bucket of chicken maybe?'

She ignores this.

'So what do you want then? What do you want to know?'

'Well, how is she? Have you spoken to her?'

'Well, she told me about the visit.'

'And?'

'I think she was pleased to see you.'

'Is she coming again?'

'She's busy, so she probably won't be round for a while – if she ever comes back at all, no offence.'

There is a feeling returning to me, I know it well. Hope. Hope at being drawn back inside. Feeling like we were when we were first in love. That her word is everything. Waiting weeks for a yes or a no. At the mercy of her approval, beyond my control like a shifting weather system.

'No, that's good.'

'I don't know what you said to her.'

'No, neither do I.'

'But she must have seen something good. Some of us do want you back, you know.'

I know some who don't.

'Even Alex and Doyle are missing you. They were talking

about you the other day, saying they wanted to take you out for a weekend to Doyle's dad's caravan in Canvey. Give you a break, have a few drinks.'

'I'm going fishing with Ray instead.'

'Who's Ray?'

'You don't know Ray? My best man. Ray's my mate, he was my best friend. Is my best friend, from the old days.'

'Well, that's good, Charlie. Listen, I've got to go.'

'Before that, I just want to say well done, congratulations and all that anyway, because I didn't get to on the wedding day.'

'Well, thank you. I like this. Very polite. The new you. You're not saying all this because you think I'm going to report back to Sarah, are you? Because I won't.'

'No. I really want you to be happy. I want everyone to be happy. It's my new thing.'

'How cool,' she says. 'That's like Buddha, isn't it?'

□

The forms could give me the answer. Give me profound insights that I could dazzle Sarah with. I sit on the bed staring at them and they look as distant as ever, cold, bureaucratic.

'I genuinely want to treat people better, I mean it,' I say out loud.

'Well, that's good,' replies my conscience.

'I'm trying.'

'I think you'll last five minutes.'

'I'll try though.'

I line up a blue biro on the chipped veneer bedside cabinet and switch off my phone. Fucking people never give you a second chance. I turn over the first page and begin.

**29**

BAM! My mind, a racing mongrel dog, catches its own tail and bites down, jerking me vertical.

'Hello, Charlie? Are you awake?'

Awake? Is it light outside? Is it morning already? Is there anyone in the room? Has someone died? Why whisper? Is my whole family dead? Am I ill? Drunk? Am I going to vomit?

'Are you awake?'

The gentle knocking persists. Tap, tap.

'Charlie?'

Constance?

I say nothing. Waking up early makes me sick. I gently shake my head from side to side. I never move too fast because any jerk, or severe pitch, could begin an unstoppable rolling nausea that would turn me over like a passenger ferry with too much water in the hold. I used to feel sick every morning. I never got hangovers, but I always seemed to be ill – tired, slow, incapable. Always with a cold on the way. Always searching around in the half-light trying to find a bucket. Drunk/sleeping/waking/blurred. Don't be afraid. Don't look in the mirror; don't check your skin, focus on the wallpaper. Be the wallpaper. Let your lids clean your eyeballs, feel the toothbrush slide across your mouth like a swab in a

Petri dish. Flex those bruised fingers, stretch that clay skin. Press your palm against the window to check the temperature outside, knowing there is no milk.

'Charlie, I need to speak to you. Charlie?'

THUMP.

A kick.

Last night I got angry. I wrote a list of all the things that really make me want my mother. I should destroy that list before it destroys me.

'Charlie.'

Louder.

'I want to speak to you.'

Constance.

Once I started to write I couldn't stop and believe me that never happens. Not in my whole life. I filled all the blanks on all my forms, crossed out lies, wrote on the flip sides, between the lines, and filled the margins with minuscule circuit board writing. I saw what was wrong. Saw it all and listed it in order of stupidity. Chrono-illogical. Everything. By 4 a.m. those pieces of paper seemed to have my whole life written on them.

'Listen, I'll see you around later.'

Her footsteps fade down the hall.

I have turned this room into one of those warehouses that house the remains of crashed airliners. I have gathered all this evidence, washed and sifted through it, a piece at a time. I spread out the papers. I can see and touch all my problems, choose any one at random. Any one I like – perfection, addiction, abandonment, guilt – and hold it up to the light.

Pots and pans slam against one another as the chef resumes his daily war against food. The kitchen is truly his battleground. The sweet doughnutty smell of burning fat seeps through the gap in my bedroom window much like the mustard gas that once swirled across Flanders' fields and is just as welcome. The residue of conflict. If I was going to be sick it would happen now. Trays of empty cups rattling on a trolley and the sway of a large woman in a big skirt, swoosh, swoosh, swoosh, her heavy old arse punishing the floorboards.

Outside the TV room Celeste tells me that I look pale. She reeks of smoke, old tobacco, wet ash and has nicotine skin. I discreetly cover my nose and mouth. Is that what I smell like? Like inherited clothes. A junk shop. She says that Constance is looking for me. That she was even up here banging on my door but no one answered.

'I can't stop,' I say.

'You should open the door if someone is banging on it,' she says. 'You owe her an explanation.'

'Why do you care?' I say.

I guess that Celeste is trying to show me how she wants to be treated herself.

'Why are you bothering me? Bother someone else.'

'You should speak to her, you know. You owe her.'

'At nine in the morning I don't owe anybody shit. Don't you know what we're doing here? I haven't got time to talk about this school-yard shit. I'm on to something.' I shake my cast at my room for drama's sake. 'If she wants to find me, she'll find me.'

'She's going to keep looking until she does,' says Celeste. 'I think she wants to apologize or something.'

'I thought you said I had to apologize to her?'

'What's an apology, really? It swings both ways,' she says.

More riddles. I walk back to my room which still smells

of doughnut grease and burnt paper and spend another hour staring at the forms. I can easily fall into some kind of trance. The hairs are gone from the back of my hand and I remember that I used all my deodorant up scorching the spiderbugs on my mattress.

My phone vibrates in my pocket.

'It's me,' she says.

'Who?' I say. 'Who's "me"? I haven't got time for this.'

'Who's that?' says the voice.

'No, who's that?' I say back. 'This is my phone.'

'It's me!'

'Don't play games!' I shout.

'It's me!' she squeals.

'Sarah?'

'Who did you think it was?' she says.

'No one, not you. I wasn't expecting anyone to call.'

'I wanted to tell you that I took a day off work. I think a bad piece of you must have rubbed off on me. I never bunk work; you know what I'm like.'

'You bunked work?'

Sarah Cane has never avoided a day of work in her life. When she signed that contract, she meant to abide by it. She probably even read it first. Not like me. It's their job to put it down in writing and your job to make a mockery of it. The importance of dodging your contract and annoying human resources departments must be equated to the efforts of those taken prisoner during the World Wars who repeatedly escaped in order to create confusion behind enemy lines. Serial absentee employees like myself do what we do for the benefit of the greater mass. So that you might have your little freedoms and continue to enjoy your way of life. Through our constant invention and cunning, company standards are often kept lower and thus more comfortable for people such as yourself. God bless you.

'I can't believe you bunked. You must be hyperventilating. Have you been sick with anxiety?'

'I'm fine,' she says.

'They'll know you've been lying. Did you submit to the company medical? I think you did. You may have been fitted with a chip.'

'Everyone has the company medical.'

'I didn't.'

'You did.'

'I didn't. That's when they microchip you and take pictures of your private parts to blackmail you with later. The chips are to track your location but they also cause embolisms.'

'Gross. When can you see me?'

'I can't. I got in trouble last time.' I'm looking down at the forms. To be friends again would be good. We could still look out for each other. 'I'll have to blow out everything I'm doing and I'm really in the middle of something here.' I mean that.

'I thought it would be nice, a surprise. I spoke to Sam. I thought you wanted to see me again.'

'Yes, I do.'

I have a sudden memory of when we were walking in the forest near her parents' house last winter. I was wearing a long coat I'd stolen from the cupboard by the front door and a hat that her mother wore to walk the dog. Even though it was a cold day we both took off a glove to hold hands, and when she wanted to kiss me she had to burrow her face through thick layers while I tried to escape. I knew that when she found warm skin she would expect me to let her bury her ice-cold nose into it. I didn't mind. No one had ever loved me like her.

My heart is still beating hard when I take a deep breath and say, 'OK. Just bell me when you get here. I'll come and find you. Don't come near the house.'

Celeste walks by me in the garden and sits on a bench opposite. I can't stay in position any longer than fifteen minutes without getting discovered. I keep moving around like Saddam Hussein.

'She's still looking for you.'

'You are, I think the word is, dogging me. You know, I need to eradicate as much outside involvement in my life as possible and therefore simplify it. So go away.'

'You only need one person in your life for it to be an utter mess. And you have two.'

'And you make three. You could help me right now by leaving me alone.'

'Fine.'

I feel ill. If I could I'd pay a man in a brown rubber apron to relieve some of the pressure on my head with a hand drill. I would.

My phone is ringing. 'Do you mind if I get this?'

She is still standing there. She says, 'Why don't you tell all these women to get fucked?'

'OK, get fucked,' I say.

I turn the corner of the building. I see the nurse's blue uniform, Constance, rumpled, trailing. I can't turn around and start walking away. There is no time. She blocks my path forcing me onto the grass. She has no concept of personal space.

'Why are you avoiding me? What have I done to you? What did I do wrong?'

With her following I make towards some mature trees, but we are still in full view of the car park. I smile and try to look casual. She is animated and violent.

'Why are you avoiding me?'

I keep walking.

'I can't do this now,' I say.

'Why?' she says from behind me, quickening her pace. 'Why are you avoiding me?'

'I'm not,' I say, looking over at the cars to see if I can find Sarah's old grey 16-valve Golf GTI. My phone rings and I'm still scanning the car park. 'I'm not, I've just had shit to do. I've got to get this,' I say.

'Can't you turn that fucking phone off when you're talking to me?'

I try again to turn away from her.

'Hello?' I say.

'Charlie?' says the compressed electronic voice. 'What are you doing over there? I'm here. Look. I can see you.'

I look up at the car park, see her waving.

'Who's that you're with? Is that the girl who I met the last time I was here? The one who cried?'

'No, yes. Can you hold on?'

Constance grabs at my phone. Again I have to move it to the other side of my head.

Constance is hissing, 'She's here, isn't she? That's her, isn't it?'

'What?'

I cover the mouthpiece as much as I can and snarl back, 'Back off.'

She follows me around the tree.

'Don't you fucking care? Everyone can see us. Are you fucking stupid?' I say.

Sarah continues: 'Hello? Charlie? Hello?'

'Is that her? Is that why you've been avoiding me? Is that it, Charlie?'

I clasp the phone in my hands behind my back. I don't want her to think I'm going to hit her.

'For fuck's sake be quiet. Do you want your nurse to hear? Is that what you want? Get us thrown out?'

'No.'

'Well, grow the fuck up.'

'Charlie? Hello, Charlie?'

I wave at Sarah, and Constance turns to see her standing by her car. Constance has tears in her eyes. 'Is that her?'

She looks like someone sat on her and squeezed out the air.

'I have to take this call, Constance.'

'That's that girl, isn't it?' says Sarah. 'Are you coming over? You told me to stay in the car; I'm here. What do you want me to do?'

'I don't know,' I say. 'Can you wait?'

'Now is a bad time, isn't it?'

'No,' I say.

'It's my fault,' she says. 'I forget you have . . . all this.'

She is backing away. She knows. She knows.

'Sarah, I'll be with you in two minutes, OK?'

'Well?' says Constance. 'What are you going to do?'

I put my phone in my shirt pocket and hold her by the shoulders. I want her to look in my eyes. See the truth.

'Last night I realized some things I can't begin to tell you, Constance. There are things that seem so clear, like black and white, like life and death, that aren't. I found out a lot last night.'

'This is bad.'

'There is no good and bad.'

'I mean bad for us.'

'Good and bad are for children who can't sleep at night. Like right and wrong.'

'What facetious shit!' she says, pushing me. This tree is an oak. I recognize the leaf from an old clothing label. I look up at the sky through the leaves, I let out a long breath and press hard against it. Constance has her back to the car park. Her nurse must know everything now. 'I thought that you didn't care about her any more? You said it was all over. If I didn't think it was, then, you know, I would have never have done it, Charlie, would I? We'd never have gone to bed.'

I look down into my pocket and see a green light flashing. I realize that I haven't hung up the connection. I pick it out and see the display blinking with Sarah's name by it.

'Hello?' I say tentatively. 'Hello,' like you'd say if you poked your head up into a dark loft. And then envisage a thickset pig-headed man sharpening a knife. You're about to die and the best thing you can come up with is 'Hello?' Schwip, schwip. You have tears in your eyes. 'Hello, is anybody there?' Schwip, schwip. Who are you kidding? If you have to ask that question then you're already dead.

'Hello, are you there?'

Please be gone.

'Charlie? What is she talking about?'

'Constance, I've got to go. Please, I promise I can explain this. Can we talk about it later, please? Can we talk about it later? I have to explain this. I have to clear this up.'

I can still hear Sarah saying, 'Answer me, Charlie.'

I leave Constance sobbing by the tree, her face buried in the crook of her arm.

Sarah has got back in her car.

'Sarah?' I knock on the glass. 'Sarah, I'm sorry.'

She is looking in her handbag. Fingers pushing aside small gold and silver tubes, brushes and pens and bottles.

'Can we talk at least?' I say.

'I am so stupid,' she shouts through the glass. 'I am so stupid.'

'Ahh shit, we were meant to be laughing. I wanted to have a good day. I needed a good day!'

I look back at Constance who is slumped against the oak and I am angry at her for not having more composure in this situation. I have a lot of anger for Constance right now.

'Sarah, please, get out of the car. This is nothing. I can explain this. Fragile people.'

'I should never have come. I thought this was a good idea, but I'm going now. I'm going. I know what that was, Charlie.'

'What? You don't know what you saw. Look at me please.'

She won't. She is staring directly into a bag on her lap.

'Please stay a while.'

'Charlie, I only came here . . . I don't know. I came here because I wanted to be honest with you. To help you get better. You know it was Sean who told me about the other girl. A couple of days after the service. When we didn't get married. I believed him.'

'Why? Why would you? I never lied to you!'

'I need you to be honest, Charlie. I need you to take responsibility for this. I'm not mad. You changed. You were different. You had secrets, Charlie, and where there's one there's another. And you know most of the time a secret is just a lie. You were already living your life apart from me. We hadn't even started.'

My face is pressed close to the glass. I can hardly hear what she's saying. This is like my wedding. Like another short soundless film projected over life, directly onto my eyeballs. An audience of one, watching a small piece centred on the collapse of me.

'Now I see you together with that girl, you know. I didn't think I'd ever . . . What's her name again?'

'Constance.'

'I feel sorry for Constance. You don't cry like that over anything but one thing, Charlie. See the way she is crying? Only people you love can make you cry like that, Charlie. I know that much.'

She turns the ignition.

'Look, she needs you. I don't. Make things right, that's what you're always saying, isn't it?'

She scrapes the gears, lets out the clutch and shoots backwards. Then she is gone.

## 30

Doyle presses his fat face to the front passenger window while the whole chassis pitches and yaws. Is this really a car? Or are we flying westwards strapped to the back of a giant goose.

'Look sheep, look cows, look a horse,' says Doyle.

The countryside oscillates sickeningly.

'And look,' he says, finger pointed straight at me. 'Look! A Charlie! I spy a Charlie! All fit and well and back to normal.'

'Get your stinking shit finger out of my face,' I say.

It's good to be engaged in something pointless again. Escaping. On the run.

'I didn't think I'd be seeing you so soon,' says Alex.

'We thought you'd be in the nut house for a long time,' says Doyle.

'I should have been.'

Alex kicks down the gears and pushes past a tanker, his foot flat on the accelerator, rain and spray washing the windscreen. No matter how fast you go in this weather it'll always seem like you're going backwards.

Doyle rummages through the tapes.

'What we got?'

'The Mondays?' says Alex.

'Shit on you. "Weekender"? Weee-ken-durr,' says Doyle.

'What do you want on, Charlie?'

'The Mondays,' I say.

'The Mondays? Maybe we should just have left him asleep. Weee-ken-dur!'

'I haven't got "Weekender",' says Alex.

'It's on this tape,' says Doyle, pressing in all the buttons at once.

'Not like that, not like that, you fucking idiot, like this,' says Alex.

'What is this German stereo shit, can't you get a Jap one like everyone else?'

The air of the motorway beats through a busted seal and cuts across the side of my face, cold and wet.

It all happened while I was sleeping. After Sarah left me in the car park I'd started walking back to where I left Constance. I had no stomach for a fight, so when I realized that she'd already gone I was glad. I was thinking about myself. I wanted to be alone. I went back to my room. I threw off my clothes and slid between the cool covers of my bed. I bunched up a pile of dirty clothes next to me to support my cast, smiled lazily at the small comfort, and slept while she cried.

Then some time later Celeste came for me, banging on my door. I went out onto the landing.

I could still feel the disturbance in the air, the footsteps and doors slamming, hands tearing at dressings, one, two, three, lift, half turns, nods and firm commands. I sat down on the stairs watching them work – the ambulance, the paramedics and the police.

'She was on her bed,' Celeste said.

'That was supposed to be her safe place, her refuge,' I said. Celeste didn't ask me how I knew.

'That's where they found her.'

In my rush to be close to her, any woman, any body, I pushed everyone else away. And all I did after that, when I got her trust, was fuck with her. Upset her. Maybe if I hadn't pushed so hard someone better would have taken my place. Someone who would have watched out for her.

'I heard there was blood all over the place but I didn't see any of it. Nothing,' said Celeste.

We walked past her room. The bedroom door was locked and there was still the same smell.

'Nivea,' said Celeste.

'What's that other smell?' I asked. 'Disinfectant?'

'Patchouli,' she said.

'I was going to go and see her when she calmed down. I was going to see her nurse as well and then explain it all to her doctor. Tell them everything.'

'I hate patchouli,' said Celeste. 'It makes me retch.'

'I was going to own up to everything.'

'That would have been stupid. It was an out-and-out suicide job,' said Celeste, trying to cool her words with an extra breath. 'You know parasuicides are a hundred times more likely to do this than normal civilians?'

'I didn't think of her like that.'

'Maybe you should have,' she said.

I tried to imagine Constance one third whiter. Drained. This is difficult to imagine. I think of her beautiful head lying gently on her green hospital pillow because I can't think of her screaming and crying.

'I'm going to my room,' I said.

'Don't you do anything stupid yet,' she said, and put her hand on my arm. 'Wait until you know the whole story.'

'Do people know?'

'Yes,' she said. 'They all know.'

'Well, that's it then. I'd better pack,' I said. 'When they ask me to go I don't want to hang around.'

'Charlie, slow down.'

'Don't worry about me.'

'You don't know how worried I am.' She tried to give me a special 'I care' look, but it just died on her.

'I should have listened to you. You were right about her. I was busy. I thought I had more time to sort this mess out than I did.'

'It wasn't your fault.'

We all know whose fault it was.

'Look at me, Charlie.'

I was ashamed.

'It wasn't your fault. You didn't make her do it. You didn't stand over her and force her.'

'It's all right. I'm too tired to do anything dangerous. I'll probably sleep, that's all.'

'Good,' she said. 'Knock on my door if you want extra pills or want to watch TV or something.'

It was like I'd pitched my tent to the side of a giant spinning top. You'd think that it would be impossible to sleep at a time like this, but the mind and body have a way of quietening in times of true crisis. It's stupid how I've been awake some nights till four or five in the morning just because Sean has been mad at me or I'd done a bad job of some work. Yet when real trouble comes I can always sleep. Shut my eyes and put a fence between the pain in my head and the pain outside.

☐

'Pick one tape,' shouts Alex. 'Put that on. You'll fuck the eject.'

'But I want to hear them all,' pleads Doyle.

'But you can't. Do you want me to crash this fucking car?'

'Yes,' he says.

'Then stop fucking around.'

Two hours after Celeste left me I came round – needing a drink more than anything else. I called Doyle and asked him when he'd be driving up to his dad's caravan and to see if he could come by and pick me up. He whined because the hospital was out of his way. Then he remembered that Alex was driving, because he'd lost his licence, and said that they'd pick me up in a couple of hours, no trouble. As soon as he hung up I started piling my clothes into different carrier bags, sorting them until I had four bags each one smelling discernibly worse than the next. In the time it took me to find anything clean enough to wear I'd begun shaking. Real DT shakes. I tried to put on a couple of extra layers of clothing but they had no effect beyond making me smell twice as bad. I wanted the cold, to feel like her, and to be close to madness again. I sat still at the end of my bed, teeth chattering, wondering why did she do it and did I really make this happen? Was this pain meant for me?

'Stop the car, I'm going to be sick,' I shout.

'Jesus! Stop the car, Alex,' says Doyle.

I'm sitting behind Doyle, so he's the one who'll get it if I'm sick.

'Have you got a bag or something?' says Alex. 'Use that one next to you.'

'I can't,' I say. 'That's my clothes.'

Alex pulls the car onto the hard shoulder and I kick the

door open, blowing out water like a humpback whale. The rain is running down my neck. How did I get from not wanting to get married to having nothing? Things can slip away from you if you're not watching. My advice at this time is to screw everything down. I feel like the man who went to scratch his head and found it was missing. I think of Sean telling Sarah about the girl. Why did he do that? You'd think I could be a little more self-aware after all the time I've spent in that hospital. But really I'm as ignorant as I ever was and Sarah is gone now. These other people, they seem so sharp. So much tougher, bigger than me, so much more willing to inflict pain. If I hurt it's because most of the time I don't know better, because I swear I have no malice in me. I get back in the car and pull the door shut. The speakers in the back of the car vibrate and my eyes shut as the tyres press into the road as the rain cries down, as this country turns grey, as I hide my face again.

**31**

'Jesus.' Alex, white hair cut jagged with £400 scissors, is pulling on one of the cupboards hard enough to bring it down from the wall.

'This is disgusting. The cooker's too close to the shitter. We'll have a rule about that,' he says.

'Eh?' says Doyle, who has emerged from the bedroom dressed in garish orange kick-boxing shorts.

'We can either shit or eat in here, not both. It's not hygienic. And you can't wear those shorts if you can't kick-box.'

'I can.'

'Then I can start wearing a black belt then. And fucking white pyjamas.'

I leave them arguing and walk back out to the car over-come with a premonition of being burnt alive. Plastic and metal melting as a leaking gas pipe creates an explosion so powerful that it blows the fire out. It would probably take a day maximum to clear our burnt dead mess away and have this place ready for the next family. Outside, the mobile homes are lined up like family tombs. Most seem to be named after myths and legends – Excaliburs, Excelsiors, Crusaders. But they are nothing more than giant elaborate porta-potties that dumb people drag behind them like all the baggage of their life.

'You can't use the cooker in here,' says Alex.

'But I've brought steaks for dinner,' says Doyle.

'Barbecue them,' says Alex. 'Do it outside, not near the toilet. And not near any other caravan's shit pipes either.'

My worst times as a kid I can clearly relate to family holidays in caravans. We never owned one ourselves. We'd rent one a couple of hundred miles away and drive to it. We'd then park up, barely survive in it for a week, and then come home again. It was a testament to human delusion that we could call that experience a holiday. You take a family from a relatively spacious three- or even four-bedroomed house and make them sleep in a rain-soaked ice box and expect them to enjoy themselves. How? The only warmth in a caravan quickly dissipates through the tin sheets that serve as walls. You get up in the morning, you are cold. You go to sleep at night, you are cold. In between you are cold. The clothes in the shoebox drawers are cold. Traditional ways of warming yourself like, say, taking a shower, can lead to critical levels of disappointment. Never try to warm up in a 'mobile home' by taking a shower; first-timers always make this mistake. You disrobe, stand in what may well be a puddle of old man's verruca water and begin rubbing your arm with a dry bar of soap. While the three needles of yellow water (one extremely hot, two freezing cold) create red and blue tattoos on your chest, the real battle is being fought elsewhere – between your arse and the shower curtain. There are two problems with your arse touching the curtain. 1) Countless arses of old men have been pressed into that curtain. 2) You touch it, just brush it, and the rest will jump on your back like an aggressive jellyfish. You will be wet and wearing a cape of old men's arses. This is something that even the most flamboyant serial killers will never experience. Then you are supposed to have a good day.

'But we haven't got a barbecue,' pleads Doyle.

'So?' says Alex. 'How hard can it be to set something on fire in a caravan site?'

I pull a box of bottles out of the boot of the car. Four bottles of Johnnie Walker, two large black Smirnoffs and a couple of bright blue bottles of a disco liquor called Kontiki – delicious alcoholic bamboo and melon tropical milk. I spin off the lid and give it a sniff. It smells like a Hawaiian ear, nose and throat clinic. I bet drinking too much of it makes you want to beat drums and do pure evil. What should I do, scream and run away waving my hands in the air? Stay calm, take time to collect my thoughts and maintain a stiff expression?

'Where's Ben?' I shout back at the caravan.

'He didn't want to come,' says Alex.

'Naargh,' says Doyle. 'He didn't want to get fucked up in a caravan. He's getting too good for us now he's deputy.'

'Leave it,' says Alex, loyal. 'Take that box off Charlie and do the drinks.'

'Yeah,' says Doyle, poking his head out of the door, 'let's get the deckchairs out.'

'Do you know where he is?' I say.

'Who?'

'Ben,' I say.

'No,' he says. 'I don't know.'

'Does he have a bird at the moment?'

'I think there's one, but I don't know her. Doyle's seen her, haven't you?'

'No, I haven't. Why would I care?'

No unconscious slips.

I have to ask myself, Would they tell me if he was with Sarah right now? Would they be able to hide that? I don't think so. Maybe they don't know anything?

Doyle pulls out two nylon chairs. His shirt rides up his back allowing his love handles to roll out.

'Doyle,' I say, 'did Ben tell you where he was going to be?'

'No, but whoever the bird is I bet she's a big one. Otherwise he would have shown her around.'

Doyle disappears back in the caravan while Alex and I sit in the chairs and look over the lumpen stagnant marsh in the direction of the sea.

It's clear neither of them knows. They would have given it away by now. You can't hide anything in a caravan; I would know already. I have to face it. Ben may be with Sarah now. I'm sure he wants to be. That much is clear. What they have together I don't know. She said it was physical. Other than that I can't imagine what's going through her mind now. I get this desire to call her, so I can listen for him in the background. Put a little pressure on both of them. Let them know that I'm not dead. But I have never shown any doubt in her. I didn't go to Africa to catch her cheating; I went there because I loved her. I'm not going to start chewing my knuckles now.

Doyle comes back outside.

'Shall I put the steaks on?'

'You just took a shit, didn't you?' says Alex.

'Yes.'

'Then no.'

'I thought you were joking.'

'No,' says Alex. 'You just took a shit. Now we have to

cook outside. The toilet will infect the cooker. It's all the same in there.'

I am inclined to believe him.

'It's like in *The Matrix*,' he says. 'You have to think about it on a molecular level. It's all around you. You see the smell for what it is. A cloud comprised of minute particles of faeces, an extension of what you flushed. If it's drifted into the kitchen, if you can actually smell it around the cooker, then we have to presume the area is contaminated.'

Doyle sits down.

'I am fucking starving,' he says.

'No,' says Alex. 'Africans starve. You have a rumbling fucking stomach.'

'I wish we could actually see the sea,' I say.

We sit in the chairs, three old ladies in a field of metal coffins.

'Where is everyone?' says Alex.

Doyle begins to make a spliff inside a copy of a magazine.

'Yeah, it's not exactly kickin' bass is thumpin'.'

I twist the top off a bottle of whisky. Both of them look at me.

'What?' I say.

'Nothing,' says Alex, pulling his head further into his jacket. 'Make mine a large one.'

Two hours later it is dark and we are inside drinking in the dining booth. Doyle is happy, he is drunk. Alex is happy, he is drunk. They are both happy, they are both drunk. I am drunk, I am unhappy. I am melancholic. My brain suffocating, aching like I'm banging it against a fridge door in a carrier bag filled with Big Gulp. Ice-cold, bruised, full up with drink. Pointless glass after pointless glass, sitting in my gut. It seems like a stupid way to take drugs. One after the other down your throat. You extract all the poison you need then you carry it all, in your blood and your bladder, to a toilet, where you have to flush it into a sewer. That's sophisticated.

The toilet is the common ground of all drug abusers. Shoot up, smoke, sniff, empty out, clean up. The toilet is where many addicts begin and end their journey. I drop my trousers and sit on the pan, kicking the door shut on the bright lights of the cabin. The music still rattles the walls which vibrate like slips of paper blown over a musical comb. There are three kicks on the door. The last pops the lock and it flips open. Doyle is standing there. 'Phone for you,' he says. He hands me my mobile phone which buzzes in my hand. Ray's name is on the display.

'Yo, Ray.'

'Yeah,' he says. 'Where are you?'

'I'm with Alex and Doyle in Doyle's dad's caravan.'

'Yeah, I've been at the hospital. And you're pissed.'

'It all went wrong, I'm sorry. I had to get away. Escape.'

'I spent all week setting this up. Getting this gear together and then you fuck off on the day.'

'Come down here in the van; we can fish here.'

'I'm not going to a fucking caravan with fucking Doyle and Alex; they're a pair of twats.'

'I'm sorry. I am.'

'Yeah, well it's not about me, is it? The point of fishing was there was no need to booze. It was going to be simple.'

'We could do that in a couple of weekends.'

'No. I fucking don't want to go fucking fishing. You've got to make your mind up.'

'What?'

'About all this. You've got to make your mind up. You

can't have it all ways. Drinking, fucking off without talking to people. It won't always be all right when you get back. People won't always be waiting. Look, life is too short for this. I don't care; I've done my best. At least I fucking made an effort, which is more than you did.'

'Ray, we can go fishing in a couple of weeks.'

'Fuck fishing.'

'I mean it.'

'Yeah, yeah. Whatever.' Ray hangs up.

Just like Williams says to Mr Han, before his violent death in the martial arts epic *Enter The Dragon*, 'Suddenly, I'd like to leave this island.'

I don't feel so good. There's no point holding all the sick in like a brave little soldier. I drop my head and vomit between my legs down into the pan.

I pull my clothes back on and make a triumphant re-entry, jumping into the corridor, the whole caravan shuddering as I land. I then do a little dance, pretending to be a fat girl for a while. You have to do this when you've been sick. To skulk back, apologizing for oneself, would exhibit a poverty of class. The main thing is to keep going and always be entertaining.

'I feel like I need a reason to drink. I never needed one before, but I do now. What are we celebrating?' I say.

'Nothing,' says Alex. 'We haven't got anything to celebrate.'

'Get fucked,' says Doyle.

Alex slaps Doyle round the face, knocking him out of the small dining booth onto the floor.

'Do you want to sit outside? Because people with foul mouths have to sit outside,' says Alex.

I look at them aping. Like they don't have a care. I think

they can do this for ever, confident in what they are. No rush to change, improve, be better. Why do I have to be different? Why can't I be like them? I feel like a housewife trying to balance her family and her own personal ambitions. What about me? How do I balance my busy life and personal happiness while managing my sanity, and get fucked up at the same time? I have to know. Should I change my shampoo?

'Alex,' I say, 'are you happy being like you are?'

'What?'

'Are you happy being what you are?'

'Am I what?'

'Gay,' says Doyle from the floor. 'Are you happy being gay?'

'Happy. Like, happy in general,' I say.

'I'm sorry,' says Doyle, 'I said are you gay?'

'I don't think so,' says Alex, not wanting to commit to either question. 'Happy? Am I happy the way I am?'

'With what you are? With what you've become?' I say.

'No one's ever asked me that. I don't know,' he says. 'No one likes to be considered happy, do they?'

'I do,' says Doyle from the floor. 'I'm a happy person. Happy all the time.'

Alex stays quiet.

'I always thought you were pretty sorted,' I say. 'You seem happy. I don't know. You and Ben. Like you have this shit worked out. That your lives are good.'

'Whose life is good? I thought you were sorted until you went to hospital. But you weren't. And I don't know about Ben; Ben's not here.'

'Miserable mean fucker,' says Doyle.

'I never knew that,' I say.

'Then you don't know much,' says Doyle, thinking I'm

replying to him not Alex. 'Don't ever think that Ben cares about you; the only person Ben cares about is himself.'

'Shut up, Doyle,' says Alex.

'It's true,' he squeals. 'Ben only cares about himself.'

'You don't know that. Nothing, no one, is perfect.'

'Not perfect. I didn't say that. I said happy.'

'What? Happy in my job? Happy in my flat? What kind of happy?'

'Everything happy. Big happy.'

'My life isn't what you obviously think it is.'

He fills his glass.

'What do you mean?'

'Shit. Do I think I drink too much?' He clinks glasses with me. 'Yes. Do I smoke too much? Maybe. Could I, could we, all work harder? Earn more money? Maybe. Maybe not Doyle. Doyle is fucked. Err, do I think I should have a better job? Own better shit? Yes, yes . . .'

'What?'

'Well, stop me when this starts sounding familiar. You shouldn't let it get stuck in your head, that's all. We all get hit by big waves of it. I want; me, me, me; depression. Whatever. Big waves, good and bad and little waves, always. Tomorrow the waves might be bigger and they also might be loaded with used tampons, plastic bottles and dead fish. Tomorrow might be better, it might be worse. Could I do better in my life? Should I ask that question every day? No.'

'I have been.'

'Don't.'

'Do you cry yourself to sleep at night?' says Doyle. 'I mean, please shut up, you miserable pair of cunts.'

'I'm sorry,' I say. 'I want to know.'

'Well, I don't. This is bringing me down,' he says.

I feel sick. I feel like vomiting again.

'I don't want to talk about this miserable shit. I haven't come here to have therapy,' says Doyle. 'I came here to have a fucking laugh. Fuck.' He tries to pull himself up using the sink. Angry. 'You bring things down; not everyone wants to get sucked up into your fucking problems. Not all of us are like you. Some of us can cope with a drink and a laugh. We don't have to go mental and get depressed and shit like that.'

'Doyle, I'm sorry.'

'No one wants to hear his miserable shit, Alex.'

Alex gets up and grabs him by the shoulders and pushes him into the lounge area. 'Calm,' he slaps him across the cheek, 'down.'

'I want to know, Doyle,' I say. 'I have to know if you're happy, if all this stuff really makes you happy, Doyle. Because it doesn't make me happy so I need to know. I need to know other people can't handle all this either. That other people are like me. I don't want to be selfish but I have to know.'

'This is stupid,' says Doyle. 'Everyone's got shit in their lives, everyone. No one has it like you think – no one's life is simple – but we don't all go round shouting and crying about it; we have a drink, and we get on. Now get off me, Alex, before I fucking flatten you.' Alex pushes Doyle into the bedroom, barricading the door.

'Shut up, you fucking potato head.' Alex is laughing. 'Don't come out till you learn to behave yourself.' He turns to me, serious now. 'What you said. All this about being happy, is that something you talk about in therapy?'

'Not happiness in particular, that's just something I get fixed on. I can't get it out of my head. It's like I want to live everyone else's life as well as my own. That I am missing out, maybe. You know, missing out by being married.'

'You made your choice.'

'And I tried to stick by it – I was going to stick by it – but that went to shit.'

'A grass is greener kind of thing.'

'I don't know if that was what I was thinking before the wedding. I was in parts. Separate pieces. There's me, Charlie. Drinking, smoking, going out, being normal. Then there's this other Charlie. The Charlie that Sarah wanted. The brighter better Charlie. And then in hospital I found another one. He is still out there, lost. Old school Charlie. Old school Charlie went missing somewhere along the way.'

'You get older, you change.'

'I wanted to get married. But I also didn't want to retire before my time. You know, before I'd had my time, had my chance. Done my own thing. You know. Been me.'

'What do you mean – like now? Like this?' Alex snorts with laughter.

'I don't know.'

'Doyle, do you think Charlie's had his chance?'

'I don't fucking care. Fuck off.'

'I didn't know. By the time it actually got through my thick head that marrying Sarah would be for ever, it was my wedding day. It was too late. I was a mess.'

He pours me another drink. I put a splash of Coke in it for my kidneys.

'I thought I hadn't seen enough, thought that I needed to have what you and Doyle have. Freedom to be. By doing this I threw that away. I think I made the wrong choice. I think you have the right balance, you know.'

'But you flipped? You thought you were OK, then you weren't. Waves. It doesn't mean you'll be happy like this either. I'm not. You know, completely.'

'What?'

'Happy like this.'

'Like what?'

'Like spending this weekend in a caravan getting shit-faced with you when I should be with a bird. Don't you think I know some people have good relationships? Spend weekends together? Live together? Have babies.'

'Do you think they're better off than us?'

'Are you mental?'

'I need to know. Do you think they're better off than you?'

'I don't know; they probably think so. How should I know? Look, when you got engaged to Sarah, there was a mixed reaction. Say, a seventy/thirty split that you were doing the right thing. I mean, it made me think. Big news is like that, always makes you think of yourself. What am I doing? Where am I? Where's my life? I can't say I felt comfortable, but I'm not sure whether I was uncomfortable with you getting married or me not having a bird.'

'That's because I was getting comfortable with your bird,' says Doyle.

Alex doesn't respond.

'It genuinely made me think, man. I had some moments. I never agreed with what you were doing. And I'm sorry about that, but it doesn't matter what I think. Ignore me. Ignore Ben and Sean and fucking Doyle. You can't live other people's lives. You can't live my life; only I can do that. You have to believe we make our own mistakes. Live your own life. Who cares what I'm doing? No one cares what I'm doing. Enough people obviously care about you. That's a start. You want to hang onto that. Because, you know, sooner or later you get old – no real ties to anything or anyone, everyone stops giving a shit. Look at Ben: no parents, no brothers or sisters, no bird. He's got no one really, just his mates.'

'Boo hoo,' says Doyle through the bedroom door. 'What mates?'

'Will you fucking shut up, large boy?' Alex's face is red. 'Bottom line, Charlie: at one point it really looked like you had it all, and you know what, I don't think some people liked that.'

'Who?'

'Use your imagination. You don't know that many people.'

'Do you know who?'

'I know nothing. I'm just being friendly.'

The weight of this presses me down onto the counter top – the ache in my legs, the smell of the drink backing up my nostrils, making me retch. I haven't got many people left; I've alienated most of them. I think that Sarah is probably with Ben now, and I haven't spoken to my mum and dad who might have left each other for all I know. And Ray. Who I was meant to be fishing with.

And Constance.

I shouldn't be here. I've got to get back. I can't run away like this. I can't be drinking, making things worse. I can't live this any more. This is drinking, smoking me. What am I doing here living this dead man's life? A man who doesn't even exist any more. I am wearing his clothes, speaking to his friends, going through the motions of his life.

I know who he is, but who am I? Who am I if every *me* I know is dead? I get up from the table. 'I've got to go. I've got to be somewhere.'

'What?'

'I have to live for now, whatever that means.'

'Sit the fuck down and finish your drink.'

'I made a promise. What time is it?'

'It's three thirty in the morning. You're not going anywhere.'

'Alex, I've got to get back to town.'

'You're pissed.'

'I'll get a cab.'

'There aren't any. Everyone goes to bed round here.'

I try to get to the door but Alex blocks the way.

'You've had too much.'

I try to speak, but there is nothing to say.

Half an hour later, Alex places a blanket around my shoulders. I have found a quiet corner and been pushed into it. I will the sun to come up and the earth to spin faster so I can get out of here.

Alex is speaking into the phone.

'He flipped out . . . I don't know.'

He turns his head. Looking uncomfortable.

'Yes, I think he had a couple of drinks.'

Whatever.

'No, he isn't,' he says.

Lies.

'Sorry again about the hour; I wasn't sure who to phone.'

Doyle walks in from outside.

'Fuck this, it's freezing.'

'Then shut the door.'

'I'm too fucked to drive, mate. I got in the wrong fucking side of the car. We'll have to go later.'

Alex leans into my face.

'Charlie, we'll have to get some sleep and that before we

go home. Is that all right? Just wait there. If you need anything bang on my door.'

I try to nod.

'Doyle,' he says, 'give *me* the keys.'

In my head the same thought is holding the paddle, punishing me. Turning over and over again. That I have been
here before. In this place, in this state. I thought this was a
place I could hide out, just be myself, but I can't even have
that any more. I am having an anxiety attack. I've learnt
about anxiety attacks, and the techniques for dealing with
them don't seem relevant to this. I try to describe the room
around me but the depth of concentration and effort this
requires makes me feel nauseous. I try to focus on particular
objects but they drag my eyeballs up and over into their
sockets as I try to track them; the sofa, kettle, teapot, TV all
climb the walls. I know this eyeball-rolling thing. I know it
well. Once it starts it doesn't stop for two, three hours. I'm
safe here. I remember being this ill before, and being wrapped
in a blanket helps. The idea that I might vomit brushes over
me. This is a weakness and, like cutting off my own head to
stop the pain, it is merely another option that I have at my
disposal. Slowly though, sunlight begins to appear through
the cracks in the curtain, eventually warming the outside
of the blanket. If I had the courage I'd let it warm my skin.
Elsewhere on the site I can hear cupboard doors closing, a
toilet flushing. And I don't have to look, but I know that the
grass is covered in a cold clear dew. I have to go back to
the city and tidy up now. I get off the floor, drunk and tired,
and start drinking glasses of water to sober up. I won't mourn
this life that's gone. It doesn't fit me any more.

# 32

If you said 'dinner party' to me I'd have thought of maybe six shit-faced people sitting around a table in a Barratt starter home, choking on takeout prawn balls and talking out the sides of their mouths about screwing and mortgages. To me the dinner party was a twilight world of kitchen arse-fondling, orange Matchmakers and empty bottles of Spew Nun that I was happy to be left out of. I didn't own slacks, boat shoes or sweaters. I didn't have wood for anyone's wife. I hated kids and long conversations, I didn't care what you were driving and I had never felt the need to equip myself with an extensive knowledge of wine. I saw as much need to read the label on a bottle of Rioja as I did the emergency instructions on the back of a bottle of bleach. If the bottle was not made of blue die-injected plastic or green with one of those duck necks for getting under the rim, then I'd drink it. I don't care who made it or where it came from. I'd drink it. So what if the grapes grew in the long shadow cast by Chris de Burgh sunbathing and were crushed by monkeys in tuxedos. I'd still drink it. I held a firm belief that anything left in a bucket for long enough would eventually turn into booze.

I had the same ignorance of food, which to me was a harder, non-alcoholic form of booze. Most British food, for instance, was flat. Most foreign food was not. It came in piles and exotic shapes like alphabetti spaghetti, and main courses were eaten from bowls. You've got your spaghetti carbonara which was white and your spaghetti bolognese was brown. How one got to be white and the other got to be brown was beyond me, but the red one with tomatoes was for students. I told Sarah before she went down the shops that I knew nothing about cooking and that I was worried about feeding her friends sparrow bones and old Castrol. But she still wanted me to cook and picked out a recipe and even bought the ingredients. 'Gnocchi in four cheeses', it said. It could be done in one pot, it said. Except the salad, which you put in a big bowl with oil and balsamic vinegar and serve with some crusty bread to mop up the sauce.

'Ow! That hurt my mouth!'

'Yes, do watch out for the needles. There are thousands of them hidden amongst the pigeon skulls.'

If I was actually cooking for normal people I could relax, sip a small glass of sherry and catch a couple of programmes on Radio 4. But her over-educated friends made me drink more than a sip. My initial shock, on meeting graduates of a real university for the first time, was that they showed no sign of mutation. This seemed deceitful to me. I was sure that evolution would furnish them with larger brain cavities. I expected thick glasses, big teeth, slicked-down hair, green Mekon skulls, cravats and ceremonial cavalry swords. I was unlucky. Apparently all this remained well hidden unless they worked at the BBC. The three boys I was to cook for were in turn slick, good-looking and rich. They all worked 'in the City'. They were clever, quick-witted young gods who balanced fortunes while I still balanced on walls. I was the

339

outsider – poorer, comparatively juvenile and technically more stupid. I felt that this made me the cheeky fox dancing on his hind legs past the chicken coop. These people all understood each other. They all went to the same college, at the same university, in the same year. And knew people who'd done the same. Two of the people I went to college with ended up selling posters in Southsea town centre; I think the rest moved into juggling.

As far as I could guess Sarah's friends were thinking, What's with her and this shit head? Does he really think he is equal to us? What can she get from him that we never gave her?

I'd be stupid if I didn't account for their territoriality. Whenever you dance with a lady, bear in mind that there is always another man, perhaps one with a big square head, who thinks he loved her more and will want to push your teeth down your throat because he once bought her jewellery.

Also I was thinking, What were Sarah and I saying to these people? That we'd got it together enough to be cooking? She hadn't even told me she loved me and we were giving dinners already. Had we moved in together? Even unofficially? My circumstances were growing surreptitiously more twee by the second. I remember looking at all the cheese she'd bought and chain-smoking from nervousness. She could see that I'd allowed myself to feel threatened, and I began accusing her of deliberately trying to upset my equilibrium. I was insecure she said. I moped. We rowed a little. She didn't seem aware that this was new to me. She expected me to know so much and be so capable and more grown-up than I was, and that expectation was making me tense.

'You'll like them; stop bitching,' she said. 'And how many cigarettes have you smoked today?'

Bitching, fucking panicking.

'I've never seen you like this.'

'I know, I know,' I said. 'I want everything right for you. I don't want them to think you're with some idiot.'

'They're not like that, I promise.'

'Right,' I said.

'They're normal. Like you.'

'Yeah.'

She slipped past me, on the way from the bathroom to the bedroom, a sweet cloud of scent evaporating behind her.

'What, you think they were all born in castles?'

I'm silent here. Compared to where I grew up they were.

'Does that mean yes?' she said. 'Well, don't think about it. They don't care where you come from.'

'Right. You're pleased with yourself today, aren't you?' I said. Half spoiling for a fight. She just smiled as she offered a silver eyelash curler up to her eye.

'They'll be interested in you.'

The white rubberized lips of the curler were already stained black from mascara.

'They'll be interested in me?' I said. 'What, in a zoo sort of way?'

She squeezed harder on the lashes. I couldn't recall the last time she'd made this much effort just for me.

'No,' she said, 'they're not interested in you in a zoo sort of way. They're interested because you're with me, darling.'

She finally took the curling machine away from her eye and blinked twice at me like an ostrich through a chain-link fence.

'Very Disney,' I said.

'You'll love them.'

She leant closer to the mirror, then sideways, examining each side of her face with a scrupulous look.

'Love them?' I said.

'They're cracking fun.'

'Don't say *cracking fun*; I feel excluded already. You can't use language like that any more. So, after dinner, are we going to run around the garden after a fox?'

'No.'

She was silent as she exchanged the shirt she was wearing to do her make-up in for a fine La Perla bra. I used to dream about women doing this kind of thing in front of me but now I just stand and whine.

'Are you going to give us a piano recital?'

'No,' she said.

'Will we play *Give Us a Clue*?'

'Charades?'

'Yes,' I said.

'No.'

'Then what do you lot do exactly?'

'Talk,' she said. 'Eat and talk.'

I should have known I was out of my depth. I was trying to cut fucking Dolcelatte into cubes when I heard the first distraught plummy voice vomiting condescension in the street. Black Saab, roof down, blue baseball cap. He looked like he'd been rolled off some production line hidden beneath Putney.

'No, you listen to me, darling, and please pay a-fucking-ttention because the last spread I made bought me this fucking Saab.'

This would have to be one of them I thought. And he was the Cheesemaster.

'I left a fucking voicemail to sell back. No, you're not listening, darling. Let me explain. No, it was a hundred and fifty at close of play. Do you think that I'm that fucking stupid? I'm not raising my voice. Other line. Bye-bye. Shit. Hello? Jerome! Hello, my friend, how are you? No. No, I was just— No. Listen. Jerooooome, other line.'

This was someone with a pathological level of confidence.

'Sarah, there's a man outside screaming into a mobile. I think it's your friend.'

'Is that him screaming?'

'I think so. He's wearing a blue baseball cap.'

'Is there anything in my teeth?' she said as she ran out of the door.

'A prawn,' I shouted as she emerged below in the gardens.

'Come upstairs,' she told him. 'You're scaring the neighbours.'

When he walked through the door he was still on his telephone and didn't even acknowledge me. He handed me his coat and I brought him a glass of chilled white wine.

'I'll have red,' he said.

'OK,' I said.

I walked back into the kitchen and swallowed his glass in one. One thing I did know for a fact was that sophisticated men of the world didn't suck their wine down in one go. At least not in company. We used to drink stuff at college that was nothing more than grape juice mixed with surgical spirit and the kind of smoke flavouring they add to fast food. It was called something like Lustbader and had a green tint even out of the bottle. Drink enough of it and you felt like you could knock down a horse with one punch. But mostly you'd end up sleeping. I wished I had some of that now.

I poured myself a glass of red and then swallowed that

in one. Then I squirted a bit of lighter fluid in the bottom of the glass, spat in it and stirred it and the wine together with my finger. Gigondas it said on the label. I poured a glass for myself, careful to keep it separate from the toxic one. It's smoky in a non-burger way and makes my face warm. Gigondas, Gigondas. I took him his new wine and then hid in the kitchen while he and Sarah got re-acquainted.

I listened to him getting louder, drinking my gob, while I waited for the cheese to boil and his enormous headache to begin.

Scott arrived next. He was different to Simon. Scott's first words when I greeted him and took his coat were, 'Now, don't drop it on the bloody floor, use a hanger.'

'Sure,' I said. 'I was going to.'

'I'm joking!' he said, and laughs even though I haven't done anything. 'So you're Charlie? Pleased to meet you. Drop that anywhere you like. Sarah's told me a lot about you.'

'Scott, shut up!'

She had to hide her face behind his shoulder. I could see she was blushing. Scott's eyes followed her. Scott was handsome. Scott probably climbed mountains and reached the summit despite serious frostbite. He gripped my shoulder with his strong hand. 'No, Sarah, tell him; he should at least have an idea of what you've got in store.'

'Shut up!' she shouted again.

'She may think I'm a bit of a bastard, Charlie, but I'm going to tell you straight. Sarah might have been with some fucking oiks in her time, but from what she's told me you're the first man she's ever been with who doesn't sound exactly like some test-tube replication of her horrible father.'

My jaw was open, my tongue drying in the warm indoor air. What should I say? Thank you?

'Now, Charlie, shall we mix some drinks? Scotch and soda for me. On the rocks if you've got.'

While Simon sounded like a seagull eating crabs from an oil barrel, Scott delicately arranged each word as though it might be the last you ever heard. He wanted to gauge your reaction while he was talking and listened when he wasn't. He didn't raise his voice, except to express surprise or joy, and appeared to be everything I wanted from my middle classes. He appeared uncomplicated and interested in Sarah. He asked her the right questions and I thought that there was something good and honest about a man who could still be interested in someone other than himself at the end of the working day. I leant against the wall in the hallway, listening. People like him and Sarah seemed to be the foundation of any modern healthy society. I liked him, which was all well and good, but I still thought dinner parties were church. How many times did you have to have them in a month? I worried about the future and watched my various cheeses amalgamate.

Greg stood in the doorway talking to Sarah for five minutes before he actually deigned to enter the flat. Mumbling and whining with waxy black curls, his eyes tracked me through the hallway as I carried more lighter-fluid wine from the kitchen for Simon. I sensed that Greg had been here before. Leant against the door frame, so angry, cocky, comfortable. I watched as Sarah took his hand and closed her own around it. She could put people at ease, always trying to give them a little of what they wanted. He looked over at me and smiled, suddenly contented at something she'd said, and I wanted to kick him down the stairs and break his fingers. Even though I'd seen this little-boy act a thousand times it was still an ugly sight to me as she coaxed him inside, he pretending to be bashful as she pulled him into the living room by his outstretched arms.

Yes, we love you. You're coming in whether you like it or not; you must join us at any cost.

Dinner came out of the oven in a big steaming pot. I cared as much as anyone could about that dangerously hot cheese. As I began to serve up stringy ladles of hot rotted dairy fats, Greg and Simon immediately struck up an old conversation. Brag, lie, brag. I drive this. I was best at sport. I went on holiday there. I bought that. You bought the wrong one. You should have waited a month and got the next one.

The bad feeling seemed to move around the table.

Greg (M3, boxing blue, holidays in Africa), affronted by my silence and maybe even my hot cheese stylings, wanted to know if I could box. This was the first thing he'd actually said to me since his smirking arrival.

'Box?' I said. This is a man who earns his living telling old ladies to buy electric, sell privatized gas and he was getting big remembering that he thumped people at school. So what? 'Do you box?' he said.

'If I have to,' I said.

'But do you know how to box?'

I was curious because he didn't have the face for it.

'I know how to fight,' I said.

'Oh do you, and where did you learn that?' He laughed and then asked Simon, 'Can you fight?'

'Boys, boys,' said Sarah. She was three large glasses into a bottle and about as persuasive as Barney the dinosaur.

'No, really,' he said. 'Can you fight?'

'Would you like to find out?' I said.

'What?'

'Would you like to find out?'

He stopped laughing. I thought that would happen. You should only ever ask someone if they'd like to fight if you're already on top of them hitting them in the head. Usually I wouldn't ask, but tonight I didn't mind getting hurt. And I wanted to see what a boxing blue could do. Especially one with floppy hair. Fucking poet warriors.

'Take off your rings and your watch. Leave them with your mate; we'll go on the grass outside. Me and you. No fuss.'

'What?' he said.

'You asked me three times if I could fight. So I said would you like to find out.'

'I was —'

'Talking shit?' I said. 'Well that's sorted that then. Would anyone like some coffee?'

Priceless. Maybe it was my apparent domesticity that confused. That or I was starting to look soft.

We had a quiet ten minutes after that as Scott told us about his new office. Then, as I was clearing the plates away feeling alone and stupid, Sarah grabbed me. She took hold of my collar and in full sight of the table gave me an inept slobbering kiss. A broken jaw, first disco, two bottles of Thunderbird and a Kit Kat open-mouth surgery. I was astounded. My stomach flipped and the three suits just faded away and I remembered again why I was there, miles away from what I knew.

I had to break her grip on my neck and push her back into her chair. 'We've got company,' I said.

'My God,' said Scott, 'you'd better go back in your box until we've gone. No more wine for you, my dear.'

'Did you know I bought a boat?' said Simon.

I flicked the kettle on as they continued on the brag, lie, brag theme. Bonuses. Models/women/cars/investments.

And then he blew it. Somewhere in the greedy clamour: 'So Sarah,' Simon said, 'have you picked up any common mannerisms from Charlie?'

'Common?' said Sarah, laughing. 'What do you mean, Simon?'

'I said, have you picked up any common habits from Charlie?'

I stood by the kettle, blushing bright and hot, glad they couldn't see this uncontrollable, running off-the-leash blushing.

'What?' She was still laughing.

I was thinking that the next one was going to cost someone. Was I going to make a deal of it, stand there and shout? I had to swallow it. They were her friends; I still wanted them to be.

Sarah told me later that Scott thought both Greg and Simon had behaved like 'pricks', blah, blah, blah. But by that point the dinner was over, and it wasn't a party because no one was having fun. Scott had said he was embarrassed, but I felt like none of this would have happened if I'd been different, if I'd been one of them. They had all got along fine before I turned up, and in many ways I couldn't agree with them more. Only I would probably never say it out loud, that's all. I knew that if I'd tried to be anything other than myself it would have been worse.

I lay down in the bedroom. I didn't want her to look at me. I stared at the ceiling, wanting to claw through it with my fingers, tear at the roof and rip up the sky.

'I've got nothing to prove to any of them.'

Angry. Lie.

'You've got me now,' she said. 'Greg . . . we went out for a time at college. It was a first-year thing. It was nothing but it meant a lot then.'

'You should have warned me.'

'You'd have overreacted. You've got more dignity and talent and love in you than all of them.'

I watched her closely, wondering if she truly believed that.

'That's right,' I said. I realized I would never know the truth in anything she ever said to me. As long as she was by my side, that's where she was. I could count on nothing else.

'You're special, Charlie, that's why I chose you. Tomorrow he'll remember what he said and he'll hate himself. I love you for letting it go. You don't need to prove anything to me, Charlie. I have you, that's all I want.'

There were tears on her face and then on my shoulder, which I put down to the drink. She pulled back, twisting out of her dress and releasing herself from her bra and slipped into the bed beside me. As I pulled the covers around her and she curled up I felt calmed by her dependent drunken breaths.

'I don't have to worry, do I?'

'No,' she said. 'I'll look after you. And you can look after me. For ever.'

'That's right,' I said straight back at her. 'For ever.'

As a kid I never got to go to the funfair much because we never had the money. Me and Ray, we'd always be stuck in the back of the car driving past these places. We'd look in and see kids flying around in giant teacups, splashing down log flumes, swinging back and forth on pirate ships bedecked in light bulbs. Go-karts, Jesus, I still love go-karts. Back then once a year was as much as we could afford, so when we did get in we had to make the most of it. Back then the funfairs operated on the ticket system. Fifteen tickets end on end was all you had to spend and you couldn't move inside the fair without tearing off at least two. At first it felt like you could make those tickets last all day – if you stayed off the big rides and threw some plywood hoops over jars at twelve goes for one ticket – or threw darts at playing cards. But you didn't come to the fair to test your hand–eye coordination in a hope-sapping game that you could play in your dad's garage. You couldn't be satisfied with shooting plastic ducks when you could hear the screams, the gears cranking chains and see upstretched arms and faces shredding the air. There was only one place for that handful of tickets. The big ride. One go. You slapped them down on the counter and shuffled up the gangway, listening to the creaking and groaning as this whole colossal machine retched forward a line of cars. The rest of the fair, you realized, was a distraction. The bar came down over your head. You started to move along the tracks with a slam, shunt, shunt and you never wanted the ride to end. You never wanted to get off. But you only got so many tickets, so many breaths, so many heartbeats.

When the ride ended you would see it and the rest of the fair for what it really was. Disposable. You now saw past the promise and the paint. Saw the things you never saw before. The rats in the rubbish, the spent tickets in the dirt, the children crawling around under the rides. Rust, loose bolts, peeling paint, grease, ripped cushions and fuck-you graffiti. There was nothing more it could offer you. You'd seen the best it had to offer and now you wanted to go home.

'This is fucked, man. We've got to get him back to the hospital. Shit, look at him. He was like that in New York and we nearly lost him then.'

'He's not that fucked. Shit, a couple of pills or what?' says Doyle.

'Chas, you had a couple of pills, right?'

I nod. They were strong pills. I shut my eyes thinking about the ride.

'He had a couple,' says Doyle. 'That means we've got one and a half left.'

If the ride was everything, what is this supposed to be?

'I've got to check my pockets,' says Alex. 'I know they're at the bottom. Hold the steering wheel.'

I say out loud, 'Some people ride on the dodgems and just want to go fast. Others want to collide with everyone. We all want to get the most we can for our money. That's right, isn't it?'

'I got ten? Didn't I? Doyle? Right?'

'I had one left over, you should have two. Give me one of yours; we'll split it,' says Doyle.

'No. You've had too much, man. Take your hands off the wheel.'

'If you put your hands back on it,' says Doyle.

'What do you think these are?' says Alex.

Doyle yelps.

'It's like you've got four arms. What are they then?'

'Those are my legs.'

'Shit, so they are,' he says.

I had the tickets, I had the tickets in my hand. They were there and then they were gone. This is what running out of tickets feels like. This is the final comedown. I blew them on the big ride.

'I'm resting my eyes,' says Doyle. He flips his seat further backwards. 'I'm resting my eyes, doing all that.'

'I blew them on the big ride,' I say, 'and then the big ride ended and now I have no tickets.'

'You're sleeping!' shouts Alex. 'Fucking sit up. I need you to watch the fucking road for me.'

'I don't want to,' says Doyle.

'You selfish cunt.'

Doyle is laughing, his pink lips stretching taut and white.

'You selfish, selfish cunt,' says Alex.

'Hah hahahaha!' laughs Doyle.

I realize that I am burbling, a strange kind of ill speak. I can taste toffee apples and smell candyfloss thick in the air. Maybe this is the smell that dogs clowns when they have a brain tumour.

'Can anyone else smell candyfloss?' I say. 'Am I the only one?'

'You irrelevant mumbling fuck.'

Am I mumbling? How fast are we going? Too fast.

'Doyle?'

'Shut up, Charlie.'

'Alex,' I say.

'What?' says Alex.

'Inside you know that something has to end just so it can begin again.'

Alex has his nose up against the glass of the windscreen.

'Alex,' says Doyle, 'where are your arms? I can't see them.'

'I can't do this on my own. I can't see straight.'

'Lean back, man. Relax. Pull over and have a drink. Something.'

This is not what I wanted. We backslide across the country in shame and confusion, the adventure in reverse. No one cares what is out of the window; what we pass we've seen before. Put all the toys back in the box. No more tickets. No more rides. I sit upright.

'I think we should put on our seat belts,' I say. 'Anyone who isn't wearing their seat belt is just asking to die.'

□

I sip the hot coffee while holding a green hand towel over my eyes. The freeze-dried flavour is like a hug from big science. I take the green hand towel off my face and look at Celeste who is sitting in a kind of visitor's chair by my bed. The kind you could grieve in comfortably for two or even three fourteen-hour shifts.

'You know what you smell like?' she says. 'You smell like a two-day-old lunch box.'

I woke up under some chairs in the TV room with my

carrier bag stuck to my face like a giant swollen eyelid. Celeste found me and put me into bed.

'That's how I found you. I smelt you first,' she says.

'What?' I say.

'I smelt you first. I wondered what the smell was, then, when I looked, I saw you under there.'

'It's my cast,' I say. 'It honks.'

I bring it up to my nose.

'Raw sausage meat,' I say.

I want to ask her about Constance but the fear of her response to the question sucks the oxygen from my lungs. Even a simple question like 'Do they know what happened?' seems funereal. Celeste is so matter-of-fact it's like she expected her to die.

I try bravado.

'Who collects on that dead girl sweepstake thing then? You, I suppose.'

'No. No one gets paid.'

'Oh, bad taste. Sorry.'

'No,' she says. 'You don't get paid for near misses. I admit I have the best statistical chance of winning.'

'What?'

'She can still die. She's in another hospital; they patched her up. She's at Saint somethings. With even more bandages.'

'She's not dead?'

'Dead? When? What last night? Today? Where did you get that from? Have I won? Shit.'

'You said she was dead.'

'I didn't. I didn't say anything. I thought she was nearly dead. We didn't know if she was or not. She was alive when she left here, she still is. They don't know what happened yet.'

'I'll tell them.'

'Why? Tell them what? I hate to break it to you, Dr Sex, but there's no cure for what she's got.'

'I have to tell them. I don't want her getting the blame.'

'Err, she did it to herself.'

'I got her there.' I did. Sure as I had my head buried in bed I may as well have handed her the razor and told her where to make the first cut. 'I should have looked in on her. I should have warned her nurse.'

'Don't flatter yourself. She could have taken up the trumpet. She didn't have to cut herself. And whatever you say to them won't change a thing for her.'

'Her parents will know.'

'Dad'll just love that story.'

'I'll tell them how I unbalanced her.'

'From bad ideas to worse, Dr Sex. Drink your coffee.'

'I don't want any more. Have you got an orange or anything like that?'

'In my room.'

'Can you bring it to me?'

'Shit.'

This weekend I had to process the thought of Constance's death, around fifty drinks, two strong pills, the death of my old life and still make it back.

She returns with the orange.

'Are you going to try and see her when you leave here?'

'Can you peel it for me?'

She blushes.

'Can I fuck.'

'Please, Celeste, I might fucking die trying to get into that orange. Don't torture me; use your fucking nails.'

'Come on . . .'

'Please, I haven't got any.' I hold up my fingers with their harmless rounded tips. 'You're blushing.'

'You sorry little shit. You'd do this for me, right?'

Her ice-pick thumb punctures the skin, spraying its zest over both of us. Most smells die a fast death against the bleached air in here, but the essence of the orange fills the room and smells like freedom.

She passes me a segment. The acidic juice stings the dried skin around my lips.

'Thanks. Tomorrow I take my shit and I'm gone. I'll meet Sklansky. Maybe I'll do a last session and try to make up for being such a dumb bastard.'

She quietly dissects the rest of the orange. All I want is my vitamin C so I can get this over with. So I can make this the last comedown of my life.

**34**

Last group and I can hardly hold my head up or keep my
feet from brushing each other or my knees from the carpet.
I keep one arm stiff against the wall, hold the door handle
like the crook of a walking stick and wait in the doorway
for Sklansky's attention while he pokes and cajoles the slow
kids. I may look broken and sick to him, but in my mind I
am strong.

'You're late,' he says.

'That would be the least of it.'

'Well?'

'Well. Can I sit down or shall we go through the usual
shit?'

He turns his back to me and carries on with the group.

'Take a seat.'

'Sure, let him in!' shouts Heinrich.

I look right at Heinrich and show him my teeth. Sklansky
looks round to check on my progress and finds me curling
my top lip like a baby giraffe.

'Sit down, Charlie. Or do you have something you'd like
to say to the group?'

Thumb inside the waistband of his trousers. Pen hanging
limp in the other.

'Like what?' I say.

'Like sorry you're late,' says Lisa.

'Sorry I'm late, group.' I smile.

This is like school again. Being judged. Kissing arse.

'Where were you at the weekend?' says SLG.

'When I should have been here?' I say. 'With you? Redeeming myself?'

'Did you go visit our little friend with the bandages?' says Lisa. 'Did anything come up that you'd like to share with the group?'

Sklansky waits. He tries to force me to speak with a silence.

'Oh yeah,' I say. 'That was what I came here to say. I'm leaving.'

'Now?' asks Sklansky.

'Today,' I say. 'Honest.'

'No one is asking you to leave,' says Sklansky.

'Yes, but it would be best. I've made up my mind. This is my last group.'

'You're sure this is what you want?'

'It's a guesstimate. You can't help me. The last three weeks you've tried and we've failed. So I'm going. I'll probably get worse. Depressed, unhappy, blah, blah, blah. But I was ill before I came here. Nothing has changed. I might even have got stronger but things, outside and inside, have gotten worse. Everything changes, nothing stays the same.'

'Why don't you tell everyone what you've done,' says Lisa, 'then maybe you'll feel better.'

'Shut up, you bitch,' says Celeste.

'Can you write it down? For me, privately?' says Sklansky.

'No. I don't want to write it down. I can't.'

He walks over with a pen and paper and hands them to me. What do I write? That we needed to fuck? That I wanted to fuck Sarah. That I used Constance. Made Constance Sarah. It's all there for the picking. Thinking of them pinches at the same black space in my gut. This is too much; this is why I have to leave. I can feel myself straightening out, growing raw. The sharp corners appearing again.

'I'm leaving.'

'What do you have to lose by staying?'

'It's what other people have to lose by me staying that concerns me.'

'Maybe you should just think about yourself right now,' says Celeste. 'Perhaps you're not in a place where you can think about other people.'

'Thanks, but I know this part off by heart. This is where you say I can't take responsibility for other people's mental states, right?'

'Yes,' she says.

'Yes, and she's absolutely right,' says Sklansky. 'You cannot take responsibility for other people's mental states. You take responsibility for your own emotions, actions and anger.'

'Don't turn this into a fucking lecture,' I say. 'That's why I'm going.'

I get out of my chair and make for the door with Sklansky in tow.

'I'm taking responsibility now.'

I pull off my jumper walking towards the door. When I get outside, the cold air chills the sweat on my face and my body. I lean my head against the wall and try and breathe as slowly as my heart will let me.

'Are you leaving now?' says Sklansky behind me.

'Yes.'

'Will you come back?'

'No,' I say.

'Will you work on those forms?'

'I might burn half of them. They're no use to me now. They're old. I've got brand-new shit to deal with.'

I want to get out of here without fainting. I'm already moving away from him, walking backwards to the exit.

'We have drop-in sessions twice a week,' he shouts. 'They're free for the first six months!'

I lean into a fire door; it sucks in air as I push against it. Back to the fair. Everything has to end so it can begin again. Why be sad?

'Sorry, Doc,' I say. 'I'm gone.'

## 35

Sean's angry words whirl around my head like a vortex of brittle autumn leaves. It's happened, I think. The big rage, the huge upset has finally hit me. It's my turn now. I've seen all this before. I've watched good people come and go. Real grown-ups, bigger than me, try to fight him in the same circumstances. Try and use words and logic only to lose to his pre-emptive paranoid screaming and plain untethered aggression.

'Who let you in? I don't recall inviting you in. Who let him in?' He switches back and forth, playing to the audience that surrounds us. White scalp and wet ginger curls. Talking about me as if I don't matter. As if I am worth so little – invisible, gone in the head, disgraced.

'C'mon, who let him in, who let him in? Fucking won't ask you again.'

There is no dignity in this. I thought I could get my things and get out. But now I see, I remember, that he always hated me. I can't remember when he began to hate me specifically, but he always treated me with contempt. Like a pig. An animal brought into the office who could deal with the rubbish and be fed on slops. From the first time I asked for a rise, he began to hate me.

He looks at me as a farmer might look at a pig. I have

turned on him and in my frenzy knocked the bucket from his hand.

'I work here. This is my office. I still work here.'

I am standing behind my desk with my pictures, with my notes still scrawled on paper scattered across it.

'No. It *was* your office. You did have a job. You left.'

I might have forgotten who or what I was, but he hadn't. He wouldn't let me change. He wouldn't let me get better. I came in here with nothing. When I forgot that, he would remind me. He never forgot. I wanted more respect? He didn't see why. I wanted some more money? I should have been happy to work for nothing – grateful because anything he gave me would be more than I had before. I wanted money and respect? I wanted too much. You are a pig. You are Charlie Big Potatoes, he said mockingly. The pig who wanted it all.

'Charlie fucking Big Potatoes, look at the fucking state of you.'

He looks around for acknowledgement. People who used to be my friends stop work to watch the argument unfold. I think if they ignored him he'd stop screaming, starved of fuel like a candle burning under an upturned glass.

'I didn't leave.'

'You didn't tell me where you were. I didn't receive a formal notification.'

'But you should have done. Everyone knew where I was.'

Doyle, dressed in a lizard-skin shirt, tries to step between us. The shirt smells like damp biscuits.

'We're all mates,' he says. 'This is not necessary.'

'No, this is business,' says Sean. 'And I did not receive a note from his doctor, which puts him in breach of his contract.'

'Let me get my stuff and I'll go and we can sort this out later when I come back to work.'

'What stuff? You have no stuff. This is all company property. It belongs to us.'

'But they are my papers. My writing, my work; it's all mine.'

'You don't listen to anyone. You don't work here. You left.'

I pull at a drawer which is falling apart under the weight of old drafts and unopened brown envelopes. I want to get everything I own within reach, because I am starting to believe that what I cannot see, touch and hold, does not exist. Only when I have everything together will I feel secure.

'I don't give a shit,' he continues. 'That's company property. Our work, we own it, written on our paper on our time. It stays here. Now get out.'

I could sit down on the edge of the desk and tell everyone how he came between Sarah and me. About how his lie hurt us at a time when we needed our friends the most. I imagine how the addition of all this to the argument would force a whole new perspective. Even now his day-one estimate of my worth endures. I don't think anyone would believe me. Or care.

I am quiet, I don't know for how long. My face is hot. I am staring at the carpet and the skin on the back of my neck is sore. I will not do this here. I shake my head.

'Well?'

'Not here,' I say.

'In my office,' he says, 'now.'

He is all swagger and violence walking into his office. I follow, obedient.

'What do you want to do this now for?' asks Doyle,

trotting along beside us. 'Let him have his stuff. This can wait.'

'And this is a private meeting,' says Sean as he slams the door in his face. Doyle will have to lie low. If I was him I'd go home now and make sure that I get in bright and early tomorrow morning. He walks quickly to the other side of his desk.

'You cunt.'

'Don't call me that,' I say.

'You came here to embarrass me, you cunt. I'll call you what I want. You walk in here and fuck with my magazine, disrupt me in the middle of production, and then tell me what I can call you. I can call you anything I want.'

He leans across, close now, and lowers his voice. Between me and him.

'What do you think people think of you now, eh? When you come in here begging? You want your job back? Is that what you want? You want money? Fuck off. You greedy cunt, can't even do your job. What do you think they think of you? Out there? You let them down and they did your work for you when you couldn't be bothered. Your friends? Do you want to know what they think of you? They hate you. They think you're greedy. A greedy cunt piece of shit.'

'I want my stuff.'

'Resign then.'

'What?'

'Resign today. Give me the letter, then you can take all your shit with you.'

'What letter? I don't have any letter.'

'Who did you give it to?'

'No one. I haven't written it yet.'

'I am giving you the opportunity to resign, now.'

'I don't want to, Sean. I can't resign. I need the job. The money.'

'Then you give me no choice. I can sack you for gross misconduct.'

'Gross misconduct? What gross misconduct?'

'Or you can resign now. Read your contract.'

'I've done nothing. You can't.'

'It's in your contract and I want your notice. Post-dated. Three weeks ago.'

He taps at a sheaf of papers on the desk.

'A resignation letter?'

'Yes.'

I'll have nothing if I resign. Whatever I do now, he'll lie about later. He'll make something up, tell people he fired me for having poor hygiene, or that I simply couldn't write. I was hitting on his secretary, I had a bad drug problem, I stole from expenses, I dealt wraps of Vim to school kids. Charlie Big Potatoes only cared about himself. Gross misconduct? Gross fucking life.

'I need that stuff. I need everything I've done. It's what I am. It's my whole life in there.' Why can't I stand up in front of him and say, 'You made this happen; you win. Let me retreat with some dignity, with something?'

'This is your last chance,' he says. 'Write the letter.'

He pushes a blank piece of paper across the table. Here of all places I should be excused for what I am, what I became. Here, where they gave me a new sense of right and wrong, new dreams, and games to play. They gave me everything but a new box to sit in and a serial number.

'Write what I say. To whom it may concern.'

'No, I can't do that.'

'To whom it may concern.'

'Sean . . .'

'In light of my unacceptable behaviour and the decline in the standard of my work and my personal conduct at this company . . .'

'No, Sean.'

His anger is a rope cutting and suffocating him. A cord pulled tight around his throat, across his back and wound up tight under his blackening arms. Constricting, gnawing at bone, cutting tendon, bending swollen veins to bursting. Bleeding inside, outside, everywhere, his wanting, his needing to hurt and win spilling out in a dark black slurry across his hands, over his desk. He takes his pen and a piece of headed notepaper from his printer tray. He draws a short line at the bottom and pushes it towards me.

'Sign it.'

'No.'

This is about shame. The shame of returning home with nothing. The shame of failing. The shame of him sending me home, back to my old life. Back to who I was.

'Are you stupid?' he says.

Please sir, I'm sorry. I admit I got a big head. I got like you.

'Write. Take the pen and write.'

Please, please.

'Write.'

I dressed like you. I drank and I took drugs like you. Isn't that enough? I wasn't trying to be better than you, it wasn't intentional. I didn't even like it myself. I wasn't trying to be clever. I apologize for any criticism that might have been implied by my decision to not be a pig any more.

I look at him writhing in his chair, his bent body, his flaccid white-bread muscles taut.

'I'm not resigning; I can't do that.'

'Then consider this a termination of your employment here. Get out. Fuck off.'

I think about holding a gun to his head and pulling the trigger. He stays behind his desk while I find the door myself. Does my anger come from pride or self-respect? One is good, one is bad. Walking out of the room I'm still thinking, is that it? Is that all I get? I just got fired. Shall I tell him to stuff it all up his arse and then threaten to kill everyone? Would that be shrewd? I should go.

'Go on!' he shouts.

'I'm going,' I say, smiling like an idiot. 'Don't worry, I'm going.'

I don't look back, I keep walking. For some dumb reason I don't want to upset him more than he is. Like it could be any worse – his insults and demands and orders.

The corporation's lobby smells of stale oxygen and Brasso. I want to make it smell of cordite and burning plastic. I want to put Sean's head on a pole in the car park still attached to his body. Alive and twitching for as long as possible. And what's more, I want to do it without permission from human resources. I want retribution.

**36**

I turn up at my nan's house with one dirty holdall and the rest of my world in a cardboard box.

'What's all that?' she says.

'My clothes in the bag and all my problems in the box, written down on bits of paper.'

'Well, for God's sake put them under the stairs,' she says. 'You don't want them lying around here when you want to get better.'

Nan is of the school of thought that there is always someone worse off than you, and this attitude has rubbed off on me. I haven't got a problem. What am I whining about? I could be on fire. I could be a refugee on fire. Or a refugee with cancer on fire (at which point the fire would probably be a blessing). The thing is, people, Nan included, like an obvious illness they can see. No one likes surreptitious pain. Secret sickness. They hate depression, bulimics and anorexics and your quiet killers – radiation, lymph node cancer, invisible sexual diseases. We are conditioned to appreciate the sight of a large plaster, casts, drips, stitches, crutches and bruises as identifiable and comforting signs of illness under control. After all, if a doctor can see it he can cure it. Plus, if you have a bandage on your head people can see you coming, and if they want to, they can run away.

This is why we like our loons dressed up as Napoleon. Not the invisible menace they are now, stabbing people on trains with bread knives. People like this need a bell round their neck, like lepers – an obvious warning to society to keep away.

Ever since I got ill I've been watching for people like me. People who might have the same kind of problems as me. I started with refugee skip divers and dirty-looking needle kids wearing V-necks stretched down to their knees, kids who make you want to cross the road so you don't have to look them in the eye. I looked at the malnourished old men holding pieces of rolled-up carpet, old men who tuck their trousers into their socks. Now I see thousands more and I don't have to look in subways and doorways. These people don't ask for spare change but are more likely to ask to borrow twenty quid. They work at your office, live in your building, sleep warm in your bed. They are your demographic, standing next to you in the supermarket every day, buying the same tuna sandwich.

Nan shows me to my room upstairs. It used to belong to my dad. I tell her that it smells like a holiday chalet and spark up a cigarette. Nan is still using a carpet sweeper, pushing around fifty years' worth of dust. I put the box in the bottom of the wardrobe and lie back on the bed, looking at it and smoking, thinking, Is this it? An empty room. What next? You have no dependants. Your distance from other human beings actually feels like an advantage. You can't hurt them, they can't hurt you. So you start avoiding these places. Anywhere with people. Maybe you start scowling more. You don't care that your jacket doesn't match your trousers. You get a seat to yourself on a packed bus. Lack of verbal contact with other people suits you. In isolation you become cynical. You are spending most of your waking time alone, watching them fill their lives and the space around them with waste and consumption. You realize that you can find what you need in what others leave behind. There's perfectly good stuff in this skip, you think. Before you know it you are tucking your trousers into your socks and climbing over the edge. Nice carpet, you think, pulling it out from under a bag of kittens stuffed in a shattered toilet pan. Strong weave, purple. Nice for the bathroom. Are you going to let anyone inside your head? Your heart? Ever? No, because hell is other people and in that hell all they do is take, take, take and blame, blame, blame. Soon your face is pressed up against the window of KFC. The last conversation you had was screamed though your letter box. You have a piece of rolled-up kennel carpet and you wonder why people insist on travelling in pairs.

Nan takes my clothes away for washing. I tell her I'll do it but she gives me a strange look. She runs me a bath, telephones my mother to tell her where I am and cooks braising steak in gravy with some boiled potatoes for dinner. Nothing else happens.

Living in my dad's old room, even for a short time, is like having my head dunked in the cold bucket of his youth. I leave the bedroom door open so I can see a little warm yellow light from the bathroom. I work out that I have a total of two possible futures. Supermarkets are unavoidable in both. In the first I'm drunk, alone, blowing whisky fumes into checkout girls' faces. I think I work for a newspaper. In the second I have cleaned up. I am standing in the same aisle looking equally doomed, with two kids, trying to find the tuna with the parrot on the can. I love these children with all my heart, but every week it's the same fucking thing with these parrot characters. In a moment of pure noise, equivalent to a monstrous amplification of dolphins screaming, I look down at myself and realize that I didn't buy any of the clothes that I am wearing. And I have beer tits. Big beer tits and a shit job.

It is 3 a.m. I'm standing by the front door wearing clothes still damp from the drier. I've got out of bed seven or eight times since midnight, each time managing to put on one more item of clothing than before. Then I get back into bed and press my face into the pillow for another twenty minutes. Then I'm by the front door again – my forehead against the wrought-iron security cage – thinking that it would be better if I just got this over with. I'm going to walk over the green, hail a cab and go to a snooker club that does after-hours drinks. Nan switches the hallway light on. Five 60-watt bulbs illuminate the corridor like a flare.

Nan is standing at the top of the stairs.

'Sorry,' I say, 'I was trying to be quiet.'

'Now,' she says, 'are you going in or going out, because I'm not going to stand here all night?'

I want to tell her that no matter how tight I try to grip it, I have this desire to get more fucked up than any drug could make me. Like blowing up the office. Killing Sean. This is beyond drugs and booze. This runs through me like rot in a peach, right through to the stone. Embedded.

'Are you or aren't you? Coming or going?'

'Nan, I don't know what to say. This is what I am. I can't live without it. I've tried and it's been shit. I want to be out there, doing it.'

'What?'

'Being large, Nan. Being silly. That's what I'm about. That's what life's all about. The rest of it. Getting married, shit. That's my old man, that's not me. Is it? Kids on your knee and baby bouncers, whatever. Rusks?'

'What are you talking about?'

'I'm a selfish little bastard.'

'You got that right.'

I turn the handle.

'For God's sakes if you need one that much you can have one here.'

She takes each stair sideways on, like Des O'Connor in slow motion.

'I've got drinks, but there's no turning back. That's a big decision to make now.'

'I know.'

'Can't you decide about that tomorrow? After a sleep, eh? Not now.'

'I'm going up the wall in that room. I'm thinking about the rest of my life, Dad's life. My life was to be lived large. Am I supposed to work all day, get home with all that shit in my head and not have a drink or smoke a joint? I can't stand it. I can't live like this – every day the same way.'

'Your father did. Had the same doubts.'

'And he's happy now, is he?'

'I didn't say he was,' she says.

'I don't want to be like him. I don't want to spend twenty or thirty years fighting with Sarah before realizing none of it was worth the effort.'

'And do nothing with your life? Have no children and love no one?' There is a harshness in her voice. 'That's not a life for any man. Where's the good in that? You're a strong boy; a man like you can work and have a family. How long do you think you can keep doing this?'

'Some of my mates are in their mid thirties and still doing it.'

'Still doing what?'

'They work, they drink, go to clubs, pull birds. Every night.'

'Every night they do that?'

'Every night!' I shout.

'The same thing? But you said you didn't want to live every day the same?'

'I don't, but I'll have a load more memories than if I was stuck in a house like this with a load of fucking kids.'

'You know that for sure?'

'Yes, I do.'

'But you haven't given this life a chance.'

'I know this life. Find a room, find a TV, sit in front of it, get unhappy.'

'How do you know you won't be happy, that your generation won't do better? I'm sixty-eight. My memory is good for the important things, Charlie. I remember your grandfather, and I remember him because he was the one I loved. Other men, other nights, are nothing but a lot of sounds and shapes. I remember your grandfather, though. That's all that's important to me now.'

She makes her way down the stairs and takes hold of my hand. Hers is small and cold but strong all the same.

'I try and think of myself smiling, laughing, doing anything. All the best times of my life and I'm holding a glass of drink. Even in restaurants with Sarah, I always had to have another bottle, another drink. And when I think of her, it seems that we're happy because we're both drunk.'

'There's no magic in that bottle. You just have what you

take to it. If you're happy it's because you're together. That's
it.'

'What have I done, Nan?'

'I don't know, Charlie. Just be grateful you're in one piece
and that it's over now. Put it all away and go to bed. Come
on. Go to sleep and dream about something nice for a
change.'

☐

The noise that wakes me the next morning sounds like one
of the best in the world. The scraping of heavy wood on a
poured concrete walkway. I look down into the garden to
see Nan setting out two deckchairs on a harsh rectangular
lawn. She looks up at me and waves her arm in the air.

'Look at that!'

'What, a pigeon?'

'No, the sky. Look how blue it is.'

The bright horizon rushes my dilated pupils and tries to
hide in my aching brain.

'Fucking hell, Nan.'

She is humming an old song: 'You Are My Sunshine'.

'This is like the fifties.'

She is laughing, reminding me of one of those golden
permawave ladies who are always getting their arses pinched
on old postcards.

'Get out here and get some colour in your cheeks.'

I can smell sausage and bacon cooking. I wouldn't be
surprised if there's a fried slice to be had as well. I close my
eyes and see her scrape the lard onto the lip of the pan with
a knife. A bottle of ice-cold gold top on cornflakes. Toast
with melting globs of rich yellow butter.

When I get downstairs, she puts a plate of it in front of

me and I fall on it like a swamp donkey on a bag of carrots.
I don't eat alone. The cat also rolls in, sounding off about
something or other. It trots past Nan and drops to the floor
licking one of the winterish twigs that it uses for a leg. Nan
cracks the seal on a tin of rank pink salmon which turns me
green.

'Are you joking?' I say, as she draws the mess onto a
cracked blue saucer. 'That is the fucking worst-smelling substance on earth.'

'Cuss mouth!'

'You could have waited,' I say, trying to hold onto my
stomach. I pick up the plate and take it out into the garden.
'You did that on purpose.'

She comes outside and sits in the chair beside me, rolling
a slosh of Bell's around a cloudy glass. 'You'll have to abide
by my rules. No drinking. No drugs, Ecstasy.'

'What!'

'I read the newspapers. You're all on the heroin, God
forbid.'

'You can talk.' I point to her whisky. 'It's a bit early, isn't
it?'

'That's my business,' she says. 'And that's another thing:
I have my own life. And I don't want to hear your opinion
on everything I do. Got that? And no more swearing. Right?'

'Yes, boss.'

She takes a sip and I pass her a cigarette.

'Now what do you plan to do?'

'I don't know. I want to get straight. I want to sort myself
out here, Nan. I haven't got anywhere else to go.'

'That's OK, I'm not pressuring you. We'll see what we
can do with each other. Why don't we make a deal?'

'You're hitting me for cash? I'm getting hit up by my own nan? You old robber.'

'Be quiet. The deal is, I won't ask you what you're going to do for another two weeks. Then, when those two weeks are up, I'll ask you again. And you're going to give me an answer. A proper one. How about that?'

'OK.'

'Nothing big. But you have to make a decision. I can't sit here and watch you stew, not getting yourself back on your feet.'

'I understand.'

'Is that a deal?'

'Yes.'

I listened to her knowing that it's best to let people believe the worst then surprise them. Keep everyone's expectations nice and low. That night I closed the door of the room and I cried because I thought everything I once had was lost. I looked at the map of my life and saw that the painfully charted contours and red lines had dropped from the page. It is now blank on both sides. After all my plans and my education, here I am, watching quiz shows with my nan, with a busted bank account and no job. If I'd wanted this kind of aimless life I would never have bothered cheating in my exams.

**37**

*Q.* What do families with no love and no stuff have?
*A.* No place in suburbia.

In my old man's garage there seemed to be a thousand old products, boxes of what you could call stuff. Over time, acquiring the stuff got more important than acquiring love, and it is indicative of nothing in particular. Except maybe greed. Call it over-providing. It makes people feel good about themselves. You need stuff when you don't have love, to show people you're making it. After all, the minimum you need to function in suburbia is a happy husband, a happy wife and one kid who makes everyone happy. If for some reason this doesn't happen, mum and dad can separate and repeat the experiment in another house. A new house filled with more new stuff. A new kitchen, a new family and a dealership-maintained automobile. Where's the love? The same thing is happening again. The new house is the same as the old one, the kids look the same and the TV is twice the size. But we must have left something in the shop with the pots and pans. Where's the love? The big love is missing. So we buy more stuff, and use that instead. To show the love we get. I love you so much that I have financed you a new kitchen. We only care about what other people can see. If you can't stick it in someone's face, on the driveway, then it has no purpose. If you can't throw it away without caring after one week then it's a burden. Anything that isn't worth an HP form is surplus; a cat for example is a burden. You can't make someone sick with envy because you've got a new cat. You can't upgrade a cat. You can't turn a new cat up really loud, or leave the box it came in out front or drive it up and down the street really fast.

And how the fuck do you get rid of it when you're bored? Cats aren't disposable enough. The ultimate suburban pet can be bought in seconds, starved in a week and buried in the back garden by a drunk man in less than half an hour. Cats, like outsized rabbits, are an enormous liability requiring an equally big hole. Everything must be readily disposable. Obviously, ponies are out. It is not acceptable to order a skip and put a dead horse into it. That would be horrible.

We can get by without love, but not a decent credit history. Suburbia has evolved to function without love, not money. I think that it has been like this for a long time. I try to remember moments of big love in my family. But all I can summon up is a memory of the togetherness that resulted from a major appliance upgrade.

One hour away from her arrival at my parents' house I was thinking that if we could treat Sarah like new white goods then we'd be OK. We were meant to be cooking her dinner, but because my father said something he shouldn't have all preparations had come to a furious halt, which was a joke as Mum only seemed to cook to spite us anyway. I wished I had a shotgun. Instead of screaming with them I'd been hiding in the garage nearly all morning. I was twenty-three years old and I wanted to marry my girlfriend, whom

I loved, but the sight of my parents continuously grating at each other like raw carrot was disturbing. I was, am, scared of becoming like them and this fear was holding me back. We had long stopped caring; we had stopped still. We didn't buy new stuff any more and the house had become like a tomb. What once lived in here was dead and we were stuck for eternity playing out our anger like a bunch of Elizabethan ghosts, pleading old woe into vacant spaces.

I remember standing in the kitchen doorway staring at my mother bent over her puzzle magazine.

The time had passed when I could depend on her for anything. She looked up at me and she whined, 'Why is she coming here today?'

Her hair was like dirty straw. Horse bedding. Damp. Mud where her brain should have been. She needed vitamins.

'It's a fucking Sunday,' I shouted. 'People visit people on Sundays!'

'It's meant to be a rest day!'

'You think if you do fuck all it won't happen. I didn't want her to come here and see this. It disgusts me how you don't give a fuck. You make me feel ashamed.'

'Watch your mouth! Harold, do something!'

'You look like shit,' I said.

'Are you ashamed of me?' she shouted back.

'Yeah, I'm ashamed,' I said. I felt no sympathy. 'I get ashamed when you get like this, and will you stop fucking drinking.'

'I'm cooking! You stop drinking!'

I was pointing at her with a half-drunk bottle of beer still in my hand.

'Why do you need to be shit-faced to cook?'

'I'm not shit-faced! I'm not shit-faced!' she screamed.

'You did this to me. You made me like this. I need my weekends and look at me now.'

'What do you need your weekends for? You don't fucking do anything! Two weeks ago I told you she was coming! Two fucking weeks ago.'

I pick up a cardboard lid from one of the packets she has in the oven. It's a Chinese party selection.

'What's this crap? Are you mental? You're making my head hurt.'

'I've cleaned this house from top to bottom.'

She started to cry after that.

I'd told her about this two weeks ago. It's like she was thinking that if she didn't cook any food then nothing was going to happen.

'She's going to be here in an hour,' I said, leaning over her. She was still crying. 'No matter what you do or don't do, she's coming.'

I could hear my old man switching the channel on the TV, looking for a something louder, maybe a Grand Prix. He did nothing for her. She sat in the kitchen filling empty boxes with tiny letters in women's weekly magazines, living an isolated, sexless life. She was frustrated. She was angry. This was not her dream, but I do not know how to help her. She got married to Harold not me. A TV and a bowl of peanuts seemed to be all he asked for from life.

'You're ashamed of us. You're ashamed of this house.'

'Did you just work that out?' I said.

'Look at yourself, you're the one with the problem. I'm not doing anything different.'

'I can fucking see that. I tell you what. Dad, what do you reckon? Do you mind if I take a few ornaments and go down to the Wimpy? I could spread them around there, warm the place up a bit. That would take fuck-all effort. And you and her could even sit at another table. Or how about when Sarah gets here I keep her standing outside and just show her some Polaroids of the family while you shout through the letter box.' Pointing my finger at her, accusing. 'You horrible cow.'

I went to the cupboard over the sink and pulled out a nasty-looking tumbler. I filled it with red wine from a brown plastic barrel and walked calmly into the garage. I could really end up hurting myself in here. I sat down and sipped at the booze and read the labels on the cans of paint, flicking through old records, waiting for the hot mist to blow away.

I'm sure now that Sarah knew that I was going to ask her to marry me. She also thought it was strange that I kept her away from my parents.

'I don't want them involved,' I said.

'But I'll have to meet them one day.'

'Why?' I said.

'You have to tell them about me. Are you crazy?'

'Why?' I say. 'Why ruin it?'

They'd been to the cash and carry and the garage was full of coffee and bog roll, which seemed like a logical progression. I bet her parents didn't hoard toilet roll. They must have had about 200 rolls in there. I thought it was bad enough buying a large nine-pack in a supermarket. But 200 rolls? People must think all you do is shit. That's enough paper to deal with a whole mountain of turd.

When she did ring on the door the house fell silent as if two barrels of a shotgun had exploded into the ceiling.

I darted out of the garage, rushing for the front door. In one look on opening that door I must have communicated to Sarah the state of mind of everyone in that house.

But she smiled, thinking that I was joking. OK, I laughed back, you think this is funny, go ahead.

'Hello, Mrs Marshall. I'm Sarah Cane,' she said. I had never seen her non-sexual, cake-baking, junior royal act before. My mum stepped forward, wrapped in one of her better cardigans, and almost bent at the knee.

'Hello, Sarah, how lovely to meet you. Do come in.'

'Thank you,' said Sarah graciously, immediately focusing on the three framed family shots kept by the telephone. I liked to think that these were the pictures we'd be happiest for the newspapers to use if we all ended up murdering each other.

'Oh what lovely pictures,' she said, gently touching my picture with the animated, delicate care of Snow White.

My mother wilted like a guard dog on receiving two pounds of drugged mince.

'This must be Charlie again,' said Sarah. Who else's kid was it going to be?

She pointed to a picture of me dressed up as Zorro. I looked like a pig with a bin lid tied to its head.

'Three?' she asked.

'Two years old in that one,' said my mum.

'Two! My goodness! And is that in the garden of this house?'

'Yes, it's a real family garden,' said my mother.

'Have you lived here long?'

'Twenty-five years,' said Mum with great pride. 'And this is my husband, Harold.'

'Hello, Mr Marshall,' she said.

'June,' he said. 'I mean, call me Harold.'

'Yes, June,' says Sarah.

We all laughed like the comedy moment at the end of

*Scooby Doo.* By the time we got to the sitting room I was ready to bite down on a grenade. Sarah and I cuddled up on one sofa, my parents on the other. Between us, a coffee table heavy with lies. Harold smiled at June. June smiled at Harold. They were now happily married again. I'd been ready to leave this all burning in flames behind me, my new life beyond their values. But I was in the midst of creating a new *Daily Mail* life. It's like suburbia had been designed especially for this moment. Animals don't do this. Bring their mates back home for approval before breeding. This meeting was way beyond biological necessity. Is this some part of evolution? Do couples who have the approval of their parents stand a better chance of survival and mating? It was fucking eugenics in action. Only those we approve of will breed!

'Charlie and I have been together a year,' she said to my mother.

'Really? Has it been that long?'

'Yes, it's dragged by for me as well.' She laughed.

June smiled knowingly at Harold.

'I don't know why he's been hiding you from us.'

'I don't know either,' said Sarah.

They both look at me, the idiot in the stocks.

June smiled again and Sarah squeezed my hand – see, it's not so bad.

'We've been busy,' I plead.

'But you don't do anything,' said Harold.

My head disintegrates in a small cloud of grey dust.

I needed Sarah to hate her but she handled my mother effortlessly. She knew what to say and how to say it. She knew what people wanted to hear.

'He really keeps himself to himself,' said my mother. 'You

know, we don't see him much any more.' She paused to look at me. 'Though that's a relief, I can tell you.'

'I can imagine!' said Sarah.

More laughter. She thinks this is amusing. She turns to me quickly and winks. There is nothing to wink about.

'Shall I make tea?' Harold, having ditched the tin of beer, was walking around with a teapot.

'And you must have some cake.'

This is insane. Is a pantomime horse going to bring in the cake, wedged in its wooden teeth? Or clowns with biscuits?

'You must come to visit my parents, Mrs Marshall, they'd love to have you.'

'Well really . . .'

'No, they really would.'

'Would you like tea?' says my mother.

'What?' I say.

Waves of heat were rising out of my shirt. My head was beginning to go light. Maybe I needed a glass of water or something. This is love I thought. For a month I'd been having these feelings, these fits. Like suffocating, drowning in the future of fear. Sometimes they happened on the train to work. One minute I'd be reading the paper and the next I'd think about Sarah and all the ifs and my arms would fly up in the air. I'd have to cuddle myself silent, shouting silent and hoarse, and get off the train when I could. This is the pressure of responsibility, I thought. I felt like I could touch my heart through the material of my shirt.

'What?' said my mum.

'What?' I said.

'What? Is that any way to speak? Did we bring you up to speak like that?'

I take a deep breath and felt the soles of my feet touch the ground.

'Of course you didn't!' said Sarah.

'No, I did not!' said June.

'You said "what" to me,' I said.

Sarah laughed and pecked me on the cheek and then followed my mother out of the room. She loved me even though I was a freak who attacked himself on the train every morning and had parents who hated each other, wanted to divorce, yet still bulk-bought toilet roll. She was beautiful and funny, and making jokes and doing her best, while I only wanted the impossible. For her to reassure me that this would not be us in twenty years' time, when I was sure this was us now.

# 38

We eat spaghetti bolognese in the garden and listen to the radio. The cricket, the snooker, horse racing and anything else we can find on medium wave. Anything but the news. When the news comes on I have to stop whatever I'm doing and find another station before she gets upset. She claims that she's heard all the news the first time round and if she hasn't heard it then it hasn't happened and can't upset her. This goes back to the missile crisis, she says. Foreign stations are best. Anything that sounds exotic enough to help her imagine that she's in Arabia with Omar Sharif or Peter O'Toole. Sometimes she'll make me get the dates from the sideboard, which look as though they might have spent decades preserved in the same lurid wax box. They look like decomposed mice.

'Oh leave it on that one, leave that on.' Some impossible Moroccan jam session wheels out of the radio's single speaker. She shuts her eyes and fills her mind with blue skies and never-ending dunes.

The music takes me back to jobs in hot places. The best of the old times. Knocked out of my head on pipes and coming to under the setting sun, red-faced and dazed.

'Jesus, Nan,' I say as she bites into one of the brown cocoons, tearing on the innards like a kestrel.

The other thing she does is play the horses. She likes to make her selections through the morning, then bet in the afternoon, usually on the last couple of races. This way she can make her money last longer and keep the buzz going all day. When I first got here she sent me to the bookie's to lay her little bets daily. I was annoyed at first because just being in a bookie's again could get me into trouble. It's not a bad way to kill a day, making little bets, drinking cheap soup. That burn you get in your stomach when you're close to the win can become addictive. Personally, I've never lost enough to truly experience that world-ending, tunnel-vision lust, not only to win but to punish the bookie, punish the casino, have it all back and more. So after I mention to her that being around a load of desperate gambling addicts might not be wise for me right now, she relents. I tell her that sooner or later I would have to lay some bets of my own, and that would be a big step back for me. I think it shocks her to see me back away from such a mundane little pleasure. I tell her I'll make it up to her but she says there's no need and makes me turn my back while she hides her pile of blank slips. I offer to set her up a phone account but she says no. I get the impression that at some point in the past the betting has been a bigger part of her life than she lets on.

When the sun shines we get out of the kitchen and lie around in the garden. It might look lush and green but the turf was probably laid over old war scrap. Even the solitary tree looks like it grew from fallen ordnance and is infested with plump wrinkled caterpillars. I remember that I always had to watch myself round here. Especially at the end of the garden where there's still a compost heap of mouldering kitchen and cat matter. There always seemed to be more splinters, bruises, scratches, thorns and nails to be found in this garden than anywhere else on earth.

Due to the risk involved we rarely make it to the grass from the security of the concrete. Instead we'll sit in deck-chairs staring at the grass, commenting on it. When we're bored of that I'll bring her cups of tea or glasses of sangria, depending on the weather, and she'll talk about Grandad, and me coming here as a kid and how beautiful everybody thought I was. I'm happy to sit by her, listening. You get told a lot of stuff by your grandparents as a kid but you never take it in. But something about the stories begins to move me. Now, I listen. These are possible eventualities. It's not just the stories about me that I suddenly care about. It's the stories in newspapers that I never would have read before. I realized yesterday that I've been secretly tracking the marriages of at least three celebrity couples. Couples close to my age. Couples with babies. With jobs and houses and all that big stuff. I want to see how they're getting on. Now when Nan talks about Grandad I listen. Not because I want to know what he did in the war, but how he did all this. Made his house, his life, his family. Nan says it was no different then, apart from the Germans and not having computers. I tell her that she is in denial about her war pain and she tells me to bugger off.

Usually we'll stay out in the sunshine until I get sore and begin to seriously dehydrate. Then I sit inside in the dark, watching her sleeping under the hot sun, skin like beaten leather. This is the best time of all. When there are no jobs to be done or bets to be laid or windows to be cleaned and I have the house to myself for a couple of hours.

When it starts to rain, then I have to play games.

'This is not your second childhood,' I tell her.

'Just play this last hand,' she says.

I hate her games. They are all bent, fixed, contorted versions of family favourites, the widely known rules and standards altered in favour of her. I try to teach her how to play dice in the covered alleyway outside the house, but it's impossible to get the betting structure and odds into her head so we end up playing Kaluki, which is a nasty old lady's version of rummy. Throughout the game she is trying to confuse me. She tells me what she's read in her supermarket paperbacks about ancient space-travelling civilizations giving us our culture. Whenever I look like I'm onto a good hand, she'll tell me that there's a giant library hidden under the Sphinx, which only the richest people in the world are allowed to enter. Enough is enough. I try to drag her out to play dice again but the only place we can play is the tunnel where the horse-dog lives and that smells of ammonia and raw mince. She also complains because you have to crouch and it's cold and damp, which is bad for her knees. I give in and as a 'compromise' she breaks out one of those mini casino compendiums – with the tiddlywinks for chips and the plastic roulette wheel. She gets to be house, and I have to buy chips from her. She rakes every hand of blackjack and she won't cover evens bets on roulette. That every game we play involves money is natural to her. Why play cards if you're not playing for money? Where's the fun? You have to risk something, she says.

Days pass and she keeps torturing me with an ongoing threat of cribbage. I also find she has a dark streak. She thinks everyone she hasn't seen in two days is dead and it doesn't upset her. Where is the paper boy? He's been run over? Where's the milkman. Have you heard an ambulance?

Have you seen Mavis over the road. Go and stick your nose in her letter box and see if you can smell something funny.

With the games and torture and the diversions she begins to crack through a shell that I hadn't even realized existed. As blind as I am, I can see I am in a place where I am served nothing but happy memories. I begin to remember times with a black and white simplicity. Times when I got to do this aimless stuff all day. Exploring, crying, playing, getting cheated out of money. Everywhere I look I can see my dad. I can see him installing the cooker. Opening a jar of cucumber relish. Painting the shed at the bottom of the garden – which he did in a dark granite hue. Nan said it looked like a mausoleum and every time she looked at it she crossed herself. I also remember crashing through the asbestos roof of the same shed and landing on an old bike. Which hurt.

When Nan's cat doesn't come back at night I have to stand around the bins under the flats whacking a tin of cat food shouting 'Davey boy' in the dark. It sounds like the worst kind of hopeful cruising. 'Davey, Davey boy!' What a way to go. Getting my head smashed in some Met no-go area for a cat with whom I have an indifferent relationship. In the cold I think of Constance. She is more like me than Sarah is, but does that mean we are more compatible? I don't know. Increasingly I think that compatibility is for throw rugs and armchairs, not for human beings. We are too complicated.

The cat doesn't show and Nan is abrupt with my failure. I have to tell her to take it somewhere else because I can't handle disapproval now. Coming from her even the smallest bad word seems like the end of the world. She is the last person I have left. I have to do right by her. But because she loves her cat she is unrelenting and fierce. I'm reduced to sulking upstairs, my fingers reeking of pink salmon. A stink that I know won't wash off.

I get out my notes from the cupboard again. Mostly I just stare at them in the pile. I know what's in there but I can't face reading them and curl up with my back to them. When I do flick through them, I skip the forms and look at the notes and the doodles that we passed back and forth. Sklansky with large testicles. Celeste with large testicles. A better one of Celeste with large testicles that was actually drawn by Celeste. There are also the notes from Constance. When I read them back, I realize how much I pursued her. A flood of notes between two scared people. Some mundane, some stupid. Nearly all seem wrong and provocative and irresponsible. We had no business behaving like this.

'What did I say that was wrong? R U OK?'

Another says, 'Yooooo Rrr Sooooooo clever!'

I'm not clever. Why didn't I write a note back saying she was wrong? I tricked her. I misrepresented myself. I did the same with Sarah. I let her think I was one thing while I was another. I am as bad as one of those men who pretend that they're in the SAS and turn up at their girlfriend's house at three in the morning claiming to have just come back from operations.

Another note reads, 'Don't you like me any more? Can we meet in TV room 8 p.m.?'

Ashamed, I want to screw it up and force it into some crack in the wall. I go downstairs and find Nan drinking sherry. She still hasn't forgiven me for not finding that cat of hers and won't switch on the TV. She wants to sit there in the dark. Which puts me in a temper. I lie back on the furry tassel-ridden lined suite with my feet up on the far arm.

Hidden in the darkness, I tell her about this space in me that I always have to fill.

'Well, if you didn't have a hole you wouldn't have room for anyone else, would you?

'What does that mean?'

'Somewhere inside there is a part of us that we keep for others.'

'What, like a lung?'

'No, not a bloody lung.'

'What then?'

'Well, it would be sweet. Like a piece of sweet fudge, a part of ourselves that's pure. Love that you can give to someone.'

'You're pissed.'

'That's what your grandfather called it: fudge. That's right, the part of us that we give when we're in love. That was his name for me, you know. I was his little piece of fudge. It's the best of us.'

'Right.'

'If you don't even believe it, then you have no hope. I throw up my hands.'

'Calm down or I'll hide the bottle.'

'It's in all of us. You have to love yourself a little, you see. That love comes from the same place. You use that to love yourself. To have dignity and respect for yourself. And it builds up until there's enough to share.'

'Like earwax?'

She eyes me suspiciously.

'You can give big, you can give small. But you can always give. But if it's not there in the first place, or you can't find it, or make jokes about it and don't believe in it then what do you really have to give? Nothing.'

'Well, if it's that sweet why would you give it away?'

'Because it's the best of us.'

'Right. So keep it. Why get hurt? Keep all the love inside.'

'But it doesn't make sense not to give it to anyone. Or even to stop wanting to give just because you are scared someone is going to . . .'

'Swallow it in one go and then fuck off.'

'Well . . .'

'Like I did to Sarah. Like she did to me?'

'Maybe. Only you know that. You see there is nothing to be frightened of because it works both ways. The love you give you always get back. You have to give.'

'Hmm.'

'And the love you'll get back should fill that empty space and then some. More than you think.'

Nan is too old and too drunk to climb the stairs on her own. I carry her the last flight and leave her sitting up in bed, fully dressed with a fag hanging out of her mouth. She looks like Ron Wood. Downstairs, I switch on the TV and go to one of the bad channels looking for any kind of distraction. I look at the TV, I look at the telephone and next to it the pottery postman. I could call Sarah. This is the first real privacy I have had since before the wedding. I need to get my stuff back. 'What do you think?' I ask the postman. The postman's alert pose, his Zen-like self-acceptance, taunts me. The thought of speaking to Sarah sends a bowling ball of acid through my digestive system. She can't be mad at me for wanting my stuff back? Can she? I turn to the bone-china Cornish milkmaid. 'Of course she can,' says the milkmaid. 'She's a woman, silly.' I'm then wracked by three back-splitting stomach cramps which I try to walk off like a dancer on an old game show, head to the side, then backwards and forwards with my hands on my hips. The last time I saw Sarah was at the hospital when she sped away from me, angry, crying. Even if she never wants to hear from me again she has to be expecting this call. My one chance. My last chance. My breath is dry and hot and burns the tip of my nose. I remove two layers of clothing. Naked with the telephone, I still have options. I do not have to dial.

'Yeah, it's me.'

'Oh,' she says. 'Hi. Hello?'

'Is it OK this?'

'Erm.'

'I mean I can call another time.'

'No. No. It's fine. I just wasn't expecting you. Are you on a payphone? I could call you back?'

'No. I've left hospital.'

'Oh right. Wow. Are you OK?'

'Yeah. I signed out a week ago. Don't tell your mother. I know she wants me in there, wired to the wall, getting shocks.'

'She does. So where are you now?'

'I'm at my nan's.'

'How is she?'

'Pissed and smoking in bed.'

'Oh that's good, so you're looking after each other.'

'That's right. I go out looking for her cat and when I find it we both get fed.'

'Sounds like your kind of arrangement. One you can handle anyway.'

'I caught that. That was you being rude.'

'Sorry. Do you think I'm getting meaner?'

'Sharper maybe. It's a new you.'

We have a silence like we used to when we could hold

the phone to our ears for hours and not even say a word, only listen to each other breathing.

'What are you doing?' I ask.

'Watching TV. A film. Channel Five.'

'Hold on, I'll switch. What's it about?'

'Well. This woman's husband has an affair and he tries to kill her. Then she ruins his life by taking over his company.'

'Oh.'

'She's just taken over. He's a real cheating bastard.'

'Yeah. I still don't know why you haven't put the phone down.'

'Neither do I,' she says.

'Do you want to?'

'No. I'll put it down when I want to and not when you tell me.'

'You sure?'

'So why are you calling me at ten o'clock? You could call me at work. What do you want?'

'I want to speak to you.'

I know she's glad I phoned. Then my courage drops away and I remember that I need my stuff.

'My stuff. It must be getting in your way. I thought now was the time to come and get it. To help you move on.'

'Move on? You haven't got any stuff.'

'My ornaments. My hats. My special blanket.'

'That's not stuff, that's jumble.'

'No. I hate to break it to you but that's all my stuff.'

'Oh right. Really?'

'Well, apart from the bag I took to hospital. I know I might have led you to believe I had better stuff somewhere else, but really that's it.'

'You haven't amassed much, have you?'

'No.'

Once I had everything in place. But everything wasn't enough. I was still unhappy. 'I just need my basics for now. I'm cutting down.'

'Oh. Like what?'

On TV a woman with giant shoulder pads, obviously a housewife, is leading a rebellion in a sweatshop which will no doubt lead to extra employee benefits and possibly crèche facilities.

'How can you watch this shit? Can't her husband just call security and get her fired?'

'He's not the boss of her now. She's the boss of him.'

'That's no answer to their problem.'

'You're right.'

'He has to learn to listen to his wife, take her on as an equal partner and stop his exploiting ways.'

'You're spoiling it.'

'Sorry. It's not going to end with a fierce gun battle, is it?'

'Don't ridicule me.'

'I wasn't. Sorry. I'm nervous, that's all.'

'What do you mean?'

I can't finish this. I . . .

'You make me nervous.'

'I make *you* nervous?'

'Well yeah. I also have to ask you something.'

'I think I can take it,' she says.

'It's like a difficult question.'

'Like what?'

There are two places I can take this conversation. I can press her for my belongings. I can go cold and find my diary and get a date and a time. Liaise with Ray to use the van. I can clean myself out of her life now and her out of mine. Do what I was going to do. I can bleach this conversation of all hope and expectation or I can keep pushing. Find that part of me I thought was gone. That sweet thing. The soul butter.

'Like do you have a man friend?'

'What's it to you?' she says.

'I need to know.'

I know Ben is gone. But I also know that he will come back when it pleases him.

'You do?'

'I have a right to know. I still have dibs on what you're doing and who you're doing it with.'

'What!' she squeals. 'I can't believe you fucking said that!'

'It's the law.'

'I don't believe you.'

'Sorry. I may not like it, you may not like it, but it is half true.'

'Charlie . . .'

'You know it. Just admit I have dibs and I'll sleep better.'

We don't have to be on the phone; we could be lying in bed talking in the darkness. Just because I can't see her, doesn't mean I can't see her.

'I'm going to put the phone down.'

'No, no, don't do that. Sorry. Have you though? Got a man friend? Just so I know for my files. There isn't some big hairy bloke with his feet up next to you, is there? Sharpening my knife collection? Called Steve? Six foot four? Ex-para? Finding it hard to adjust to life on Civvy Street?'

'I'm not sure you have a right to ask me that.'

'I'm looking out for you.'

'Now you're looking out for me?'

'Yes. I am.'

Her voice turns red.

'It's a little late for that, isn't it, Charlie?'

'I still love you. I still care about you.'

'What about that girl? Shouldn't you be looking out for her?'

'I was never seeing her.'

'Well, what was that then?'

'You want me to tell you?'

'You don't have to tell me if you don't want to.'

'This isn't easy for me.'

I'm ashamed to have to tell her how it failed. How there was nothing there and I mistook this girl for her. I have to take a breath between each word. 'She. I used her. I want you to know the truth. I was stupid. I thought there was something real between us.'

'Right.'

'But all the emotions were feelings I had for you. She was a replacement for you. A replacement, that's all. I mean she was beautiful like you and reminded me of you and I had this crush infatuation, for her.'

'And now?'

'She is messed up. She was, is. I hurt her, like you said that day in the car park. When I hurt you as well.'

The words are coming out smaller and smaller.

'People around me get hurt. I have the best intentions, I don't know why.' I can't hear my own words. 'I'm sorry,' I whisper. 'I want to have people in my life, but I don't know how to without hurting them.'

'You didn't have to tell me all that.'

'No, I did. You should know it all,' I say.

Call waiting sounds in the background.

'Thank you for being honest.'

Can she even hear me? I feel so tired.

'I do have to speak to you about my stuff. Can I call you back again? Another time?'

'Charlie?'

'No, really, it's cool. I'm sorry.'

Call waiting again.

'Charlie, I don't want to leave you like this.'

'Babe,' I say, not even looking at the handset, 'you already did.'

I switch calls.

'Charlie?'

'Ray.'

'All right?'

I get up out of the chair still feeling hot and walk to the kitchen window, stretching. Outside I see an old lady who could be Nan struggling with two bulky carrier bags filled with cheap meat and vegetables in the dark street. She turns to look at me and smiles. I smile at her back and think about waving until I realize that I'm naked.

'Paintball,' he says.

I walk backwards from the window.

'Paintball with a broken arm? When?'

'Tomorrow,' he says. 'I'm a man down and I thought it would be good for you to get outdoors. Run around the forest shooting people in the head.'

'I'm not the type,' I say.

'What type do you have to be, tell me?'

'I don't know. Nerds with fat arses who couldn't get in the paras. Blokes who shoot cats with air rifles. Middle management gun freaks who fantasize about proving themselves in war and know how to build squirrel traps. Blokes with tricked out Vauxhall Corsas with dumb-bells in their bedrooms who probably read *Club International*. Men with bushy moustaches who smell of massage oil. And anyone bi-curious who owns a rubber knife. Them mostly.'

'Do you want to come or not? It'll be me and you and some mates, normal blokes. Yes or no.'

'Ray, you're putting me on the spot here what with the arm and everything.'

'Yes or no.'

'I haven't even got a beard.'

I never expected him to forgive me again. I let him down time after time and he always comes back. I think he must want me to go or he wouldn't call. I could do this for him; it would be a start. It's not like anyone will actually know I've been paintballing except Ray's weird mates.

'Yes or no?' he says. 'I have got other people who want to come.'

'I'll do it,' I say. 'Count me in.'

'I'll pick you up at 7.30 a.m.'

'When?'

'7.30 a.m. tomorrow morning.'

'Tomorrow morning? That's in six hours.'

'Well, you better get some sleep then.'

I can't imagine the kind of blokes who want to be out of bed at 7.30 a.m. on a Saturday morning. What do they have – yellow beaks and orange feathers?

**39**

We are sitting at picnic tables set in a forest clearing, eating stale sausage sandwiches and drinking weak tea. Ray says that I'm trying to wind him up on purpose, but all I'm trying to do is establish the acceptable behavioural parameters of paintball.

'Can I drop the gun and do karate at close quarters?'

'No.'

'Can I use a rubber knife on people?'

'No.'

'Do you have a rubber knife?'

'No.'

'Can I jump on people from trees?'

'No.'

'Can I hide in the trees then?'

'No.'

'Can I bury myself in a wall of clay then jump out when you walk past, like a clay man, surprising you, because you thought I was just a wall of mud and clay and then kill you?'

'No,' says Ray. 'This is sport, not combat. You have to use the paint gun. You can't use anything else.'

'That's not true,' says Ray's mate, Steve. 'They sell paint grenades here.'

Grenades!

'Ray, can I get a grenade and bite down on it when my base gets stormed, rather than be taken alive?' I say.

'No,' says Ray, while Steve applies orange tape to his upper arm. 'The grenades are four pound a go and they haven't got any in stock.'

Eric, another of Ray's friends, brings him a bacon roll. I think I could easily fit two of my fingers inside only one of Eric's giant nostrils.

'So what's the plan?' he says.

Ray obviously has some kind of reputation here. They ask his opinion on everything from tactics to goggle management. He squints like Clint Eastwood. He uses phrases like 'weaver stance'. As we get up to ready ourselves for game one, he takes me aside.

'What do you think of the boys?' he asks me.

'Good,' I say, suspicious of the question. What he meant to say was, 'What's the problem, aren't they cool enough for you?' He knows that ordinarily I'd have classified them mostly as nerds. Self-conscious/awkward would be one way of putting it. And since working at the magazine I've got used to a higher grade of idiot in the shape of Alex, Ben and Doyle. Sharper, faster and meaner with it. Every one of us the class joker. Every word spoken drop-dead funny, spot on, flawless.

'You seem a little hyper,' he says.

'Me? Hyper?' I say.

'Yeah,' he says, 'hyper. You know, you can relax. No one knows anything about you. You can be yourself here.'

'Be myself?'

'I get the same around strangers, don't worry. Now put your goggles on.' He pulls aside a large piece of netting so I can walk through to another section. 'We're going to get our guns now.'

Ray is hiding behind a tree stump. I think I can walk through the middle of the forest, tree to tree, picking off the opposition as I go. I get about twenty yards before someone on the other team goes for a head shot and taps me three times. Once in the temple, and twice in the neck. It's like having a tennis ball served directly into the side of my head.

Behind me, in the distance, I can hear Ray screaming. He is already compensating for my failure to obey orders by pushing Steve and Eric down my flank. Phut, phut, phut. Yellow paintballs splatter the trees, splitting apart in the scrub around my head. I am hit another five times and wriggling for cover when my assailant starts to scream in an unbroken voice, 'Steward! Steward! Paint check, paint check!'

I am nonsensical with pain. I want to hear the comforting sound of chopper blades whup, whup, whupping overhead but instead I get a nineteen-year-old in an orange vest telling me to leave the game.

'Get up,' he says, kicking me in the leg. 'Bloody get up, you're out.' Ray, meanwhile, continues the fight, running and hiding like victory is freedom's last hope.

When we meet up for lunch the rest of the team can hardly believe the injustice of my being asked to leave combat.

'Head shots are illegal,' says Steve. 'They should have put you straight back in after the paint check.'

I didn't want to stay in. I felt a faint embarrassment. I'd been shot in the throat. It hurt.

'Shit, I forgot head shots were illegal,' I say. 'If I'd known that then I would have gone back in.'

'No, you did the right thing,' says Ray, adding to my spurious defence. 'You can't be shot in the head and be allowed back in; rules or no rules, a head shot has to count. In a real war that would have been it.' He points at the paint splatter directly over his solar plexus. 'I have to come to terms with the fact that in a real war I could be missing a large piece of my spine now.'

'But you're not and it's not real. It's a game,' says Steve's mate, Eric, who sounds like a bassoon thanks to his huge bony nose. 'I mean, in the next round we could all be Ewoks for what it matters to the reality of it.'

'That's what you'd like, isn't it?' says Ray. 'To be one of the little monkeys in *Star Wars*? Singing little songs. Wee, wee, wee. Dancing round a fire. Look at me, I'm an Ewok.'

'Fuck off,' says Eric, blowing his words through his musical nose. 'I didn't mean that and you know it.' Eric, who is obviously a *Star Wars* geek, walks off to the snack hut in disgust and it starts to drizzle. We all begin to load up on pellets and clean our masks for the afternoon session.

The conversation is more relaxed than any I've known in a long time. It's like people can say what they are thinking without being humiliated. It is not a test and you're not likely to be cross-examined on what you say.

In the confusion of activity I slip out. I'm glad I came, but running around with a cast on my arm and firing the gun one-handed is too much for me. I stagger to the car park thinking that I can sleep in the back of Ray's van for a couple of hours. As the rain begins to get heavier, I find the doors locked and instead crawl underneath. The boiler suit that I'm wearing, the protective balaclava and the remaining heat of the engine are enough to keep me warm and dry. I lie there in the mud and grit, watching the raindrops begin to fill the potholes in the dirt track, my eyes slowly closing, my body heavy, my clothes snug, the forest turning darker, more silent.

I'm woken up by Ray pulling me out from under the van by my ankles.

'I was under there thinking what a good set of mates you have,' I say.

'Sleeping under vehicles is fucking dangerous. What the fuck are you doing; do you want to do this or not?'

'Don't be fucked off, Ray. I'm loving it, I am.'

'Then why are you sleeping under the van?'

'Because I'm tired, I've got a broken arm and I haven't done any exercise in two years. I'm not up to it. I'm waddling around like Steven Seagal in there.'

'You're a real twat, you know that?'

'What? Ray, relax.'

'I get you out here, you say you'll do it, then you just don't bother. How do you think that makes me look?'

'Ray,' I plead from the floor, 'I'm loving it, I really am. I like being here. This is me relaxing. I swear I'm not hiding. It's the opposite. I'm chilled. I like your mates.' This doesn't sound honest. I'm so cynical most of the time that people just don't believe me when I'm being sincere any more. 'I'm having a great day, I swear. I can relax here. You know how it is when you feel that you're being watched. Well, it's hard to explain, Ray, but I feel the opposite with your mates. I'm sorry about falling asleep; I couldn't help it. If there's another game going I'd like to play. Help me up.'

He grabs my good arm and pulls.

'I don't suppose it is all that practical, is it?'

'What?' I say.

'You running around a wet forest with your arm in a cast.'

'Fuck it, Ray, when did I ever do the sensible thing?'

'Are you sure you're good?'

'Yes, I'm sure. I came here to, er, paintball, and that's what I'm going to do. I just felt sleepy, and even though your mates are all freaks and Ewok-lovers you can still be my red leader any time.'

He eyes me more suspiciously than ever.

'I'm trying to communicate with you here. I am not being sarcastic; tell me what I have to do.'

'Just stick close to me,' he shouts.

'Oh my God, I can't believe you said that. I think I'm blushing. Don't say anything like that again.'

'C'mon, Charlie, on me!' He starts running towards the woods.

I am glad that we are friends again. But I am even more relieved that there are no women around to see or hear any of this.

At the hospital a stink like the bottom of an old steel bin is coming from inside my cast. The radiographer places my arm on the bench and retreats behind his screen. I wish I could leave my arm here and join him. Still visible is a faint outline of a squirrel with giant balls. It seems almost inconceivable that my arm has set correctly. However, despite my own early attempts at home surgery, the pictures he takes reveal good things.

'What have you been doing to this?' says the nurse, who is very pretty.

There are six deep diagonal scars cut into the plaster, one for each big sin. My little reminders. She takes a pair of cutters and starts to work down.

'Be careful,' I say.

'Don't worry. It looks worse than it is.'

I hate it that she's so pretty. No one wants to be near a pretty woman when their arm smells this bad.

'I think there might be a family of mice in there,' I say.

'Are you sure?' she says. 'My money would be on prawns.'

I'm still laughing when she finishes cutting. Mostly from embarrassment. She helps me wash my arm clean.

'Do you want to keep it?' she says, pointing at the cast, wincing.

'Why?'

'Some people like to keep it as a souvenir.'

I am looking at my arm. I haven't seen it since the wedding. It's like a part of me has been encapsulated, blindfolded and is ignorant of all the change. Does that make it worse than the rest of me or better? I was hardly conscious of its breaking. And then the bones that were separated came together again, meshed, re-wove themselves as one, better and stronger even than before. I look at my arm, intent on finding a truth hidden in its mending.

'I can see you're having a bit of a moment.'

'We've been through a lot,' I say.

The nurse takes the cast and places it on the side table.

I look at it. The mess of pocks, dinks and harsh furrows carved into it. I think about it sitting in a hazmat bin.

'You know that broken bones heal stronger,' she says.

'Yeah,' I say. 'I know that already.'

Yesterday I got a call from a car magazine about coming up with some feature ideas. I think about the easy salary and writing long pompous articles criticizing gears and clutch ratios, oversteer and shafts and pistons. I imagine spending my days reviewing giant inferiority-complex 4×4s, tweaking switches that wreak unseen environmental damage in Third World trade zones. Flicking switches that operate automatic wife-opinion control. Sitting on leather stained with dog turds collected by small children.

I'd have to start drinking again. It would be a side door into the same circus of freebies and drunken junkets. We'd overlap, me and the old crew. And I could do a lot more damage to myself and others behind the wheel of a borrowed

Maserati. I took the last job because I wanted a good time and it took me. I don't care now. What I used to think was a good time is nothing more tangible than a picture projected onto smoke, dispersed with one faint breath.

Whilst I am experiencing this intense sensation of resurrection, Nan is in the kitchen pulling the insides out of a chicken. I tell her that I am on my way back. She says that she cannot see why, if that's true, I haven't got a job. She says that it's all noise. That I could prove it by finding some work.

'You can't run away,' she says, shattering the chicken's legs with the blunt side of the cleaver.

I realize now that a simple life, a strong mind, a single purpose is like an asbestos suit in a firestorm.

She also tells me that she wants me to be quieter at night. She is getting militant about me not sleeping. Since I spoke to Sarah two nights ago I have been mostly awake. I used to fear the night, try and hide from it with drink and pills. Now I excavate the kitchen cupboards and I sit there eating fruit chews, pear drops, crackers and garibaldis. I drink endless bottles of water rereading old hospital forms and sometimes I even sleep. Each burst of activity is punctuated by me making noises in the bathroom like a small pony.

Slooooooooooosh.

I hold more water than a family bathtub and I never feel truly tired. I am well aware of the obligation to sleep but mostly I stay up late just so I can glide through the next day with my eyes half shut, horizontal on the sofa and watching some programme about carpet factories – perfect in the absence of Valium or any other sedative.

'You don't sleep because you don't do anything. I told you I'd be sticking my oar in after two weeks. Well I am now. There is no reason for a strong young man to be inside all day and now that bloody smelly thing is off your arm I can't see any reason for you not to be working.'

'I'll get a job.'

She waits. 'Well, go on.'

'Now?'

'Now.'

'And you need a place to live. I suggest you start working on both because you're out of here in two weeks.'

'What?'

'Buy a paper. Look in the small ads. You've got two weeks. There are things that are important to all good men. And you won't find them living with an old woman like me. This is the last piece of advice that you're getting out of me. Pack your kit, get your belongings out of Sarah's flat and then you can go ask your father for a job. Put your money where your mouth is.'

It took me months to sneak my things past Sarah. My giant sponge, my red cape, my collection of hats, they all arrived under my coat. I'd dreamed that one day I would have a place for my best things, and thought this was it. I couldn't understand what her problem was. I would bring something in, wave it around, sometimes even plug it in and show her how amusing it was. But she never wanted any of it. She would just yank it away from me, often putting it by the front door. No conversation. Every day I brought something new. There was so much incoming and outgoing jumble, she soon lost any point of reference and my stuff began to stick. Much of it requiring a plug socket, blinking and whirring and interconnected. The key was to make sure it was cleverly hidden behind her stuff. Wires criss-crossed. I tightly packed everything together so as to make simple removal of it impossible. All excess shelf space was utilized. All her property moved forwards by a minimum of three inches. The picture on the mantelpiece of the college spring ball? The one about to teeter over and smash? Behind it you'll find a Bruce Lee memorial vase fashioned to hold a single plastic lily (head missing). Why do the shampoo bottles keep falling in the bath? That would be my 'Sing-a-Song-a-Soap-Monster, The World's Largest Musical Soap Dish' and my bath-time buddy.

I don't want to move any of this stuff. I didn't move it in to move it out again, but when I call her I will be emotionless. I'll make this easy. I'll tell her that I'm coming to get it and I need a date.

'Don't rush me,' she says. 'I have things I need to say to you. Things about Ben and me that I want you to know, Charlie.'

'Look. This doesn't have to be said,' I say. 'I called to get a date for my stuff.'

'I made a mistake and I want to apologize now. You have to listen to me. I am sorry. Sorry that I listened to Sean and believed him over you. I am sorry that I believed him. Sorry that it had to be Ben. I needed someone. Someone I trusted.'

'I can't hear this.'

'And we knew each other so well. I didn't have to play any games with him. We knew what we wanted from each other.'

'What are you trying to do to me? Do you want me to put the phone down?'

'I want to be honest with you, like you've been honest with me, baby, so please listen. I thought he would make me feel better. Like me again. Not like a dumped bride, but a woman. I didn't want to sit at home and cry for you; I wanted to have the life you promised. I wanted to have fun. And you know I did and it was easy for me. And—'

'Please don't say any more.'

'But we have to be honest.'

'Sarah, these are things about you I don't ever want to know.'

'But I thought you wanted us to move on. We can't go on if we hide all this from each other and resent each other.'

'I do. I admit that I did you a lot of damage. I rang because I'm coming to get my things.'

'Why rush, Charlie? I'm not pushing for this. Why are you talking like nothing I've said matters? Like I don't exist?'

'I have to get on with my life. I have to look out for both of us. Just like if we were married. Except like this, I keep my distance and you keep happy.'

'I don't want that. I never said I wanted that. Stop thinking for me. I know myself better than you.'

'It's for the best,' I say. 'Well, give me a date.'

She pauses, quiet.

'But how are you going to live? Where are you going to go?'

'I'm going to clear my stuff out of your flat and see my old man about a job.'

'I'm not throwing you out on the street. I'm not even living there at the moment. You could use it. I could give you the keys. I'm not throwing you out. I'm not.'

'I know you aren't. I know you wouldn't do that. That's why I'm doing it for you. You need to be away from me. Please, let's get this over with. Let's move on. Let's set a date.'

We were sitting in the treeline on the edge of the bright white beach wrapped in thick towels; our bodies were wet and cold, the ocean darkening. She looked up at me and then at the rain clouds amassed on the horizon. I could hear the knock and clack of the thick palms as the monsoon winds began their rush across the water. She pulled in her arms and burrowed her head into my chest and the fear disappeared. She wanted to be kissed and held and kept safe. On that beach her need enabled me to exist. Made me feel necessary. I could warm her cold skin. I could use my body to heat hers and if anything threatened us I could beat it back. And when the storm came we would endure it together.

When I told everyone at work we were going on this enormous holiday they said it was mistake. Sean said that I'd be better off playing with someone my own age. Alex and Doyle didn't like her. Did I know what I was letting myself get into? Did I know what I was doing? What it meant? They said that fast is bad. But fast felt good to me. Even so, their words sunk deep inside. These people took risks with drugs and booze but they took none with life. Yeah, they could sit in a small room and do crack. Tramlines off a stainless-steel sink. Smoke smack off a piece of foil in a public toilet. But not life. That scared them so bad they couldn't even watch other people do it. However much they recognized or thought that they saw true horror in my decision their overreaction was just an echo, an automatic reverberation from their own lives. I wasn't hiding indoors with six rocks.

'We've booked it already,' I said.

Sean walked away in disgust. Ben said he knew what it was like to get carried away with a bird – he'd been there – but I had to slow down because I didn't know what I was letting myself in for. That this Holiday of a Lifetime wasn't me. I was more the Med, Greek islands, £250 a week, bangers and couscous. I was stupid. Wasting my time. I had them all telling me what I was and none of it was good. Then I had this woman who was showing me what I could be. My life was splitting open.

The holiday itself could have been a honeymoon. A dry run. One island, nowhere to hide. We ate and slept and drank and talked and spent every waking minute with each other. Sharing everything. Part of each other. I couldn't remember experiencing that before. Not since I was a baby and my mother held me in her arms. Before, we were two people who only joined up together for hours at a time in bedrooms or in restaurants. Now we allowed ourselves to become open and the same. We opened our hearts, surrendered, and grew stronger. Maybe I wasn't ready to have my emotions returned. And how I made her feel was incomprehensible to me. I tried to accept that I could have that effect on someone else but I was always waiting for her to start loathing me. Realize that she'd made a mistake and walk away. I liked this man I found on the tropical beach, protecting this beautiful woman. Surely that was me? Surely the past was irrelevant?

I was ready to throw so much of that away. It was as if I had never existed at all. I had shed that boy's skin. And as long as she was there in my arms I would never have to be him again, ever, not for the rest of my life.

**42**

Just because Nan said I should go and ask my old man for a job doesn't mean I can just roll up to the office, walk in and sit down at the third-best desk. This is not a white-collar industry. It's the building trade. This is not like stepping over Davis in accounts, exchanging some brisk emails, then having to avoid him in the staff kitchenette for a couple of months. The last time I worked for my old man and did someone better than me out of a job they bent coat hangers around my head, wired me up to a generator and gave me moderate to severe electric shocks for an hour. Besides, Nan's request also implies that he'd be happy to give me a job. I know if it was down to him and if no one else was listening, the answer would be an unequivocal no. Ideally, he wants me a hundred miles away from where he works. He does not want everyone to know what a flake his son is. This is the double-edged sword of success. You are now a magnet for failures. He knows he can't put me in the office, give me a computer and make me vice-president of downloading pictures of naked ladies. He knows I could water the plants, but that would shame him. He also knows I can't work on site because I'm too clumsy and not strong enough in the right places. And we both know that within a couple of days in any job I'll end up with thousands of little cuts. And then get a really deep one and have to go to hospital, bleeding like a punctured paddling pool. My only real option is painting and decorating. That way, most of the damage I do to myself and others can be undone with white spirit.

When I called him last night he said we should meet in the pub so that I could buy him a pint. I've never bought him a pint in my life and I don't drink any more. I say can we go to a café, but he says we can eat in the pub. For the first time I notice the rank smell. The stench of urine, the combination of dirty carpets, fag ash and slops. It's the smell of old age, heart disease, emphysema. You can associate that smell with cancer like fried bacon with an English breakfast. I have to wait outside. Why does he want me to buy him a drink in this stinky boozer, this damp bear's arsehole? So we can pretend to be normal?

I see him walking up towards me and try to make it look like I haven't seen him. I don't have the energy for pre-conversation facial expressions.

'Charlie.'

'All right, Dad.'

I shake a large cold hand. He looks overworked and the daylight shows a bloody marbling of vessels beneath his skin. Without being morbid, these things are the ordinary indicators of death happening. I know he isn't going to live for ever. I am over that, or at least I am deluded enough to think I am. As he pushes straight through the saloon door with his free hand I realize that after so many years the smell of this bar and my father are the same thing. This is him, this is me. This smell I hate is what little boys are made of.

'Two pints and a Wintermann's,' he says.

'I'm not drinking,' I say.

'Still?'

'Yeah,' I say, 'I have a problem.'

'Is that what the doctors say?'

'Well, we all worked it out together. But they suggested it first. Based on the evidence that I wanted to be pissed for the rest of my life.'

'You're your own man; who you believe is your choice.'

That's grown-up. Intelligent.

'So you're saying I should ignore doctors? Where did you hear that? A *Carry On* film?'

He shrugs non-committally. I want to hit him.

'I've got my problems,' I say. 'At least I know what some of them are. At least I'm dealing with them.'

He retreats under sustained fire and pauses to direct the barmaid towards the red tin of plastic-wrapped cigars.

'Well, that can't be bad,' he says.

'Do you think I'm making this up?'

He looks round. I'm ready with more. He can see that. Let's see how much he wants.

'No,' he says.

'Jesus.'

'Don't get angry with me. Your mother and I aren't to blame.'

'Fuck blame. I'm not blaming you.'

'You know what your mother says. She says that she didn't get you hooked on bloody drugs.'

'Right. OK, you're doing my head in. I didn't come here to accuse you of anything. I don't want to blame anyone any more. Not even me. Right now I want to find a solution. Then later when I'm all better I might try and work out what went wrong. When I've got a job and a roof over my head. Right now I'm trying to be practical. One step at a time.'

'Practical?'

'Yes. And it would help me if you could at least agree there is a problem.'

'Wasn't that the point of the hospital, all that money?'

'To find the problem,' I say.

'Not the cure?'

'You find the problem when you admit there's a problem,' I say.

'Right. That makes sense.'

I realize how difficult this is for him. I was really only thinking of me. No one wants to have their son screaming accusations at them in their local.

'We should sit in the garden,' I say. 'More private.'

He looks at outside like it's contagious.

'I suppose.'

We sit in the garden alone, at a picnic table that smells like it was stained with creosote. There is a thin partition fence and a row of leylandii between us and the main road. The heavy traffic that thunders along from the industrial park has to change gear for the lights opposite the pub either to speed up or slow down. Large haulage trucks and fully loaded tankers groaning, V8s grumbling, hydraulic brakes spitting and hissing. No one could overhear us even if they wanted to.

'I'm here for a couple of reasons. First, I want to say sorry for what I put you and Mum through with the wedding.'

He shuffles his large frame further along the bench. The movement creates a see-saw effect, raising me off the ground.

'Right,' he says.

'Right?' I say.

'I accept your apology,' he says. 'Thank you.'

Ray drives past in a white van. We share eye contact. My dad waves. And this strikes me as extraordinarily gay.

'Ray was going to come in for one but he had to shoot off at the last minute.' He peels the plastic off his cigar. 'So what's the other thing?'

'A job.'

'A job! I never thought I'd hear that.'

'Well, can I have one?'

'Doing what?'

He smiles, challenging me to put a name, a value on my services.

'Painting or something?'

'Right.' He smirks.

'I'll do it properly. I know Ray's got a couple of sites that need some work.'

'I'll have to talk to him, see what he says.'

'Cheers.'

I sip my soda and lime. I hate buying soda and lime because the bar staff always seem to think you're only drinking it because you're skint. I hate that.

'Ray's doing well then?'

'Ray's doing very well; he's a good boy is Ray, works hard.'

'You wish Ray was your son, don't you?'

'No.'

'Yes, you do.'

'No, I don't. He looks like a wolf.'

We both laugh.

'So, can I have a job or what?'

'Christ. Only temporary.'

'If I didn't think this was temporary I wouldn't be asking you.'

I offer him a light.

'Those things smell like a burning mattress,' I say.

'You'll only fuck it up.'

'I'd appreciate it. It'll get my full attention. I need this. I won't let you down.'

'Your nan put you up to this, didn't she?'

'She gave me a push.'

'Yeah, I bet she did. She kicking you out?'

'Yeah.'

'After, wassit? Two weeks?'

'Two weeks.'

'She can be a hard cow,' he says. The wind picks up and seems even colder for passing over the industrial estate on its way to us.

'I've packed my bags already,' I say.

'Where do you plan on going?'

'Nowhere,' I say. 'She won't throw me out if I'm paying her rent. That's gambling cash.'

'She will, believe me. And don't encourage her gambling.'

'You're kidding me? She's into me for about five hundred quid. She's a nightmare.'

'You can live with Ray? Have a proper bachelor pad.'

'I don't know. I'm not through with some of the old stuff yet. Nan's is good for thinking.'

'What, the wedding? That's gone. Leave it alone. I couldn't tell anyone but when that wedding fell through I was relieved for you. To say the least. I thought you were better off out of it.'

'Me? Or Sarah? Or both?'

'Marriage is hard work. A lot of hard work. Not everyone wants that these days. Spend their life making sacrifices.'

'So what do you do?'

'Get on with it.'

'What? That's it? You get on with it?'

'Yep.' He takes a long drink.

'Even with you and Mum?'

'Things will sort themselves out with your mother, find their own level.'

'But don't you think you could be happy?'

'I could be.'

'With Dennis living under your roof.'

He winces. And shakes his head. Don't go there.

'Jesus. So after all this you didn't think I should get married. You could have said something.'

'All that matters is that it's come out now and you don't have to go through forty years regretting it.'

'We'd have split.'

'My generation was different. We stick with our decisions.'

'Your entire generation is divorced.'

'Not me and your mother.'

'And that's supposed to be a good thing?'

Because of the large percentage of my parents' friends who divorced while I was still at school the spectre of this possibility had long hung over me like the prospect of my dad's redundancy or either Mum or Dad going down with a major illness. Now I know how difficult it must have been for them to stay together. Looking at my old man, I don't think there's ever been a time when I thought he didn't regret being with my mother, and vice versa. The snide asides, the looks of resentment on long car journeys. No conversation. Life as one long forfeit.

I see the way they have lived and I see its reflection in my own attempts at countering it. They starved their relationship to death. We are all capable of it. Handing our relationships small moments of death on a daily basis as we deprive ourselves and other people of our life and our touch. In hospital they asked me how many drinks were too many. Well they should have also asked how many rounds of golf or TV channels were too many. One round of golf, one TV channel is too many if you are using it to ignore your girlfriend, your wife. We all have different ways of hiding, reducing our impact. People need us to be there for them. And the more we retreat, the more they are starved and we starve ourselves. Is one method saner than another? I don't think so. These are all small forms of suicide. We don't have to be like that. Like our parents were. We can be better.

Four days ago I pulled on the company uniform. The Teflon-dipped tan trousers with the stitched-in front crease and the acidic-yellow polo shirt. Sunshine and shit, the corporate colour scheme. We arranged that Ray would pick me up and drive me to work in the morning, then collect me and drop me back at Nan's each night. These are the measures we have taken to bring my life back to order. He is my minder. He does not pack me a lunch.

Throughout the working day I am locked away from the world in a room on my own. I do not see daylight. Sometimes I am underground seven out of eight hours, painting pipes in car parks and the insides of rooms that no one cares about. But for my promise to the old man, this would be carte blanche to sleep on the job. I am the only person other than Ray who appears to know what I am supposed to be doing. During my lunch hour I find a cheap sandwich shop where I can get thick, stale baguettes filled with bacon, and large polystyrene buckets of tea. After eating I go walking. Too tired to pull off my overalls I lie down on a patch of grass somewhere and try to catch the last of the summer sun. Even if I fall asleep, I am never late back for work.

I like what I do – standing halfway up a ladder, staring at a blank wall, my painting hand slowly turning grey. You've got a lot of time to think with floors and walls. I ask myself undemanding questions. Is the brush getting dry? Or do I have enough paint for the wall? Previously I would have used this time to torture myself about failing. When I catch myself on the attack I fight it. I'm not better than this. I never was. I like having both my arms back and I like doing something physical with them. I already have about a tablespoon of camouflage-grey paint in my hair, more in the creases in my knuckles and under my fingernails.

Four days and bets are being won and lost all over the company because I still haven't fucked up. There have been no deaths or lawsuits. I like carrying around pots and cans. If there is any heavy work, I want it. I'm not scared of hurting my arm because broken bones heal stronger. If anything needs lifting, I want to lift it. Matter lodged in a pipe? I have my hand in there first. Ray loves this new Charlie. It's like I've finally endorsed his life. He appears at the end of every day still neat and tidy, in a well-pressed brand-new uniform, groomed hair and clean shoes, to check that I'm working and finds that I am. And when he sees me happy and knackered at the end of the day, I love it. I lay into him about the shit music and how tired I am, and he laughs. It's a good sound and I never want to make him feel less than me ever again. This is the way I want it to be. I am sick of playing the big man.

☐

Chops and mash for dinner with Mum, Dad and Dennis. Then when Ray hears we are having chops he starts to pull these butcher's dog expressions and makes me phone Mum for a plus one.

'Chops and mash, chops and mash,' sings Ray on the way. His favourite.

Mum does them in a big oven tray with tomatoes and oily gravy. They take about a week to get out of your teeth and when you eat them you can't help but make a noise like a Labrador chewing on a dried pig's ear. When I get through to Mum she says it's all right to bring Ray round if he stops singing.

'There's always enough,' she says.

By the time we arrive, Dennis and Dad are already sitting at the table. Mum takes Ray's plate and begins to fill it with meat. He gets two chops. She takes Dad's plate and he also gets a couple. Then I get two, and she gets two and then she takes Dennis's. He gets three. I've never seen that before. The remaining chop already assigned. With only two chops to play with, Ray's face hits the table.

Dennis smiles at her and immediately begins to tuck in. The gravy is thick and salty and the mash comes straight from the pan, which has been set down in the middle of the table.

'Lovely chops, June, very tender.'

He doesn't realize that we are all staring at him. He is wearing a light V-neck jumper over his work shirt, having removed his tie.

'I hear you're back working for your father?' he says, smiling.

Whatever.

'Mum, can you tell me why Dennis is getting three chops and everyone else is getting two?'

'What do you care?' she says.

'I'm saying you should leave that other chop to the end and whoever needs it the most, gets it.'

I'm looking at Ray. He really needs it the most.

'Dennis,' I say, 'give Ray your chop; you don't need it.'

'Please, Dennis,' says Ray.

'No,' says Dennis, straight back at him.

'Dennis pays for it,' says Mum.

'So what? So does Dad.'

'Dennis pays for it, so Dennis gets the extra.'

'Is that true, Dennis, are you paying for it?'

He looks at me, his mouth full of tough fibrous pork, sweet nothings to my mother and lies.

'Do you get enough for your money, Dennis?'

What does he want from us?

'Do you think that you're getting value for your pound here? Is it stretching as far as you'd like? How's the service? Has my family home lived up to your expectations? Or could we do more?' He puts down his knife and fork, still chewing. 'Do you get value for your money, Dennis? Is there anything I can do for you later? Perhaps a rub down and a handjob?'

'Charlie!' Dad hits the table with his fist.

'Come on, Dennis,' I say. 'You can tell me. Or should I call you Dad? What else do you want? Do you want me to call you Daddy Dennis?'

He stands up. 'This is not the time or the place.'

'Sit down and finish your fucking tea.'

He does so immediately.

Ray starts laughing nervously. 'Fucking hell, Dennis, I just wanted that chop.'

'And what do you get for his money, Mum? Are you enjoying Dennis's company? I bet the money comes in useful, doesn't it?'

'The money comes in useful,' she whispers.

'Does it, Dad?'

Dad reaches over and grabs the top of my arm. 'What are you trying to prove?' he whispers.

'Come on, Dad, does the money come in useful?'

'No, it doesn't, not any more, not really,' says Dad.

'There you go. I didn't think so. So what is he doing here? Why is he still here? Why hasn't he moved on? Dennis?'

He says nothing and Dad removes his hand from my arm.

'Mum, anything to add?'

'We need the money.'

'Bullshit. Tell the truth, Mum. Is it that you like another man around the house?'

'No!'

'Be honest.'

'No.'

'Tell the truth, Mum.'

'Please stop, Charlie.'

'What is he even doing here? I mean, I look at him sitting there, he's a joke. Dennis,' I say, 'you're a joke.'

'Charlie, that is enough.'

'Sorry, Mum, I'm going to have to ask Dennis to get his stuff together and get out.'

'You have no right to do that,' she says.

'Dennis, you have one week.'

'I think that's for June to decide, not you.'

'One week.'

'You don't even live here.'

'If you're not gone inside that time, I'll come and get you, and your stuff and put you in the back of the van.'

'You can't threaten him like that!'

'All you have to do is leave, Dennis. I'll drive you any-where you want to go.'

'Don't threaten me. I'll call the police.'

'Don't bitch. You know where the phone is.'

'It isn't his fault!' shouts Mum. 'It's not fair.'

This cut was a scar long before he came along and opened it again.

'I don't care, Mum. I don't care about him. He's nothing. You and Dad need to talk. Alone. And Dennis, if you interfere I will break your fucking legs.'

Ray shakes a mash-smothered knife at him. 'Dennis, I'd pack up my shit if I was you. And I'll have that chop as well.'

He leans over and jabs his fork into it.

'Charlie, please,' says Mum.

'Sorry, Mum, this is the way it's got to be. You can stay and talk things through or you can join him in the back of the van. I've fucking had it with all this pissing around.'

'Harold, say something.'

Dad has his head in his hands. This has been a long time coming.

'I'm sorry, Dad. It has to be said. He has to go, she has to make a decision.'

He doesn't look well.

'Jesus, Charlie,' he says.

Mum is crying. Turned side on to the table pulling balls of tissue from her cardigan sleeves.

'You talk now. You can't both want to go on like this. You're wasting your own lives and mine. How did you get like this? How did it get this far? Your lives didn't end when you got married but you both act like it. Like you stole something from each other you can never give back. The way you are now, you'd be better off dead tomorrow. Go upstairs and get it sorted. When you've worked out what you want, tell each other so you can do something about it. No more lies. No more hiding.'

□

It takes three hours to reach the hospital and we park in a quiet lane. Ray took the two remaining chops from his plate and ate them, including pieces of kitchen roll, on the way here. I ruined his dinner, he says. He is reconsidering the offer he was going to make to let me sleep on his floor. I tell him that it is the sign of a true scoundrel to withdraw offers you haven't even made. Part of his fightback is a double playing of Katrina and the Waves' 'I'm Walking On Sunshine', which he claims is to cheer himself up. When I get back in that van I'm going to jam that tape in his ear.

'Oh shit. When you phoned I thought you were joking.'

I am standing beneath Constance's window. If I wanted to I could jump up and pull myself in.

'Hello.'

'My God, Charlie. How romantic. Are you stalking me?'

I think she is slightly stoned on her pills. When I called her mobile to tell her I was coming she asked me if I'd been drinking. Between now and then she must have gone back to sleep. She leans further out of her window. I could reach round the back of her head and kiss her.

'Thanks,' I say.

'I didn't think you'd come back. No one could bring me back here. Except myself obviously.'

'I was always going to come back. To see you anyway.'

'No note, no letter.'

'Nothing, I'm sorry.'

'Yeah, right.'

She disappears back inside her room and comes back to the window with a cigarette lit.

'Are you staying? I mean coming in?'

'You want me to come in?'

'If you want.'

'That would be, well, you know,' I say.

'What?'

We are almost nose to nose. She smells of bed. Of sleep.

'Come on up.'

She winks and clicks her cheek. I laugh. I want to.

'No, this is a quick visit.'

'Oh.'

'I mean it's not like that.'

She blows a long agitated stream of smoke up at the moon.

'Constance, I'm sorry I took advantage of you.'

'You didn't. I'm not a child. What we did was consensual.'

'I mean emotionally.'

'Oh. Emotionally.'

She leans back into her room, takes another pull on her cigarette.

'Oh you lied.'

'I didn't mean to. I just want you to hear from me that I apologize, and that I care about you. I want you to be all right.'

'So you can feel better, right?'

'No, no.'

'You think that you did this?'

She sticks her arms out of the window. They are fully wrapped.

'You think you made me cut myself?'

'Maybe I had something to do with it.'

'What, you think I did that from a broken heart?'

'I don't know.'

'Then you came here so I could forgive you and you could carry on with your life, happy and safe, and all tucked up nicely with her, right?'

'No. I'm here because I care about you. I came here to tell you that I care about what happened. That you're better off without me. You know that.'

'Sure, I believe you.'

Strands of her hair brush my cheek. I can feel her, parts of her, underneath me.

'You were always with her.'

'Maybe I was but didn't want to admit it.'

'You are stupid.'

'You can have anyone you want when you're ready.'

'You sound like my mother.'

'And if they hurt you or anyone hurts you again then you call me. I'll be your big brother when you need me. I'll fucking scratch them. I owe you but I don't want to hear from you for months.'

'But you will be with her.'

'I don't know. Even if I am, I promise, when the time does come that you need me I will be there. I'm not going to abandon you. You won't be alone.'

**44**

Ray spins the van violently through the short burst of country lanes before the city ring road. We are the accident you will drive past tomorrow morning. The upturned grey belly, muddy tyres and bent-up roof in the ploughed field. The stereo spits Tiffany's 'I Think We're Alone Now' and instinctively I stamp down on the phantom brake I wish I had. Eventually, we will be a gap in the hedgerow marked by a cheap white crucifix and a couple of bunches of rotting petrol-station flowers. The tape stops and turns over. It begins playing '99 Luftballons'. Ray drums the steering wheel, the car sashays. He tries to sing along in German. In a woman's voice. I close my eyes and ask Jesus to surround me in a protective blanket of love.

It is almost midnight when I call Sarah. I want to ask her if she still wants to spend time with me. If I can still come and get my stuff in the next couple of days and if so then I can ask her whether we can still have lunch once in a while.

'Hello?'

'Charlie?'

'Sarah?'

'Andrea.'

Shit. I wonder how strong her powers are? If she can actually see me and Ray now, driving through these woods?

How many times do you think she has to stir her finger in that smoking cauldron of hers before she conjures up an image of me?

'Oh. Hello, Andrea. Would it be possible for me to speak to Sarah, please?'

'She isn't here.'

'Could you please put her on the phone.'

'I asked you not to telephone this house again.'

'I'm sorry. I wouldn't have called if it wasn't important.'

'How many times do you have to be told? Are you stupid?'

So we're never going to hang out, read *Lady* magazine, punch each other in the arm, spot for each other in the weight room, or become spit brothers. Not as long as she wants to rake out my internal organs and pound them flat with a length of lead pipe. Not as long as I remind her of all the things she hates about herself.

'You're working on a building site, aren't you? I knew you'd come to nothing.'

'Friends don't keep telling other friends that they've come to nothing.'

'We're . . . not . . . friends.' She says that, but her intense, phobic reaction to my presence is probably the only real obstacle that prevents us from being major buddies.

'I'm sorry you don't think we're friends, Andrea. But could you tell her I called all the same?'

'She is out for the evening. At an awards ceremony.'

The awards? I forgot about the awards.

'She loathes you. Why don't you leave her alone?'

'I can't, Andrea. Even though she loathed me. She was right to. And I love her.'

'What?'

'You should listen to her. I still love her very much. I didn't ever stop. And she still loves me.'

Teacups shattering, a nest of tables separating, show dogs imploding, underdone brûlée and sex on a Wednesday. This is Andrea's whole world turning upside down. Charlie still loves Sarah. Sarah still loves Charlie.

I will have to spend the rest of my life looking over my shoulder for a kidnap squad of monkey soldiers with wings.

□

Rain water shines the cobbles, greasy. The last time I was here my arm was twisted back and I was being stretchered into the back of an ambulance. There is a piece of paper with the magazine's name on it pinned to the club door – the writing blurred by rivulets of dirty rain water. I walk in unchallenged. No sharp-looking door controllers with council badges. No earpieces and clipboards. Just a twenty-stone man slumped in a chair at the foot of a long staircase. It's difficult to tell if he's alive or dead.

At the top the main room is only a quarter lit but you can make out enough to see the waiting faces. Coming up, coming down, checking their pockets, hands moving back and forth. Boozing and snorting and smoking. Same again, please. Fill my emptiness. The frenzy becomes everything. Take in more expensive high-tax booze and fags until they can't even taste or smell, trying to plug a hole that is continuously swelling beyond your control. Somebody please kill me so I can sleep.

Or you can stop.

Doyle is standing at the end of the bar wearing a bright polyester shirt two sizes too small. He looks like a runaway fruit machine. I barely know the person standing next to him. Everyone in this room feels like a stranger to me.

'Oh shit,' he says. 'What are you doing here?'

'I wanted to know if I won the prize; did I?'

'You didn't. You weren't even entered.'

'Shit. So where's Ben?'

I lean in closer to hear his answer but someone is pulling on my arm.

'Charlie, come and have a line.'

'What?'

'Have you got any?'

'What?'

'Got a line?'

I pull my arm away from him, looking for someone recognizable in the mass.

'Fuck off.'

He trips over his feet and falls between two tables. The mound by the door doesn't even move. I turn to Doyle for an answer but he is already talking to someone else. I am standing with my back pressed against the wall when I hear his voice.

'Well, if it isn't Charlie Big Potatoes.'

Sean steps out from between the bodies. He is three kilos uncut, two-machine-guns-at-the-top-of-the-stairs out of his mind on coke. He is jagged and white. Sarah steps out from behind him. She double takes. My expression is probably the same as that night on the beach with the fire bell. I don't want to find her with somebody else again. See her leave with somebody else. She splits off from Sean and takes me by the elbow, walking me away.

'What are you doing here?' she says.

'What are you doing here?' I say.

'What am I doing here? I don't have to tell you.'

'Where's Ben?' I say.

'You don't get it, do you?'

'No, you don't get it. Where is he?'

'It was never about him. Don't you see that? Please don't start anything.'

'You know this is where I set Sean's head on fire the last time . . . And I broke my arm down those steps. We were getting married then.'

'My God, please go.'

'What happened? Jesus.'

This still shocks me. I hide my face in my hands. Embarrassment becomes shame. The tears I hold back swell inside me.

'Charlie.'

'I want you in my life. But there are too many people in the way. Would it be that bad for us to be together? Tell me that it's right? That all this has been for a cause or something. I don't even know how we got here. With him in between us.'

The music is so loud.

'With who? With Ben? Charlie? Is that what you think all this has been about?'

'There are too many people who tell us what we can be.'

'Just leave here, now. With me.'

Sean is laughing to himself, propped up against a wall. 'Don't go, babe. Ben'll be back in a minute.'

Sarah touches my face.

'Oi! Charlie Big Potatoes! Aren't you a fucking decorator?'

'Please,' she says.

'I can't do that,' I say.

Sean looks over at Ben, who then looks at me, nods arrogantly and continues walking into the toilets. Sarah tries to grab my arm.

'Charlie, don't!'

I push past Sarah and Sean and make my way through the crowd towards the toilets.

Inside, I feel bodies close the doorway behind me as they crowd around the single cubicle. I thought Ben would hide in there but instead he stands at the urinal, like a king in a shining-wet throne room. I try to find the words. A way of letting him know how much his betrayal hurt me, but nothing comes. After everything he has done to me, giving me the overdose, taking my woman – I can think of nothing I have to say. Nothing that could ever make him understand how I feel about the rip that runs through my life. Why should his life continue the same? No consequences. What troubles him? His conscience? Nothing.

My anger is a scream. My lost pride is a fist. My humiliation is his pain. I walk up behind him, crouch, grab his ankles and pull his legs out from under him. He drops onto his face, hard, his hands slipping down the white porcelain wall, gripping the trough at the bottom of the urinal, hands deep in the yellow liquid, the swirls of bubbles and white foam. As I drag him backwards over the wet tiles towards the cubicle I kick him hard between the legs and think how much I trouble him now. I walk out back to the bar.

Sean turns around, nodding his head. He has dribble down his chin. You cannot hit a man with dribble over his chin. He smiles and beckons me over. I don't feel better yet. I don't suppose I ever will. That was not for gain, but for equality. I think about Ben trying to claw his way out of that cubicle. The mess. A little blood.

Sean tilts his head back, sniffing the cold liquid in his nasal cavity all the way down.

'Charlie,' he says. 'So what are you doing here then? Do you want to come and work for me again, eh?' He starts laughing. Brain damage. 'You don't like me, do you?' he says. 'Why don't you like me?'

He picks up laughing again.

I nod and look around the room for Sarah.

'Don't mind all that shit,' he continues. 'We could let bygones be bygones, have a drink – me and you and Ben. Get Ben. Where is he?' I shrug and take the position at the bar next to him. 'Fuck that whore, eh?' he says when he sees I can't find Sarah. 'What do you want to drink?'

I wonder what his pulse is at. If I hit him hard in the centre of the chest would he have a heart attack?

'Have a cigar.'

Sean has never seen me grin like this and there is no desk between us.

'A cigar and a brandy.'

He's flagging. His wet waxy skin shines like a bowl of eels. It is almost impossible to hear what he is saying. My hands are still wet from the cistern water.

The barman puts the brandy in front of me. I watch Sean aimlessly tip his down his neck.

He turns to me. 'What's wrong with you?' he says.

There is no concise answer to that question.

Alex appears with Doyle.

Sean rambles at Alex because he was supposed to buy champagne.

'Ben's been assaulted,' Alex interrupts Sean.

'What?'

Doyle leans in.

439

'He got his head flushed down the toilet; he's covered in piss.'

Sean looks disbelieving.

'What?'

'He's been in a fight,' says Doyle. 'Or something. He's covered in piss.'

'I've seen him,' I say. 'He's going to be fine. Though he'll need to go to the hospital and get some jabs.'

Sean looks at me and I smile. I show him my wet arms, pick my wet shirt from my skin. I lean over and whisper in his ear, 'You know, Sean, the last time me and you were in here, I set your head on fire.'

Doyle pulls on my shirt.

'Get out of here.'

'Not yet. Sean and I were talking about Sarah, weren't we, Sean. Eh?'

'What?'

'About Sarah. You said she was a whore. Do you really think Sarah's a whore? I want to know. While Alex and Doyle are here, all us boys having a drink.'

'I don't know.'

'Is she?' I say.

'I don't know.'

'Is she?'

He looks sick.

'No, she's not.'

'Who is not what, Sean?'

I have his collar.

'Who is not what, Sean?'

'Sarah.'

'Go on.'

'Sarah is not a whore.'

'No, she isn't.'

I rattle his head a bit.

'No.'

'Will you talk about me behind my back or come near my friends again?'

'No.'

'Will you stay away?'

'No. Yes.'

'Or?'

'I don't know.'

'Or?'

'I don't know!'

'Or one day I'll spike your fucking drugs and kill you. Do you understand?'

I am strong, this is not me.

I am not a thug.

I let go of his collar and his head springs backwards.

I will not become like them.

I will not become like Ben.

I am leaving.

The cab driver gets lost twice on the way to my nan's house, which is in a grey part of town that always seems to be to the left of wherever you want to go.

The time driving down half-lit back streets gives me all the time I need to turn against myself. I already feel ashamed. Playing it over and over, wondering whether or not I gave him a bruised brain. Thinking of him in a chair, getting fed mushy peas by his mother for the rest of his life. I wonder if I could plead diminished responsibility.

'Look at the state of you,' says Nan, pointing at buttons missing from the middle of my shirt.

I throw a fast bap-bap-bap combination of punches in the air.

'I've got quick hands.'

'You silly sod. You're lucky you're not sitting in the back of a police van right now.'

She kisses her teeth loudly and hands me her empty glass for a refill.

'And your dad phoned and told me about the performance you made at dinner.'

'Jesus, that feels like two nights ago. Did he say anything about Mum and Dennis?'

'Nope. He didn't want to talk about it.'

'What a shock. No one ever talks. No one has any problems.'

'Not everyone has problems.'

I hand her the drink.

You've got to love people with no problems. You think, If I could make my life like theirs, if I mimic what they do, I will become like them. Yet the closer you get, the more fucked-up you realize they are. Take tonight. I was in a room with 300 people. I saw myself 300 times over. So intent and so professional in the pursuit of happiness, yet so fucked-up and empty. The people who I used to think had the perfect balance, I now wouldn't want to be in a thousand years. Because I began asking questions. Now if I come across someone who wants me to think they have it all worked out I assume that I don't know enough about them yet. That if I knew them better I could see through the lie. I mean who are these perfect people? I have grown up idolizing drunk actors and glam addict rock gods, whose danger and reckless abandon is probably derived from some unprocessed old pain that originated with their grandparents. When they aren't strutting around on stage sucking an arena's worth of love into a bottomless hole, they armour themselves with booze and drugs and swearing. You rock the mic? All I see is some little baby desperate to be picked up and held. All they really needed – Hendrix, Moon, Morrison, Cobain – was a cuddle from Mum and a long sleep under a tree.

'Nan. There are no perfect people with no problems. I set up my perfect life. I had everything in place, worked it out. I had the job and the clothes and I was going for the whole lifestyle.'

'Really, you had everything in place?'

'I can see where I went wrong,' I say. 'I can rebuild.'

'It's all about you still. All about making your life right. What is perfect for you, not Sarah.'

'No, it's not.'

'Well, answer me this. Can you make a sacrifice, Charlie? I don't mean share. I don't mean give, I mean sacrifice. This is not like giving when you're going to get something back in return. Or handing over something, an emotion you already half-own. I mean, are you really ready to give yourself to Sarah? Give without requiring anything back in return.'

'I don't know. If I loved her enough. Yes.'

'Are you sure? Love is sacrifice. Love is sacrifice, or otherwise you're just using people. You have to give her more than you take. If you don't, then you'll be using her, using Sarah like you use everything else.'

More filling for that empty hole.

'I'm not talking about Sarah.'

'Rubbish. Who else are we talking about? You be honest now. You must love her as right and as well as you can. Every day you have to try and give her the same or a little more. And always love her. Always show her what can be done. Show her the possibilities so that she might return them to you.'

'That's a lot to ask.'

'Well, that's what love is. If you think it's anything less than that, you should leave her be.'

'You think so? I loved her. She is everything to me. I still love her.'

That's what Sarah was to me: everything. It is there in my own words. Everything. She was everything to me. My goddess, my princess, my entertainment system, my sister, my mother, my best friend. But what was I to her? What did I give?

Nan holds the now empty glass in her lap and stares into the wall. It is clear that the conversation is over. I have not seen her show hurt before. Or this kind of anger. Real, private anger. The anger you don't show anyone. Is that really what I was doing to Sarah? Do we really treat other people like that? People we think we love? Was she going to be my first wife? Number one in a series of consumable, collectable, disposable marriages?

'Nan,' I say, 'I think I'm going to have to start all over again.'

**46**

On the train out of the city I am so busy picking the scales of blue paint off my arms – grooming myself like a giant ape – that I forget to have my customary panic attack. Instead, I can feel each breath's smooth passage, the oxygen flowing into my blood. I pull my shoulders back and push my chin up, straightening my spine. I feel like I can take care of myself now. My eyes flick to the six people sitting opposite. They look scuffed, beaten and preyed upon. Left out in the garden. Ignored. They need haircuts, baths, surgical procedures and new shoes. They have subjugated their dreams and needs to those of others. And they have suffered because they never had a chance to tell the world what they really wanted.

It happens to all of us. We live our lives consumed with small choices, not realizing that the big decisions have already been made for us. I don't know when it's supposed to hit you, but most of us must wake up at the wheel of an estate car or something like that. That's when you realize that somewhere along the way you lost your original dream. The sweater you're wearing, the car you're driving or even the two children in the back. You don't remember wanting any of this. As you grip that steering wheel you're really holding on to everything you know. Holding on to your schedules, your wife, your children. The pillars of your existence, built on the foundation of other people's dreams. Grip it tighter. Everything you have achieved has been a reaction to decisions made for you by other people – since you were a child. Will you have the courage now to look for your original dream which lies buried in the foundations of this life? Will you threaten all this? Or will you replace it instead with jewellery and a big-screen TV? A new car? A new nose? More drugs.

I blink and five more stops fly past.

Did you get it? Did you get what you wanted? And did it disappear down the hole?

Grip the wheel. Don't say a word to anyone. Hide that thought because what you really want could destroy your life. A new partner? No partner? What's your secret? If you don't tell us we can't help you. Does it shake your code? Is it causing conflict? Are you ashamed? Too scared to tell? To ask? Keep quiet. Lose yourself in something stupid.

Blink again, another five.

Sarah never told me what she wanted, and I never told her because I couldn't be honest. I couldn't tell her what I thought I wanted to be because it would have destroyed her. Or that's what I thought. I mean, who confronts that? I walked slowly into hell before I was honest.

Reality, dreams and desire fighting like scissors, rock and paper. Face her with the truth after all we'd built together? Because I had some childish desire to be heard and be free? And will I be too frightened to ask myself again in ten years' time? And then ask her if her dreams are still the same? If she has what she needs and if she still needs me? Will we have the courage to follow our own paths no matter what? To free each other?

In the warped window of the train, in the yellow light, I can focus on this new version of myself.

My telephone buzzes in my pocket as we sit at a station. Dad says that Dennis is packed, ready to go and making a real deal of it. Mum is crying and he doesn't know what to say to her. She was crying all night and she was still crying this morning and it's my fault. I ask him how long they've been married. Twenty-five years he says. I say that's what she is crying for. The last twenty years of their marriage. All he has to do is sit down next to her and listen to what she has to say. The rest they can work out later.

'That's all?' he says.

'Yeah,' I say, 'for now.'

He thought I was going to tell him to go and buy her something nice.

'Do you want to be in the same place in five years' time? You'll be two stone fatter and at least five times more sick in the head.'

'No, I don't want that,' he says.

I have to apply this same kick-ass methodology to my own life.

As the train moves north, the last of the city stations deplete the train of the lower classes. Only high-calibre people remain for the final shuddering push into deep suburbia. Heavy heads loll backwards on tired necks. Limbs unfold. Drink cans are kicked the length of the compartment, spilling last drops. I think we have a chance at knowing what people really need by those they choose to have around them. We will never know the truth of why we are chosen. The question 'Tell me why you love me?' will never receive an honest answer. Is it the shape of my neck or the face I make when I submerge my head in the bath? Broken down into its component parts, love begins to sound so arbitrary. Is it her smile, which is like sunshine? Lips you could bite? Or is it

the scent of her hair in the morning or the way she can say
'Do me, baby' in Russian? Are these song lyrics the real truth
about love? Or would a more honest chorus be something
along the lines of 'I love you because you're a warped clone
of my mother, without the excessive demands and bad
temper, who I can have sex with.' This may be nearer the
truth but it isn't getting everyone on the dance floor at the end
of the evening, is it?

Click. Last stop.

Unless we are honest with ourselves we are not even
giving other people a chance.

I ring the video buzzer at the gate, which they've installed
since my last visit. I feel a small prick of pride at being
personally responsible for rich people upgrading their
security system. I hit the buzzer and smile into the camera
knowing this image will be broadcast simultaneously on
small screens around the house – from the kitchen up to the
master bedroom. I give them both sides in full profile.

'Guess who!'

No answer.

'Can Sarah come out and play?'

A click and . . .

'What do you want?'

'Good evening, Andrea.'

'Good evening.'

'How are you? Would you tell Sarah I'm here.'

'What am I going to do about you?'

'I don't want to come in. I'll stay out here.'

Have you considered snipers?

'Are you going to leave my daughter alone?'

'Only if she wants me to.'

'Ha!' She suffocates a laugh. 'How many times have you said that!'

Sarah appears at the front door. She walks ten steps towards me and then turns to offer a silent scream at the house before continuing to walk up to the gate.

'Try taking a deep breath,' I say, hands fixed to the bars on the gate.

'You've got paint in your hair,' she says.

'What do you want? It's my new job; I work with paint.'

'Doctors don't finish work with syringes and plasters stuck to their heads,' she says.

She reaches through the bars and pulls at a dollop.

'You always get in a mess. Some of these are like iced gems.'

I can feel her trying to get her nails underneath the paint.

'Ow!'

'Did you get any on the brush?'

'Ouch. Shit. I'm better than you'd think,' I say.

'Sorry, baby, I know you're working hard.'

I feel the gentle pressure of her arm, the perfume on her clothes. I close my eyes and remember her lying next to me. Our sheets. Our bedroom. The way we made it feel when we were in there alone.

She pulls back her hand and I open my eyes.

'Keep going. I like it,' I say.

'Did you get in a fight with Ben?'

'Not exactly. Is that why you left?'

'I didn't want to see you hurt.'

'It's over now,' I say.

I lean my head forward into the gap between the bars. I have to take a couple of long and slow breaths, like the doctors said, to keep calm, but I can only draw jagged tugs of air. I look up at her and her eyes focus on mine and I feel like I exist again.

'This is a big job,' she says.

'Well, keep going.'

'No matter how much it hurts? It could take a long time.'

'Do you want it?'

'What?' she says.

'The job,' I say.

She continues grooming me, picking at the paint.

'I do miss it,' she says.

I reach up and touch the patch on my head that she was working on. It feels wet. I think I'm bleeding. 'I miss you.'

'What?'

'I miss you. I miss everything about you.'

'You do?'

'I didn't do it right before. I didn't tell you how I felt. I wasn't honest with you. I've said a lot. But I wasn't honest. As honest as I could have been. We have to tell each other what we really want.'

'And then?'

'Then we can be whatever we want to be.'

'Whatever we want to be?'

'We don't have to be like our parents. If we start right we don't have to make the mistakes that they made. I know there are no guarantees.'

'No, there aren't.'

'I mean, we have to like what each other wants to be, but if we're honest and we like what we hear . . .'

'You've been thinking.'

'I have thought so hard that my brain has grown another ring round it. Like a tree. I think I've grown up.'

Her hand slips through the gate and touches my cheek.

'You're you again.'

'I am?'

'This is the Charlie I fell in love with.'

'I'm not making much sense.'

'You never did.'

'I want to be honest,' I say. 'There are so many things I want to say to you.'

'There's time,' she says.

'I can't do it from behind this gate.'

I jog ten paces back.

'Charlie?'

I turn and run as fast as I can, and jump at the gate. I get a foothold and swing a leg over between the spikes, which are blunted with layers of thick lead paint. With one leg either side I roll myself sideways in a cartwheel, head first. Gripping the bars in each hand on my way down, pulling my other leg over as I go.

The world turns upside down.

I land a couple of feet from her and brush the dust from my hands.

'So that's how you do it,' she says. 'I always wondered.'

'Last time I did that I landed on my head.'

'Shit,' she says, looking me up and down. I am suddenly ashamed of how scruffy I am.

My nasty uniform, cheap polyester shirt. I stand there before her, waiting, foolish.

'You're back then,' she says.

She throws her arms out wide and presses her whole body against mine.

'I got lost,' I say.

She kisses me.

I hold her, frightened to pull back in case her expression

or her mood changes. I want us to stay like this. I know we can't, that this embrace will have to end and so will this kiss, night, and us, eventually.

'Let's run away,' she says, crushing my lips.

But this is our moment, now. Our time.

'I didn't get better just to run away again,' I say. 'I got better to be alive and be here, with you.'

'Well, what do we do now?' she says.

'I don't know,' I say as we begin to spin round faster and faster, two objects joined in space, momentarily hurtling in the same direction. 'Maybe we can go bowling.'